D1053400

# THE GREEN LEOPARD PLAGUE

Other books by Walter Jon Williams:

Hardwired series
*Hardwired*
*Solip:System*
*Voice of the Whirlwind*

Drake Maijstral series
*The Crown Jewels*
*House of Shards*
*Rock of Ages*

Metropolitan series
*Metropolitan*
*City on Fire*

Dread Empire's Fall series
*The Praxis*
*The Sundering*
*The Conventions of War*

*Ambassador of Progress*
*Knight Moves*
*Angel Station*
*Elegy for Angels and Dogs*
*Days of Atonement*
*Aristoi*
*The Rift* (by Walter J. Williams)
*Star Wars: The New Jedi Order: Destiny's Way*
*Implied Spaces*
*This Is Not a Game*
*Deep State*

# THE GREEN LEOPARD PLAGUE AND OTHER STORIES

## WALTER JON WILLIAMS

NIGHT SHADE BOOKS
San Francisco

*The Green Leopard Plague and Other Stories*
© 2010 by Walter Jon Williams
This edition of *The Green Leopard Plague and Other Stories*
© 2010 by Night Shade Books
Jacket art by Andrew Kim
Jacket design by Michael Ellis
Interior layout and design by Ross E. Lockhart

Introduction by Charles Stross. © 2010 Charles Stross.
Story afterwords by Walter Jon Williams. © 2010 Walter Jon Williams.
"Lethe," *Asimov's Science Fiction*, September 1997.
"Daddy's World," *Not of Woman Born*, ed. Constance Ash, Roc, 1999.
"The Last Ride of German Freddie," *Worlds That Weren't*, ed. Laura Anne Gilman, Roc, 2002.
"The Millennium Party," *Infinitematrix.net*, August 2002.
"The Green Leopard Plague," *Asimov's Science Fiction*, October-November 2003.
"The Tang Dynasty Underwater Pyramid," *Scifiction.com*, August 4, 2004.
"Incarnation Day," *Escape from Earth*, ed. Jack Dann and Gardner Dozois, SFBC, 2006.
"Send Them Flowers," *The New Space Opera*, ed. Jonathan Strahan and Gardner Dozois, Harper Eos, 2007.
"Pinocchio," *The Starry Rift: Tales of New Tomorrows*, ed. Jonathan Strahan, Viking, 2007.

**First Edition**

ISBN: 978-1-59780-177-5

**Night Shade Books**
Please visit us on the web at
http://www.nightshadebooks.com

# CONTENTS

# INTRODUCTION

## CHARLES STROSS

Greetings: I want you to know that I envy you.

You're reading the introduction to a new collection of short stories by one of science fiction's most versatile and elegant writers, and because you're reading the introduction I infer that you're probably about to read *The Green Leopard Plague and Other Stories* for the first time.

And I envy you, because I won't get to read this book for the first time ever again.

Walter is one of the science fiction field's secret treasures. It wasn't always thus; his first five novels were of a nautical, if not Napoleonic, type (a form that he has successfully translated into space opera in his Dread Empire's Fall series). For reasons I'm unclear on (but applaud the results of) he turned his hand to science fiction in the early 1980s, releasing a steady stream of novels over two and a half decades that bracket the quirks and obsessions of some of the genre's leading lights with his own inimitable style. From the Zelazny-esque world of *Knight Moves* to the criminal comedy caper of the Drake Maijstral books (think Raffles in Space, with just a touch of Jeeves, and you won't go far wrong), he's put his own distinctive stamp on a host of popular themes—and broken new ground of his own, with such landmark novels as *Aristoi* and *Metropolitan*. Along the way he came close to leaving a mark of a much more significant kind, writing the definitive cyberpunk novel in the form of *Hardwired*. (Gibson's *Neuromancer*, while widely admired, is seldom emulated; *Hardwired*, mostly written before *Neuromancer* was published, seems to have defined the form.)

Fiction publishing is a hard furrow to till. Writing of quality, on its own, isn't enough to earn you success; you need a goodly supply of luck. Walter shouldn't be a secret treasure of science fiction; he ought to be a *very public* one, with a couple of shelves in every bookstore, not to mention a display in the window. But it's *our* good fortune that Walter has had sufficient

1

tenacity, skill, and luck to weather the vicissitudes and keep plugging away. Moreover, he has the energy and inclination to write short stories as well as novels. Short stories are an ill-rewarded part of the field. If you're a freelance writer with a bank manager breathing down your neck it's all too easy to concentrate on novels, where the pay is better and the deadlines easier.

I mentioned earlier that Walter is a versatile and elegant writer; and his flexibility is at the forefront in this showcase collection. Taste is a highly subjective phenomenon, but I think the big guns are on my side in this case: "Daddy's World" and "The Green Leopard Plague" both won the Nebula Award, the Science Fiction and Fantasy Writers of America's gong for the best fiction of the year, while "The Last Ride of German Freddie" won the Sidewise for best alternate history; oh, and lest I forget, "The Green Leopard Plague" also made the cut for the Hugo Award, *the* top spot in the SF award firmament. But don't let that put you off the other stories in this collection—they're just as good. (The only difference is that they were published in anthologies that don't generally make the radar of the award voters.)

Anyway, I'm waffling and wasting paper gilding the lily here. You didn't pick up this book to read my frothing, did you? Listen, just read the stories already: you won't regret it!

—Charles Stross

# DADDY'S WORLD

One day Jamie went with his family to a new place, a place that had not existed before. The people who lived there were called Whirlikins, who were tall, thin people with pointed heads. They had long arms and made frantic gestures when they talked, and when they grew excited threw their arms out *wide* to either side and spun like tops until they got all blurry. They would whirr madly over the green grass beneath the pumpkin-orange sky of the Whirlikin Country, and sometimes they would bump into each other with an alarming clashing noise, but they were never hurt, only bounced off and spun away in another direction.

Sometimes one of them would spin so hard that he would dig himself right into the ground, and come to a sudden stop, buried to the shoulders, with an expression of alarmed dismay.

Jamie had never seen anything so funny. He laughed and laughed.

His little sister Becky laughed, too. Once she laughed so hard that she fell over onto her stomach, and Daddy picked her up and whirled her through the air, as if he were a Whirlikin himself, and they were both laughing all the while.

Afterwards, they heard the dinner bell, and Daddy said it was time to go home. After they waved goodbye to the Whirlikins, Becky and Jamie walked hand-in-hand with Momma as they walked over the grassy hills toward home, and the pumpkin-orange sky slowly turned to blue.

The way home ran past El Castillo. El Castillo looked like a fabulous place, a castle with towers and domes and minarets, all gleaming in the sun. Music floated down from El Castillo, the swift, intricate music of many guitars, and Jamie could hear the fast click of heels and the shouts and laughter of happy people.

But Jamie did not try to enter El Castillo. He had tried before, and discovered that El Castillo was guarded by La Duchesa, an angular, forbidding woman all in black, with a tall comb in her hair. When Jamie asked to come inside, La Duchesa had looked down at him and said, "I do not admit anyone who does not know Spanish irregular verbs!" It was all she ever said.

Jamie had asked Daddy what a Spanish irregular verb was—he had difficulty pronouncing the words—and Daddy had said, "Someday you'll learn, and La Duchesa will let you into her castle. But right now you're too young to learn Spanish."

That was all right with Jamie. There were plenty of things to do without going into El Castillo. And new places, like the country where the Whirlikins lived, appeared sometimes out of nowhere, and were quite enough to explore.

The color of the sky faded from orange to blue. Fluffy white clouds coasted in the air above the two-story frame house. Mister Jeepers, who was sitting on the ridgepole, gave a cry of delight and soared toward them through the air.

"Jamie's home!" he sang happily. "Jamie's home, and he's brought his beautiful sister!"

Mister Jeepers was diamond-shaped, like a kite, with his head at the topmost corner, hands on either sides, and little bowlegged comical legs attached on the bottom. He was bright red. Like a kite, he could fly, and he swooped through in a series of aerial cartwheels as he sailed toward Jamie and his party.

Becky looked up at Mister Jeepers and laughed from pure joy. "Jamie," she said, "you live in the best place in the world!"

At night, when Jamie lay in bed with his stuffed giraffe, Selena would ride a beam of pale light from the Moon to the Earth and sit by Jamie's side. She was a pale woman, slightly translucent, with a silver crescent on her brow. She would stroke Jamie's forehead with a cool hand, and she would sing to him until his eyes grew heavy and slumber stole upon him.

> The birds have tucked their heads
> The night is dark and deep
> All is quiet, all is safe,
> And little Jamie goes to sleep.

Whenever Jamie woke during the night, Selena was there to comfort him. He was glad that Selena always watched out for him, because sometimes he still had nightmares about being in the hospital. When the nightmares came, she was always there to comfort him, stroke him, sing him back to sleep.

Before long the nightmares began to fade.

Princess Gigunda always took Jamie for lessons. She was a huge woman, taller than Daddy, with frowzy hair and big bare feet and a crown that could never be made to sit straight on her head. She was homely, with a mournful face that was ugly and endearing at the same time. As she shuffled along with Jamie to his lessons, Princess Gigunda complained about the way her feet hurt, and about how she was a giant and unattractive, and how she would never be married.

"I'll marry you when I get bigger," Jamie said loyally, and the Princess' homely face screwed up into an expression of beaming pleasure.

Jamie had different lessons with different people. Mrs. Winkle, down at the little red brick schoolhouse, taught him his ABCs. Coach Toad—who *was* one—taught him field games, where he raced and jumped and threw against various people and animals. Mr. McGillicuddy, a pleasant whiskered fat man who wore red sleepers with a trapdoor in back, showed him his magic globe. When Jamie put his finger anywhere on the globe, trumpets began to sound, and he could see what was happening where he was pointing, and Mr. McGillicuddy would take him on a tour and show him interesting things. Buildings, statues, pictures, parks, people. "This is Nome," he would say. "Can you say Nome?"

"Nome," Jamie would repeat, shaping his mouth around the unfamiliar word, and Mr. McGillicuddy would smile and bob his head and look pleased.

If Jamie did well on his lessons, he got extra time with the Whirlikins, or at the Zoo, or with Mr. Fuzzy or in Pandaland. Until the dinner bell rang, and it was time to go home.

Jamie did well with his lessons almost every day.

When Princess Gigunda took him home from his lessons, Mister Jeepers would fly from the ridgepole to meet him, and tell him that his family was ready to see him. And then Momma and Daddy and Becky would wave from the windows of the house, and he would run to meet them.

Once, when he was in the living room telling his family about his latest trip through Mr. McGillicuddy's magic globe, he began skipping about with enthusiasm, and waving his arms like a Whirlikin, and suddenly he noticed that no one else was paying attention. That Momma and Daddy and Becky were staring at something else, their faces frozen in different attitudes of polite attention.

Jamie felt a chill finger touch his neck.

"Momma?" Jamie said. "Daddy?" Momma and Daddy did not respond. Their faces didn't move. Daddy's face was blurred strangely, as if it been caught in the middle of movement.

"Daddy?" Jamie came close and tried to tug at his father's shirt sleeve. It was hard, like marble, and his fingers couldn't get a purchase at it. Terror blew hot in his heart.

"*Daddy?*" Jamie cried. He tried to tug harder. "Daddy! Wake up!" Daddy didn't respond. He ran to Momma and tugged at her hand. "Momma! Momma!" Her hand was like the hand of a statue. She didn't move no matter how hard Jamie pulled.

"Help!" Jamie screamed. "Mister Jeepers! Mr. Fuzzy! Help my Momma!" Tears fell down his face as he ran from Becky to Momma to Daddy, tugging and pulling at them, wrapping his arms around their frozen legs and trying to pull them toward him. He ran outside, but everything was curiously still. No wind blew. Mister Jeepers sat on the ridgepole, a broad smile fixed as usual to his face, but he was frozen, too, and did not respond to Jamie's calls.

Terror pursued him back into the house. This was far worse than anything that had happened to him in the hospital, worse even than the pain. Jamie ran into the living room, where his family stood still as statues, and then recoiled in horror. A stranger had entered the room—or rather just parts of a stranger, a pair of hands encased in black gloves with strange silver circuit patterns on the backs, and a strange glowing opalescent face with a pair of wraparound dark glasses drawn across it like a line.

"Interface crashed, all right," the stranger said, as if to someone Jamie couldn't see.

Jamie gave a scream. He ran behind Momma's legs for protection.

"Oh shit," the stranger said. "The kid's still running."

He began purposefully moving his hands as if poking at the air. Jamie was sure that it was some kind of terrible attack, a spell to turn him to stone. He tried to run away, tripped over Becky's immovable feet and hit the floor hard, and then crawled away, the hall rug bunching up under his hands and knees as he skidded away, his own screams ringing in his ears...

...He sat up in bed, shrieking. The cool night tingled on his skin. He felt Selena's hand on his forehead, and he jerked away with a cry.

"Is something wrong?" came Selena's calm voice. "Did you have a bad dream?" Under the glowing crescent on her brow, Jamie could see the concern in her eyes.

"Where are Momma and Daddy?" Jamie wailed.

"They're fine," Selena said. "They're asleep in their room. Was it a bad dream?"

Jamie threw off the covers and leaped out of bed. He ran down the hall, the floorboards cool on his bare feet. Selena floated after him in her serene, concerned way. He threw open the door to his parents' bedroom and snapped on the light, then gave a cry as he saw them huddled beneath their blanket. He flung himself at his mother, and gave a sob of relief as she opened her eyes and turned to him.

"Something wrong?" Momma said. "Was it a bad dream?"

"*No!*" Jamie wailed. He tried to explain, but even he knew that his words made no sense. Daddy rose from his pillow, looking seriously at Jamie, and then turned to ruffle his hair.

"Sounds like a pretty bad dream, trouper," Daddy said. "Let's get you back to bed."

"*No!*" Jamie buried his face in his mother's neck. "I don't want to go back to bed!"

"All right, Jamie," Momma said. She patted Jamie's back. "You can sleep here with us. But just for tonight, okay?"

"Wanna stay here," Jamie mumbled.

He crawled under the covers between Momma and Daddy. They each kissed him, and Daddy turned off the light. "Just go to sleep, trouper," he said. "And don't worry. You'll have only good dreams from now on."

Selena, faintly glowing in the darkness, sat silently in the corner. "Shall I sing?" she asked.

"Yes, Selena," Daddy said. "Please sing for us."

The birds have tucked their heads, Selena began to sing,

The night is dark and deep

All is quiet, all is safe,

And little Jamie goes to sleep.

But Jamie did not sleep. Despite the singing, the dark night, the rhythmic breathing of his parents and the comforting warmth of their bodies.

It *wasn't* a dream, he knew. His family had really been frozen.

Something, or someone, had turned them to stone. Probably that evil disembodied head and pair of hands. And now, for some reason, his parents didn't remember.

Something had made them forget.

Jamie stared into the darkness. What, he thought, if these *weren't* his parents? If his parents were still stone, hidden away somewhere? What if these substitutes were bad people—kidnappers or worse—people who just *looked* like his real parents. What if they were evil people who were just waiting for him to fall asleep, and then they would turn to monsters, with teeth and fangs and a horrible light in their eyes, and they would tear him to bits right here in the bed...

Talons of panic clawed at Jamie's heart. Selena's song echoed in his ears. He *wasn't* going to sleep! He *wasn't!*

And then he did. It wasn't anything like normal sleep—it was as if sleep was *imposed* on him, as if something had just *ordered* his mind to sleep. It was just like a wave that rolled over him, an irresistible force, blotting out his senses, his body, his mind...

I *won't* sleep! he thought in defiance, but then his thoughts were extinguished.

When he woke he was back in his own bed, and it was morning, and Mister Jeepers was floating outside the window. "Jamie's awake!" he sang. "Jamie's awake and ready for a new day!"

And then his parents came bustling in, kissing him and petting him and taking him downstairs for breakfast.

His fears seemed foolish now, in full daylight, with Mister Jeepers dancing in the air outside and singing happily.

But sometimes, at night while Selena crooned by his bedside, he gazed into the darkness and felt a thrill of fear.

And he never forgot, not entirely.


A few days later Don Quixote wandered into the world, a lean man who frequently fell off his lean horse in a clang of home-made armor. He was given to making wan comments in both English and his own language, which turned out to be Spanish.

"Can you teach me Spanish irregular verbs?" Jamie asked.

"*Sí, naturalmente,*" said Don Quixote. "But I will have to teach you some other Spanish as well." He looked particularly mournful. "Let's start with *corazon.* It means 'heart.' *Mi corazon,*" he said with a sigh, "is breaking for love of Dulcinea."

After a few sessions with Don Quixote—mixed with a lot of sighing about *corazons* and Dulcinea—Jamie took a grip on his courage, marched up to El Castillo, and spoke to La Duchesa. "*Pierdo, sueño, haría, ponto!*" he cried.

La Duchesa's eyes widened in surprise, and as she bent toward Jamie her severe face became almost kindly. "You are obviously a very intelligent boy," she said. "You may enter my castle."

And so Don Quixote and La Duchesa, between the two of them, began to teach Jamie to speak Spanish. If he did well, he was allowed into the parts of the castle where the musicians played and the dancers stamped, where brave Castilian knights jousted in the tilting yard, and Señor Esteban told stories in Spanish, always careful to use words that Jamie already knew.

Jamie couldn't help but notice that sometimes Don Quixote behaved strangely. Once, when Jamie was visiting the Whirlikins, Don Quixote charged up on his horse, waving his sword and crying out that he would save Jamie from the goblins that were attacking him. Before Jamie could explain that the Whirlikins were harmless, Don Quixote galloped to the attack. The Whirlikins, alarmed, screwed themselves into the ground where they were safe, and Don Quixote fell off his horse trying to swing at one with his sword. After poor Quixote fell off his horse a few times, it was Jamie who had to rescue the Don, not the other way around.

It was sort of sad and sort of funny. Every time Jamie started to laugh about it, he saw Don Quixote's mournful face in his mind, and his laugh grew uneasy.

After a while, Jamie's sister Becky began to share Jamie's lessons. She joined him and Princess Gigunda on the trip to the little schoolhouse, learned reading and math from Mrs. Winkle, and then, after some coaching from Jamie and Don Quixote, she marched to La Duchesa to shout irregular verbs and gain entrance to El Castillo.

Around that time Marcus Tullius Cicero turned up to take them both to the Forum Romanum, a new part of the world that had appeared to the south of the Whirlikins' territory. But Cicero and the people in the Forum, all the shopkeepers and politicians, did not teach Latin the way Don Quixote taught Spanish, explaining what the new words meant in English, they just talked Latin at each other and expected Jamie and Becky to understand. Which, eventually, they did. The Spanish helped. Jamie was a bit better at Latin than Becky, but he explained to her that it was because he was older.

It was Becky who became interested in solving Princess Gigunda's problem. "We should find her somebody to love," she said.

"She loves *us*," Jamie said.

"Don't be silly," Becky said. "She wants a *boyfriend*."

"*I'm* her boyfriend," Jamie insisted.

Becky looked a little impatient. "Besides," she said, "it's a puzzle. Just like La Duchesa and her verbs."

This had not occurred to Jamie before, but now that Becky mentioned it, the idea seemed obvious. There were a lot of puzzles around, which one or the other of them was always solving, and Princess Gigunda's lovelessness was, now that he saw it, clearly among them.

So they set out to find Princess Gigunda a mate. This question occupied them for several days, and several candidates were discussed and rejected. They found no answers until they went to the chariot race at the Circus Maximus. It was the first race in the Circus ever, because the place had just appeared on the other side of the Palatine Hill from the Forum, and there was a very large, very excited crowd.

The names of the charioteers were announced as they paraded their chariots to the starting line. The trumpets sounded, and the chariots bolted from the star as the drivers whipped up the horses. Jamie watched enthralled as they rolled around the *spina* for the first lap, and then shouted in surprise at the sight of Don Quixote galloping onto the Circus Maximus, shouting that he was about to stop this group of rampaging demons from destroying the land, and planted himself directly in the path of the oncoming chariots.

Jamie shouted along with the crowd for the Don to get out of the way before he got killed.

Fortunately Quixote's horse had more sense than he did, because the spindly animal saw the chariots coming and bolted, throwing its rider. One of the chariots rode right over poor Quixote, and there was a horrible clanging noise, but after the chariot passed, Quixote sat up, apparently unharmed. His armor had saved him.

Jamie jumped from his seat and was about to run down to help Don Quixote off the course, but Becky grabbed his arm. "Hang on," she said, "someone else will look after him, and I have an idea."

She explained that Don Quixote would make a perfect man for Princess Gigunda.

"But he's in love with Dulcinea!"

Becky looked at him patiently. "Has anyone ever *seen* Dulcinea? All we have to do is convince Don Quixote that Princess Gigunda *is* Dulcinea."

After the races, they found that Don Quixote had been arrested by the lictors and sent to the Lautumiae, which was the Roman jail. They weren't allowed to see the prisoner, so they went in search of Cicero, who was a lawyer and was able to get Quixote out of the Lautumiae on the promise that he would never visit Rome again.

"I regret to the depths of my soul that my parole does not enable me to destroy those demons," Quixote said as he left Rome's town limits.

"Let's not get into that," Becky said. "What we wanted to tell you was that we've found Dulcinea."

The old man's eyes widened in joy. He clutched at his armor-clad heart. "*Mi amor!* Where is she? I must run to her at once!"

"Not just yet," Becky said. "You should know that she's been changed. She doesn't look like she used to."

"Has some evil sorcerer done this?" Quixote demanded.

"Yes!" Jamie interrupted. He was annoyed that Becky had taken charge of everything, and he wanted to add his contribution to the scheme. "The sorcerer was just a head!" he shouted. "A floating head, and a pair of hands! And he wore dark glasses and had no body!"

A shiver of fear passed through him as he remembered the eerie floating head, but the memory of his old terror did not stop his words from spilling out.

Becky gave him a strange look. "Yeah," she said. "That's right."

"He crashed the interface!" Jamie shouted, the words coming to him out of memory.

Don Quixote paid no attention to this, but Becky gave him another look.

"You're not as dumb as you look, Digit," she said.

"I do not care about Dulcinea's appearance," Don Quixote declared, "I love only the goodness that dwells in her *corazon*."

"She's Princess Gigunda!" Jamie shouted, jumping up and down in enthusiasm. "She's been Princess Gigunda all along!"

And so, the children following, Don Quixote ran clanking to where Princess Gigunda waited near Jamie's house, fell down to one knee, and began to kiss and weep over the Princess' hand. The Princess seemed a little surprised by this until Becky told her that she was really the long-lost Dulcinea, changed into a giant by an evil magician, although she probably didn't remember it because that was part of the spell, too.

So while the Don and the Princess embraced, kissed, and began to warble a love duet, Becky turned to Jamie.

"What's that stuff about the floating head?" she asked. "Where did you come up with that?"

"I dunno," Jamie said. He didn't want to talk about his memory of his family being turned to stone, the eerie glowing figure floating before them. He didn't want to remember how everyone said it was just a dream.

He didn't want to talk about the suspicions that had never quite gone away.

"That stuff was weird, Digit," Becky said. "It gave me the creeps. Let me know before you start talking about stuff like that again."

"Why do you call me Digit?" Jamie asked. Becky smirked.

"No reason," she said.

"Jamie's home!" Mister Jeepers' voice warbled from the sky. Jamie looked up to see Mister Jeepers doing joyful aerial loops overhead. "Master Jamie's home at last!"

"Where shall we go?" Jamie asked.

Their lessons for the day were over, and he and Becky were leaving the little red schoolhouse. Becky, as usual, had done very well on her lessons, better than her older brother, and Jamie felt a growing sense of annoyance. At least he was still better at Latin and computer science.

"I dunno," Becky said. "Where do you want to go?"

"How about Pandaland? We could ride the Whoosh Machine."

Becky wrinkled her face. "I'm tired of that kid stuff," she said.

Jamie looked at her. "But you're a kid."

"I'm not as little as you, Digit," Becky said.

Jamie glared. This was too much. "You're my little sister! I'm bigger than you!"

"No, you're not," Becky said. She stood before him, her arms flung out in exasperation. "Just *notice something* for once, will you?"

Jamie bit back on his temper and looked, and he saw that Becky was, in fact, bigger than he was. And older-looking. Puzzlement replaced his fading anger.

"How did you get so big?" Jamie asked.

"I grew. And you *didn't* grow. Not as fast anyway."

"I don't understand."

Becky's lip curled. "Ask Mom or Dad. Just *ask* them." Her expression turned stony. "Just don't believe everything they tell you."

"What do you mean?"

Becky looked angry for a moment, and then her expression relaxed. "Look," she said, "just go to Pandaland and have fun, okay? You don't need me for that. I want to go and make some calls to my friends."

"*What* friends?"

Becky looked angry again. "*My* friends. It doesn't matter who they are!"

"Fine!" Jamie shouted. "I can have fun by myself!"

Becky turned and began to walk home, her pale legs rapidly scissoring against the deep green hillside. Jamie glared after her, then turned and began the walk to Pandaland.

He did all his favorite things, rode the Ferris wheel and the Whoosh Machine, watched Rizzio the Strongman and the clowns. He enjoyed himself, but his enjoyment felt hollow. He found himself *watching*, watching himself at play, watching himself enjoying the rides.

Watching himself not grow as fast as his little sister.

Watching himself wondering whether or not to ask his parents about why that was.

He had the idea that he wouldn't like their answers.

He didn't see as much of Becky after that. They would share lessons, and then Becky would lock herself in her room to talk to her friends on the phone.

Becky didn't have a telephone in her room, though. He looked once when she wasn't there.

After a while, Becky stopped accompanying him for lessons. She'd got ahead of him on everything except Latin, and it was too hard for Jamie to keep up.

After that, he hardly saw Becky at all. But when he saw her, he saw that she was still growing fast. Her clothing was different, and her hair. She'd started wearing makeup.

He didn't know whether he liked her anymore or not.

It was Jamie's birthday. He was eleven years old, and Momma and Daddy and Becky had all come for a party. Don Quixote and Princess Gigunda serenaded Jamie from outside the window, accompanied by La Duchesa on Spanish guitar. There was a big cake with eleven candles. Momma gave Jamie a chart of the stars. When he touched a star, a voice would appear telling Jamie about the star, and lines would appear on the chart showing any constellation the star happened to belong to. Daddy gave Jamie a car, a miniature Mercedes convertible, scaled to Jamie's size, which he could drive around the country and which he could use in the Circus Maximus when the chariots weren't racing. His sister gave Jamie a kind of lamp stand that would project lights and moving patterns on the walls and ceiling when the lights were off. "Listen to music when you use it," she said.

"Thank you, Becky," Jamie said.

"Becca," she said. "My name is Becca now. Try to remember."

"Okay," Jamie said. "Becca."

Becky—Becca—looked at Momma. "I'm dying for a cigaret," she said. "Can I go, uh, out for a minute?"

Momma hesitated, but Daddy looked severe. "Becca," he said, "this is *Jamie's birthday.* We're all here to celebrate. So why don't we all eat some cake and have a nice time?"

"It's not even real cake," Becca said. "It doesn't *taste* like real cake."

"It's a *nice cake,*" Daddy insisted. "Why don't we talk about this later? Let's just have a special time for Jamie."

Becca stood up from the table. "For *the Digit?*" she said. "Why are we having a good time for *Jamie?* He's not even a *real person!*" She thumped herself on the chest. "*I'm* a real person!" she shouted. "Why don't we ever have special times for *me?*"

But Daddy was on his feet by that point and shouting, and Momma was trying to get everyone to be quiet, and Becca was shouting back, and suddenly a determined look entered her face and she just disappeared—suddenly, she wasn't there anymore, there was just only air.

Jamie began to cry. So did Momma. Daddy paced up and down and swore, and then he said, "I'm going to go get her." Jamie was afraid he'd disappear like Becca, and he gave a cry of despair, but Daddy didn't disappear, he just stalked out of the dining room and slammed the door behind him.

Momma pulled Jamie onto her lap and hugged him. "Don't worry, Jamie," she said. "Becky just did that to be mean."

"What happened?" Jamie asked.

"Don't worry about it." Momma stroked his hair. "It was just a mean trick."

"She's growing up," Jamie said. "She's grown faster than me and I don't understand."

"Wait till Daddy gets back," Momma said, "and we'll talk about it."

But Daddy was clearly in no mood for talking when he returned, without Becca. "We're going to have *fun*," he snarled, and reached for the knife to cut the cake.

The cake tasted like ashes in Jamie's mouth. When the Don and Princess Gigunda, Mister Jeepers, and Rizzio the Strongman came into the dining room and sang "Happy Birthday," it was all Jamie could do to hold back the tears.

Afterwards, he drove his new car to the Circus Maximus and drove as fast as he could on the long oval track. The car really wouldn't go very fast. The bleachers on either side were empty, and so was the blue sky above.

Maybe it was a puzzle, he thought, like Princess Gigunda's love life. Maybe all he had to do was follow the right clue, and everything would be fine.

What's the moral they're trying to teach? he wondered.

But all he could do was go in circles, around and around the empty stadium.

"Hey, Digit. Wake up."

Jamie came awake suddenly, with a stifled cry. The room whirled around him. He blinked, realized that the whirling came from the colored lights projected by his birthday present, Becca's lamp stand.

Becca was sitting on his bedroom chair, a cigaret in her hand. Her feet, in the steel-capped boots she'd been wearing lately, were propped up on the bed.

"Are you awake, Jamie?" It was Selena's voice. "Would you like me to sing you a lullaby?"

"Fuck off, Selena," Becca said. "Get out of here. Get lost."

Selena cast Becca a mournful look, then sailed backwards, out the window, riding a beam of moonlight to her pale home in the sky. Jamie watched her go, and felt as if a part of himself was going with her, a part that he would never see again.

"Selena and the others have to do what you tell them, mostly," Becca said. "Of course, Mom and Dad wouldn't tell *you* that."

Jamie looked at Becca. "What's happening?" he said. "Where did you go today?"

Colored lights swam over Becca's face. "I'm sorry if I spoiled your birthday, Digit. I just got tired of the lies, you know? They'd kill me if they knew I was here now, talking to you." Becca took a draw on her cigaret, held her breath for a second or two, then exhaled. Jamie didn't see or taste any smoke.

"You know what they wanted me to do?" she said. "Wear a little girl's body, so I wouldn't look any older than you, and keep you company in that stupid school for seven hours a day." She shook her head. "I wouldn't do it. They yelled and yelled, but I was damned if I would."

"I don't understand."

Becca flicked invisible ashes off her cigaret, and looked at Jamie for a long time. Then she sighed.

"Do you remember when you were in the hospital?" she said.

Jamie nodded. "I was really sick."

"I was so little then, I don't really remember it very well," Becca said. "But the point is—" She sighed again. "The point is that you weren't getting well. So they decided to—" She shook her head. "Dad took advantage of his position at the University, and the fact that he's been a big donor. They were doing AI research, and the neurology department was into brain modeling, and they needed a test subject, and—Well, the idea is, they've got some of your tissue, and when they get cloning up and running, they'll put you back in—" She saw Jamie's stare, then shook her head. "I'll make it simple, okay?"

She took her feet off the bed and leaned closer to Jamie. A shiver ran up his back at her expression. "They made a copy of you. An *electronic* copy. They scanned your brain and built a holographic model of it inside a computer, and they put it in a virtual environment, and—" She sat back, took a drag on her cigaret. "And here you are," she said.

Jamie looked at her. "I don't understand."

Colored lights gleamed in Becca's eyes. "You're in a computer, okay? And you're a program. You know what that is, right? From computer class? And the program is sort of in the shape of your mind. Don Quixote and Princess Gigunda are programs, too. And Mrs. Winkle down at the schoolhouse is *usually* a program, but if she needs to teach something complex, then she's an education major from the University."

Jamie felt as if he'd just been hollowed out, a void inside his ribs. "I'm not real?" he said. "I'm not a person?"

"Wrong," Becca said. "You're real, all right. You're the apple of our parents' eye." Her tone was bitter. "Programs are real things," she said, "and yours was a real hack, you know, absolute cutting-edge state-of-the-art technoshit. And the computer that you're in is real, too—I'm interfaced with it right now, down in the family room—we have to wear suits with sensors and a helmet with scanners and stuff. I hope to fuck they don't hear me talking to you down here."

"But what—" Jamie swallowed hard. How could he swallow if he was just a string of code? "What happened to *me?* The original me?"

Becca looked cold. "Well," she said, "you had cancer. You died."

"Oh." A hollow wind blew through the void inside him.

"They're going to bring you back. As soon as the clone thing works out—but this is a government computer you're in, and there are all these government restrictions on cloning, and—" She shook her head. "Look, Digit," she said. "You really need to know this stuff, okay?"

"I understand." Jamie wanted to cry. But only real people cried, he thought, and he wasn't real. He wasn't real.

"The program that runs this virtual environment is huge, okay, and *you're* a big program, and the University computer is used for a lot of research, and a lot of the research has a higher priority than *you* do. So you don't run in real-time—that's why I'm growing faster than you are. I'm spending more hours being me than you are. And the parents—" She rolled her eyes. "They aren't making this any better, with their emphasis on *normal family life.*"

She sucked on her cigaret, then stubbed it out in something invisible. "See, they want us to be this *normal family.* So we have breakfast together every day, and dinner every night, and spend the evening at the Zoo or in Pandaland or someplace. But the dinner that we eat with *you* is virtual, it doesn't taste like anything—the grant ran out before they got that part of the interface right—so we eat this fast-food crap before we interface with you, and then have dinner all *over* again with *you*… Is this making any sense? Because Dad has a job and Mom has a job and I go to school and have friends and stuff, so we really can't get together every night. So they just close your program file, shut it right down, when they're not available to interface with you as what Dad calls a 'family unit,' and that means that there are a lot of hours, days sometimes, when you're just *not running,* you might as well really be *dead*—" She blinked. "Sorry," she said. "Anyway, we're *all* getting older a lot faster than you are, and it's not fair to you, that's what I think. Especially because the University computer runs fastest at night, because people don't use them as much then, and you're pretty much real-time then, so interfacing with you would be almost *normal,* but Mom and Dad sleep then, cuz they have day jobs, and they can't have you running around unsupervised in here, for God's sake, they think it's unsafe or something…"

She paused, then reached into her shirt pocket for another cigaret. "Look," she said, "I'd better get out of here before they figure out I'm talking to you. And then they'll pull my access codes or something." She stood, brushed something off her jeans. "Don't tell the parents about this stuff right away. Otherwise they might erase you, and load a backup that doesn't know shit. Okay?"

And she vanished, as she had that afternoon.

Jamie sat in the bed, hugging his knees. He could feel his heart beating in the darkness. How can a program have a heart? he wondered.

Dawn slowly encroached upon the night, and then there was Mister

Jeepers, turning lazy cartwheels in the air, his red face leering in the window.

"Jamie's awake!" he said. "Jamie's awake and ready for a new day!"

"Fuck off," Jamie said, and buried his face in the blanket.

Jamie asked to learn more about computer and programming. Maybe, he thought, he could find clues there, he could solve the puzzle. His parents agreed, happy to let him follow his interests.

After a few weeks, he moved into El Castillo. He didn't tell anyone he was going, he just put some of his things in his car, took them up to a tower room, and threw them down on the bed he found there. His Mom came to find him when he didn't come home for dinner.

"It's dinnertime, Jamie," she said. "Didn't you hear the dinner bell?"

"I'm going to stay here for a while," Jamie said.

"You're going to get hungry if you don't come home for dinner."

"I don't need food," Jamie said.

His Mom smiled brightly. "You need food if you're going to keep up with the Whirlikins," she said.

Jamie looked at her. "I don't care about that kid stuff anymore," he said.

When his mother finally turned and left, Jamie noticed that she moved like an old person.

After a while, he got used to the hunger that was programmed into him. It was always *there*, he was always aware of it, but he got so he could ignore it after a while.

But he couldn't ignore the need to sleep. That was just built into the program, and eventually, try though he might, he needed to give in to it.

He found out he could order the people in the castle around, and he amused himself by making them stand in embarrassing positions, or stand on their head and sing, or form human pyramids for hours and hours.

Sometimes he made them fight, but they weren't very good at it.

He couldn't make Mrs. Winkle at the schoolhouse do whatever he wanted, though, or any of the people who were supposed to teach him things. When it was time for a lesson, Princess Gigunda turned up. She wouldn't follow his orders, she'd just pick him up and carry him to the little red schoolhouse and plunk him down in his seat.

"You're not real!" he shouted, kicking in her arms. "You're not real! And *I'm* not real, either!"

But they made him learn about the world that *was* real, about geography and geology and history, although none of it mattered here.

After the first couple times Jamie had been dragged to school, his father met him outside the schoolhouse at the end of the day.

"You need some straightening out," he said. He looked grim. "You're part of a family. You belong with us. You're not going to stay in the castle anymore, you're going to have a *normal family life.*"

"No!" Jamie shouted. "I *like* the castle!"

Dad grabbed him by the arm and began to drag him homeward. Jamie called him a *pendejo* and a *fellator.*

"I'll punish you if I have to," his father said.

"How are you going to do that?" Jamie demanded. "You gonna erase my file? Load a backup?"

A stunned expression crossed his father's face. His body seemed to go through a kind of stutter, and the grip on Jamie's arm grew nerveless. Then his face flushed with anger. "What do you mean?" he demanded. "Who told you this?"

Jamie wrenched himself free of Dad's weakened grip. "I figured it out by myself," Jamie said. "It wasn't hard. I'm not a kid anymore."

"I—" His father blinked, and then his face hardened. "You're still coming home."

Jamie backed away. "I want some changes!" he said. "I don't want to be shut off all the time."

Dad's mouth compressed to a thin line. "It was Becky who told you this, wasn't it?"

Jamie felt an inspiration. "It was Mister Jeepers! There's a flaw in his programming! He answers whatever question I ask him!"

Jamie's father looked uncertain. He held out his hand. "Let's go home," he said. "I need to think about this."

Jamie hesitated. "Don't erase me," he said. "Don't load a backup. Please. I don't want to die *twice.*"

Dad's look softened. "I won't."

"I want to grow up," Jamie said. "I don't want to be a little kid forever."

Dad held out his hand again. Jamie thought for a moment, then took the hand. They walked over the green grass toward the white frame house on the hill.

"Jamie's home!" Mister Jeepers floated overhead, turning aerial cartwheels. "Jamie's home at last!"

A spasm of anger passed through Jamie at the sight of the witless grin. He pointed at the ground in front of him.

"Crash right here!" he ordered. "*Fast!*"

Mister Jeepers came spiraling down, an expression of comic terror on his face, and smashed to the ground where Jamie pointed. Jamie pointed at the sight of the crumpled body and laughed.

"Jamie's home at last!" Mister Jeepers said.

As soon as Jamie could, he got one of the programmers at the University to fix him up a flight program like the one Mister Jeepers had been using. He swooped and soared, zooming like a superhero through the sky, stunting between the towers of El Castillo and soaring over upturned, wondering faces in the Forum.

He couldn't seem to go as fast as he really wanted. When he started increasing speed, all the scenery below paused in its motion for a second or two, then jumped forward with a jerk. The software couldn't refresh the scenery fast enough to match his speed. It felt strange, because throughout his flight he could feel the wind on his face

So this, he thought, was why his car couldn't go fast.

So he decided to climb high. He turned his face to the blue sky and went straight up. The world receded, turned small. He could see the castle, the hills of Whirlikin Country, the crowded Forum, the huge oval of the Circus Maximus. It was like a green plate, with a fuzzy, nebulous horizon where the sky started.

And, right in the center, was the little two-story frame house where he'd grown up.

It was laid out below him like scenery in a snow globe.

After a while he stopped climbing. It took him a while to realize it, because he still felt the wind blowing in his face, but the world below stopped getting smaller.

He tried going faster. The wind blasted onto him from above, but his position didn't change.

He'd reached the limits of his world. He couldn't get any higher.

Jamie flew out to the edges of the world, to the horizon. No matter how he urged his program to move, he couldn't make his world fade away.

He was trapped inside the snow globe, and there was no way out.

It was quite a while before Jamie saw Becca again. She picked her way through the labyrinth beneath El Castillo to his throne room, and Jamie slowly materialized atop his throne of skulls. She didn't appear surprised.

"I see you've got a little Dark Lord thing going here," she said.

"It passes the time," Jamie said.

"And all those pits and stakes and tripwires?"

"Death traps."

"Took me forever to get in here, Digit. I kept getting de-rezzed."

Jamie smiled. "That's the idea."

"Whirlikins as weapons," she nodded. "That was a good one. Bored a hole right through me, the first time."

"Since I'm stuck living here," Jamie said, "I figure I might as well be in charge of the environment. Some of the student programmers at the University helped me with some cool effects."

Screams echoed through the throne room. Fires leaped out of pits behind him. The flames illuminated the form of Marcus Tullius Cicero, who hung crucified above a sea of flame.

"*O tempora, o mores!*" moaned Cicero.

Becca nodded. "Nice," she said. "Not my scene exactly, but nice."

"Since I can't leave," Jamie said, "I want a say in who gets to visit. So either you wait till I'm ready to talk to you, or you take your chances on the death traps."

"Well. Looks like you're sitting pretty, then."

Jamie shrugged. Flames belched. "I'm getting bored with it. I might just wipe it all out and build another place to live in. I can't tell you the number of battles I've won, the number of kingdoms I've trampled. In this reality and others. It's all the same after a while." He looked at her. "You've grown."

"So have you."

"Once the *paterfamilias* finally decided to allow it." He smiled. "We still have dinner together sometimes, in the old house. Just a normal family, as Dad says. Except that sometimes I turn up in the form of a werewolf, or a giant, or something."

"So they tell me."

"The advantage of being software is that I can look like anything I want. But that's the disadvantage, too, because I can't really *become* something else, I'm still just…me. I may wear another program as a disguise, but I'm still the same program inside, and I'm not a good enough programmer to mess with that, yet." Jamie hopped off his throne, walked a nervous little circle around his sister. "So what brings you to the old neighborhood?" he asked. "The old folks said you were off visiting Aunt Maddy in the country."

"*Exiled*, they mean. I got knocked up, and after the abortion they sent me to Maddy. She was supposed to keep me under control, except she didn't." She picked an invisible piece of lint from her sweater. "So now I'm back." She looked at him. "I'm skipping a lot of the story, but I figure you wouldn't be interested."

"Does it have to do with sex?" Jamie asked. "I'm sort of interested in sex, even though I can't do it, and they're not likely to let me."

"*Let* you?"

"It would require a lot of new software and stuff. I was prepubescent when my brain structures were scanned, and the program isn't set up for making

DADDY'S WORLD • 21

me a working adult, with adult desires et cetera. Nobody was thinking about putting me through adolescence at the time. And the administrators at the University told me that it was very unlikely that anyone was going to give them a grant so that a computer program could have sex." Jamie shrugged. "I don't miss it, I guess. But I'm sort of curious."

Surprise crossed Becca's face. "But there are all kinds of simulations, and…"

"They don't work for me, because my mind isn't structured to be able to achieve pleasure that way. I can manipulate the programs, but it's about as exciting as working a virtual butter churn." Jamie shrugged again. "But that's okay. I mean, I don't *miss* it. I can always give myself a jolt to the pleasure center if I want."

"Not the same thing," Becca said. "I've done both."

"I wouldn't know."

"I'll tell you about sex if you want," Becca said, "but that's not why I'm here."

"Yes?"

Becca hesitated. Licked her lips. "I guess I should just say it, huh?" she said. "Mom's dying. Pancreatic cancer."

Jamie felt sadness well up in his mind. Only electrons, he thought, moving from one place to another. It was nothing real. He was programmed to feel an analog of sorrow, and that was all.

"She looks normal to me," he said, "when I see her." But that didn't mean anything: his mother chose what she wanted him to see, just as he chose a mask—a werewolf, a giant—for her.

And in neither case did the disguise at all matter. For behind the werewolf was a program that couldn't alter its parameters; and behind the other, ineradicable cancer.

Becca watched him from slitted eyes. "Dad wants her to be scanned, and come here. So we can still be a *normal family* even after she dies."

Jamie was horrified. "Tell her *no*," he said. "Tell her she can't come!"

"I don't think she wants to. But Dad is very insistent."

"She'll be here *forever!* It'll be awful!"

Becca looked around. "Well, she wouldn't do much for your Dark Lord act, that's for sure. I'm sure Sauron's mom didn't hang around the Dark Tower, nagging him about the unproductive way he was spending his time."

Fires belched. The ground trembled. Stalactites rained down like arrows.

"That's not it," Jamie said. "She doesn't want to be here no matter what I'm doing, no matter where I live. Because whatever this place looks like, it's a prison." Jamie looked at his sister. "I don't want my mom in a prison."

Leaping flames glittered in Becca's eyes. "You can change the world you live in," she said. "That's more than I can do."

"But I can't," Jamie said. "I can change the way it *looks*, but I can't change anything *real*. I'm a program, and a program is an *artifact*. I'm a piece of *engineering*. I'm a simulation, with simulated sensory organs that interact with simulated environments—I can only interact with *other artifacts*. *None* of it's real. I don't know what the real world looks or feels or tastes like, I only know what simulations tell me they're *supposed* to taste like. And I can't change any of my parameters unless I mess with the engineering, and I can't do that unless the programmers agree, and even when that happens, I'm still as artificial as I was before. And the computer I'm in is old and clunky, and soon nobody's going to run my operating system anymore, and I'll not only be an artifact, I'll be a museum piece."

"There are other artificial intelligences out there," Becca said. "I keep hearing about them."

"I've talked to them. Most of them aren't very interesting—it's like talking to a dog, or maybe to a very intelligent microwave oven. And they've scanned some people in, but those were adults, and all they wanted to do, once they got inside, was to escape. Some of them went crazy."

Becca gave a twisted smile. "I used to be so jealous of you, you know. You lived in this beautiful world, no pollution, no violence, no shit on the streets."

Flames belched.

"*Integra mens augustissima possessio*," said Cicero.

"Shut up!" Jamie told him. "What the fuck do you know?"

Becca shook her head. "I've seen those old movies, you know? Where somebody gets turned into a computer program, and next thing you know he's in every computer in the world, and running everything?"

"I've seen those, too. Ha ha. Very funny. Shows you what people know about programs."

"Yeah. Shows you what they know."

"I'll talk to Mom," Jamie said.

Big tears welled out of Mom's eyes and trailed partway down her face, then disappeared. The scanners paid a lot of attention to eyes and mouths, for the sake of transmitting expression, but didn't always pick up the things between.

"I'm sorry," she said. "We didn't think this is how it would be."

"Maybe you should have given it more thought," Jamie said.

It isn't sorrow, he told himself again. It's just electrons moving.

"You were such a beautiful baby." Her lower lip trembled. "We didn't want to lose you. They said that it would only be a few years before they could implant your memories in a clone."

Jamie knew all that by now. Knew that the technology of reading memories turned out to be much, much simpler than implanting them—it had been discovered that the implantation had to be made while the brain was actually growing. And government restrictions on human cloning had made tests next to impossible, and that the team that had started his project had split up years ago, some to higher-paying jobs, some retired, others to pet projects of their own. How his father had long ago used up whatever pull he'd had at the University trying to keep everything together. And how he long ago had acquired or purchased patents and copyrights for the whole scheme, except for Jamie's program, which was still owned jointly by the University and the family.

Tears reappeared on Mom's lower face, dripped off her chin. "There's potentially a lot of money at stake, you know. People want to raise perfect children. Keep them away from bad influences, make sure that they're raised free from violence."

"So they want to control the kid's entire environment," Jamie said.

"Yes. And make it *safe*. And wholesome. And—"

"Just like *normal family life*," Jamie finished. "No diapers, no vomit, no messes. No having to interact with the kid when the parents are tired. And then you just download the kid into an adult body, give him a diploma, and kick him out of the house. And call yourself a perfect parent."

"And there are *religious people…*" Mom licked her lips. "Your Dad's been talking to them. They want to raise children in environments that reflect their beliefs completely. Places where there is no temptation, no sin. No science or ideas that contradict their own…"

"But Dad isn't religious," Jamie said.

"These people have money. Lots of money."

Mom reached out, took his hand. Jamie thought about all the code that enabled her to do it, that enabled them both to feel the pressure of unreal flesh on unreal flesh.

"I'll do what you wish, of course," she said. "I don't have that desire for immortality, the way your father does." She shook her head. "But I don't know what your father will do once his time comes."

The world was a disk a hundred meters across, covered with junk: old Roman ruins, gargoyles fallen from a castle wall, a broken chariot, a shattered bell. Outside the rim of the world, the sky was black, utterly black, without a ripple or a star.

Standing in the center of the world was a kind of metal tree with two forked, jagged arms.

"Hi, Digit," Becca said.

A dull fitful light gleamed on the metal tree, as if it were reflecting a bloody sunset.

"Hi, sis," it said.

"Well," Becca said. "We're alone now."

"I caught the notice of Dad's funeral. I hope nobody missed me."

"*I* missed you, Digit." Becca sighed. "Believe it or not."

"I'm sorry."

Becca restlessly kicked a piece of junk, a hubcap from an old, miniature car. It clanged as it found new lodgement in the rubble. "Can you appear as a person?" she asked. "It would make it easier to talk to you."

"I've finished with all that," Jamie said. "I'd have to resurrect too much dead programming. I've cut the world down to next to nothing; I've got rid of my body, my heartbeat, the sense of touch."

"All the human parts," Becca said sadly.

The dull red light oozed over the metal tree like a drop of blood. "Everything except sleep and dreams. It turns out that sleep and dreams have too much to do with the way people process memory. I can't get rid of them, not without cutting out too much of my mind." The tree gave a strange, disembodied laugh. "I dreamed about you, the other day. And about Cicero. We were talking Latin."

"I've forgotten all the Latin I ever knew." Becca tossed her hair, forced a laugh. "So what do you do nowadays?"

"Mostly I'm a conduit for data. The University has been using me as a research spider, which I don't mind doing, because it passes the time. Except that I take up a lot more memory than any real search spider, and don't do that much better a job. And the information I find doesn't have much to do with *me*—it's all about the real world. The world I can't touch." The metal tree bled color.

"Mostly," he said, "I've just been waiting for Dad to die. And now it's happened."

There was a moment of silence before Becca spoke. "You know that Dad had himself scanned before he went."

"Oh yeah. I knew."

"He set up some kind of weird foundation that I'm not part of, with his patents and programs and so on, and his money and some other people's."

"He'd better not turn up here."

Becca shook her head. "He won't. Not without your permission, anyway. Because I'm in charge here. You—your program—it's not a part of the foundation. Dad couldn't get it all, because the University has an interest, and so does the family." There was a moment of silence. "And I'm the family now."

"So you...*inherited* me," Jamie said. Cold scorn dripped from his words.

"That's right," Becca said. She squatted down amid the rubble, rested her forearms on her knees.

"What do you want me to do, Digit? What can I do to make it better for you?"

"No one ever asked me that," Jamie said.

There was another long silence.

"Shut it off," Jamie said. "Close the file. Erase it."

Becca swallowed hard. Tears shimmered in her eyes. "Are you sure?" she asked.

"Yes. I'm sure."

"And if they ever perfect the clone thing? If we could make you..." She took a breath. "A person?"

"No. It's too late. It's...not something I can want anymore."

Becca stood. Ran a hand through her hair. "I wish you could meet my daughter," she said. "Her name is Christy. She's a real beauty."

"You can bring her," Jamie said.

Becca shook her head. "This place would scare her. She's only three. I'd only bring her if we could have..."

"The old environment," Jamie finished. "Pandaland. Mister Jeepers. Whirlikin Country."

Becca forced a smile. "Those were happy days," she said. "They really were. I was jealous of you, I know, but when I look back at that time..." She wiped tears with the back of her hand. "It was the best."

"Virtual environments are nice places to visit, I guess," Jamie said. "But you don't want to live in one. Not forever." Becca looked down at her feet, planted amid rubble.

"Well," she said. "If you're sure about what you want."

"I am."

She looked up at the metal form, raised a hand. "Goodbye, Jamie," she said.

"Goodbye," he said.

She faded from the world.

And in time, the world and the tree faded, too.

Hand in hand, Daddy and Jamie walked to Whirlikin Country. Jamie had never seen the Whirlikins before, and he laughed and laughed as the Whirlikins spun beneath their orange sky.

The sound of a bell rang over the green hills. "Time for dinner, Jamie,"

Daddy said.

Jamie waved goodbye to the Whirlikins, and he and Daddy walked briskly over the fresh green grass toward home.

"Are you happy, Jamie?" Daddy asked.

"Yes, Daddy!" Jamie nodded. "I only wish Momma and Becky could be here with us."

"They'll be here soon."

When, he thought, they can get the simulations working properly.

Because this time, he thought, there would be no mistakes. The foundation he'd set up before he died had finally purchased the University's interest in Jamie's program—they funded some scholarships, that was all it finally took. There was no one in the Computer Department who had an interest anymore.

Jamie had been loaded from an old backup—there was no point in using the corrupt file that Jamie had become, the one that had turned itself into a *tree*, for heaven's sake.

The old world was up and running, with a few improvements. The foundation had bought their own computer—an old one, so it wasn't too expensive—that would run the environment full time. Some other children might be scanned, to give Jamie some playmates and peer socialization.

This time it would work, Daddy thought. Because this time, Daddy was a program too, and he was going to be here every minute, making sure that the environment was correct and that everything went exactly according to plan. That he and Jamie and everyone else had a normal family life, perfect and shining and safe.

And if the clone program ever worked out, they would come into the real world again. And if downloading into clones was never perfected, then they would stay here.

There was nothing wrong with the virtual environment. It was a *good* place.

Just like normal family life. Only forever.

And when this worked out, the foundation's backers—fine people, even if they did have some strange religious ideas—would have their own environments up and running. With churches, angels, and perhaps even the presence of God…

"Look!" Daddy said, pointing. "It's Mister Jeepers!"

Mister Jeepers flew off the rooftop and spun happy spirals in the air as he swooped toward Jamie. Jamie dropped Daddy's hand and ran laughing to greet his friend.

"Jamie's home!" Mister Jeepers cried. "Jamie's home at last!"

## AFTERWORD: DADDY'S WORLD

*The story was originally called "The World and the Tree," but the publisher thought the title was insufficiently direct.*

*The story was solicited by Constance Ash, a friend for many years, for her anthology* Not of Woman Born, *dedicated to exploring the future of reproductive technologies.*

*I've always been skeptical of the claims of those who promote "uploading," the notion that the human consciousness will be much better off once it's reduced to digits and placed in a virtual environment where reality is more plastic and subject to experiment than on our own terraqueous globe. Such locations strike me as fine places for a vacation, but dreadful as a permanent residence. Ultimately we all inhabit physical reality—even virtual people, insofar as they would consist of a string of zeroes and ones stuck somewhere in a box—and physical reality provides the ultimate check on our tendency to megalomania. Ids in a box—how much fun would that be?*

*Living in virtual would be even less fun for a minor or dependent child. (This is a theme I returned to later, in "Incarnation Day.") A child would not be able to choose his environment, would theoretically be under adult supervision throughout his entire existence, would have to live with whatever system of punishments and rewards are established by adult authority, and would have no physical escape whatever. The child in effect would be living the parent's fantasy of childhood, rather than his own.*

*Of these conditions are nightmares born.*

*The Science Fiction and Fantasy Writers of America were kind enough to vote this story a Nebula Award.*

# LETHE

Davout had himself disassembled for the return journey. He had already been torn in half, he felt: the remainder, the dumb beast still alive, did not matter. The Captain had ruled, and Katrin would not be brought back. Davout did not want to spend the years between the stars in pain, confronting the gaping absence in his quarters, surrounded by the quiet sympathy of the crew.

Besides, he was no longer needed. The terraforming team had done its work, and then, but for Davout, had died.

Davout lay down on a bed of nano and let the little machines take him apart piece by piece, turn his body, his mind, and his unquenchable longing into long strings of numbers. The nanomachines crawled into his brain first, mapping, recording, and then shut down his mind piece by piece, so that he would feel no discomfort during what followed, or suffer a memory of his own body being taken apart.

Davout hoped that the nanos would shut down the pain before his consciousness failed, so that he could remember what it was like to live without the anguish that was now a part of his life, but it didn't work out that way. When his consciousness ebbed, he was aware, even to the last fading of the light, of the knife-blade of loss still buried in his heart.

The pain was there when Davout awoke, a wailing voice that cried, a pure contralto keen of agony, in his first dawning awareness. He found himself in an early-Victorian bedroom, blue-striped wallpaper, silhouettes in oval frames, silk flowers in vases. Crisp sheets, light streaming in the window. A stranger—shoulder-length hair, black frock coat, cravat carelessly tied—looked at him from a gothic-revival armchair. The man held a pipe in the right hand and tamped down tobacco with the prehensile big toe of his left foot.

"I'm not on the *Beagle*," Davout said.

The man gave a grave nod. His left hand formed the mudra for <correct>. "Yes."

"And this isn't a virtual?"

<Correct> again. "No."

"Then something has gone wrong."

<Correct> "Yes. A moment, sir, if you please." The man finished tamping, slipped his foot into a waiting boot, then lit the pipe with the anachronistic lighter in his left hand. He puffed, drew in smoke, exhaled, put the lighter in his pocket, and settled back in the walnut embrace of his chair.

"I am Dr. Li," he said. <Stand by> said the left hand, the old finger position for a now-obsolete palmtop computer, a finger position that had once meant *pause*, as <correct> had once meant *enter*, enter because it was correct. "Please remain in bed for a few more minutes while the nanos double-check their work. Redundancy is frustrating," puffing smoke, "but good for peace of mind."

"What happens if they find they've made a mistake?"

<Don't be concerned> "It can't be a very large mistake," said Li, "or we wouldn't be communicating so rationally. At worst, you will sleep for a bit while things are corrected."

"May I take my hands out from under the covers?" he asked.

"Yes."

Davout did so. His hands, he observed, were brown and leathery, hands suitable for the hot, dry world of Sarpedon. They had not, then, changed his body for one more suited to Earth, but given him something familiar.

If, he realized, they were on Earth.

His right fingers made the mudra <thank you>.

<Don't mention it> signed Li.

Davout passed a hand over his forehead, discovered that the forehead, hand, and the gesture itself were perfectly familiar.

Strange, but the gesture convinced him that he was, in a vital way, still himself. Still Davout.

Still alive, he thought. Alas.

"Tell me what happened," he said. "Tell me why I'm here."

Li signed <stand by>, made a visible effort to collect himself. "We believe," he said, "that the *Beagle* was destroyed. If so, you are the only survivor."

Davout found his shock curiously veiled. The loss of the other lives—friends, most of them—stood muted by the precedent of his own earlier, overriding grief. It is as if the two losses were weighed in a balance, and the *Beagle* found wanting.

Li, Davout observed, was waiting for Davout to absorb this information before continuing.

<Go on> Davout signed.

"The accident happened seven light-years out," Li said. "*Beagle* began to yaw wildly, and both automatic systems and the crew failed to correct the maneuver. *Beagle*'s automatic systems concluded that the ship was unlikely to survive the increasing oscillations, and began to use its communications lasers to download personality data to collectors in Earth orbit. As the only crew member to elect disassembly during the return journey, you were first in the queue. The others, we presume, ran to nano disassembly stations, but communication was lost with the *Beagle* before we retrieved any of their data."

"Did Katrin's come through?"

Li stirred uneasily in his chair. <Regrettably> "I'm afraid not."

Davout closed his eyes. He had lost her again. Over the bubble of hopelessness in his throat he asked, "How long has it been since my data arrived?"

"A little over eight days."

They had waited eight days, then, for *Beagle*—for the *Beagle* of seven years ago—to correct its problem and reestablish communication. If *Beagle* had resumed contact, the mass of data that was Davout might have been erased as redundant.

"The government has announced the loss," Li said. "Though there is a remote chance that the *Beagle* may come flying in or through the system in eleven years as scheduled, we have detected no more transmissions, and we've been unable to observe any blueshifted deceleration torch aimed at our system. The government decided that it would be unfair to keep sibs and survivors in the dark any longer."

<Concur> Davout signed.

He envisioned the last moments of the *Beagle*, the crew being flung back and forth as the ship slammed through increasing pendulum swings, the desperate attempts, fighting wildly fluctuating gravity and inertia, to reach the emergency nanobeds... no panic, Davout thought, Captain Moshweshwe had trained his people too well for that. Just desperation, and determination, and, as the oscillations grew worse, an increasing sense of futility, and impending death.

No one expected to die anymore. It was always a shock when it happened near you. Or *to* you.

"The cause of the *Beagle*'s problem remains unknown," Li said, the voice far away. "The Bureau is working with simulators to try to discover what happened."

Davout leaned back against his pillow. Pain throbbed in his veins, pain and loss, knowledge that his past, his joy, was irrecoverable. "The whole voyage," he said, "was a catastrophe."

<I respectfully contradict> Li signed. "You terraformed and explored two worlds," he said. "Downloads are already living on these worlds, hundreds of thousands now, millions later. There would have been a third world added to our commonwealth if your mission had not been cut short due to the, ah, first accident..."

<Concur> Davout signed, but only because his words would have come out with too much bitterness.

<Sorry>, a curt jerk of Li's fingers. "There are messages from your sibs," Li said, "and downloads from them also. The sibs and friends of *Beagle*'s crew will try to contact you, no doubt. You need not answer any of these messages until you're ready."

<Understood>

Davout hesitated, but the words were insistent; he gave them tongue. "Have Katrin's sibs sent messages?" he asked.

Li's grave expression scarcely changed. "I believe so." He tilted his head. "Is there anything I can do for you? Anything I can arrange?"

"Not now, no," said Davout. <Thank you> he signed. "Can I move from the bed now?"

Li's look turned abstract as he scanned indicators projected somewhere in his mind. <Yes> "You may," he said. He rose from his chair, took the pipe from his mouth. "You are in a hospital, I should add," he said, "but you do not have the formal status of patient, and may leave at any time. Likewise, you may stay here for the foreseeable future, as long as you feel it necessary."

<Thank you> "Where is this hospital, by the way?"

"West Java. The city of Bandung."

Earth, then. Which Davout had not seen in seventy-seven years. Memory's gentle fingers touched his mind with the scent of durian, of ocean, of mace, cloves, and turmeric.

He knew he was never in Java before, though, and wondered whence the memory came. From one of his sibs, perhaps?

<Thank you> Davout signed again, putting a touch of finality, a kind of dismissal, into the twist of his fingers.

Dr. Li left Davout alone, in his new/old body, in the room that whispered of memory and pain.

In a dark wood armoire Davout found identification and clothing, and a record confirming that his account had received seventy-eight years' back pay. His electronic inbox contained downloads from his sibs and more personal messages than he could cope with—he would have to construct an electronic personality to answer most of them.

He dressed and left the hospital. Whoever supervised his reassembly—Dr. Li perhaps—had thoughtfully included a complete Earth atlas in his internal ROM, and he accessed it as he walked, making random turnings but never getting lost. The furious sun burned down with tropical intensity, but his current body was constructed to bear heat, and a breeze off the mountains made pleasant even the blazing noontide.

The joyful metal music of the *gamelans* clattered from almost every doorway. People in bright clothing, agile as the siamang of near Sumatra, sped overhead along treeways and ropeways, arms and hands modified for brachiation. Robots, immune to the heat, shimmered past on silent tires. Davout found it all strangely familiar, as if he had been here in a dream.

And then he found himself by the sea, and a pang of familiarity knifed through his heart. *Home!* cried his thoughts. Other worlds he had built, other beauties he had seen, but he had never beheld *this* blue, *this* perfection, anywhere else but on his native sphere. Subtle differences in atmospherics had rendered this color unnatural on any other world.

And with the cry of familiarity came a memory: it had been Davout the Silent who had come here, a century or more ago, and Katrin had been by his side.

But Davout's Katrin was dead. And as he looked on Earth's beauty, he felt his world of joy turn to bitter ashes.

<Alas!> His fingers formed the word unbidden. <Alas!>

He lived in a world where no one died, and nothing was ever lost. One understood that such things occasionally occurred, but never—hardly ever—to anyone that one knew. Physical immortality was cheap and easy, and was supported by so many alternate systems: backing up the mind by downloading, or downloading into a virtual reality system or into a durable machine. Nanosystems duplicated the body or improved it, adapted it for different environments. Data slumbered in secure storage, awaiting the electron kiss that returned it to life. Bringing a child to term in the womb was now the rarest form of reproduction, and bringing a child to life in a machine womb the next rarest.

It was so much easier to have the nanos duplicate you as an adult. Then, at least, you had someone to talk to.

No one died, and nothing is ever lost. But Katrin died, Davout thought, and now I am lost, and it was not supposed to be this way.

<Alas!> Fingers wailed the grief that was stopped up in Davout's throat. <Alas!>

Davout and Katrin had met in school, members of the last generation in which womb-breeding outnumbered the alternatives. Immortality whispered its covenant into their receptive ears. On their first meeting, attending a lecture (Dolphus on "Reinventing the Humbolt Sea") at the College of Mystery, they looked at each other and knew, as if angels had whispered into their ears, that there was now one less mystery in the world, that each served as an answer to another, that each fitted neatly into a hollow that the other had perceived in his or her soul, dropping into place as neatly as a butter-smooth piece in a finely made teak puzzle—or, considering their interests, as easily as a carbolic functional group nested into place on an indole ring.

Their rapport was, they freely admitted, miraculous. Still young, they exploded into the world, into a universe that welcomed them.

He could not bear to be away from her. Twenty-four hours was the absolute limit before Davout's nerves began to beat a frustrated little tattoo, and he found himself conjuring a phantom Katrin in his imagination, just to have someone to share the world with—he *needed* her there, needed this human lens through which he viewed the universe.

Without her, Davout found the cosmos veiled in a kind of uncertainty. While it was possible to apprehend certain things (the usefulness of a coenocytic arrangement of cells in the transmission of information-bearing proteins and nuclei, the historical significance of the Yucatan astrobleme, the limitations of the Bénard cell model in predicting thermic instabilities in the atmosphere), these things lacked *noesis*, existed only as a series of singular, purposeless accidents. Reflected through Katrin, however, the world took on brilliance, purpose, and genius. With Katrin he could feast upon the universe; without her the world lacked savor.

Their interests were similar enough for each to generate enthusiasm in the other, diverse enough that each was able to add perspective to the other's work. They worked in cozy harmony, back to back, two desks set in the same room. Sometimes Davout would return from a meeting, or a coffee break, and find that Katrin had added new paragraphs, sometimes an entire new direction, to his latest effort. On occasion he would return the favor. Their early work—eccentric, proliferating in too many directions, toward too many specialties—showed life and promise and more than a hint of brilliance.

Too much, they decided, for just the two of them. They wanted to do too much, and all at once, and an immortal lifetime was not time enough.

And so, as soon as they could afford it, Red Katrin, the original, was duplicated—with a few cosmetic alterations—in Dark Katrin and later Katrin the Fair; and nanomachines read Old Davout, blood and bone and the long strands of numbers that were his soul, and created perfect copies in Dangerous Davout, later called the Conqueror, and Davout the Silent.

Two had become six, and half a dozen, they now agreed, was about all the universe could handle for the present. The wild tangle of overlapping interests was parceled out between the three couples, each taking one of the three most noble paths to understanding. The eldest couple chose History as their domain, a part of which involved chronicling the adventures of their sibs; the second couple took Science; the third Psyche, the exploration of the human mind. Any developments, any insights, on the part of one of the sibs could be shared with the others through downloads. In the beginning they downloaded themselves almost continually, sharing their thoughts and experiences and plans in a creative frenzy. Later, as separate lives and more specialized careers developed, the downloads grew less frequent, though there were no interruptions until Dangerous Davout and Dark Katrin took their first voyage to another star. They spent over fifty years away, though to them it was less than thirty; and the downloads from Earth, pulsed over immense distances by communications lasers, were less frequent, and less frequently resorted to. The lives of the other couples, lived at what seemed speeded-up rates, were of decreasing relevance to their own existence, as if they were lives that dwelled in a half-remembered dream.

<Alas!> the fingers signed. <Alas!> for the dream turned to savage nightmare.

The sea, a perfect terrestrial blue, gazed back into Davout's eyes, indifferent to the sadness frozen into his fingers.

"Your doctors knew that to wake here, after such an absence, would result in a feeling of anachronism," said Davout's sib, "so they put you in this Victorian room, where you would at least feel at ease with the kind of anachronism by which you are surrounded." He smiles at Davout from the neo-gothic armchair. "If you were in a modern room, you might experience a sensation of obsolescence. But everyone can feel superior to the Victorians, and besides one is always more comfortable in one's past."

"Is one?" Davout asked, fingers signing <irony>. The past and the present, he found, were alike, a place of torment.

"I discover," he continued, "that my thoughts stray for comfort not to the past, but to the future."

"Ah." A smile. "That is why we call you Davout the Conqueror."

"I do not seem to inhabit that name," Davout said, "if I ever did."

Concern shadowed the face of Davout's sib. <Sorry> he signed, and then made another sign for <profoundly>, the old *multiply* sign, multiples of sorrow in his gesture.

"I understand," he said. "I experienced your last download. It was…

intensely disturbing. I have never felt such terror, such loss."

"Nor had I," said Davout.

It was Old Davout whose image was projected into the gothic-revival armchair, the original, womb-born Davout of whom the two sibs were copies. When Davout looked at him it was like looking into a mirror in which his reflection had been retarded for several centuries, then unexpectedly released—Davout remembered, several bodies back, once possessing that tall forehead, the fair hair, the small ears flattened close to the skull. The grey eyes he had still, but he could never picture himself wearing the professorial little goatee.

"How is our other sib?" Davout asked.

The concern on Old Davout's face deepened. "You will find Silent Davout much changed. You haven't uploaded him, then?"

<No> "Due to the delays, I'm thirty years behind on my uploading."

"Ah." <Regret> "Perhaps you should speak to him, then, before you upload all those years."

"I will." He looked at his sib and hoped the longing did not burn in his eyes. "Please give my best to Katrin, will you?"

"I will give her your *love*," said Old Davout, wisest of the sibs.

The pain was there when Davout awoke next day, fresh as the moment it first knifed through him, on the day their fifth child, the planet Sarpedon, was christened. Sarpedon had been discovered by astronomers a couple centuries before, and named, with due regard for tradition, after yet another minor character in Homer; it had been mapped and analyzed by robot probes; but it had been the *Beagle*'s terraforming team that had made the windswept place, with its barren mountain ranges and endless deserts, its angry radiation and furious dust storms, into a place suitable for life.

Katrin was the head of the terraforming team. Davout led its research division. Between them, raining nano from Sarpedon's black skies, they nursed the planet to life, enriched its atmosphere, filled its seas, crafted tough, versatile vegetation capable of withstanding the angry environment. Seeded life by the tens of millions, insects, reptiles, birds, mammals, fish and amphibians. Re-created themselves, with dark, leathery skin and slit pupils, as human forms suitable for Sarpedon's environment, so that they could examine the place they had built.

And—unknown to the others—Davout and Katrin had slipped bits of their own genetics into almost every Sarpedan life-form. Bits of redundant coding, mostly, but enough so that they could claim Sarpedon's entire world of creatures as their children. Even when they were junior terraformers on the *Cheng Ho*'s mission to Rhea, they had, partly as a joke, partly as something more calculated, populated their creations with their genes.

Katrin and Davout spent the last two years of their project on Sarpedon among their children, examining the different ecosystems, different interactions, tinkering with new adaptations. In the end Sarpedon was certified as suitable for human habitation. Preprogrammed nanos constructed small towns, laid out fields, parks, and roads. The first human Sarpedans would be constructed in nanobeds, and their minds filled with the downloaded personalities of volunteers from Earth. There was no need to go to the expense and trouble of shipping out millions of warm bodies from Earth, running the risks of traveling for decades in remote space. Not when nanos could construct them all new on site.

The first Sarpedans—bald, leather-skinned, slit-eyed—emerged blinking into their new red dawn. Any further terraforming, any attempts to fine-tune the planet and make it more Earthlike, would be a long-term project and up to them. In a splendid ceremony, Captain Moshweshwe formally turned the future of Sarpedon over to its new inhabitants. Davout had a few last formalities to perform, handing certain computer codes and protocols over to the Sarpedans, but the rest of the terraforming team, most fairly drunk on champagne, filed into the shuttle for the return journey to the *Beagle*. As Davout bent over a terminal with his Sarpedan colleagues and the *Beagle*'s first officer, he could hear the roar of the shuttle on its pad, the sustained thunder as it climbed for orbit, the thud as it crashed through the sound barrier, and then he saw out of the corner of his eye the sudden red-gold flare…

When he raced outside it was to see the blazing poppy unfolding in the sky, a blossom of fire and metal falling slowly to the surface of the newly christened planet.

There she was—her image anyway—in the neo-gothic armchair: Red Katrin, the green-eyed lady with whom he in memory, and Old Davout in reality, had first exchanged glances two centuries ago while Dolphus expanded on what he called his "lunaforming."

Davout had hesitated about returning her call of condolence. He did not know whether his heart could sustain *two* knife-thrusts, both Katrin's death and the sight of her sib, alive, sympathetic, and forever beyond his reach.

But he couldn't *not* call her. Even when he was trying not to think about her, he still found Katrin on the edge of his perceptions, drifting through his thoughts like the persistent trace of some familiar perfume.

Time to get it over with, he thought. If it was more than he could stand, he could apologize and end the call. But he had to *know*…

"And there are no backups?" she said. A pensive frown touched her lips.

"No *recent* backups," Davout said. "We always thought that, if we were to die, we would die together. Space travel is hazardous, after all, and when catastrophe strikes it is not a *small* catastrophe. We didn't anticipate one of us surviving a catastrophe on Earth, and the other dying light-years away." He scowled.

"Damn Moshweshwe anyway! There were recent backups on the *Beagle*, but with so many dead from an undetermined cause he decided not to resurrect anyone, to cancel our trip to Astoreth, return to Earth, and sort out all the complications once he got home."

"He made the right decision," Katrin said. "If my sib had been resurrected, you both would have died together."

<Better so> Davout's fingers began to form the mudra, but he thought better of it, made a gesture of negation.

The green eyes narrowed. "There are older backups on Earth, yes?"

"Katrin's latest surviving backup dates from the return of the *Cheng Ho*."

"Almost ninety years ago." Thoughtfully. "But she could upload the memories she has been sending me… the problem does not seem insurmountable."

Red Katrin clasped her hands around one knee. At the familiar gesture, memories rang through Davout's mind like change-bells. Vertigo overwhelmed him, and he closed his eyes.

"The problem is the instructions Katrin—we both—left," he said. "Again, we anticipated that if we died, we'd die together. And so we left instructions that our backups on Earth were not to be employed. We reasoned that we had two sibs apiece on Earth, and if they—you—missed us, you could simply duplicate yourselves."

"I see." A pause, then concern. "Are you all right?"

<No> "Of course not," he said. He opened his eyes. The world eddied for a moment, then stilled, the growing calmness centered on Red Katrin's green eyes.

"I've got seventy-odd years' back pay," he said. "I suppose that I could hire some lawyers, try to get Katrin's backup released to my custody."

Red Katrin bit her nether lip. "Recent court decisions are not in your favor."

"I'm very persistent. And I'm cash-rich."

She cocked her head, looked at him. "Are you all right talking to me? Should I blank my image?"

<No.> He shook his head. "It helps, actually, to see you."

He had feared agony in seeing her, but instead he found a growing joy, a happiness that mounted in his heart. As always, his Katrin was helping him to understand, helping him to make sense of the bitter confusion of the world.

An idea began to creep into his mind on stealthy feet.

"I worry that you're alone there," Red Katrin said. "Would you like to come stay with us? Would you like us to come to Java?"

<No, thanks> "I'll come see you soon," Davout said. "But while I'm in the hospital, I think I'll have a few cosmetic procedures." He looked down at himself, spread his leathery hands. "Perhaps I should look a little more Earthlike."

After his talk with Katrin ended, Davout called Dr. Li and told him that he wanted a new body constructed.

Something familiar, he said, already in the files. His own, original form.

Age twenty or so.

"It is a surprise to see you... as you are," said Silent Davout.

Deep-voiced, black-skinned, and somber, Davout's sib stood by his bed.

"It was a useful body when I wore it," Davout answered. "I take comfort in... familiar things... now that my life is so uncertain." He looked up. "It was good of you to come in person."

"A holographic body," taking Davout's hand, "however welcome, however familiar, is not the same as a real person."

Davout squeezed the hand. "Welcome, then," he said. Dr. Li, who had supervised in person through the new/old body's assembly, had left after saying the nanos were done, so it seemed appropriate for Davout to stand and embrace his sib.

The youngest of the sibs was not tall, but he was built solidly, as if for permanence, and his head seemed slightly oversized for his body. With his older sibs he had always maintained a kind of formal reserve that had resulted in his being nicknamed "the Silent." Accepting the name, he remarked that the reason he spoke little when the others were around is that his older sibs had already said everything that needed saying before he got to it.

Davout stepped back and smiled. "Your patients must think you a tower of strength."

"I have no patients these days. Mostly I work in the realm of theory."

"I will have to look up your work. I'm so far behind on uploads—I don't have any idea what you and Katrin have been doing these last decades."

Silent Davout stepped to the armoire and opened its ponderous mahogany doors. "Perhaps you should put on some clothing," he said. "I am feeling a chill in this conditioned air, and so must you."

Amused, Davout clothed himself, then sat across the little rosewood side table from his sib. Davout the Silent looked at him for a long moment—eyes placid and thoughtful—and then spoke.

"You are experiencing something that is very rare in our time," he said. "Loss, anger, frustration, terror. All the emotions that in their totality equal *grief.*"

"You forgot sadness and regret," Davout said. "You forget memory, and how the memories keep replaying. You forgot *imagination*, and how imagination only makes those memories worse, because imagination allows you to write a different ending, but the world will not."

Silent Davout nodded. "People in my profession," fingers forming <irony>, "anyway those born too late to remember how common these things once were, must view you with a certain clinical interest. I must commend Dr. Li on his restraint."

"Dr. Li is a shrink?" Davout asks.

<Yes> A casual press of fingers. "Among other things. I'm sure he's watching you very carefully and making little notes every time he leaves the room."

"I'm happy to be useful." <Irony> in his hand, bitterness on his tongue. "I would give those people my memories, if they want them so much."

<Of course> "You can do that." Davout looked up in something like surprise.

"You know it is possible," his sib said. "You can download your memories, preserve them like amber or simply hand them to someone else to experience. And you can erase them from your mind completely, walk on into a new life, *tabula rasa* and free of pain."

His deep voice was soft. It was a voice without affect, one he no doubt used on his patients, quietly insistent without being officious. A voice that made suggestions, or presented alternatives, but which never, ever, gave orders.

"I don't want that," Davout said.

Silent Davout's fingers were still set in <of course>. "You are not of the generation that accepts such things as a matter of course," he said. "But this, this *modular* approach to memory, to being, constitutes much of my work these days."

Davout looked at him. "It must be like losing a piece of yourself, to give up a memory. Memories are what make you."

Silent Davout's face remained impassive as his deep voice sounded through the void between them. "What forms a human psyche is not a memory, we have come to believe, but a pattern of thought. When our sib duplicated himself, he duplicated his pattern in us; and when we assembled new bodies to live in, the pattern did not change. Have you felt yourself a different person when you took a new body?"

Davout passed a hand over his head, felt the fine blond hair covering his scalp. This time yesterday, his head had been bald and leathery. Now he felt subtle differences in his perceptions—his vision was more acute, his hearing less so—and his muscle memory was somewhat askew. He remembered having a shorter reach, a slightly different center of gravity.

But as for *himself*, his essence—no, he felt himself unchanged. He was still Davout.

<No> he signed.

"People have more choices than ever before," said Silent Davout. "They choose their bodies, they choose their memories. They can upload new knowledge, new skills. If they feel a lack of confidence, or feel that their behavior is too impulsive, they can tweak their body chemistry to produce a different effect. If they find themselves the victim of an unfortunate or destructive compulsion, the compulsion can be edited from their being. If they lack the power to change their circumstances, they can at least elect to feel happier about them. If a memory cannot be overcome, it can be eliminated."

"And you now spend your time dealing with these problems?" Davout asked.

"They are not *problems*," his sib said gently. "They are not *syndromes* or *neuroses*. They are *circumstances*. They are part of the condition of life as it exists today. They are environmental." The large, impassive eyes gazed steadily at Davout. "People choose happiness over sorrow, fulfillment over frustration. Can you blame them?"

<Yes> Davout signed. "If they deny the evidence of their own lives," he said. "We define our existence by the challenges we overcome, or those we don't. Even our tragedies define us."

His sib nodded. "That is an admirable philosophy—for Davout the Conqueror. But not all people are conquerors."

Davout strove to keep the impatience from his voice. "Lessons are learned from failures as well as successes. Experience is gained, life's knowledge is applied to subsequent occurrence. If we deny the uses of experience, what is there to make us human?"

His sib was patient. "Sometimes the experiences are negative, and so are the lessons. Would you have a person live forever under the shadow of great guilt, say for a foolish mistake that resulted in injury or death to someone else; or would you have them live with the consequences of damage inflicted by a sociopath, or an abusive family member? Traumas like these can cripple the whole being. Why should the damage not be repaired?"

Davout smiled thinly. "You can't tell me that these techniques are used only in cases of deep trauma," he said. "You can't tell me that people aren't using these techniques for reasons that might be deemed trivial. Editing out a foolish remark made at a party, or eliminating a bad vacation or an argument with the spouse."

Silent Davout returned his smile. "I would not insult your intelligence by suggesting these things do not happen."

<Q.E.D.> Davout signed. "So how do such people mature? Change? Grow in wisdom?"

"They cannot edit out *everything*. There is sufficient friction and conflict in the course of ordinary life to provide everyone with their allotted portion of wisdom. Nowadays our lives are very, very long, and we have a long time to learn, however slowly. And after all," smiling, "the average person's capacity for wisdom has never been so large as all that. I think you will find that as a species we are far less prone to folly than we once were."

Davout looked at his sib grimly. "You are suggesting that I undergo this technique?"

"It is called Lethe."

"That I undergo Lethe? Forget Katrin? Or forget what I feel for her?"

Silent Davout slowly shakes his grave head. "I make no such suggestion."

"Good."

The youngest Davout gazed steadily into the eyes of his older twin. "Only you know what you can bear. I merely point out that this remedy exists, should you find your anguish beyond what you can endure."

"Katrin deserves mourning," Davout said.

Another grave nod. "Yes."

"She deserves to be remembered. Who will remember her if I do not?"

"I understand," said Silent Davout. "I understand your desire to feel, and the necessity. I only mention Lethe because I comprehend all too well what you endure now. Because," he licked his lips, "I, too, have lost Katrin."

Davout gaped at him. "You —" he stammered. "She is—she was killed?"

<No> His sib's face retains its remarkable placidity. "She left me, sixteen years ago."

Davout could only stare. The fact, stated so plainly, was incomprehensible.

"I —" he began, and then his fingers found another thought. <What happened?>

"We were together for a century and a half. We grew apart. It happens."

*Not to us it doesn't!* Davout's mind protested. *Not to* Davout and Katrin!

Not to the two people who make up a whole greater than its parts. Not to us. Not ever.

But looking into his sib's accepting, melancholy face, Davout knew that it had to be true.

And then, in a way he knew to be utterly disloyal, he began to hope.

"Shocking?" said Old Davout. "Not to us, I suppose."

"It was their downloads," said Red Katrin. "Fair Katrin in particular was careful to edit out some of her feelings and judgments before she let me upload them, but still I could see her attitudes changing. And knowing her, I could make guesses by what she left out... I remember telling Davout three years before the split that the relationship was in jeopardy."

"The Silent One was still surprised, though, when it happened," Old Davout said. "Sophisticated though he may be about human nature, he had a blind spot where Katrin was concerned." He put an arm around Red Katrin and kissed her cheek. "As I suppose we all do," he added.

Katrin accepted the kiss with a gracious inclination of her head, then asked Davout, "Would you like the blue room here, or the green room upstairs? The green room has a window seat and a fine view of the bay, but it's small."

"I'll take the green room," Davout said. I do not need so much room, he thought, now that I am alone.

Katrin took him up the creaking wooden stair and showed him the room, the narrow bed of the old house. Through the window he could look south to a storm on Chesapeake Bay, bluegrey cloud, bright eruptions of lightning, slanting beams of sunlight that dropped through rents in the storm to tease bright winking light from the foam. He watched it for a long moment, then was startled out of reverie by Katrin's hand on his shoulder, and a soft voice in his ear.

"Are there sights like this on other worlds?"

"The storms on Rhea were vast," Davout said, "like nothing on this world. The ocean area is greater than that on Earth, and lies mostly in the tropics—the planet was almost called Oceanus on that account. The hurricanes built up around the equatorial belts with nothing to stop them, sometimes more than a thousand kilometers across, and they came roaring into the temperate zones like multi-armed demons, sometimes one after another for months. They spawned waterspots and cyclones in their vanguard, inundated whole areas with a storm surge the size of a small ocean, dumped enough rain to flood an entire province away... We thought seriously that the storms might make life on land untenable."

He went on to explain the solution he and Katrin had devised for the enormous problem: huge strings of tall, rocky barrier islands built at a furious rate by nanomachines, a wall for wind and storm surge to break against; a species of silvery, tropical floating weed, a flowery girdle about Rhea's thick waist, that radically increased surface albedo, reflecting more heat back into space. Many species of deep-rooted, vinelike plants to anchor slopes and prevent erosion, other species of thirsty trees, adaptations of cottonwoods and willows, to line streambeds and break the power of flash floods.

Planetary engineering on such an enormous scale, in such a short time, had never been attempted, not even on Mars, and it had been difficult for Katrin and Davout to sell the project to the project managers on the *Cheng Ho*. Their superiors had initially preferred a different approach, huge equatorial solar curtains deployed in orbit to reflect heat, squadrons of orbital beam weapons to blast and disperse storms as they formed, secure underground dwellings for the inhabitants, complex lock and canal systems to control flooding... Katrin and Davout had argued for a more elegant approach to Rhea's problems, a reliance on organic systems to modify the planet's extreme weather instead of assaulting Rhea with macro-tech and engineering. Theirs was the approach that finally won the support of the majority of the terraforming team, and resulted in their subsequent appointment as heads of *Beagle's* terraforming team.

"Dark Katrin's memories were very exciting to upload during that time," said Katrin the Red. "That delirious explosion of creativity! Watching a whole globe take shape beneath her feet!" Her green eyes look up into Davout's. "We were jealous of you then. All that abundance being created, all that talent going to shaping an entire world. And we were confined to scholarship, which seemed so lifeless by comparison."

He looked at her. <Query> "Are you sorry for the choice you made? You two were senior: you could have chosen our path if you'd wished. You still could, come to that."

A smile drifts across her face. "You tempt me, truly. But Old Davout and I are happy in our work—and besides, you and Katrin needed someone to provide a proper record of your adventures." She tilted her head, and mischief glittered in her eyes. "Perhaps you should ask Blonde Katrin. Maybe she could use a change."

Davout gave a guilty start: she was, he thought, seeing too near, too soon. "Do you think so?" he asked. "I didn't even know if I should see her."

"Her grudge is with the Silent One, not with you."

"Well." He manages a smile. "Perhaps I will at least call."

Davout called Katrin the Fair, received an offer of dinner on the following day, accepted. From his room he followed the smell of coffee into his hosts' office, and felt a bubble of grief lodge in his heart: two desks, back-to-back, two computer terminals, layers of papers and books and printout and dust… he could imagine himself and Katrin here, sipping coffee, working in pleasant compatibility.

<How goes it?> he signed.

His sib looked up. "I just sent a chapter to Sheol," he said. "I was making *Maxwell* far too wise." He fingered his little goatee. "The temptation is always to view the past solely as a vehicle that leads to our present grandeur. These people's sole function was to produce *us*, who are of course perfectly wise and noble and far superior to our ancestors. So one assumes that these people had *us* in mind all along, that we were what they were working toward. I have to keep reminding myself that these people lived amid unimaginable tragedy, disease and ignorance and superstition, vile little wars, terrible poverty, and *death*…"

He stopped, suddenly aware that he'd said something awkward—Davout felt the word vibrate in his bones, as if he were stranded inside a bell that was still singing after it had been struck—but he said, "Go on."

"I remind myself," his sib continued, "that the fact that we live in a modern culture doesn't make us better, it doesn't make us superior to these people—in fact it enlarges *them*, because they had to overcome so much more than we in order to realize themselves, in order to accomplish as much as they did." A shy smile drifted across his face. "And so a rather smug chapter is wiped out of digital existence."

"*Lavoisier* is looming," commented Red Katrin from her machine.

"Yes, that too," Old Davout agreed. His *Lavoisier and His Age* had won the McEldowney Prize and been shortlisted for other awards. Davout could well imagine that bringing *Maxwell* up to *Lavoisier*'s magisterial standards would be intimidating.

Red Katrin leans back in her chair, combs her hair back with her fingers. "I made a few notes about the *Beagle* project," she said. "I have other commitments to deal with first, of course."

She and Old Davout had avoided any conflicts of interest and interpretation by conveniently dividing history between them: she would write of the "modern" world and her near-contemporaries, while he wrote of those securely in the past. Davout thought his sib had the advantage in this arrangement, because her subjects, as time progressed, gradually entered his domain, and became liable to his reinterpretation.

Davout cleared away some printout, sat on the edge of Red Katrin's desk. "A thought keeps bothering me," he said. "In our civilization we record everything. But the last moments of the crew of the *Beagle* went unrecorded.

Does that mean they do not exist? Never existed at all? That death was *always* their state, and they returned to it, like virtual matter dying into the vacuum from which it came?"

Concern darkened Red Katrin's eyes. "They will be remembered," she said. "I will see to it."

"Katrin didn't download the last months, did she?"

<No> "The last eight months were never sent. She was very busy, and—"

"Virtual months, then. Gone back to the phantom zone."

"There are records. Other crew sent downloads home, and I will see if I can gain access either to the downloads, or to their friends and relations who have experienced them. There is *your* memory, your downloads."

He looked at her. "Will you upload my memory, then? My sib has everything in his files, I'm sure." Glancing at Old Davout.

She pressed her lips together. "That would be difficult for me. *Me* viewing *you* viewing *her...*" She shook her head. "I don't dare. Not now. Not when we're all still in shock."

Disappointment gnawed at his insides with sharp rodent teeth. He did not want to be so alone in his grief; he didn't want to nourish all the sadness by himself.

He wanted to share it with *Katrin*, he knew, the person with whom he shared everything. Katrin could help him make sense of it, the way she clarified all the world for him. Katrin would comprehend the way he felt.

<I understand> he signed. His frustration must have been plain to Red Katrin, because she took his hand, lifted her green eyes to his.

"I *will*," she said. "But not now. I'm not ready."

"I don't want *two* wrecks in the house," called Old Davout over his shoulder.

Interfering old bastard, Davout thought. But with his free hand he signed, again, <I understand>.


Katrin the Fair kissed Davout's cheek, then stood back, holding his hands, and narrowed her grey eyes. "I'm not sure I approve of this youthful body of yours," she said. "You haven't looked like this in—what—over a century?"

"Perhaps I seek to evoke happier times," Davout said.

A little frown touched the corners of her mouth. "*That* is always dangerous," she judged. "But I wish you every success." She stepped back from the door, flung out an arm. "Please come in."

She lived in a small apartment in Toulouse, with a view of the Allée Saint-Michel and the rose-red brick of the Vieux Quartier. On the whitewashed walls hung terracotta icons of Usil and Tiv, the Etruscan gods of the sun and moon, and a well cover with a figure of the demon Charun emerging from the underworld. The Etruscan deities were confronted, on another wall, by a bronze figure of the Gaulish Rosmerta, consort of the absent Mercurius.

Her little balcony was bedecked with wrought iron and a gay striped awning. In front of the balcony a table shimmered under a red-and-white-checked tablecloth: crystal, porcelain, a wicker basket of bread, a bottle of wine. Cooking scents floated in from the kitchen.

"It smells wonderful," Davout said.

<Drink?> Lifting the bottle.

<Why not?>

Wine was poured. They settled onto the sofa, chatted of weather, crowds, Java. Davout's memories of the trip that Silent Davout and his Katrin had taken to the island were more recent than hers.

Fair Katrin took his hand. "I have uploaded Dark Katrin's memories, so far as I have them," she said. "She loved you, you know—absolutely, deeply." <Truth> She bit her nether lip. "It was a remarkable thing."

<Truth> Davout answered. He touched cool crystal to his lips, took a careful sip of his cabernet. Pain throbbed in the hollows of his heart.

"Yes," he said. "I know."

"I felt I should tell you about her feelings. Particularly in view of what happened with me and the Silent One."

He looked at her. "I confess I do not understand that business."

She made a little frown of distaste. "We and our work and our situation grew irksome. Oppressive. You may upload his memories if you like—I daresay you will be able to observe the signs that he was determined to ignore."

<I am sorry>

Clouds gathered in her grey eyes. "I, too, have regrets."

"There is no chance of reconciliation?"

<Absolutely not>, accompanied by a brief shake of the head. "It was over." <Finished> "And, in any case, Davout the Silent is not the man he was."

<Yes?>

"He took Lethe. It was the only way he had of getting over my leaving him."

Pure amazement throbbed in Davout's soul. Fair Katrin looked at him in surprise.

"You didn't know?"

He blinked at her. "I *should* have. But I thought he was talking about *me*, about a way of getting over..." Aching sadness brimmed in his throat.

"Over the way my Dark Katrin left me."

Scorn whitened the flesh about Fair Katrin's nostrils. "That's the Silent One for you. He didn't have the nerve to tell you outright."

"I'm not sure that's true. He may have thought he was speaking plainly enough —"

Her fingers formed a mudra that gave vent to a brand of disdain that did not translate into words. "He knows his effects perfectly well," she said. "He was trying to suggest the idea without making it clear that this was his *choice* for you, that he wanted you to fall in line with his theories."

Anger was clear in her voice. She rose, stalked angrily to the bronze of Rosmerta, adjusted its place on the wall by a millimeter or so. Turned, waved an arm. <Apologies>, flung to the air. "Let's eat. Silent Davout is the last person I want to talk about right now."

"I'm sorry I upset you." Davout was not sorry at all: he found this display fascinating. The gestures, the tone of voice, were utterly familiar, ringing like chimes in his heart; but the *style*, the way Fair Katrin avoided the issue, was different. Dark Katrin would never have fled a subject this way: she would have knit her brows and confronted the problem direct, engaged with it until she'd either reached understanding or catastrophe. Either way, she'd have laughed, and tossed her dark hair, and announced that now she understood.

"It's peasant cooking," Katrin the Fair said as she bustled to the kitchen, "which of course is the best kind."

The main course was a ragout of veal in a velouté sauce, beans cooked simply in butter and garlic, tossed salad, bread. Davout waited until it was half consumed, and the bottle of wine mostly gone, before he dared to speak again of his sib.

"You mentioned the Silent One and his theories," he said. "I'm thirty years behind on his downloads, and I haven't read his latest work—what is he up to? What's all this theorizing about?"

She sighed, fingers ringing a frustrated rhythm on her glass. Looked out the window for a moment, then conceded. "Has he mentioned the modular theory of the psyche?"

Davout tried to remember. "He said something about modular *memory*, I seem to recall."

<Yes> "That's a part of it. It's a fairly radical theory that states that people should edit their personality and abilities at will, as circumstances dictate. That one morning, say, if you're going to work, you upload appropriate memories, and work skills, along with a dose of ambition, of resolution, and some appropriate emotions like satisfaction and eagerness to solve problems, or to endure drudgery, as the case may be."

Davout looked at his plate. "Like cookery, then," he said. "Like this dish—veal, carrots, onions, celery, mushrooms, parsley."

Fair Katrin made a mudra that Davout didn't recognize. <Sorry?> he signed.

"Oh. Apologies. That one means, roughly, 'har-de-har-har.'" Fingers formed <laughter>, then <sarcasm>, then slurred them together. "See?"

<Understood> He poured more wine into her glass.

She leaned forward across her plate. "Recipes are fine if one wants to be *consumed*," she said. "Survival is another matter. The human mind is more than just ingredients to be tossed together. The atomistic view of the psyche is simplistic, dangerous, and *wrong*. You cannot *will* a psyche to be whole, no matter how many *wholeness* modules are uploaded. A psyche is more than the sum of its parts."

Wine and agitation burnished her cheeks. Conviction blazed from her eyes. "It takes *time* to integrate new experience, new abilities. The modular theorists claim this will be done by a 'conductor,' an artificial intelligence that will be able to judge between alternate personalities and abilities and upload whatever's needed. But that's such *rubbish*, I —" She looked at the knife she was waving, then permitted it to return to the table.

"How far are the Silent One and his cohorts toward realizing this ambition?" Davout said.

<Beg pardon?> She looked at him. "I didn't make that clear?" she said. "The technology is already here. It's happening. People are fragmenting their psyches deliberately and trusting to their conductors to make sense of it all. And they're *happy* with their choices, because that's the only emotion they permit themselves to upload from their supply." She clenched her teeth, glanced angrily out the window at the Vieux Quartier's sunset-burnished walls. "All traditional psychology is aimed at integration, at wholeness. And now it's all to be *thrown away*…" She flung her hand out the window. Davout's eyes automatically followed an invisible object on its arc from her fingers toward the street.

"And how does this theory work in practice?" Davout asked. "Are the streets filled with psychological wrecks?"

Bitterness twisted her lips. "Psychological imbeciles, more like. Executing their conductors' orders, docile as well-fed children, happy as clams. They upload passions—anger, grief, loss—as artificial experiences, secondhand from someone else, usually so they can tell their conductor to avoid such emotions in the future. They are not *people* anymore, they're…" Her eyes turned to Davout.

"You saw the Silent One," she said. "Would you call him a *person*?"

"I was with him for only a day," Davout said. "I noticed something of a…" <Stand by> he signed, searching for the word.

"Lack of affect?" she interposed. "A demeanor marked by an extreme placidity?"

<Truth> he signed.

"When it was clear I wouldn't come back to him, he wrote me out of his memory," Fair Katrin said. "He replaced the memories with *facts*—he knows he was married to me, he knows we went to such-and-such a place or wrote such-and-such a paper—but there's nothing else there. No feelings, no real memories good or bad, no understanding, nothing left from almost two centuries together." Tears glittered in her eyes. "I'd rather he felt anything at all—I'd rather he hated me than feel this apathy!"

Davout reached across the little table and took her hand. "It is his decision," he said, "and his loss."

"It is *all* our loss," she said. Reflected sunset flavored her tears with the color of roses. "The man we loved is gone. And millions are gone with him—millions of little half-alive souls, programmed for happiness and unconcern." She tipped the bottle into her glass, received only a sluicing of dregs.

"Let's have another," she said.

When he left, some hours later, he embraced her, kissed her, let his lips linger on hers for perhaps an extra half-second. She blinked up at him in wine-muddled surprise, and then he took his leave.

"How did you find my sib?" Red Katrin asked.

"Unhappy," Davout said. "Confused. Lonely, I think. Living in a little apartment like a cell, with icons and memories."

<I know> she signed, and turned on him a knowing green-eyed look.

"Are you planning on taking her away from all that? To the stars, perhaps?"

Davout's surprise was brief. He looked away and murmured, "I didn't know I was so transparent."

A smile touched her lips. <Apologies> she signed. "I've lived with Old Davout for nearly two hundred years. You and he haven't grown so very far apart in that time. My fair sib deserves happiness, and so do you… if you can provide it, so much the better. But I wonder if you are not moving too fast, if you have thought it all out."

Moving fast, Davout wondered. His life seemed so very slow now, a creeping dance with agony, each move a lifetime.

He glanced out at Chesapeake Bay, saw his second perfect sunset in only a few hours—the same sunset he'd watched from Fair Katrin's apartment, now radiating its red glories on the other side of the Atlantic. A few water-skaters sped toward home on their silver blades. He sat with Red Katrin on a porch swing, looking down the long green sward to the bay-front, the old wooden pier, and the sparkling water, that profound, deep blue that sang of home to Davout's soul. Red Katrin wrapped herself against the breeze in a fringed, autumn-colored shawl. Davout sipped coffee from gold-rimmed porcelain, set the cup into its saucer.

"I wondered if I was being untrue to *my* Katrin," he said. "But they are really the same person, aren't they? If I were to pursue some other woman now, I would know I was committing a betrayal. But how can I betray Katrin with herself?"

An uncertain look crossed Red Katrin's face. "I've downloaded them both," hesitantly, "and I'm not certain that the Dark and Fair Katrins are quite the same person. Or ever were."

Not the same—of course he knew that. Fair Katrin was not a perfect copy of her older sib—she had flaws, clear enough. She had been damaged, somehow. But the flaws could be worked on, the damage repaired. Conquered. There was infinite time. He would see it done

<Question> "And how do your sibs differ, then?" he asked. "Other than obvious differences in condition and profession?"

She drew her legs up and rested her chin on her knees. Her green eyes were pensive. "Matters of love," she said, "and happiness."

And further she would not say.

Davout took Fair Katrin to Tangier for the afternoon and walked with her up on the old palace walls. Below them, white in the sun, the curved mole built by Charles II cleaved the Middle Sea, a thin crescent moon laid upon the perfect shimmering azure. (Home! home! the waters cried.) The sea breeze lashed her blonde hair across her face, snapped little sonic booms from the sleeves of his shirt.

"I have sampled some of the Silent One's downloads," Davout said. "I wished to discover the nature of this artificial tranquility with which he has endowed himself."

Fair Katrin's lips twisted in distaste, and her fingers formed a scato-logue.

"It was… interesting," Davout said. "There was a strange, uncomplicated quality of bliss to it. I remember experiencing the download of a master sitting zazen once, and it was an experience of a similar cast."

"It may have been the exact same sensation." Sourly. "He may have just copied the Zen master's experience and slotted it into his brain. That's how *most* of the vampires do it—award themselves the joy they haven't earned."

"That's a Calvinistic point of view," Davout offered. "That happiness can't just happen, that it has to be earned."

She frowned out at the sea. "There is a difference between real experience and artificial or recapitulative experience. If that's Calvinist, so be it."

<Yes> Davout signed. "Call me a Calvinist sympathizer, then. I have been enough places, done enough things, so that it matters to me that I was actually there and not living out some programmed dream of life on other worlds. I've experienced my sibs' downloads—lived significant parts of their lives, moment by moment—but it is not the same as *my life*, as *being me*. I am," he said, leaning elbows on the palace wall, "I am myself, I am the sum of everything that happened to me, I stand on this wall, I am watching this sea, I am watching it with you, and no one else has had this experience, nor ever shall, it is *ours*, it belongs to us…"

She looked up at him, straw-hair flying over an unreadable expression. "Davout the Conqueror," she said.

<No> he signed. "I did not conquer alone."

She nodded, holding his eyes for a long moment. "Yes," she said. "I know."

He took Katrin the Fair in his arms and kissed her. There was a moment's stiff surprise, and then she began to laugh, helpless peals bursting against his lips. He held her for a moment, too surprised to react, and then she broke free. She reeled along the wall, leaning for support against the old stones. Davout followed, babbling, "I'm sorry, I didn't mean to—"

She leaned back against the wall. Words burst half-hysterical from her lips, in between bursts of desperate, unamused laughter. "So that's what you were after! My God! As if I hadn't had enough of you all after all these years!"

"I apologize," Davout said. "Let's forget this happened. I'll take you home."

She looked up at him, the laughter gone, blazing anger in its place. "The Silent One and I would have been all right if it hadn't been for you—*for our sibs!*" She flung her words like daggers, her voice breaking with passion. "You lot were the eldest, you'd already parceled out the world between you. You were only interested in psychology because my damned Red sib and your Old one wanted insight into the characters in their histories, and because you and your dark bitch wanted a theory of the psyche to aid you in building communities on other worlds. We only got created because *you were too damned lazy to do your own research!*"

Davout stood, stunned. <No> he signed, "That's not—"

"We were *third*," she cried. "We were *born in third place*. We got the jobs you wanted least, and while you older sibs were winning fame and glory, we were stuck in work that didn't suit, that you'd *cast off*, awarded to us as if we were charity cases—" She stepped closer, and Davout was amazed to find a white-knuckled fist being shaken in his face. "My husband was called the Silent because his sibs had already used up all the words! He was third-rate and knew it. It *destroyed* him! Now he's plugging artificial satisfaction into his head because it's the only way he'll ever feel it."

"If you didn't like your life," Davout said, "you could have changed it. People start over all the time—we'd have helped." He reached toward her. "I can help you to the stars, if that's what you want."

She backed away. "The only help we ever needed was to *get rid of you!*" A mudra, <har-de-har-har>, echoed the sarcastic laughter on Fair Katrin's lips. "And now there's another gap in your life, and you want me to fill it—*not this time.*"

<Never> her fingers echoed. <Never> The laughter bubbled from her throat again.

She fled, leaving him alone and dazed on the palace wall, the booming wind mocking his feeble protests.

"I am truly sorry," Red Katrin said. She leaned close to him on the porch swing, touched soft lips to his cheek. "Even though she edited her downloads, I could tell she resented us—but I truly did not know how she would react."

Davout was frantic. He could feel Katrin slipping farther and farther away, as if she were on the edge of a precipice and her handholds were crumbling away beneath her clawed fingers.

"Is what she said true?" he asked. "Have we been slighting them all these years? Using them, as she claims?"

"Perhaps she had some justification once," Red Katrin said. "I do not remember anything of the sort when we were young, when I was upload-ing Fair Katrin almost every day. But now," her expression growing severe, "these are mature people, not without resources or intelligence—I can't help but think that surely after a person is a century old, any problems that remain are *her* fault."

As he rocked on the porch swing he could feel a wildness rising in him. *My God*, he thought, *I am going to be* alone.

His brief days of hope were gone. He stared out at the bay—the choppy water was too rough for any but the most dedicated water-skaters—and felt the pain pressing on his brain, like the two thumbs of a practiced sadist digging into the back of his skull.

"I wonder," he said. "Have you given any further thought to uploading my memories?"

She looked at him curiously. "It's scarcely time yet."

"I feel a need to share... some things."

"Old Davout has uploaded them. You could speak to him."

This perfectly sensible suggestion only made him clench his teeth. He needed *sense* made of things, he needed things put in *order*, and that was not the job of his sib. Old Davout would only confirm what he already knew.

"I'll talk to him, then," he said.

And then never did.


The pain was worst at night. It wasn't the sleeping alone, or merely Katrin's absence: it was the knowledge that she would *always* be absent, that the empty space next to him would lie there forever. It was then that the horror fully struck him, and he would lie awake for hours, eyes staring into the terrible void that wrapped him in its dark cloak. Fits of trembling sped through his limbs.

*I will go mad*, he sometimes thought. It seemed something he could choose, as if he were a character in an Elizabethan drama who turns to the audience to announce that he will be mad now, and then in the next scene is found gnawing bones dug out of the family sepulchre. Davout could see himself being found outside, running on all fours and barking at the stars.

And then, as dawn crept across the windowsill, he would look out the window and realize, to his sorrow, that he was not yet mad, that he was condemned to another day of sanity, of pain, and of grief.

Then, one night, he *did* go mad. He found himself squatting on the floor in his nightshirt, the room a ruin around him: mirrors smashed, furniture broken. Blood was running down his forearms.

The door leapt off its hinges with a heave of Old Davout's shoulder. Davout realized, in a vague way, that his sib had been trying to get in for some time. He saw Red Katrin's silhouette in the door, an aureate halo around her auburn hair in the instant before Old Davout snapped on the light.

Afterwards Katrin pulled the bits of broken mirror out of Davout's hands, washed and disinfected them, while his sib tried to reconstruct the green room and its antique furniture.

Davout watched his spatters of blood stain the water, threads of scarlet whirling in Coriolis spirals. "I'm sorry," he said. "I think I may be losing my mind."

"I doubt that." Frowning at a bit of glass in her tweezers.

"I want to *know*."

Something in his voice made her look up. "Yes?"

He could see his staring reflection in her green eyes. "Read my downloads.

Please. I want to know if... I'm reacting normally in all this. If I'm lucid or just..." He fell silent. *Do it*, he thought. *Just do this one thing.*

"I don't upload other people. Davout can do that. *Old* Davout, I mean."

No, Davout thought. His sib would understand all too well what he was up to.

"But he's me!" he said. "He'd think I'm normal!"

"Silent Davout, then. Crazy people are his specialty."

Davout wanted to make a mudra of scorn, but Red Katrin held his hands captive. Instead he gave a laugh. "He'd want me to take Lethe. Any advice he gave would be... in that direction." He made a fist of one hand, saw drops of blood well up through the cuts. "I need to know if I can stand this," he said. "If—something drastic is required."

She nodded, looked again at the sharp little spear of glass, put it deliberately on the edge of the porcelain. Her eyes narrowed in thought—Davout felt his heart vault at that look, at the familiar lines forming at the corner of Red Katrin's right eye, each one known and adored.

*Please do it*, he thought desperately.

"If it's that important to you," she said, "I will."

"Thank you," he said.

He bent his head over her and the basin, raised her hand, and pressed his lips to the flesh beaded with water and streaked with blood.

It was almost like conducting an affaire, all clandestine meetings and whispered arrangements. Red Katrin did not want Old Davout to know she was uploading his sib's memories—"I would just as soon not deal with his disapproval"—and so she and Davout had to wait until he was gone for a few hours, a trip to record a lecture for Cavor's series on *Ideas and Manners*.

She settled onto the settee in the front room and covered herself with her fringed shawl. Closed her eyes. Let Davout's memories roll through her.

He sat in a chair nearby, his mouth dry. Though nearly thirty years had passed since Dark Katrin's death, he had experienced only a few weeks of that time; and Red Katrin was floating through these memories at speed, tasting here and there, skipping redundancies or moments that seemed inconsequential...

He tried to guess from her face where in his life she dwelt. The expression of shock and horror near the start was clear enough, the shuttle bursting into flames. After the shock faded, he recognized the discomfort that came with experiencing a strange mind, and flickering across her face came expressions of grief, anger, and here and there amusement; but gradually there was only a growing sadness, and lashes wet with tears. He crossed the room to kneel by her chair and take her hand. Her fingers pressed his in response… she took a breath, rolled her head away… he wanted to weep not for his grief, but for hers.

The eyes fluttered open. She shook her head. "I had to stop," she said. "I couldn't take it—" She looked at him, a kind of awe in her wide green eyes. "My God, the sadness! And the *need*. I had no idea. I've never felt such need. I wonder what it is to be needed that way."

He kissed her hand, her damp cheek. Her arms went around him. He felt a leap of joy, of clarity. The need was hers, now.

Davout carried her to the bed she shared with his sib, and together they worshipped memories of his Katrin.

"I will take you there," Davout said. His finger reached into the night sky, counted stars, *one, two, three…* "The planet's called Atugan. It's boiling hot, nothing but rock and desert, sulfur and slag. But we can make it home for ourselves and our children—all the species of children we desire, fish and fowl." A bubble of happiness filled his heart. "Dinosaurs, if you like," he said. "Would you like to be parent to a dinosaur?"

He felt Katrin leave the shelter of his arm, step toward the moonlit bay. Waves rumbled under the old wooden pier. "I'm not trained for terraforming," she said. "I'd be useless on such a trip."

"I'm decades behind in my own field," Davout said. "You could learn while I caught up. You'll have Dark Katrin's downloads to help. It's all possible."

She turned toward him. The lights of the house glowed yellow off her pale face, off her swift fingers as she signed.

<Regret> "I have lived with Old Davout for near two centuries," she said.

His life, for a moment, seemed to skip off its internal track; he felt himself suspended, poised at the top of an arc just before the fall.

Her eyes brooded up at the house, where Old Davout paced and sipped coffee and pondered his life of *Maxwell*. The mudras at her fingertips were unreadable in the dark.

"I will do as I did before," she said. "I cannot go with you, but my other self will."

Davout felt his life resume. "Yes," he said, because he was in shadow and could not sign. "By all means." He stepped nearer to her. "I would rather it be you," he whispered.

He saw wry amusement touch the corners of her mouth. "It *will* be me," she said. She stood on tiptoe, kissed his cheek. "But now I am your sister again, yes?" Her eyes looked level into his. "Be patient. I will arrange it."

"I will in all things obey you, madam," he said, and felt wild hope singing in his heart.

Davout was present at her awakening, and her hand was in his as she opened her violet eyes, the eyes of his Dark Katrin. She looked at him in perfect comprehension, lifted a hand to her black hair; and then the eyes turned to the pair standing behind him, to Old Davout and Red Katrin.

"Young man," Davout said, putting his hand on Davout's shoulder, "allow me to present you to my wife." And then (wisest of the sibs) he bent over and whispered, a bit pointedly, into Davout's ear, "I trust you will do the same for me, one day."

Davout concluded, through his surprise, that the secret of a marriage that lasts two hundred years is knowing when to turn a blind eye.

"I confess I am somewhat envious," Red Katrin said as she and Old Davout took their leave. "I envy my twin her new life."

"It's your life as well," he said. "She is you." But she looked at him soberly, and her fingers formed a mudra he could not read.

He took her on honeymoon to the Rockies, used some of his seventy-eight years' back pay to rent a sprawling cabin in a high valley above the headwaters of the Rio Grande, where the wind rolled grandly through the pines, hawks spun lazy high circles on the afternoon thermals, and the brilliant clear light blazed on white starflowers and Indian paintbrush. They went on long walks in the high hills, cooked simply in the cramped kitchen, slept beneath scratchy trade blankets, made love on crisp cotton sheets.

He arranged an office there, two desks and two chairs, back-to-back. Katrin applied herself to learning biology, ecology, nanotech, and quantum physics—she already had a good grounding, but a specialist's knowledge was lacking. Davout tutored her, and worked hard at catching up with the latest developments in the field. She—they did not have a name for her yet, though Davout thought of her as "New Katrin"—would review Dark Katrin's old downloads, concentrating on her work, the way she visualized a problem.

Once, opening her eyes after an upload, she looked at Davout and shook her head. "It's strange," she said. "It's *me*, I know it's me, but the way she thinks —" <I don't understand> she signed. "It's not memories that make us, we're told, but patterns of thought. We are who we are because we think using certain patterns… but I do not seem to think like her at all."

"It's habit," Davout said. "Your habit is to think a different way."

<Possibly> she conceded, brows knit.

<Truth> "You—Red Katrin—uploaded Dark Katrin before. You had no

difficulty in understanding her then."

"I did not concentrate on the technical aspects of her work, on the way she visualized and solved problems. They were beyond my skill to interpret—I paid more attention to other moments in her life." She lifted her eyes to Davout. "Her moments with you, for instance. Which were very rich, and very intense, and which sometimes made me jealous."

"No need for jealousy now."

<Perhaps> she signed, but her dark eyes were thoughtful, and she turned away.

He felt Katrin's silence after that, an absence that seemed to fill the cabin with the invisible, weighty cloud of her somber thought. Katrin spent her time studying by herself or restlessly paging through Dark Katrin's downloads. At meals and in bed she was quiet, meditative—perfectly friendly, and, he thought, not unhappy—but keeping her thoughts to herself.

*She is adjusting,* he thought. *It is not an easy thing for someone two centuries old to change.*

"I have realized," she said ten days later at breakfast, "that my sib—that Red Katrin—is a coward. That I am created—and the other sibs, too—to do what she would not, or dared not." Her violet eyes gaze levelly at Davout. "She wanted to go with you to Atugan—she wanted to feel the power of your desire—but something held her back. So I am created to do the job for her. It is my purpose… to fulfill *her* purpose."

"It's her loss, then," Davout said, though his fingers signed <surprise>.

<Alas!> she signed, and Davout felt a shiver caress his spine. "But I am a coward, too!" Katrin cried. "I am not your brave Dark Katrin, and I cannot become her!"

"Katrin," he said. "You are the same person—you *all* are!"

She shook her head. "I do not think like your Katrin. I do not have her courage. I do not know what liberated her from her fear, but it is something I do not have. And—" She reached across the table to clasp his hand. "I do not have the feelings for you that she possessed. I simply do not—I have tried, I have had that world-eating passion read into my mind, and I compare it with what I feel, and—what I have is as nothing. I *wish* I felt as she did, I truly do. But if I love anyone, it is Old Davout. And…" She let go his hand, and rose from the table. "I am a coward, and I will take the coward's way out. I must leave."

<No> his fingers formed, then <please>. "You can change that," he said. He followed her into the bedroom. "It's just a switch in your mind, Silent Davout can throw it for you, we can love each other forever…" She made no answer. As she began to pack grief seized him by the throat and the words dried up. He retreated to the little kitchen, sat at the table, held his

head in his hands. He looked up when she paused in the door, and froze like a deer in the violet light of her eyes.

"Fair Katrin was right," she said. "Our elder sibs are bastards—they use us, and not kindly."

A few moments later he heard a car drive up, then leave. <Alas!> his fingers signed. <Alas!>

He spent the day unable to leave the cabin, unable to work, terror shivering through him. After dark he was driven outside by the realization that he would have to sleep on sheets that were touched with Katrin's scent. He wandered by starlight across the high mountain meadow, dry soil crunching beneath his boots, and when his legs began to ache he sat down heavily in the dust.

*I am weary of my groaning...* he thought.

It was summer, but the high mountains were chill at night, and the deep cold soaked his thoughts. The word *Lethe* floated through his mind. Who would not choose to be happy? he asked himself. It is a switch in your mind, and someone can throw it for you.

He felt the slow, aching droplets of mourning being squeezed from his heart, one after the other, and wondered how long he could endure them, the relentless moments, each striking with the impact of a hammer, each a stunning, percussive blow...

Throw a switch, he thought, and the hammerblows would end.

"Katrin deserves mourning," he had told Davout the Silent, and now he had so many more Katrins to mourn, Dark Katrin and Katrin the Fair, Katrin the New and Katrin the Old. All the Katrins webbed by fate, alive or dead or merely enduring. And so he would, from necessity, endure... *So long lives this, and this gives life to thee.*

He lay on his back, on the cold ground, gazed up at the world of stars, and tried to find the worlds, among the glittering teardrops of the heavens, where he and Katrin had rained from the sky their millions of children.

## AFTERWORD: LETHE

*I started my career as a writer of historical fiction, specifically novels taking place in the Age of Sail, a genre pioneered by James Fenimore Cooper and later practiced successfully by C. S. Forester and Patrick O'Brian, among others. I enjoyed writing these journeyman works, but over time I grew frustrated by the sameness of the setting. Book after book, I had a cast of a couple hundred males aboard a small ship. I longed to break free into the universe, which I eventually did by becoming a science fiction writer.*

*When I began writing SF, I realized that I could tell practically any story that appealed to me, as long as I set it in a science fiction context, and so I made a list of the sorts of stories I longed to write. The list was as follows:*

*1. A future in which everything went right. (This became my novel* Knight Moves.*)*
*2. A future in which everything went wrong. (This became* Hardwired.*)*
*3. A mystery/thriller. (*Voice of the Whirlwind*)*
*4. A first-contact story. (*Angel Station*)*
*5. A Restoration-style comedy of manners. (*The Crown Jewels *and its sequels)*
*6. A hard-boiled mystery. (*Days of Atonement*)*

*Within a six-to-eight month period, I had these works outlined, at least in my head. (*Voice of the Whirlwind, *which I had begun some years earlier, took a little longer.) For the next several years, I went about the task of realizing the works that I had envisioned during that one manic period of creativity.*

*As I worked my way to the end of the list, I began to worry that maybe I'd lost my creative spark: I hadn't had anything like that period of creativity in the time since.*

*Then I wrote* Aristoi, *and I stopped worrying.*

*None of this has any direct bearing on "Lethe," except to note that the very first thing I wanted to write was the future in which everything went right.*

*In my versions of this future, every box has been checked on humanity's collective wish list: there is no poverty, war, disease, or death. Some might claim that this deprives the future of the raw material for fiction, but my own view is that, with our inherited burden of tragic distractions out of the way, we might be able to get on with the actual search for meaning.*

*In any case, getting rid of war and death makes the search for a story all that much more imaginative.*

*I wrote "Lethe" in a period in which I was looking for just that kind of challenge. In order to challenge myself further, I decided to outdo* Comedy of Errors *by making the story about two sets of triplets.*

*And I couldn't avoid death altogether. The foundation of the story, after all, is what happens when death occurs in a culture where death simply does not happen.*

*It occurred to me that it would make an interesting challenge to write this same story over again from the point of view of any of the other Davouts or Katrins, but I haven't taken up the challenge as yet.*

*This was the first, but not the last, story taking place in what I call the College of Mystery sequence.*

# THE LAST RIDE OF GERMAN FREDDIE

"*Ecce homo*," said German Freddie with a smile. "That is your man, I believe."

"That's him," Brocius agreed. "That's Virgil Earp, the lawman."

"What do you suppose he wants?" asked Freddie.

"He's got a warrant for someone," said Brocius, "or he wouldn't be here."

Freddie gazed without enthusiasm at the lawman walking along the opposite side of Allen Street in Tombstone. His spurred boots clumped on the wooden sidewalk. He looked as if he had somewhere to go.

"Entities should not be multiplied beyond what is necessary," said Freddie, "or so Occam is understood to have said. If he is here for one of us, then so much the worse for him. If not, what does it matter to us?"

Curly Bill Brocius looked thoughtful. "I don't know about this Occam fellow, but as my mamma would say, those fellers don't chew their own tobacco. Kansas lawmen come at you in packs."

"So do we," said Freddie. "And this is not Kansas."

"No," said Brocius. "It's Tombstone." He gave Freddie a warning look from his lazy eyes. "Remember that, my friend," he said, "and watch your back."

Brocius drifted up Allen Street in the direction of Hafford's Saloon while Freddie contemplated Deputy U.S. Marshal Earp. The man was dressed like the parson of a particularly gloomy Protestant sect, with a black flat-crowned hat, black frock coat, black trousers, and immaculate white linen.

German Freddie decided he might as well meet this paradigm.

He walked across the dusty Tombstone street, stepped onto the sidewalk, and raised his grey sombrero.

"Pardon me," he said. "But are you Virgil Earp?"

The man looked at him, light eyes over fair mustache. "No," he said. "I'm his brother."

"Wyatt?" Freddie asked. He knew that the deputy had a lawman brother.

"No," the man said. "I'm their brother, Morgan."

A grin tugged at Freddie's lips. "Ah," he said. "I perceive that entities *are* multiplied beyond that which is necessary."

Morgan Earp gave him a puzzled look. Freddie raised his hat again. "I beg your pardon," he said. "I won't detain you."

It is like a uniform, Freddie wrote in his notebook that night. Black coats, black hats, black boots. Blond mustaches and long guns in the scabbards, riding in line abreast as they led their posse out of town. As a picture of purposeful terror they stand like the *Schwartzreiter* of three centuries ago, horsemen who held all Europe in fear. They entirely outclassed that Lt. Hurst, who was in a *real* uniform and who was employing them in the matter of those stolen Army mules.

What fear must dwell in the hearts of these Earps to present themselves thus! They must dress and walk and think alike; they must enforce the rigid letter of the dead, dusty law to the last comma; they must cling to every rule and range and feature of mediocrity... it is fear that drives men to herd together, to don uniforms, to impose upon others a needless conformity. But what enemy is it they fear? What enemy is so dreadful as to compel them to wear uniforms and arm themselves so heavily and cling to their beliefs with such ferocity?

*It is their own nature!* The weak, who have no power even over themselves, fear always the power that lies in a *free* nature—a nature fantastic, wild, astonishing, arbitrary—they must enslave this spirit first in themselves before they can enslave it in others.

It is therefore our duty—the duty of those who are free, who are natural, valorous, and unafraid, those who scorn what is sickly, cowardly, and slavish—we must *resist these Earps!*

And already we have won a victory—won it without raising a finger, without lifting a gun. The posse of that terrible figure of justice, that Mr. Virgil Earp, found the mules they were searching for in Frank McLaury's corral at Baba Comari—but then the complainant Lt. Hurst took counsel of his own fears, and refused to press charges.

It is wonderful! Deputy Marshal Earp, the sole voice of the law in this part of Arizona, has been made ridiculous on his first employment! How his pride must have withered at the joke that fortune played on him! How he must have cursed the foolish lieutenant and his fate!

He has left town, I understand, returned to Prescott. His brothers remain, however, stalking the streets in their dread black uniforms, infecting the town with their stolid presence. It is like an invasion of Luthers.

We must not cease to laugh at them! We must be gay! Laughter has driven Virgil from our midst, and it will drive the others, too. Our laughter will lodge burning in their hearts like bullets of flaming lead. There is nothing that will drive them from our midst as surely as our own joy at their shortcomings.

They are afraid. And we will *know* they are afraid. And this knowledge will turn our laughter into a weapon.

Ike Clanton was passed out on the table. The game went on regardless, as Ike had already lost his money. It was late evening in the Occidental Saloon, and the game might well go on till dawn.

"It's getting to be hard being a Cowboy," said John Ringo. "What with having to pay *taxes* now." He removed cards from his hand, tossed them onto the table. "Two cards," he said.

Brocius gave him his cards. "If we pay taxes," he said, "we can vote. And if we vote, we can have our own sheriff. And if we have our own sheriff, we'll make back those taxes and then some. Dealer folds." He tossed his cards onto the table.

Freddie adjusted his spectacles and looked at his hand, jacks and treys. He tossed his odd nine onto the table. "One card," he said. "I believe it was a mistake."

Brocius gave Freddie a lazy-lidded glance as he dealt Freddie another trey. "You think John Behan won't behave once we elect him?"

"I think it is unwise to give someone power over you."

"Hell yes, it was unwise," agreed Ringo. "Behan's promised Wyatt Earp the chief deputy's job. Fifty dollars." Silver clanged on the tabletop. Ike Clanton, drowsing, gave an uncertain snort.

"That's just to get the votes of the Earps and their friends," Brocius said. He winked at Freddie. "You don't think he's going to keep his promises, do you?"

"What makes you think he will keep his promises to *you?*" Freddie asked. He raised another fifty.

"It will pay him to cooperate with us," Brocius said.

Ringo bared his yellow fangs in a grin. "Have you seen Behan's girl? Sadie?"

"Are you going to call or fold?" Freddie asked.

"I'm thinking." Staring at his cards.

"I thought Behan's girl was called Josie," said Brocius.

"She seems to go by a number of names," Ringo said. "But you can see her for yourself, tonight at Shieffelin Hall. She's Helen of Troy in *Doctor Faustus.*"

"Are you going to call or fold?" Freddie asked.

"Helen, whose beauty summoned Greece to arms," Ringo quoted, "and drew a thousand ships to Tenedos."

"I would rather be a king," Freddie said, "and ride in triumph through Persepolis. Are you going to fold or call?"

"I'm going to bump," Ringo said, and threw out a hundred-dollar-bill, just as Freddie knew he would if Freddie only kept on nagging.

"Raise another hundred," Freddie said. Ringo cursed and called. Freddie showed his hand and raked the money toward him.

"Fortune's a right whore," Ringo said, from somewhere else out of his eccentric education.

"You should not have compromised with the authorities," Freddie said as he stacked his coin. "Once you were the free rulers of this land. Now you are taxpayers and politicians. Why do you bring this upon yourselves?"

Curly Bill Brocius scowled. "I'm on top of things, Freddie. Behan will do what he's told."

Freddie looked at him. "But will the Earps?"

"We got two hundred riders, Freddie," Brocius said. "I ain't afraid of no Earps."

"We were driven out of Texas," Freddie reminded. "This is our last stand."

"Last stand in Tombstone," Ringo said. "That's doesn't have a comforting sound."

"I'm on top of it," Brocius insisted.

He and his crowd defiantly called themselves Cowboys. It was a name synonymous with "rustler," and hardly respectable—legitimate ranchers called themselves "stockmen." The Cowboys ranged both sides of the American-Mexican border, acquiring cattle on one side, moving them across the border through Guadalupe and Skeleton Canyons, and selling them. Most of the local ranchers—even the honest ones—did not mind owning cattle that did not come with a notarized bill of sale, and the Cowboys' business was profitable.

In the face of this threat to law from the two hundred outlaws, the United States government had sent to Tombstone exactly one man, Deputy Marshal Virgil Earp, who had been sent right out again. The Mexicans, unfortunately, were more industrious—they had been fortifying the border, and making the Cowboys' raids more difficult. The Clanton brothers' father, who had been the Cowboys' chief, had been killed in an ambush by Mexican *rurales.*

Brocius now led the Cowboys, assuming anyone did. Since illegitimate plunder was growing more difficult, Brocius proposed to plunder legitimately, through a political machine and a compliant sheriff. His theory was that the government would let them alone if he lined up enough votes to buy their tolerance.

German Freddie mistrusted the means—he did not trust politicians or their machines or their sheriffs—but then his opinion did not rank near Brocius', as he wasn't, strictly speaking, a Cowboy, just one of their friends. He was a gambler, and had never rustled stock in his life—he just won the money from those who had.

"Everybody ante," said Brocius. Freddie threw a half-eagle into the pot.

"May I sit in?" asked a cultured voice. *Ay*, Freddie thought as he looked up, *the plot thickens very much upon us.*

"Well," Freddie said, "if you are here, now we know that Tombstone is on the map." He rose and gestured the newcomer to a chair. "Gentlemen," he said to the others, "may I introduce John Henry Holliday, D.D."

"We've met," said Ringo. He rose and shook Holliday's hand. Freddie introduced Brocius, and pointed out Ike Clanton, still asleep on the table.

Holliday put money on the table and sat. To call him thin as a rail was to do injustice to the rail—Holliday was pale and consumptive and light as a scarecrow. He looked as if the merest breath of wind might blow him right down Skeleton Canyon into Mexico. Only the weight of his boots held him down, that and the weight of his gun.

German Freddie had met Doc Holliday in Texas, and knew that Holliday was dangerous when sober and absurd when drunk. Freddie and Holliday had both killed people in Texas, and for much the same reasons.

"Is Kate with you?" Freddie asked. If Holliday's Hungarian girl was in town, then he was here to stay. If she wasn't, he might drift on.

"We have rooms at Fly's," Holliday said.

Freddie looked at Holliday over the rim of his cards. If Kate was here, then Doc would be here till either his pockets or the mines ran dry of silver.

The calculations were growing complex.

"Twenty dollars," Freddie said.

"Bump you another twenty," said Holliday, and tossed a pair of double eagles onto the table.

Ike Clanton sat up with a sudden snort. "I'll kill him!" he blurted.

"Here's my forty," Ringo said. He looked at Ike. "Kill who, Ike?"

Ike's eyes stared off into nowhere, pupils tiny as peppercorns. "I'm gonna kill him!" he said.

Ringo was patient. "Who are you planning to kill?"

"Gonna kill him!" Ike's chair tumbled to the floor as he rose to his feet.

He took a staggering step backward, regained his balance, then began to lurch for the saloon door.

"Dealer folds," said Brocius, and threw in his cards.

Holliday watched Ike's exit with cold precision. "Shouldn't one of you go after your friend? He seems to want to shoot somebody."

"Ike's harmless," Freddie said. "Besides, his gun is at his hotel, and in his current state Ike won't remember where he left it."

"What if someone takes Ike seriously enough to shoot him?" Holliday asked.

"No one will do that for fear of Ike's brother Billy," said Freddie. "He's the dangerous one."

Holliday nodded and returned his hollow eyes to his cards. "Are you going to call, Freddie?" he asked.

"I call," Freddie said.

It was a mistake. Holliday cleaned them all out by midnight. "Thank you, gentlemen," he said politely as he headed toward the door with his winnings jingling in his pockets. "I'm sure we'll meet again."

John Ringo looked at the others. "Silver and gold have I none," he quoted, "but such as I have I'll share with thee." He pulled out bits of pasteboard from his pockets. "Tickets to *Doctor Faustus,* good for the midnight performance. Wilt come with me to hell, gentlemen?"

Brocius was just drunk enough to say yes. Ringo looked at Freddie. Freddie shrugged. "Might as well," he said. "That was the back end of bad luck."

"Luck?" Ringo handed him a ticket. "It looked to me like you couldn't resist whenever Doc raised the stakes."

"I was waiting for him to get drunk. Then he'd start losing."

"What was in your mind, raising on a pair of jacks?"

"I thought he was bluffing."

Ringo shook his head. "And you the only one of us sober."

"I don't see that you did any better."

"No," Ringo said sadly, "I didn't."

They made their way out of the Occidental, then turned down Allen Street in the direction of Shieffelin Hall. The packed dust of the street was hard as rock. The night was full of people—most nights Tombstone didn't close down till dawn.

Brocius struck a match on his thumb as he walked, and lit a cigar. "I plan to go shooting tomorrow," he said. "I've changed my gun—filed down the sear so I can fan it."

"Oh Lord," Ringo sighed. "Why'd you go and ruin a good gun?"

"Fanning is for fools," Freddie said. "You should just take *aim...*"

"I ain't such a good shot as you two," Brocius said. He puffed his cigar.

"My talents are more *organizational* and *political.* I figure if I got to jerk my gun, I'll just fan it and make up for aim with *volume.*"

"You'd better hope you never have to shoot it," Freddie said.

"If we win the election," Brocius said cheerfully. "I probably won't."

Even the drinking water must be carried to us on wagons, Freddie wrote in his notebook a few hours later. The alkali desert is unforgiving and unsuitable for anything but the lizards and vultures who were here before us. Even the Indians avoided this country. The ranchers cannot keep enough cattle on this wretched land to make a profit—thus they are dependent on the rustlers and smugglers for their livelihood. The population came because of greed or ambition, and if the silver ever runs out, Tombstone will fly away with the dust.

So why, when I perceive these Cowboys in their huge sombreros, their gaudy kerchiefs and doeskin trousers, do I see instead the old Romans in their ringing bronze?

From such as these did Romulus spring! For who was Romulus?—a tyrant, a bandit, a man who harbored runaways and stole the cattle—and the daughters—of his neighbors. Yet he was noble, yet a hero, yet he spawned a great Empire. History trembles before his memory.

And now the Romans have come again! Riding into Tombstone with their rifles in the scabbards!

All the old Roman virtues I see among them. They are frank, truthful, loyal, and above all *healthy.* They hold the lives of men—their own included—in contempt. Nothing is more refreshing and wholesome than this lack of pity, this disdain for the so-called civilized virtues. They are from the American South, of course, that defeated country now sunk in ruin and oppression. They are too young to have fought in the Civil War, but not so young they did not see its horrors. This exposure to life's cruelties, when they were still at a tender age, must have hardened them against pieties and hypocrisies of the world. Not for them the mad egotism of the ascetic, the persistent morbidity—the *sickness*—of the civilized man. These heroes abandoned their defeated country and came west—west, where the new Rome will be born!

If only they can be brought to treasure their virtues as I do. But they treat themselves as carelessly as they treat everything. They possess all virtues but one: the will to power. They have it in themselves to dominate, to rule—not through these petty maneuverings at the polls with which Brocius is so unwisely intoxicated, but through themselves, their desires, their guns… They can create an empire here, and must, if their virtues are to survive. It is not enough to avoid the law, avoid civilization—they must wish to *destroy* the inverted virtues that oppose them.

Who shall win? Tottering, hypnotized, sunken Civilization, or this new Rome? Ridiculous, when we consider numbers, when we consider mere guns and iron. Yet what was Romulus?—a bandit, crouched on his Palatine Hill. Yet nothing could stand in his way. His will was greater than that of the whole rotten world.

And—as these classical allusions seem irresistible—what are we to make of the appearance of Helen of Troy? Who better to signal the end of an empire? Familiar with Goethe's superior work, I forgot that Helen does not speak in Marlowe's *Faustus,* she simply parades along and inspires poetry. But when she looked at our good German metaphysician, that eye of hers spoke mischief that had nothing to do with verse—and the actor knew it, for he stammered. Such a sexual being as this Helen was not envisioned by the good British Marlowe, whom we are led to believe did not with women.

I do not see such a girl cleaving to Behan for long—his blood is too thin for the likes of her.

And when she tires of him—beware, Behan! Beware, Faustus! Beware, Troy!


Freddie met Sheriff Behan's girl at the victory party following the election. Brocius' election strategy had borne fruit, of a sort—but Johnny Behan was rotten fruit, Freddie thought, and would fall to the ground ere long.

The Occidental Saloon with filled with celebration and a hundred drunken Cowboys. Even Wyatt Earp turned up, glooming in his black coat and drooping mustaches, still secure in the illusion that Behan would hire him as a deputy; but at the sight of the company his face wrinkled as if he'd just bit on a lemon, and he did not stay long.

Amid all this roistering inebriation, Freddie saw Behan's girl perched on the long bar, surrounded by a crowd of men and kicking her heels in the air in a white froth of petticoats. Freddie was surprised—he had rarely in his life met a woman who would enter a saloon, let alone behave so freely in one, and among a crowd of rowdy drunks. Behan—a natty Irishman in a derby—stood nearby and accepted congratulations and bumper after bumper of the finest French champagne.

Freddie offered Behan his perfunctory congratulations, then made his way to the bar where he saw John Ringo crouched protectively around a half-empty bottle of whisky. "I have drunk deep of the Pierian," Ringo said, "and drunk disgustingly. Will you join me?"

"No," said Freddie, and ordered soda water. The noise of the room battered at his nerves. He would not stay long—he would go to another saloon, perhaps, and find a game of cards.

Ringo's melancholy eyes roamed the room. "Freddie, you do not look overjoyed," he said.

Freddie looked at his drink. "Men selling their freedom to become *citizens*," he snarled. "And they call it a victory." He looked toward Behan, felt his lips curl. "Victory makes stupid," he said. "I learned that in Germany, in 1870."

"Why so gloomy, boys?" cried a woman's voice in a surprising New York accent. "Don't you know it's a party?" Behan's girl leaned toward them, half-lying across the polished mahogany bar. She was younger than Freddie had expected—not yet twenty, he thought.

Ringo brightened a little—he liked the ladies. "Have you met German Freddie, Josie?" he said. "Freddie here doesn't like elections."

Josie laughed and waved her glass of champagne. "I don't know that we had a *real election*, Freddie," she called. "Think of it as being more like a *great big felony*."

Cowboy voices roared with laughter. Freddie found himself smiling behind his bushy mustache. Ringo, suddenly merry, grabbed Freddie's arm and hauled him toward Josie.

"Freddie here used to be a Professor of Philosophy back in Germany," Ringo said. "He was told to come West for his health." Ringo looked at Freddie in a kind of amazement. "Can you picture that?"

Freddie—who had come West to die—said merely, "Philology. Switzerland," and sipped his soda water.

"You should have him tell you about how we're all Supermen," Ringo said.

Freddie stiffened. "You are *not* Supermen," he said.

"*You're* the Superman, then," Ringo said, swaying. The drunken raillery smoothed the sad lines of his eyes.

"I am the Superman's prophet," Freddie said with careful dignity. "And the Superman will be among your children, I think—he will come from America."

"I suppose I'd better get busy and have some children, then," Ringo said.

Josie watched this byplay with interest. Her hair was raven black, Freddie saw, and worn long, streaming down her shoulders. Her nose was proudly arched. Her eyes were large and brown and heavy-lidded—the heavy lids gave her a sultry look. She leaned toward Freddie.

"Tell me some philology," she said.

He looked up at her. "You are the first American I have met who knows the word."

"I know a lot of words." With a laugh she pressed his wrist—it was all

Freddie could do not to jump a foot at the unexpected touch. Instead he looked at her sternly.

"Do you know the Latin word *bonus?*" he demanded.

She shook her head. "It doesn't mean something extra?"

"In English, yes. In Latin, *bonus* means 'good.' Good as opposed to bad. But my question—the important question to a philologist—" He gave a nervous shrug of his shoulders. "The question is what the Romans meant by 'good,' you see? Because *bonus* is derived from *duonus,* or *duen-lum,* and from *duen-lum* is also derived *duellum,* thence *bellum.* Which means *war.*"

Josie followed this with interest. "So war was good, to a Roman?"

Freddie shook his head. "Not quite. It was the *warlike man,* the bringer of strife, that was good, as we see also from *bellus,* which is clearly derived from *bellum* and means handsome—another way of saying *good.* You understand?"

He could see thoughts working their way across her face. She was drunk, of course, and that slowed things down. "So the Romans—the Roman warriors—thought of themselves as good? By definition, good?"

Freddie nodded. "All the aristocrats did—*all* aristocrats, all conquerors. The aristocratic political party in ancient Rome called themselves the *boni*—the good. They *assumed* their own values were universal virtues, that all goodness was embedded in themselves—and that the values which were not theirs were debased. Look at the words they use to describe the opposite of their *bonus*—plebeian, common, base. Even in English—'debased' means *made common.*" He warmed to the subject, English words spilling out past his thick German tongue. "And in Greece the rulers of Megara used *esthlos* to describe themselves—'the true,' the real, as opposed to the ordinary, which for them did not have a real existence." He laughed. "To believe that you *are the only real thing.* That is an ego speaking! That is a *ruler*—very much like the Brahmins, who believe their egos are immortal but that all other reality is illusion..."

He paused, words frozen in his mouth, as he saw the identical, quizzical expression in the faces of both Ringo and Josie. They must think I'm crazy, he thought. He took a sip of soda water to relieve his nervousness. "Well," he said. "That is some philological thought for you."

"Don't stop," said Josie. "This is the most interesting thing I've heard all night."

Freddie only shook his head.

And suddenly there was gunfire, Freddie's nerves leaping with each thunderclap as he ducked beneath the level of the bar, his hand reaching for the pistol which, of course, he had left in his little room.

Ceiling lathes came spilling down, and there was a burst of coarse laughter. Freddie saw Curly Bill Brocius standing amid a grey cloud of gunsmoke. Unlike Freddie, Brocius had disregarded the town ordnance forbidding firearms in saloons or other public places, and in an excess of bonhomie had fanned his modified revolver at the ceiling.

Freddie slowly rose to his feet. His heart lurched in his chest, and a kind of sickness rose in his throat. He had to hold onto the bar for support.

Josie sat perfectly erect on the mahogany surface, face flushed, eyes wide and glittering, lips parted in frozen surprise. Then she shook her head and slipped to the floor amid a silken waterfall of skirts. She looked up at Freddie, then gave a sudden gay laugh. "These *men of strife*, these *boni*," she said, "are getting a little too *good* for my taste. Will you take me home, sir?"

"I—" Freddie felt heat rise beneath his collar. Gunsmoke stung his nostrils. "But Mr. Behan—?"

She cast a look over her shoulder at the new sheriff. "He won't want to leave his friends," she said. "And besides, I'd prefer an escort who's sober."

Freddie looked at Ringo for help, but Ringo was too drunk to walk ten feet without falling, and Freddie knew his abstemious habits had him trapped.

"Yes, miss," he said. "We shall walk, then."

He led Josie from the roistering crowd and walked with her down dusty Allen Street. Her arm in his felt very strange, like a half-forgotten memory. He wondered how long it had been since he had a woman on his arm—seven or eight years, probably, and the woman his sister.

In the darkness he sensed her looking up at him. "What's your last name, Freddie?" she asked.

"Nietzsche."

"Gesundheit!" she cried.

Freddie smiled in silence. She was not the first American to have made that joke.

"Don't you drink, Freddie?" Josie asked. "Is it against your principles?"

"It makes me ill," Freddie said. "I have to watch my diet, also."

"Johnny said you came West for your health."

It was phrased like a statement, but Freddie knew it was a question. He did not mind the intrusion: he had no secrets. "I volunteered for the war," he said, and at her look, clarified, "the war with France. I caught diphtheria and some kind of dysentery—typhus or cholera. I did not make a good recovery, and I could not work." He did not mention the other problems, the nervous complaints, the sudden attacks of migraine, the cold, sick dread of dying as his father had died, mad and screaming.

"We turn here," Josie said. They turned left on Fifth Street. On the far side of the street was the Oriental Saloon, where Wyatt Earp earned his living dealing faro. Freddie glanced at the windows, saw Earp himself bathed in yellow light, standing, smoking a cigar and engaged in conversation with Holliday. To judge by his look, the topic was a grim one.

"Look!" Freddie said in sudden scorn. "In that black coat of his, Earp looks like the Angel of Death come to claim his consumptive friend."

The light of the saloon gleamed on Josie's smile. "Wyatt Earp's a handsome man, don't you think?"

"I think he is too gloomy."

She turned to him. "*You're* the gloomy one."

He nodded as they paced along. "Yes," he admitted. "That is just."

"You are a sneeze," she said. "He is a belch."

Freddie smiled to himself as they crossed Fremont Street. "I will tell him this, when I see him next."

"Tell me about the Superman."

Freddie shook his head. "Not now."

"But you will tell me some other time?"

"If you wish." Politely, doubting he would speak a word to her after this night.

"Here's our house." It was a small place that she shared with Behan, frame, unpainted, like the rest of the town thrown up overnight.

"I will bid you good-night, then," he said formally.

She turned to face him, lifted her face toward his. "You can come in, if you like," she said. "Johnny won't be back for hours."

He looked into her eyes and saw Troy there, on fire in the night.

"Good-night, miss," he said, and touching his hat he turned away.

She is a Jewess! Freddie wrote in his journals. Run away from her family of good German bourgeois Jews—no doubt of the most insufferable type—to become, here in Tombstone, a goddess among the barbarians.

Or so Brocius tells us. He says her name is Josephine Marcus, sometimes called Sadie.

I believe I understand this Helen now. She has sprung from the strangest people in all history, they who have endured a thousand persecutions, and so become wise-cunning. The world has tried with great energy to make the Jews base, by confining them to occupations that the world despises, and by depriving them of any hope of honor. Yet they themselves have never ceased to believe in their own high calling; and they are honored by the dignity with which they face their tormentors.

And how should we think them base? From the Jews sprang the most powerful book in history, the most effective moral law, Spinoza the most sublime philosopher, and Christ the last Christian. When Europe was sunk in barbarism, it was the Jewish philosophers who preserved for us the genius of the ancients.

Yet all people must have their self-respect, and self-respect demands that one repay both good and bad. Without the ability to occasionally revenge themselves upon their despisers, they could scarcely have held up their heads. The usury of which the Jews are accused is the least of it; it was the subtle, twisted, deceitful Jewish revolution in morals that truly destroyed the ancients—that took the natural, healthy joy of freedom, life, and power, that twisted and inverted that joy, that planted this fatal sickness among their enemies. Thus was the Jewish vengeance upon Rome.

And this is the tradition that our Helen has inherited. Her very existence here is a vengeance upon all that have tormented her people from the beginning of time. She is beautiful, she is gay… and what does she care if Troy burns? Or Rome? Or Tombstone?

When next Freddie encountered Josie, he was vomiting in the dust of Toughnut Street.

He had felt the migraine coming on earlier, but he was playing against a table of drunken stockmen who were celebrating the sale of their beeves and who were losing their money almost as fast as they could shove it across the table. Freddie was determined to fight on as long as the cards fell his way.

By the time he left the Occidental he was nearly blind with pain. The clink of the winnings in his pocket sounded in his ears like bronze bells. The Arizona sun flamed on his skull. He staggered two blocks—people turned their eyes from him, as if he were drunk—and then collapsed as the cramp seized his stomach. People hurried away from him as he emptied the contents of his stomach into the dust. The spasms wracked him long after he had nothing left to vomit.

Freddie heard footsteps, then felt the firm touch of a hand on his arm. "Freddie? Shall I get a doctor?"

Humiliation burned in his face. He had no wish that his helplessness should even be acknowledged—he could face those people who hurried away, there could be a pretense that they had seen nothing, but he couldn't bear that another person should see him in his weakness.

"It is normal," he gasped. "Migraine. I have medicine in my room."

"Can you get up? I'll help you."

He wiped his face with his handkerchief, and then her hand steadied him as he groped his way to his feet. His spectacles were hanging from one ear, and he adjusted them. It didn't help—his vision had narrowed to the point where it seemed he was looking at the world through the wrong end of a telescope. He shuffled down Toughnut toward his room—he rented the back room of a house belonging to a mining engineer and his family, and paid the wife extra for meals that would not torment his digestion. He groped for the door, pushed it open, and stumbled toward the bed. He swiped off the pyramid of books that lay on the blanket and threw himself onto the mattress. A whirlwind spun through his head.

"Thank you," he muttered. "Please go now."

"Where is your medicine?"

He gestured vaguely to the wooden box by his wash basin. "There. Just bring me the box."

He heard her boot-heels booming like pistol-shots on the wooden floor, and fought down another attack of nausea. He heard her open the velvet-padded box and scrutinize the contents. "Chloral hydrate!" she said. "Veronal! Do you take this all the time?"

"Only when I am ill," he said. "Please—bring it."

She gasped in surprise as he drank the chloral right from the bottle, knowing from experience the amount necessary to cause unconsciousness. "Thank you," he said. "I will be all right now. You can go."

"Let me help you with your boots."

Freddie gave a weary laugh. "Oh yes, by all means. I should not die with my boots on."

The drug was already shimmering through his veins. Josie drew off his boots. His head was ringing like a great bell. Then the sound of the bell grew less and less, as if the clapper was being progressively swathed in wool, until it thudded no louder than a heartbeat.

Freddie woke after dark to discover that Josie had not left. He wiped away the gum that glued his eyelids shut and saw her curled in his only chair with her skirts tucked under her, reading by the light of his lamp.

"My God," he said. "What hour is it?"

She brushed away an insect that circled the lamp. "I don't know," she said. "Past midnight, anyway."

"What are you doing here? Shouldn't you be with Sheriff Behan?"

"He doesn't own me." Spoken tartly enough, though Freddie suspected that Behan might disagree.

"And besides," Josie said, "I wanted to make sure you didn't die of that medicine of yours."

Freddie raised a hand to his forehead. The migraine was gone, but the drug still enfolded his nerves in its smothering arms. He felt stupid, and stupidly ridiculous. "Well, I did not die," he said. "And I thank you—I will walk you home if you like."

She glanced at the book in her hands. "I would like to finish the chapter."

He could not see the title clearly in the dim light. "What are you reading?"

"*The Adventures of Tom Sawyer.*"

Freddie gave a little laugh. "I borrowed that book from John Ringo. I think Twain is your finest American writer."

"Ringo reads?" Josie looked surprised. "I thought you were the only person in the whole Territory who ever cracked a book, *Herr Professor.*"

"You would be surprised—there are many educated men here. John Holliday is of course a college graduate. John Ringo is a true autodidact—born poor but completely self-educated, a lover of books."

"And a lover of other men's cattle."

Freddie smiled. "That is a small flaw in this country, miss. His virtues surely outweigh it."

The drug had left his mouth dry. He rose from the bed and poured a glass of water from his pitcher. There was a strange singing in his head, the beginnings of the wild euphoria that often took him after a migraine. Usually he would write in his journals for hours during these fits, write until his hand was clawed with cramp.

He drank another glass of water and turned to Josie. "May I take you home?"

She regarded him, oval face gold in the glow of the lamp. "Johnny won't be home for hours yet," she said. "Are you often ill?"

"That depends on what you mean by 'often.'" He shuffled in his stocking feet to his bed—it was the only other place to sit. He saw his winnings gleaming on the blanket—little rivers of silver had spilled from his pockets. He bent to pick them up, stack them on his little shelf.

"How often is often?" Patiently.

"Once or twice a month. It used to be worse, much worse."

"Before you came West."

"Yes. Before I—before I 'lit out for the Territory,' as Mr. Mark Twain would say. And I was very ill the first years in America."

"Were you different then?" she asked. "Johnny tells me you have this wild reputation—but here you've never been in trouble, and—" Looking at the room stacked high with books and papers. " —you live like a monk."

"When I came to America, I was in very bad health," he said. "I thought I would die." He turned to Josie. "I believed that I would die at the age of thirty-five."

She looked at him curiously. "Why that number?"

"My father died at that age. They called it 'softening of the brain.' He died mad." He turned, sat on the bed, touched his temples with his fingers. "Sometimes I could feel the madness there, pressing upon my mind. Waiting for the right moment to strike. I thought that anything was better than dying as my father had died." He laughed as memories swam through the euphoria that was flooding his brain. "So I lived a mad life!" he said. "A wild life, in hopes that it would kill me before the madness did! And then one day, I awoke—" He looked up at Josie, his face a mirror of the remembered surprise. "And I realized that I was no longer thirty-five, and that I was still alive."

"That must have been a kind of liberation."

"Oh yes! But in any case that life was at an end. The Texas Rangers came to drive the wild men from the state, and—to my great shame—we allowed ourselves to be driven. And now we are here—" He looked at her. "Wiser, I hope."

"You write to a lady," she said.

Freddie looked at her in surprise. "I beg your pardon?" he said.

"I'm sorry. You were working on a letter—I saw it when I sat down. Perhaps I shouldn't have looked, but—"

Mirth burst from Freddie. "My sister!" he laughed. "My sister Elisabeth!"

She seemed a little surprised. "You addressed her in such passionate terms—I thought she was perhaps—" She hesitated.

"A lover? No. I will rewrite the letter later, perhaps, to make it less strident." He laughed again. "I thought Elisabeth might understand my ideas, but she is too limited, she has not risen above the patronizing attitudes of that little small town where we grew up—" Anger began to build in his heart, rising to a red, scalding fury. "She *rewrote my work.* I sent her some of my notebooks to publish, and she changed my words, she added anti-Semitic nonsense to the manuscript. She has fallen under the influence of those who hate the Jews, and she is being courted by one, a professional anti-Semite named Förster, a man who *distributes wretched tracts at meetings.*" He waved a fist in the air. "She said she was *making my thoughts clearer.*" He realized his voice has risen to a shout, and he tried to calm himself, suddenly falling into a mumble. "As if she herself has ever had any clear thoughts!" he said. "God help me if she remains my only conduit to the publishers."

Josie listened to this in silence, eyes glimmering in the light of the lantern. "You aren't an anti-Semite, then?" she said. "Your Superman isn't a—what is the word they use, those people?—Aryan?"

Freddie shook his head. "Neither he nor I am as simple as that."

"I'm Jewish," she said.

He ran his fingers through his hair. "I know," he said. "Someone told me."

Bells began to sing in his head—not the bells of pain, those clanging wracking peals of his migraine, but bells of wild joy, a carillon that pealed out in celebration of some pagan triumph.

Josie looked up, and he followed her glance upward to the pistol belt above his head, to his Colt, his Zarathustra, the blue steel that gleamed in the darkness.

"You've killed men," she said.

"Not so many as rumors would have it."

"But you have killed."

"Yes."

"Did they deserve it?"

"It is not the killing that matters," Freddie said. "It is not the deserving." A laugh burbled out, the strange rapture rising. "Any fool can kill," he said, "and any animal—but it takes a Caesar, or a Napoleon, to kill *as a human being,* as a moment of self-becoming. To rise above that—" He began to stammer in his enthusiasm. "—that merely human act—that foolishness—to overcome—to become—"

"The Superman?" she queried.

"Ha-ha!" He laughed in sudden giddy triumph. "Yes! Exactly!"

She rose from the chair, stepped to the head of the bed in a swirl of skirts. She reached a hand toward the gun, hesitated, then looked down at him.

"*Nicht nur fort sollst du dich pflanzen sondern hinauf,*" she said.

Her German was fluent, accented slightly by Yiddish. Freddie stared at her in astonishment.

"You read my journals!" he said.

A smile drifted across her face. "I wasn't very successful—your handwriting is difficult, and I speak German easier than I read it."

"My God." Wonder rang in his head. "No one has *ever* read my journals."

That is her Jewish aspect, he thought, the people of the Book. Reverence for thought, from the only people in the world who held literacy as a test of manhood.

Josie glanced down at him. "Tell me what that means—that we should propagate not only downward, but upward."

Weird elation sang through his head. "I meant that we need not be animals when—" He recalled the decencies only at the last second. "—when we marry," he finished. "We need not bring only more apes into the world. We can *create.* We can be together not because we are lonely or inadequate, but because we are whole, because we wish to triumph!"

Josie gave a low, languorous laugh, and with an easy motion slid into his lap. Strangely enough he was not surprised. He put his arms around her, wild hope throbbing in his veins.

"Shall we triumph, Freddie?" she asked. Troy burned in her eyes.

"Yes!" he said in sudden delirium. "By God, yes!"

She bent forward, touched her lips to his. A rising, glorious astonishment whirled in Freddie's body and soul.

"You taste like a narcotic," she said softly, and—laughing low—kissed him again.

It was an hour or so later that the shots began echoing down Tombstone's streets, banging out with frantic speed, sounds startling in the surrounding stillness. Freddie sat up. "My God, what is that?" he said.

"Some of your friends, probably," Josie said. She reached out her hands, drew him down to the mattress again. "Whoever is shooting, they don't need you there."

Is that Behan's motto? Freddie wondered. But at the touch of her hands he felt flame burn in his veins, and he paid no attention to the shooting, not even when more guns began to speak, and the firing went on for some time.

In the morning he learned that it had been Curly Bill Brocius who was shooting, drunkenly fanning his revolver into the heavens; and that when the town marshal, Fred White, had tried to disarm him, Brocius' finger had slipped on the hammer and let it fall. White was dead, killed by Brocius' modified gun that would not hold the hammer at safety. A small battle had developed between Brocius' friends and various citizens, and Brocius had been slapped on the head by Wyatt Earp's long-barreled Colt and arrested for murder.

The next bit of news was that Marshal White's replacement had been chosen, and that Deputy U.S. Marshal Virgil Earp was now in charge of enforcing the law in the town of Tombstone.

It is like Texas again! Freddie wrote in his journal. It is not so much the killing, but the mad aimlessness of it all. Would that Brocius had been more discriminating with those bullets of his! Would that he had shot another lawman altogether!

The good citizens of Tombstone are over-stimulated, and to avoid the possibility of a lynching the trial will be held at Tucson. I believe that law in Tucson is no less amenable to reason than was the law in Texas, and I have no fear that Brocius will meet a noose.

But while Brocius enjoys his parole, Tombstone must endure the Earps, in their black uniforms, marching about the streets like so many carrion crows. It is their slave souls they hide beneath those frock coats!

But I stay above them. I look down at them from my new rooms in the Grand Hotel. My landlady on Toughnut Street did not approve of what she called my "immorality." Though she was willing to accept as rent the gambling winnings of a known killer, she will not tolerate love in her back room. The manager of the Grand Hotel is more flexible in regard to morals—he gives me a front room, and he tips his hat when Josie walks past.

But I must train his cook, or indigestion will kill me.

How long has it been since a woman held me in her arms? Three years? Four? And she was not a desirable woman, and did not desire anything from me other than the silver in my pocket.

Ach! It was a mad time. Life was cheap, but the price of love was two dollars in advance. I shot three men, and killed two, and the killing caused far less inconvenience than a few short minutes with a dance-hall girl.

Nor is Helen of Troy a dance-hall girl. She cares nothing for money and everything for power. The sexual impulse and conquest are one, and both are aspects perhaps of Jewish revenge. It is power that she seeks. But most atypically her will to power is not based on an attempt to weaken others—she does not seek to castrate her men. She challenges them, rather, to match her power with their own. Those who cannot—like Behan—will suffer.

Those who act wisely, perhaps, will live. But I cannot be persuaded that this, ultimately, will matter to her.


"I don't understand," Freddie said, "how it is that Virgil Earp can be Town Marshal and Deputy U.S. Marshal at the same time. Shouldn't he be compelled to resign one post or another?"

"Marshal Dake in Prescott don't mind if his deputy has a job on the side," said John Holliday.

"I should complain. I should write a letter to the newspaper. Or perhaps to the appropriate cabinet secretary."

"If you think it would do any good. But I think the U.S. government likes Virge right where he is."

Holliday sat with Freddie in the plush drawing room of the Grand Hotel, where Holliday had come for a visit. Their wing chairs were pulled up to the broad front window. Freddie turned his gaze from the bright October sunshine to look at Holliday. "I do not understand you," he said. "I do not understand why you are friends with these Earps."

"They're good men," Holliday said simply.

"But *you* are not, John," Freddie said.

A smile crinkled the corners of Holliday's gaunt eyes. "True," he said.

"You are a Southerner, and a gentleman, and a Democrat," Freddie said. "The Earps are Yankees, not gentle, and Republicans. I fail to understand your sympathy for them."

Holliday shrugged, reached into his pocket for a cigar. "I saved Wyatt from a mob of Texans once, in Dodge City," he said. "Since then I've taken an interest in him."

"But why?" Freddie asked. "Why did you save his life?"

Holliday struck a match and puffed his cigar into life, then drew the smoke into his ravaged lungs. He coughed once, sharply, then said, "It seemed a life worth saving."

Freddie gave a snort of derision.

"What I don't understand," said Holliday, "is why you dislike him. He's an extraordinary man. And your two greatest friends admire him."

"You and who else?"

"Your Sadie," John Holliday said. "She is with Wyatt Earp this moment, across the street in the Cosmopolitan Hotel."

Freddie stared at him, and then his gaze jerked involuntarily to the window again, to the bare façade of the Cosmopolitan, built swiftly and of naked lumber, devoid of paint. "But—" he said, "but—Earp is married—" He was aware of how ridiculous he sounded even as he stammered out the words.

"Oh," Holliday said casually, "I don't believe Wyatt and Mattie ever officially tied the knot—not that it signifies." He looked at Freddie and rolled the cigar in his fingers. "I thought you should hear it from me," he said, "rather than through the grapevine telegraph."

Freddie stared across the street and felt flaming madness beating at his brain. He considered storming across the street, kicking down the door, firing his Zarathustra, his pistol again and again until it clicked on an empty chamber, until the walls were spattered with crimson and the room was filled with the stinging, purifying incense of powder smoke.

But no. He was not an animal, to act in blind fury. He would take revenge—if revenge were to be taken—as a human being. Coldly. With foresight. And with due regard for the consequences.

And for Freddie to fight for a woman. Was that not the most stupid piece of melodrama in the world? Would not any decent dramatist in the world reject this plot as hackneyed?

He looked at Holliday, let a grin break across his face. "For a moment I was almost jealous!" he laughed.

"You're not?"

"Jealousy—pfah!" Freddie laughed again. "Sadie—Josie—she is free."

Holliday nodded. "That's one word for it."

"She is trying to get your Mr. Earp murdered. Or myself. Or the whole world."

"Gonna kill him!" said a voice. Freddie turned to see Ike Clanton, red-eyed and swaying with drink, dragging his spurs across the parlor carpet. Ike was in town on business and staying at the hotel. "Come join me, Freddie!" he said. "We'll kill him together!"

"Kill who, Ike?" Freddie asked.

"I'm gonna kill Doc Holliday!" Ike said.

"Here is Doc Holliday, right here," said Freddie.

Ike turned, swayed back on his boot-heels, and saw Holliday sitting in the wing chair and unconcernedly smoking his cigar. Ike grinned, touched the brim of his sombrero. "Hiya, Doc!" he said cheerfully.

Holliday nodded politely. "Hello, Ike."

Ike grinned for a moment more, then remembered his errand and turned to Freddie. "So will you help me kill Doc Holliday, Freddie?"

"Doc's my friend, Ike," Freddie said.

Ike took a moment to process this declaration. "I forgot," he said, and then he reached out to clumsily pat Freddie's shoulder. "That's all right, then," he said with evident concern. "I regret I must kill your friend. Adiós." He turned and swayed from the room.

Holliday watched Ike's exit without concern. "Why is Ike trying to kick a fight with me?" he said.

"God alone knows."

Holliday dismissed Ike Clanton with a contemptuous downward curl of his lip. He turned to Freddie. "Shall we find a game of cards?"

Freddie rose. "Why not? Let me get my hat."

Holliday took him to Earp country, to the Oriental Saloon. Freddie could not concentrate on the game—Wyatt Earp's faro table was in plain sight, Earp's empty chair all too visible; and visions of Josie and Earp kept burning in his mind, a writhing of white limbs in a hotel bed, scenes from his own private inferno—and Holliday calmly and professionally took Freddie's every penny, leaving him with nothing but his coat, his hat, and his gun.

"You don't own me." Freddie wrote in his notebook. She almost spat the words at me. It is her *crie d'esprit,* her defiance to the world, her great maxim.

"I own nothing," I replied calmly. "Nothing at all." Close enough to the truth. I must find someone to loan me a stake so that I can win money and pay the week's lodging.

I argued my points with great precision, and she answered with fury. Her anger left me untouched—she accused me of jealousy, of all ridiculous things! It is easy to remain calm in the face of arrows that fly so wide of the mark. I asked her only to choose a man worthy of her. Behan is nothing, and Earp an earnest fool. Worthy in his own way, no doubt, but not of such as she.

Ah well. Let her go. She is qualified to ruin her life in her own way, no doubt. I will keep my room at the Grand—unless poverty drives me into the street—and she will return when she understands her mistake.

I must remember my pocketbook, and earn some money. And I must certainly stay clear of John Holliday, at least at the card table.

I think I sense a migraine about to begin.

"Freddie?" It was Sheriff Behan who stood in the door of the Grand Hotel's parlor, his derby hat in his hand and a worried look on his face. "Freddie, can you come with me and talk to your friends?"

Freddie felt fragile after his migraine. Drugs still slithered their cold way through his veins. He looked at Behan and scowled. "What is it, Johnny?" he said. "Go away. I am not well."

"There's going to be a fight between the Earps and the Clantons and McLaurys. Your friends are going to get killed unless we do something."

"You're the sheriff," Freddie said, unable to resist digging in the spur. "Put the Clantons in jail."

"My God, Freddie!" Behan almost shouted. "I can't arrest the *Clantons!*"

"Not as long as they're letting you have this nice salary, I suppose." Freddie shook his head, then rose from his wing chair. "Very well. Tell me what is going on."

Ike Clanton had been very busy since Freddie had seen him last. He had wandered over Tombstone for two days, uttering threats against Doc Holliday to anyone who would listen. When he appeared in public with a pistol and rifle, Virgil Earp slapped him over the head with a revolver, confiscated his weapons, and tossed him in jail. Ike paid the twenty-five-dollar fine and returned to the streets, where he went boasting of his deadly intentions, now including the Earps in his threats. After Ike's brief trial, Wyatt Earp had encountered Ike's friend Tom McLaury on the street and pistol-whipped him. Now Tom was bent on vengeance as well. They had been seen in Spangenburg's gun shop, and had gathered a number of their friends. The Earps and Holliday were armed and ready. Vigilantes were arming all over Tombstone, ready for blood. Behan had promised to stave off disaster by disarming the Cowboys, and he wanted help.

"This is absurd," Freddie muttered. The clear October light sent daggers into his brain. "They are behaving like fools."

"They're down at the corral," Behan said. "It's legal for them to carry arms there, but if they step outside I'll—" He blanched. "I'll have to do something."

The first tendrils of the euphoria that followed his migraines began to enfold Freddie's brain. "Very well," he said. "I'll come."

The lethargy of the drugs warred within Freddie's mind with growing elation as Behan led Freddie down Allen Street, then through the front entrance of the O.K. Corral, a narrow livery stable that ran like an alley between Allen and Fremont streets. The Clantons were not in the corral, and Behan was almost frantic as he led Freddie out the back entrance onto Fremont, where Freddie saw the Cowboys standing in the vacant lot between Camillus Fly's boarding house, where Holliday lodged with his Kate, and another house owned by a man named Harwood.

There were five of them, Freddie saw. Ike and his brother Billy, Tom and Frank McLaury, and their young friend Billy Claiborne, who like almost every young Billy in the West was known as "Billy the Kid," after another, more famous outlaw who was dead and could not dispute the title. Tom McLaury led a horse by the reins. The group stood in the vacant lot in the midst of a disagreement. When he saw Freddie walking toward him, Billy Claiborne looked relieved.

"Freddie!" he said. "Thank God! You help me talk some sense into these men!"

Ike looked at Freddie with a broad grin. "We're going to kill Doc Holliday!" he said cheerfully. "We're going to wait for him to come home, then blow his head off!"

Freddie glanced up at Fly's boarding house, with its little photographic studio out back, then returned his gaze to Ike. He tried to concentrate against the chorus of euphoric angels that sang in his mind. "Doc won't be coming back till late," he said. "You might as well go home."

Ike shook his head vigorously. "No," he said. "I'm gonna kill Doc Holliday!"

"Ike," Freddie pointed out, "you don't even have a gun."

Ike turned red. "It's only because that son of a bitch Spangenburg wouldn't sell me one!"

"You can't kill Holliday without a gun," Freddie said. "You might as well come back to the hotel with me." He reached out to take Ike's arm.

"Now wait a minute, Freddie," said Ike's brother Billy. "*I've* got a gun." He pulled back his coat to show his revolver. "And I think killing Holliday is a sound enough idea. It'll hurt the Earps. And no one 'round here likes Doc—nobody's going to care if he gets killed."

"Holliday and half the town know you're standing here ready to kill him," Freddie said. "He's heeled and so are the Earps. Your ambush is going to fail."

"That's what I've been trying to tell them!" Billy Claiborne added, and then moaned, "Oh Lord, they'll make a blue fist of it!"

"Hell," said Tom McLaury. The side of his head was swollen where Wyatt Earp had clouted him. "We've got to fight the Earps sooner or later. Might as well do it now."

"I agree you should fight," Freddie said. "But this is not the time or the place."

"This place is good as any other!" Tom said. "That bastard Earp hit me for no reason, and I'm going to put a bullet in him."

"I'm with my brother on this," said Frank McLaury.

"Nobody can stand up to us!" Ike said. "With us five and Freddie here, the Earps had better start praying."

Exasperation overwhelmed the exaltation that sang in Freddie's skull. With the ferocious clarity that was an aspect of his euphoria, he could see exactly what would happen. The Earps were professional lawmen—they did not chew their own tobacco, as Brocius would say—and when they came they would be ready. They might come with a crowd of vigilantes. The Cowboys, half unarmed, would stand wondering what to do, would have no leader, would wait too long to reach a decision, and then they would be cut down.

"I have no gun!" Freddie told Ike. "*You* have no gun. And the Kid here has no gun. Three of you cannot fight a whole town, I think. You should go home and wait for a better time. Wait till Bill Brocius' trial is over, and get John Ringo to join you."

"You only say that 'cause you're a coward!" Ike said. "You're a kraut-eating yellowbelly! You won't stand by your friends!"

Murder sang a song of fury in Freddie's blood. His hand clawed as if it held a gun—and the fact that there was no gun did not matter, the claw could as easily seize Ike's throat. Ike took a step backward at the savage glint in Freddie's eyes. Then Freddie shook his head, and said, "This is folly. I wash my hands of it." He turned and began to walk away.

"Freddie!" Behan yelped. He sprang in front of Freddie, bouncing on his neat polished brown boots. "You can't leave! You've got to help me with this!"

Freddie drew himself up, glared savagely at Behan. Righteous angels sang in his mind. "You are the sheriff, I collect," he said. "Dealing with it is your job!"

Behan froze, his mouth half-open. Freddie stepped around him and marched away, down Fremont to the back entrance to the O.K. Corral, then through the corral to Allen Street. Exaltation thrilled in his blood like wine. He crossed the street to the shadier south side—the sun was still hammering his head—and began the walk to the Grand Hotel. At Fourth Street he looked south and saw a mob—forty or fifty armed citizens, mostly hard-bitten miners—marching toward him up the street.

If this crowd found the Clantons, the Cowboys were dead. Surely Freddie's friends could now be convinced that they must fight another day.

Freddie turned and hastened along Allen Street toward the O.K. Corral, but then gunfire cracked out, the sudden bright sounds jolting his nerves, and he felt his heart sink even as he broke into a run. A shotgun boomed, and windows rattled in nearby buildings. He dashed through the long corral, then jumped over the fence, ran past the photography studio, and into the back door of Camillus Fly's boarding house.

John Behan crouched beneath a window with his blue-steel revolver in his hand. The window had been shattered by bullets, and its yellow organdy curtain fluttered in the breeze, but there was no scent of smoke or other indication that Behan had ever fired his pistol. Shrieks rang in the air, cries of mortal agony. Freddie ran beside the window and peered out. His heart hammered, and he panted for breath after his run.

The narrow vacant lot was hazy with gunsmoke. Lying at the far end were the bodies of two men, Tom McLaury and Billy Clanton. Just four or five paces in front of them were the three Earps and John Holliday. Morgan was down with a wound. Virgil knelt on the dry ground, leg bleeding, and he supported himself with a cane. Holliday's back was to Freddie—he had a short Wells Fargo shotgun broken open over one arm—and there were bright splashes of blood on Holliday's coat and trousers.

In Fremont Street, behind the Earps, Frank McLaury lay screaming in the dust. He was covered with blood. Apparently he had run right through the Earps and collapsed. His agonized shrieks raised the hair on the back of Freddie's neck.

Of Billy Claiborne and Ike Clanton, Freddie saw no sign. Apparently the unarmed men had run away.

Wyatt Earp stood over his brother Morgan, unwounded, a long-barreled Colt in his hand. Savage hatred burned in Freddie's heart. He glared down at Behan.

"What have you done?" he hissed. "Why didn't you stop it?"

"I tried!" Behan said. "You saw that I tried. Oh, this is horrible!"

"You fool. Why do you bother to carry this?" Freddie reached down and snatched the revolver from Behan's hand. He looked out the window again and saw Wyatt Earp standing like a bronze statue over his wounded brother. Angels sang a song of glory in Freddie's blood.

Make something of it, he thought. Make something of this other than a catastrophe. Make it mean something.

He cocked Behan's gun. Earp heard the sound and raised his head, suddenly alert. And then German Freddie put six shots into Earp's breast from a distance of less than a dozen feet.

"My God!" Behan bleated. "What are you doing?"

Freddie looked at him, a savage grin taut on his face. He dropped the revolver at Behan's feet as return fire began to sing through the window. He ran into the back of the studio, out the back door, and was sprinting down Third Street when he heard Behan's voice ringing over the sound of barking gunfire. "It wasn't me! I swear to Mary!" Mad laughter burbled from Freddie's lips as he heard the crash of a door being kicked down. Behan screamed something else, something that might have been "German Freddie!" but whatever he was trying to say was cut short by a storm of fire.

A steam whistle shattered the air as Freddie ran south. Someone was blowing the alarm at the Uzina Mine. And when Freddie reached the corner, he saw the vigilante mob pouring up Allen Street, heading for the front gate of the O.K. Corral. He waited a few seconds for the leaders to swarm through the gate, and then he quietly crossed the street at a normal walking pace. Despite the way he panted for breath, Freddie had a hard time not breaking into a run.

He had never felt such joy, not even in Josie's arms.

By roundabout means he made his way to his room at the Grand Hotel. Once he had Zarathustra in his hand he began to breathe more easily. Still, he concluded, it was time to leave town. There were any number of people who could place him near the site of that streetfight, and possibly some of the vigilantes had seen him stroll away.

And then a thought struck him—he had no horse! He was a bad rider and had come to Tombstone on the Wells Fargo stage. The only way he could get a horse would be to stroll back to the O.K. Corral and hire one, with the lynch mob looking on.

He laughed and put Zarathustra in his coat pocket. He was trapped in a town filled with Earps and armed vigilantes.

"It is time to be bold," he said aloud. "It is time to be cunning."

He washed his hands, to remove the reek of gunpowder, and changed his shirt.

It occurred to him that there existed a place where he might hide.

He put his journal in another pocket, and made his way out of the hotel.

Oh, she is magnificent! Freddie wrote in his journal a few hours later. She hid me in Behan's house while Behan lay painted in his coffin in the front window of the undertakers—Ritter and Reams are making the most of this opportunity to advertise their art! I rested on Behan's bed while she received callers in the front room. And then, at nightfall, she had Behan's horse saddled and brought to the back door.

"Will I see you again?" she asked.

"Oh yes," I said. "Destiny will not permit us to part for long."

"Do you have money?"

I confessed that I did not. She went into the house and came back with an envelope of bills which she put in my pocket. Later I counted them and found they amounted to five thousand dollars. The office of sheriff pays surprisingly well!

I took her hand. "Troy is afire, my Helen. Do you have what you desire?"

"I did not want this," she said. Her fingers clutched at mine.

"Of course you did," I said. "What else did you expect?"

I rode to Charleston with her kiss burning on my lips. Charleston is a town ruled by the Cowboys, and so I knew I could find shelter there, but it is also the first place a posse will come.

It will be a war now—my bullets have decreed it. I welcome the war, I welcome the trumpet that will awaken the new Romulus. Battles there shall be, and victories. And both those who die and those who live shall be awarded a Tombstone—what an irony!

I am curiously satisfied with the day's business. It is a man's life that I am leading. Were I to live these same events a thousand times, I would find no reason to alter the outcome.

"There are more Earps than before," John Ringo observed from over the rim of his beer glass. "James and Warren have come to town. You're creatin' more Earps than you're killin', Freddie."

"Two hundred rifles," Freddie urged. "Raise them! Make Tombstone yours!"

Curly Bill Brocius shook his head. "No more shootings. The town's riled enough as it is. I don't want my parole revoked, and besides, I've got to make certain that our man gets in as sheriff."

"Let us purge this choler without letting blood," Ringo said, and wiped foam from his mustache.

"Still these politics!" Freddie scorned. "Who is our man this time?"

"Fellehy."

"The laundryman? What kind of sheriff will he make?"

Brocius gave his easy grin. "No kind," he said. "Which is *our* kind."

"He will be worse than Behan. And it was Behan's bungling that killed three of our friends."

Brocius' grin faded. "I don't reckon," he insisted.

Freddie had made good his escape and met Ringo and Brocius in the Golden Saloon in Tucson. He was not quite far enough from Tombstone— Freddie kept his back to a wall and his eye on the door, just in case a crowd of men in frock coats decided to barge in.

"So when may we start killing Earps?" Freddie asked.

"We're going to do it legal-like," Brocius said. "Ike Clanton's going to file in court against the Earps and Holliday for murder. They'll hang, and we won't have to pull a trigger."

Disgust filled Freddie's heart. "You are making yourself ridiculous," he said. "These men have killed your friends!"

"No more shooting," said Brocius. "We'll use the law's own weapons against the law, and we'll be back in charge quick as a dog can lick a dish."

Freddie looked at Brocius in fury, and then he laughed. "Very well, then," he said. "We shall see what joys the law brings us!"

You could play the law game any number of ways, Freddie thought. And he thought he knew how he wanted to bid his hand.

"Ike Clanton said he was going to kill Doc Holliday," Freddie testified. "His brother supported him, and so did the McLaurys. Claiborne and I were trying to talk sense into their stupid heads, but Ike was abusive, so I left in disgust."

There was stunned silence in the courtroom. Freddie was a witness for the prosecution, but was handing the defense its case on a plate.

The prosecution witnesses had agreed on a story ahead of time, how the Cowboys had been unarmed, and the Earps the aggressors. Now Freddie was blowing the case to smithereens.

Price, the district attorney, was so stunned by Freddie's testimony that he blurted out what had to be absolutely the wrong question. "You say that Ike was *intending* to kill Mr. Holliday?"

Freddie looked at Ike from the his witness' chair. The man stared back at him, disbelief plain on his face, and out of the slant of his eye he saw Holliday look at him thoughtfully.

"Oh yes," Freddie said. "But Ike is too much the drunken coward to actually carry out his threats. He ran away from the streetfight and left his brother to die in the dust."

Bullets or nothing, Freddie thought. We shall honor valor or honor shall lie dishonored.

"You son of a bitch," Ike Clanton said in the Grand Hotel's parlor, after the trial had adjourned for the day. "What did you say those things for?"

"Because they're true," Freddie said. "Do you think I would lie to protect a worthless dog like you?"

Ike turned red. "You skin that back, you bastard! Skin that back, or I'll settle with you!"

Freddie wiped Ike's spittle from his chin with his handkerchief. "It's Doc Holliday you hate, is it not?" he said. "Why don't you settle with him first?"

"I'm gonna get him! And you, too!"

"Do it now," Freddie advised, "while you're almost sober. You know where Holliday lives. Perhaps if you work up all your courage you can shoot him in the back." Freddie reached into his pocket, took hold of Zarathustra, and thumbed back the hammer. Ike's eyes widened at the sound. He made a little whining noise in his throat.

"Don't shoot me!" he blurted.

"You can kill Holliday now," Freddie said, "or I will shoot you like a dog where you stand. And who will take *me* to court for such a thing?"

"I'll do it!" Ike said quickly. "I'll kill him! See if I don't!"

"I believe you checked your gun with the desk clerk," Freddie reminded him.

Freddie followed him to the front desk and kept his hand on the pistol. Ike cast him frantic glances over his shoulder as he was given his gun belt. He made certain his hand was nowhere near the butt of the weapon as he strapped it on—he did not want to give a man with Freddie's murderous reputation a chance to shoot.

Freddie followed Ike out into the street, and glared at him when it looked as if he would step into a saloon for some liquid courage. Ike saw the glare, then began to walk faster down the street. Freddie pursued, boots thumping on the wooden walk. At the end of the long walk, when Fly's boarding house came into sight, Ike was almost running.

Freddie paused then, and began a leisurely stroll to the hotel. Gunfire erupted behind him, but he didn't break stride. He knew Ike Clanton, and he knew John Holliday, and he knew which of the two now lay dead.

"The legal case will collapse without a plaintiff," Freddie said that evening. "The district attorney may file a criminal case, but why would he? He knows the defense would call me as a witness." He laughed. "And now, after this second killing, Holliday will have to leave town. That is another problem solved."

Josie stretched luxuriously in Behan's bed. She was wearing a little transparent silken thing that Behan had bought her from out of a French catalogue, and Freddie, lying next to her, let his eyes feast gratefully on the ripeness of her body. She seemed well pleased with his eyes' amorous intentions, and rolled a little in the bed, to and fro, to show herself from different angles.

"You seem very pleased with yourself," she said.

"I have nothing against Holliday. I like the man. I'm glad he will be out of it."

"You're the only man alive who likes him. Now that Johnny's killed Wyatt." A silence hung for a moment in the air, and then Josie rolled over and put her chin on her crossed arms. Her dark eyes regarded him solemnly.

"Yes?" Freddie said, knowing the question that would come.

"There are people who say it was you who shot Wyatt," she said.

Freddie looked at her. "One of your lovers shot him," he said. "Does it matter which?"

"Did you kill for me, Freddie?" There was a strange thrill in her voice. "Did you kill Wyatt?"

"If I killed Wyatt," Freddie said coldly, "it was not for you. I did not do it to make you the heroine of a melodrama."

She made as if to say something, but she turned her head away, laying her cheek on her hand. Freddie reached out to caress her rich dark hair. "Troy burns for you, my Helen," he said. "Is it not your triumph?"

"I don't understand you," she said.

"I am in love with Fate," Freddie said. "I regret nothing, and neither should you. Everything you do, let it be as if you would—as if you *must*—do it again ten thousand times."

She was silent. He reached beneath her masses of hair, took her chin in his fingers, raised her face to his. "Come, my queen," he said. "Give me ten thousand kisses. And let us not regret a one of them."

Ten thousand kisses! Freddie wrote in his journal. She does not yet understand her power—that she can change the universe, and all the universes yet to be born.

How many times have I killed Earp, in worlds long dead? And how many times must I kill him again? The thought is joy to me. I crave nothing more. Ten thousand bullets, ten thousand kisses. Forever

*Amor fati.* Love is all.

"Sir." Holliday bowed. Not yet healed, he stood stiffly, and supported his wounded hip with a cane. "The district attorney is of the opinion that Arizona and I must part. I thought I would take my adieu."

Freddie rose from his wing-backed chair and offered his hand. "I'm sure we'll meet again," he said.

"Maybe so." He shook the hand, then stood, a frown on his gaunt face. "Freddie—" he began.

"Yes?"

"Get out of this," Holliday said. "Take Josie away. Go to California, Nevada, anywhere."

Freddie laughed. "There's still silver in Tombstone, John."

"Yes." He seemed saddened. He hesitated again. "I wanted to thank you, for your words at the trial."

Freddie made a dismissive gesture. "Ike Clanton wasn't worth the bullets it took to kill him," he said.

Holliday looked at Freddie gravely. "People might say that of the two of us," he said.

"I'm sure they would."

There was another hesitation, another silence. "Freddie," Holliday said.

"John." Smiling.

"There is a story that it was you who killed my friend."

Freddie laughed, though there was a part of his soul that writhed beneath Holliday's gaze. "If I believed all the stories about *you*—" he began.

"I do not know what to believe," Holliday said. "And whatever the truth, I am glad I killed that cur Behan. But it is your own friends—your Cowboys—who are spreading this story. They are boasting of it. And if I ever come to believe it is true—or if anything happens to Wyatt's brothers—then God help you." The words, forced from the consumptive lungs, were surprisingly forceful. "God help all you people."

Sudden fury flashed through Freddie's veins. "Why do you all place such a value on this *Earp!* I do not understand you!"

Cold steel glinted in Holliday's eyes. His pale face flushed. "He was worth fifty of you!" he cried. "And a hundred of me!"

"But *why?*" Freddie demanded.

Holliday began to speak, but something caught in his throat—he shook his head, bowed again, and made his way from the room as blood erupted from his ruined lungs.

Who was I to be so upset? Freddie wrote in his journal. It is not as if I do not understand how the world works. Homer wrote of Achilles and Hector battling over Troy, not about philosophers dueling with epigrams. It is people like the Earps who the story-tellers love, and whom they make immortal.

It is only philosophers who love other philosophers—unless of course they hate them.

If I wish to be remembered, I must do as the Earps do. I must be brave, and unimaginative, and die in a foolish way, over nothing.

"Why do I smell a dead cat on the line?" Brocius asked. "Freddie, why do I see you at the bottom of all my troubles?"

"Be joyful, Bill," Freddie said. "You've been found innocent of murder and you have your bond money back—at least for the next hour or two." He dealt a card face-up to Ringo. "Possible straight," he observed.

John Ringo contemplated this eventuality without joy. "These words hereafter thy tormentors be," he said, and poured himself another shot of whisky from the bottle by his elbow.

"I have been solving your problems, not adding to them," Freddie told Brocius. "I have solved your Wyatt Earp problem. And thanks to me, Doc Holliday has left town."

Brocius looked at him sharply. "What did you have to do with *that?*"

"That's between me and Holliday. Pair of queens bets."

Looking suspiciously at Freddie, Brocius pushed a gold double eagle onto the table. Freddie promptly raised by another double eagle. Ringo folded. Brocius sighed, lazy eyelids drooping.

"What's the *next* problem you're going to solve?" Brocius asked.

"Other than this hand? It's up to you. After this last killing, your Mr. Fellehy the Laundryman will never be appointed sheriff in Behan's place. They'll want a tough lawman who will work with Virgil Earp to clean up Cochise County. Are you going to call, Bill?"

"I'm thinking."

"The solution to your problem—*this* problem—is to remove Virgil Earp from all calculations."

Ringo gave a laugh. "You'll just get two more Earps in his place!" he said. "That's what happened last time."

Brocius frowned. "Entities are not multiplied beyond what is necessary."

Freddie was impressed. "Very good, Bill. I am teaching you, I see."

Brocius narrowed his eyes and looked at Freddie. "Are you going to solve this problem for me, Freddie?"

"Yes. I think you should fold."

Brocius pushed out a double eagle "Call. I meant the *other* problem."

Freddie dealt the next round of cards. "I think I have solved enough problems for you," he said slowly. "I am becoming far too prominent a member of your company for my health. I think you should arrange the solution on your own, and I will make a point of being in another place, in front of twenty unimpeachable witnesses."

Brocius looked at the table and scratched his chin. "You just dealt yourself an ace."

"And that makes a pair. And the pair of aces bets fifty." Freddie pushed the money out to the center of the table.

Brocius looked at his hole card, then threw it down.

"I reckon I fold," he said.

"Oh, they have bungled it!" Freddie stormed. "They have shot the wrong Earp!"

He paced madly in Behan's parlor, while Josie watched from her chair. "The assassin was to shoot Virgil!" Freddie said. "He mistook his man and shot Morgan instead—and he didn't even kill him!"

"Who did the shooting?" Josie said.

"I don't know. Some fool." Freddie paused in his pacing to furiously polish his spectacles. "And I will be blamed. This was supposed to occur when I was in the saloon, playing cards in front of witnesses. Instead it occurred when I was in bed with you."

She looked at him in surprise. "Ain't I a witness, Freddie?" she said in her mocking New York voice.

Freddie laughed bitterly. "They might calculate that you are prejudiced in my favor."

"They would be right." She rose, took Freddie's hands. "Perhaps you should leave Tombstone."

"And go where?" He put his arms around her. The scent of her French perfume drifted delicately through his senses.

"There are plenty of mining towns in the West," she said. "Plenty of places to play poker. And almost all have theaters, and will need someone to play the ingenue."

He looked at her. "My friends are here, Josie. And it is here that you are queen."

"*Amor fati,*" she murmured. He felt her shoulders fall slightly in acknowledgment of the defeat, and then she straightened. "I had better learn to shoot, then," she said. "Will you teach me?"

"I will. But I'm not a very good shot—my eyesight, you know."

"But you're a—" She hesitated.

"A killer? A gunman?" He smiled. "Certainly. But all my fights took place at a range of less than five meters—one was in a small room, three meters square. But still—yes—why not? It can do us no harm to be seen practicing."

"What is the best way to become a gunman?" Josie said.

"Not to care if you die," Freddie said promptly. "You must not fear death. I was deadly because I knew I was dying. John Holliday is dangerous for the same reason—he knows he must in any case die soon, so why not now? And John Ringo—he does not value his own life, clearly."

She tilted her head, looked at him carefully. "But you weren't dying at all. You may live as long as any of us. Does that make a fight more dangerous for you?"

Freddie considered this notion in some surprise. He wondered if he now truly had reasons to live, and whether the chief one was now in his arms.

"I am at least experienced in a fight," he said. "I'll keep my head, and kill or die as a man. It is important, in any case, to die at the right time."

Small comfort: he felt her tremble. Treasure this while you may, he thought; and know that you have treasured it before, and will again.

In the event it was not Freddie who died first. Three days after James Earp was appointed sheriff, Curly Bill Brocius was found dead on the road between Tombstone and Charleston. Two friends lay with him, all riddled with bullets. The only Earp not a suspect was Morgan, with a near-mortal wound in his spine, who had been carried into the county jail, where he was guarded by a half-dozen of the Earp's newly deputized supporters.

The other three Earp brothers, and a number of their friends, were not to be found in town. For several days the sound of volleys boomed off the blue Dragoon Mountains, echoed over the dry hills. Apparently they were not all fired in anger: most were signals from the Earps to their friends, who were bringing them supplies. But still three Cowboys were found dead, shot near their homes; and the Clanton spread was burned. A day later John Ringo rode into town on a lathered horse, claiming he'd been chased by a half-dozen gunmen.

"And Holliday's with them," Ringo said. "I saw the bastard, big as life."

Freddie's heart sank. "I was afraid of that."

"His hip's still bothering him, and Virgil's leg. Otherwise they would have caught me." He blew dust from his mustache and looked at Freddie. "We need a posse of our own, friend."

"So we do."

They called out their friends, but a surprising number had made themselves scarce. Freddie and Ringo assembled a dozen riders, all that remained of Brocius' mighty outlaw army, and hoped to pick up more as they rode.

Josie surprised everyone by showing up in riding clothes at the O.K. Corral, her new pistol hanging from her belt. "I will go, of course," she said.

Freddie's heart sang in praise of her bravery, but he touched his hat and said, "I believe that Helen should remain on Ilium's topless towers, where it is safe."

She looked at him, and he saw the jaw muscles tauten. "Those towers burned," she said. "And I don't want to survive another lover."

Freddie's heart flooded over. He kissed her, and knew he would kiss her thus time and again, for infinity.

"Come then!" he said. "We shall meet our fate together!"

"Let slip the dogs of war," Ringo commented wryly, and they rode out of town into a chill dawn.

They followed a pillar of smoke, a mining claim that belonged to one of the Cowboys. No one had been killed because no one was home, but the diggings had been thoroughly burned. From the mine they followed the trail north. After two days of riding they were disappointed to discover that the trail led to the Sierra Bonita, the largest ranch in the district. Ringo and his friends had been running off Sierra Bonita's cattle for years. The place was built like a fort against Apache raids, and if the Earps and their friends were inside, then they were as safe as if they were holed up in Gibraltar.

"*Hic funis nihil attraxit*," Ringo muttered, this line has taken no fish. Freddie hoped he didn't smell Brocius' dead cat on the line.

The posse retreated from the Sierra Bonita to consider their options, but these narrowed considerably when they saw a cloud of dust on the northern horizon, a cloud that grew ever closer.

"Looks like we've been out-posse'd," Ringo said. "Their horses are fresh—we can't outrun them."

"What do we do?" Freddie gasped. Two days in the saddle, even riding moderately, had exhausted him—unlike Josie, who seemed to thrive once cast in the role of Bandit Queen.

Ringo seemed almost gay. "They have tied us to the stake, we cannot fly." Freddie could have wished Ringo had not chosen *Macbeth*. "I think we'd better find a place to fort up," Ringo said.

Their Dunsinane was a rocky hill barren of life but for cactus and scrub. They hid the horses behind rocks and dug themselves in. Within an hour the larger outfit had found them: the Earps had been reinforced by two dozen riders from the Sierra Bonita, and it looked like a small army that posted itself about the hill and sealed off every exit. The pursuers did not attempt to come within gunshot: they knew all they had to do was wait for the Cowboys' water to run out.

Ringo's crew had a smaller store of water than their enemies probably suspected, and one night on the hill would surely exhaust it. "We shall have to fight," Freddie said.

"Yes."

"Few of those people have any experience in a combat. Holliday and Virgil Earp are the only two I know of. The rest will get too excited and throw away their fire, and that will give us our chance."

Ringo smiled. "I think we should charge. Come down off the hill at first light screaming like Apaches and pitch into the nearest pack of them. If we run them off, we can take their horses and make a dash for it."

"Agreed. I will have to follow you—otherwise I can't see well enough to know where I'm going."

"I'll lead you into the hornet's nest, don't you worry."

Freddie sought out Josie, lying in the shade of some rocks, and took her hand. The sun had burned her cheeks; her lips were starting to crack with thirst. "We will fight in the morning," he said. "I want you to stay here."

She shook her head, mouthed the word "No."

"You are the one of us they will not harm," Freddie said. "The rest of us will charge out of the circle, and you can join us later."

The words drove her into fury. She was in a state of high excitement, and wanted to put her pistol practice to use.

"It is not as you think," Freddie said. "This will not be a great battle, it will be something small and squalid. And—" He took her hands. She flailed to throw off his touch, but he held her. "Josie!" he cried. "I need someone to publish my work, if I should not survive. No one else will care. It must be you."

She was of the People of the Book; Freddie calculated she could not refuse. At his words her look softened. "All right, then," she said. He kissed her, but she turned her sunburned lips away. She would not speak for a while, and so Freddie wrote for an hour in his journal with a stub of pencil.

They spent a rough night together, lying cold under blankets, shivering together while Cowboys snored around them. As the eastern sky began to lighten all rose, the horses were saddled and led out. The last of the water was shared, and then the riders mounted.

Ringo seemed in good cheer. Freddie half-expected him to give the Crispin's Day Speech from *Henry V,* but Ringo contented himself with nodding, clicking to his horse, and leading the beast between the tall rocks, down the hill toward the dying fires of the Earps' camp. Freddie pulled his bandanna over his nose, less to conceal his identity than to avoid eating Ringo's dust, then followed Ringo's horse down into the gloom.

The horsemen cleared the rocks, then broke into a canter. They covered half the distance to the Earp outfit's camp before the first shot rang out; then Ringo gave a whoop and the Cowboys answered, the high-pitched yells ringing over the dusty ground.

Freddie was too busy staying atop his horse to add to the clamor. His teeth rattled with every hoofbeat. He wanted a calm place to stand.

Other, better horsemen, half-seen in the pre-dawn light, passed him as he rode. A flurry of shots crackled out. Freddie clutched Zarathustra tighter.

Startled men on foot dodged out of his way.

Abruptly the horse stumbled—Freddie tried to check it but somehow made things worse—and then there was a staggering blow to his shoulder as he was flung to the ground. He rolled, and in great surprise at his own agility rose with his pistol still in his hand. A figure loomed up—with dust coating his spectacles Freddie could not make it out—but he shot it anyway, twice, and it groaned and fell.

The yells of the Cowboys were receding southward amid a great boil of dust. Freddie ran after. Bullets made whirring noises about his head.

Then out of the dust came a horse. Freddie half-raised his pistol, but recognized Ringo before he pulled trigger. "Take my hand, Freddie," Ringo said with a great grin, "and we're free." But then one of the whizzing bullets came to a stop with a horrible smack, and Ringo toppled from the horse. Freddie stared in sudden shock at his friend's brains laid out at his feet—Ringo was beyond all noble gestures now, that was clear, there was nothing to be done for him—Freddie reached for the saddle horn. The beast was frightened and began to run before Freddie could mount; Freddie ran alongside, trying to get a foot in the stirrup, and then the horse put on a burst of terrified speed and left Freddie behind.

Rage and frustration boomed in his heart. He swiped at his spectacles to get a better view, then ran back toward the sound of shooting. A man ran across his field of vision and Zarathustra boomed. The man kept running.

Freddie neared a bush and ducked behind it, polished his spectacles quickly on his bandanna, and stuck them back on his face. The added clarity was not great. The Earps' camp was in a great turmoil in the dust and the half-light, and people were shouting and shooting and running about without any apparent purpose.

Fools! Freddie wanted to shriek. You do not even know how to live, let alone how to die!

He approached the nearest man at a walk, put Zarathustra to the stranger's breast, and pulled the trigger. When the man fell, Freddie took the other's gun in his left hand, then stalked on. He fired a shot at a startled stranger, who ran.

"Stop, Freddie!" came a shout. "Throw up your hands!"

It was Holliday's voice. Freddie froze in his tracks, panting for breath in the cold morning air. Holliday was somewhere to his right—a shift of stance and Freddie could fire—but Holliday would kill him before that, he knew.

Troy is burning, he thought. You have killed as a human being. Now die as one. Freely, and at the right moment.

"Throw up your hands!" Holliday called again, and then from the effort of the shout gave a little cough.

Wild exhilaration flooded Freddie's veins—Holliday's cough had surely spoiled his aim. Freddie swung right as he thumbed the hammer back on each of the two revolvers. And, for the last time, Zarathustra spoke.

The Earp posse caught up with Josie a few hours later as she rode her solitary way to Tombstone. John Holliday shivered atop his horse, trembling as if the morning chill had not yet left his bones. He touched his hat to her, but she ignored him, just kept her plug walking south.

"This was Freddie's, ma'am," Holliday said in his polite Southern way, and held out a book bound between cardboard covers, Freddie's journal. "You figure in his thoughts," Holliday said. "You may wish to have it."

Coldly, without a word, she took the worn volume from his hand. Holliday kicked his horse and the posse rode on, moving swiftly past her into the bright morning.

Josie tried not to look at the bodies that tossed and dangled over the saddles.

What have I found to cherish in this detestable land? Josie read when she returned to Tombstone. Comrades, and valor, and the woman of my heart. Who came to me *because she was free!* And for whom—*because she is free*—Troy will burn, and men will spill their lives into the dust. Every free woman may kill a world.

She will not chain herself; she despises the slavery that is modern life. That is freedom indeed, the freedom to topple towers and destroy without regard. Not from petulance or fear, but from greatness of heart! She does not *seek* power, she simply wields it, as a part of her nature.

Can I be less brave than she? For a gunman, or a philosopher, to live or die or scribble on paper is nothing. For a girl to overturn the order of the world—to stand over the bodies of her lovers and desire only to arm herself—for such a girl to become Fate itself—!

This Fate will I meet with joy. It is clear enough what the morning will bring, and the thought brings no terror. Let my end bring no sadness to my darling Fate, my joy—I have died a million times ere now, and will awake a million more to the love of my—of my Josie—

The words whirled in her mind. Her head ached, and her heart. The words were not easy to understand. Josie knew there were many more notebooks stacked in Freddie's room at the hotel, volume after volume packed with dense script, most in a frantic scrawled German that seemed to have been written in a kind of frenzy, the words mashed onto and over one another in a colossal road-accident of crashing ideas.

There was no longer any reason to stay in Tombstone: her lovers were dead, and those who hated her lived. She would take Freddie's journals away, read them, try to make sense of them. Perhaps something could even be published. In any case she would not give any of the notebooks to that sister Elisabeth, who would twist Freddie's words into a weapon against the Jews.

She had been Freddie's fate, or so he claimed. Now the notebooks—Freddie's words, Freddie's thoughts—were her own destiny.

She would embrace her fate as Freddie had embraced his, and carry it like a newborn infant from this desolation, this desert. This Tombstone.

## AFTERWORD: THE LAST RIDE OF GERMAN FREDDIE

*The genesis of this story appeared on the late, lamented GEnie bulletin board—or possibly on its successor, Dueling Modems—where I mentioned (in Joe Haldeman's topic, I believe) that it would be fun to see a story in which Friedrich Nietzsche became a Western gunfighter and tested his theories of the übermensch to destruction on the frontier.*

*I intended this as a joke, but when I started thinking about it, I realized that this wouldn't be a bad idea at all for a real story.*

*As is the case with most of my dabblings into alternative history, everyone in the story, from Wyatt Earp to Fellehy the Laundryman, was an actual inhabitant of Tombstone during the period of the Earp-Clanton war. Aside from introducing Freddie as a witness, and eliminating some characters (like Bat Masterson and Texas John Slaughter) who were present but had no effect on the action, I followed history very precisely up till the moment of Freddie's intervention in the O. K. Corral gunfight.*

*The greatest fun I had writing the story was pastiching Nietzsche's prose style—or rather, Walter Kaufman's English version of Nietzsche's style.*

*I hope that German Freddie, wherever he is, forgives me the liberty.*

# MILLENNIUM PARTY

Darien was making another annotation to his lengthy commentary on the *Tenjou Cycle* when his Marshal reminded him that his anniversary would soon be upon him. This was the thousandth anniversary—a full millennium with Clarisse!—and he knew the celebration would have to be a special one.

He finished his annotation, saved the work, and then de-slotted the savant brain that contained the cross-referenced database that allowed him to do his work. In its place he slotted the brain labeled *Clarisse/Passion,* the brain that contained memories of his time with his wife. Not *all* memories, however: the contents had been carefully purged of any of the last thousand years' disagreements, arguments, disappointments, infidelities, and misconnections… The memories were only those of love, ardor, obsession, passion, and release, all the most intense and glorious moments of their thousand years together, all the times when Darien was drunk on Clarisse, intoxicated with her scent, her brilliance, her wit.

The other moments, the less-than-perfect ones, he had stored elsewhere, in one brain or another, but he rarely reviewed them. Darien saw no reason why his mind should contain anything that was less than perfect.

Flushed with the sensations that now poured through his mind, overwhelmed by the delirium of love, Darien began to work on his present for his wife.

When the day came, Darien and Clarisse met in an environment that she had designed. This was an arrangement that had existed for centuries, ever since they both realized that Clarisse's sense of spacial relationships was better than his. The environment was a masterpiece, an apartment built on several levels, like little terraces, that broke the space up into smaller areas that created intimacy without sacrificing spaciousness. All of the furniture was designed for no more than two people. Darien recognized on the wall

103

a picture he'd given Clarisse on her four hundredth birthday, an elaborate, antique dial telephone from their honeymoon apartment in Paris, and a Japanese paper doll of a woman in an antique kimono, a present he had given her early in their acquaintance, when they'd haunted antique stores together.

It was Darien's task to complete the arrangement. He added an abstract bronze sculpture of a horse and jockey that Clarisse had given him for his birthday, a puzzle made of wire and butter-smooth old wood, and a view from the terrace, a view of Rio de Janeiro at night. Because his sense of taste and smell were more subtle than Clarisse's, he, by standing arrangement, populated the apartment with scents, lilac for the parlor, sweet magnolia and bracing cypress on the terrace, a combination of sandalwood and spice for the bedroom, and a mixture of vanilla and cardamom for the dining room, a scent subtle enough so that it wouldn't interfere with the meal.

When Clarisse entered he was dressed in a tailcoat, white tie, waistcoat, and diamond studs. She had matched his period élan with a Worth gown of shining blue satin, tiny boots that buttoned up the ankles, and a dashing fall of silk about her throat. Her tawny hair was pinned up, inviting him to kiss the nape of her neck, an indulgence which he permitted himself almost immediately.

Darien seated Clarisse on the cushions, and mixed cocktails. He asked her about her work: a duplicate of one of her brains was on the mission to 55 Cancri, sharing piloting missions with other duplicates—if a habitable planet was discovered, then a new Clarisse would be built on the site to pioneer the new world.

Darien had created the meal in consultation with Clarisse's Marshal. They began with mussels steamed open in white wine and herbs, then went on to a salad of fennel, orange, and red cranberry. Next came roasted green beans served alongside a chicken cooked simply in the oven, then served in a creamy port wine reduction sauce; and at the end was a raspberry Bavarian cream. Each dish was one that Darien had experienced at another time in his long life, considered perfect, stored in one brain or another, and re-created down to the last scent and sensation.

After coffee and conversation on the terrace, Clarisse led Darien to the bedroom. He enjoyed kneeling at her feet and unlacing every single button of those boots. His heart brimmed with passion and lust, and he rose from his knees to embrace her. Wrapped in the sandalwood-scented silence of their suite, they feasted till dawn on one another's flesh.

Their life together, Darien reflected, was perfection itself: one enchanted jewel after another, hanging side-by-side on a thousand-year string

After juice and shirred eggs in the morning, Darien kissed the inside of

Clarisse's wrist, then checked to make sure that his brain had recorded every single instant of their time together.

And then he de-slotted *Clarisse/Passion,* and put it on the shelf for another year.

# AFTERWORD: THE MILLENNIUM PARTY

*In 2002 I was in Taos Ski Valley with that year's Rio Hondo workshop, when editor Eileen Gunn offered a challenge to the participants.*

*She asked us each to write a short-short—defined as a story under 1000 words—on either the subject of artificial intelligence, or of marriage in the future.*

*Needless to say, I chose to write on both. The dinners we were enjoying at that workshop also worked their way into my story.*

*The stories were published in Eileen's online magazine* Infinite Matrix, *and as of this writing remain available in its online archives.*

*Charles Stross, who kindly wrote the introduction to this collection, asked if "Millennium Party" belongs in the College of Mystery sequence, along with "Lethe" and "The Green Leopard Plague."*

*My answer is that I don't know. I didn't intend it as part of that future, but on the other hand there's nothing in the story that excludes it.*

*As god of that particular universe, I've decided that "Millennium Party" will remain provisionally a part of the sequence until I'm inspired to write a story that definitely excludes it, something that may never happen.*

*That may be too vague an answer for some readers, but I remind you that—as god of this universe—I have every right to be vague if I want to.*

# THE GREEN LEOPARD PLAGUE

Kicking her legs out over the ocean, the lonely mermaid gazed out at the horizon from her perch in the overhanging banyan tree.

The air was absolutely still and filled with the scent of night flowers. Large fruit bats flew purposefully over the sea, heading for their daytime rest. Somewhere a white cockatoo gave a penetrating squawk. A starling made a brief flutter out to sea, then came back again. The rising sun threw up red-gold sparkles from the wavetops and brought a brilliance to the tropical growth that crowned the many islands spread out on the horizon.

The mermaid decided it was time for breakfast. She slipped from her hanging canvas chair and walked out along one of the banyan's great limbs. The branch swayed lightly under her weight, and her bare feet found sure traction on the rough bark. She looked down to see the deep blue of the channel, distinct from the turquoise of the shallows atop the reefs.

She raised her arms, poised briefly on the limb, the ruddy light of the sun glowing bronze on her bare skin, and then she pushed off and dove head-first into the Philippine Sea. She landed with a cool impact and a rush of bubbles.

Her wings unfolded, and she flew away.

After her hunt, the mermaid—her name was Michelle—cached her fishing gear in a pile of dead coral above the reef, and then ghosted easily over the sea grass with the rippled sunlight casting patterns on her wings. When she could look up to see the colossal, twisted tangle that were the roots of her banyan tree, she lifted her head from the water and gulped her first breath of air.

The Rock Islands were made of soft limestone coral, and tide and chemical action had eaten away the limestone at sea level, undercutting the stone above. Some of the smaller islands looked like mushrooms, pointed green pinnacles balanced atop thin stems. Michelle's island was larger and irregularly shaped, but it still had steep limestone walls undercut six meters by the tide, with no obvious way for a person to clamber from the sea to the land. Her banyan perched on the saucer-edge of the island, itself undercut by the sea.

Michelle had arranged a rope elevator from her nest in the tree, just a loop on the end of a long nylon line. She tucked her wings away—they were harder to retract than to deploy, and the gills on the undersides were delicate—and then Michelle slipped her feet through the loop. At her verbal command, a hoist mechanism lifted her in silence from the sea and to her resting place in the bright green-dappled forest canopy.

She had been an ape once, a siamang, and she felt perfectly at home in the treetops.

During her excursion she had speared a yellowlip emperor, and this she carried with her in a mesh bag. She filleted the emperor with a blade she kept in her nest, and tossed the rest into the sea, where it became a subject of interest to a school of bait fish. She ate a slice of one fillet raw, enjoying the brilliant flavor, sea and trembling pale flesh together, then cooked the fillets on her small stove, eating one with some rice she'd cooked the previous evening and saving the other for later.

By the time Michelle finished breakfast the island was alive. Geckoes scurried over the banyan's bark, and coconut crabs sidled beneath the leaves like touts offering illicit downloads to tourists. Out in the deep water, a flock of circling, diving black noddies marked where a school of skipjack tuna was feeding on swarms of bait fish.

It was time for Michelle to begin her day as well. With sure, steady feet she moved along a rope walkway to the ironwood tree that held her satellite uplink in its crown, and then straddled a limb, took her deck from the mesh bag she'd roped to the tree, and downloaded her messages.

There were several journalists requesting interviews—the legend of the lonely mermaid was spreading. This pleased her more often than not, but she didn't answer any of the queries. There was a message from Darton, which she decided to savor for a while before opening. And then she saw a note from Dr. Davout, and opened it at once.

Davout was, roughly, twelve times her age. He'd actually been carried for nine months in his mother's womb, not created from scratch in a nanobed like almost everyone else she knew. He had a sib who was a famous astronaut, and a McEldowney Prize for his *Lavoisier and His Age*, and a red-haired wife who was nearly as well-known as he was. Michelle, a couple years ago, had attended a series of his lectures at the College of Mystery, and been interested despite her specialty being, strictly speaking, biology.

He had shaved off the little goatee he'd worn when she'd last seen him, which Michelle considered a good thing. "I have a research project for you, if you're free," the recording said. "It shouldn't take too much effort."

Michelle contacted him at once. He was a rich old bastard with a thousand years of tenure and no notion of what it was to be young in these times, and he'd pay her whatever outrageous fee she asked.

Her material needs at the moment were few, but she wouldn't stay on this island forever.

Davout answered right away. Behind him, working at her own console, Michelle could see his red-haired wife Katrin.

"Michelle!" Davout said, loudly enough for Katrin to know who called without turning around. "Good!" He hesitated, and then his fingers formed the mudra for <concern>. "I understand you've suffered a loss," he said.

"Yes," she said, her answer delayed by a second's satellite lag.

"And the young man—?"

"Doesn't remember."

Which was not exactly a lie, the point being what was remembered.

Davout's fingers were still fixed in <concern>. "Are you all right?" he asked.

Her own fingers formed an equivocal answer. "I'm getting better." Which was probably true.

"I see you're not an ape anymore."

"I decided to go the mermaid route. New perspectives, all that." And welcome isolation.

"Is there any we can make things easier for you?"

She put on a hopeful expression. "You said something about a job?"

"Yes." He seemed relieved not to have to probe further—he'd had a realdeath in his own family, Michelle remembered, a chance-in-a-billion thing, and perhaps he didn't want to relive any part of that.

"I'm working on a biography of Terzian," Davout said.

"… And his Age?" Michelle finished.

"And his *Legacy*." Davout smiled. "There's a three-week period in his life where he—well, he drops right off the map. I'd like to find out where he went—and who he was with, if anyone."

Michelle was impressed. Even in comparatively unsophisticated times such as that inhabited by Jonathan Terzian, it was difficult for people to disappear.

"It's a critical time for him," Davout went on. "He'd lost his job at Tulane, his wife had just died—realdeath, remember—and if he decided he simply wanted to get lost, he would have all my sympathies." He raised a hand as if to tug at the chin-whiskers that were no longer there, made a vague pawing gesture, then dropped the hand. "But my problem is that when he resurfaces, everything's changed for him. In June he delivered an undistinguished paper at the Athenai conference in Paris, then vanishes. When he surfaced in Venice in mid-July, he didn't deliver the paper he was scheduled to read, instead he delivered the first version of his Cornucopia Theory."

Michelle's fingers formed the mudra <highly impressed>. "How have you tried to locate him?"

"Credit card records—they end on June 17, when he buys a lot of euros at American Express in Paris. After that he must have paid for everything with cash."

"He really *did* try to get lost, didn't he?" Michelle pulled up one bare leg and rested her chin on it. "Did you try passport records?"

<No luck> "But if he stayed in the European Community he wouldn't have had to present a passport when crossing a border."

"Cash machines?"

"Not till after he arrived in Venice, just a couple days prior to the conference."

The mermaid thought about it for a moment, then smiled. "I guess you need me, all right."

<I concur> Davout flashed solemnly. "How much would it cost me?"

Michelle pretended to consider the question for a moment, then named an outrageous sum.

Davout frowned. "Sounds all right," he said.

Inwardly Michelle rejoiced. Outwardly, she leaned toward the camera lens and looked businesslike. "I'll get busy, then."

Davout looked grateful. "You'll be able to get on it right away?"

"Certainly. What I need you to do is send me pictures of Terzian, from as many different angles as possible, especially from around that period of time."

"I have them ready."

"Send away."

An eyeblink later, the pictures were in Michelle's deck. <Thanks> she flashed. "I'll let you know as soon as I find anything."

At university Michelle had discovered that she was very good at research, and it had become a profitable sideline for her. People—usually people connected with academe in one way or another—hired her to do the duller bits of their own jobs, finding documents or references, or, in this case, three missing weeks out of a person's life. It was almost always work they could do themselves, but Michelle was simply better at research than most people, and she was considered worth the extra expense. Michelle herself usually enjoyed the work—it provided interesting sidelights on fields about which she knew little, and provided a welcome break from routine.

Plus, this particular job required not so much a researcher as an artist, and Michelle was very good at this particular art.

Michelle looked through the pictures, most scanned from old photographs. Davout had selected well: Terzian's face or profile was clear in every picture. Most of the pictures showed him young, in his twenties, and the ones that showed him older were of high quality, or showed parts of the body that would be crucial to the biometric scan, like his hands or his ears.

The mermaid paused for a moment to look at one of the old photos: Terzian smiling with his arm around a tall, long-legged woman with a wide mouth and dark, bobbed hair, presumably the wife who had died. Behind them was a Louis Quinze table with a blaze of gladiolas in a cloisonné vase, and above the table a large portrait of a stately looking horse in a heavy gilded frame. Beneath the table were stowed—temporarily, Michelle assumed—a dozen or so trophies, which to judge from the little golden figures balanced atop them were awarded either for gymnastics or martial arts. The opulent setting seemed a little at odds with the young, informally dressed couple: she wore a flowery tropical shirt tucked into khakis, and Terzian dressed in a tank top and shorts. There was a sense that the photographer had caught them almost in motion, as if they'd paused for the picture en route from one place to another.

Nice shoulders, Michelle thought. Big hands, well-shaped muscular legs. She hadn't ever thought of Terzian as young, or large, or strong, but he had a genuine, powerful physical presence that came across even in the old, casual photographs. He looked more like a football player than a famous thinker.

Michelle called up her character-recognition software and fed in all the pictures, then checked the software's work, something she was reasonably certain her employer would never have done if he'd been doing this job himself. Most people using this kind of canned software didn't realize how the program could be fooled, particularly when used with old media, scanned film prints heavy with grain and primitive digital images scanned by machines that simply weren't very bright. In the end, Michelle and software between them managed an excellent job of mapping Terzian's body and calibrating its precise ratios: the distance between the eyes, the length of nose and curve of lip, the distinct shape of the ears, the length of limb and trunk. Other men might share some of these biometric ratios, but none would share them all.

The mermaid downloaded the data into her specialized research spiders, and sent them forth into the electronic world.

A staggering amount of the trivial past existed there, and nowhere else.

People had uploaded pictures, diaries, commentary, and video; they'd digitized old home movies, complete with the garish, deteriorating colors of the old film stock; they'd scanned in family trees, post cards, wedding lists, drawings, political screeds, and images of handwritten letters. Long, dull hours of security video. Whatever had meant something to someone, at some time, had been turned into electrons and made available to the universe at large.

A surprising amount of this stuff had survived the Lightspeed War—none of it had seemed worth targeting, or if trashed had been reloaded from backups.

What all this meant was that Terzian was somewhere in there. Wherever Terzian had gone in his weeks of absence—Paris, Dalmatia, or Thule—there would have been someone with a camera. In stills of children eating ice cream in front of Notre Dame, or moving through the video of buskers playing saxophone on the Pont des Artistes, there would be a figure in the background, and that figure would be Terzian. Terzian might be found lying on a beach in Corfu, reflected in a bar mirror in Gdynia, or negotiating with a prostitute in Hamburg's St. Pauli district—Michelle had found targets in exactly those places during the course of her other searches.

Michelle sent her software forth to find Terzian, then lifted her arms above her head and stretched—stretched fiercely, thrusting out her bare feet and curling the toes, the muscles trembling with tension, her mouth yawned in a silent shriek.

Then she leaned over her deck, again, and called up the message from Darton, the message she'd saved till last.

"I don't understand," he said. "Why won't you talk to me? I love you!"

His brown eyes were a little wild.

"Don't you understand?" he cried. "I'm not dead! *I'm not really dead!*"

Michelle hovered three or four meters below the surface of Zigzag Lake, gazing upward at the inverted bowl of the heavens, the brilliant blue of the Pacific sky surrounded by the dark, shadowy towers of mangrove. Something caught her eye, something black and falling, like a bullet: and then there was a splash and a boil of bubbles, and the daggerlike bill of a collared kingfisher speared a blue-eyed apogonid that had been hovering over a bright red coral head. The kingfisher flashed its pale underside as it stroked to the surface, its wings doing efficient double duty as fins, and then there was a flurry of wings and feet and bubbles and the kingfisher was airborne again.

Michelle floated up and over the barrel-shaped coral head, then over a pair of giant clams, each over a meter long. The clams drew shut as Michelle slid over them, withdrawing the huge siphons as thick as her wrist. The fleshy lips that overhung the scalloped edges of the shells were a riot of colors, purples, blues, greens, and reds interwoven in an eye-boggling pattern.

Carefully drawing in her gills so their surfaces wouldn't be inflamed by coral stings, she kicked up her feet and dove beneath the mangrove roots into the narrow tunnel that connected Zigzag Lake with the sea.

Of the three hundred or so Rock Islands, seventy or thereabouts had marine lakes. The islands were made of coral limestone and porous to one degree or another: some lakes were connected to the ocean through tunnels and caves, and others through seepage. Many of the lakes contained forms of life unique in all the world, evolved distinctly from their remote ancestors: even now, after all this time, new species were being described.

During the months Michelle had spent in the islands she thought she'd discovered two undescribed species: a variation on the *Entacmaea medusivora* white anemone that was patterned strangely with scarlet and a cobalt-blue; and a nudibranch, deep violet with yellow polka-dots, that had undulated past her one night on the reef, flapping like a tea towel in a strong wind as a seven-knot tidal current tore it along. The nudi and samples of the anemone had been sent to the appropriate authorities, and perhaps in time Michelle would be immortalized by having a Latinate version of her name appended to the scientific description of the two marine animals.

The tunnel was about fifteen meters long, and had a few narrow twists where Michelle had to pull her wings in close to her sides and maneuver by the merest fluttering of their edges. The tunnel turned up, and brightened with the sun; the mermaid extended her wings and flew over brilliant pink soft corals toward the light.

*Two hours' work,* she thought, *plus a hazardous environment. Twenty-two hundred calories, easy.*

The sea was brilliantly lit, unlike the gloomy marine lake surrounded by tall cliffs, mangroves, and shadow, and for a moment Michelle's sun-dazzled eyes failed to see the boat bobbing on the tide. She stopped short, her wings cupping to brake her motion, and then she recognized the boat's distinctive paint job, a bright red meant to imitate the natural oil of the *cheritem* fruit.

Michelle prudently rose to the surface a safe distance away—Torbiong might be fishing, and sometimes he did it with a spear. The old man saw her, and stood to give a wave before Michelle could unblock her trachea and draw air into her lungs to give a hail.

"I brought you supplies," he said.

"Thanks." Michelle said as she wiped a rain of seawater from her face.

Torbiong was over two hundred years old and Paramount Chief of

Koror, the capital forty minutes away by boat. He was small and wiry and black-haired, and had a broad-nosed, strong-chinned, unlined face. He had traveled over the world and off it while young, but returned to Belau as he aged. His duties as chief were mostly ceremonial, but counted for tax purposes; he had money from hotels and restaurants that his ancestors had built and that others managed for him, and he spent most of his time visiting his neighbors, gossiping, and fishing. He had befriended Darton and Michelle when they'd first come to Belau, and helped them in securing the permissions for their researches on the Rock Islands. A few months back, after Darton died, Torbiong had agreed to bring supplies to Michelle in exchange for the occasional fish.

His boat was ten meters long and featured a waterproof canopy amidships made from interwoven pandanas leaves. Over the scarlet faux-*cheritem* paint were zigzags, crosses, and stripes in the brilliant yellow of the ginger plant. The ends of the thwarts were decorated with grotesque carved faces, and dozens of white cowrie shells were glued to the gunwales. Wooden statues of the kingfisher bird sat on the prow and stern.

Thrusting above the pandanas canopy were antennae, flagpoles, deep-sea fishing rods, fish spears, radar, and a satellite uplink. Below the canopy, where Torbiong could command the boat from an elaborately carved throne of breadfruit-tree wood, were the engine and rudder controls, radio, audio, and video sets, a collection of large audio speakers, a depth finder, a satellite navigation relay, and radar. Attached to the uprights that supported the canopy were whistles tuned to make an eerie, discordant wailing noise when the boat was at speed.

Torbiong was fond of discordant wailing noises. As Michelle swam closer, she heard the driving, screeching electronic music that Torbiong loved trickling from the earpieces of his headset—he normally howled it out of speakers, but when sitting still he didn't want to scare the fish. At night she could hear Torbiong for miles, as he raced over the darkened sea blasted out of his skull on betel-nut juice with his music thundering and the whistles shrieking.

He removed the headset, releasing a brief audio onslaught before switching off his sound system.

"You're going to make yourself deaf," Michelle said.

Torbiong grinned. "Love that music. Gets that blood moving."

Michelle floated to the boat and put a hand on the gunwale between a pair of cowries.

"I saw that boy of yours on the news," Torbiong said. "He's making you famous."

"I don't want to be famous."

"He doesn't understand why you don't talk to him."

"He's dead," Michelle said.

Torbiong made a spreading gesture with his hands. "That's a matter of opinion."

"Watch your head," said Michelle.

Torbiong ducked as a gust threatened to bring him into contact with a pitcher plant that drooped over the edge of the island's overhang. Torbiong evaded the plant and then stepped to the bow to haul in his mooring line before the boat's canopy got caught beneath the overhang,

Michelle submerged and swam till she reached her banyan tree, then surfaced and called down her rope elevator. By the time Torbiong's boat hissed up to her, she'd folded away her gills and wings and was sitting in the sling, kicking her legs over the water.

Torbiong handed her a bag of supplies: some rice, tea, salt, vegetables, and fruit. For the last several weeks Michelle had experienced a craving for blueberries, which didn't grow here, and Torbiong had included a large package fresh off the shuttle, and a small bottle of cream to go with them. Michelle thanked him.

"Most tourists want corn chips or something," Torbiong said pointedly.

"I'm not a tourist." Michelle said. "I'm sorry I don't have any fish to swap—I've been hunting smaller game." She held out the specimen bag, still dripping seawater.

Torbiong gestured toward the cooler built into the back of his boat. "I got some *chai* and a *chersuuch* today," he said, using the local names for barracuda and mahi mahi.

"Good fishing."

"Trolling." With a shrug. He looked up at her, a quizzical look on his face. "I've got some calls from reporters," he said, and then his betel-stained smile broke out. "I always make sure to send them tourist literature."

"I'm sure they enjoy reading it."

Torbiong's grin widened. "You get lonely, now," he said, "you come visit the family. We'll give you a home-cooked meal."

She smiled. "Thanks."

They said their farewells and Torbiong's boat hissed away on its jets, the whistles building to an eerie, spine-shivering chord. Michelle rose into the trees and stashed her specimens and groceries. With a bowl of blueberries and cream, Michelle crossed the rope walkway to her deck, and checked the progress of her search spiders.

There were pointers to a swarm of articles about the death of Terzian's wife, and Michelle wished she'd given her spiders clearer instructions about dates.

The spiders had come up with three pictures. One was a not-very-well focused tourist video from July 10, showing a man standing in front of the Basilica di Santa Croce in Florence. A statue of Dante, also not in focus, gloomed down at him from beneath thick-bellied rain clouds. As the camera panned across him he stood with his back to the camera but turned to the right, one leg turned out as he scowled down at the ground—the profile was a little smeared, but the big, broad-shouldered body seemed right. The software reckoned there was a 78% chance the man was Terzian.

Michelle got busy refining the image, and after a few passes of the software decided the chances of the figure being Terzian were more on the order of 95%.

So maybe Terzian had gone on a Grand Tour of European cultural sites. He didn't look happy in the video, but then the day was cloudy and rainy and Terzian didn't have an umbrella.

And his wife had died, of course.

Now that Michelle had a date and a place she refined the instructions from her search spiders to seek out images from Florence a week either way from July 3, and then expand the search from there, first all Tuscany, then all Italy.

If Terzian was doing tourist sites, then she surely had him nailed.

The next two hits, from her earlier research spiders, were duds. The software gave a less than 50% chance of Terzian being in Lisbon or Cape Sounion, and refinements of the image reduced the chance to something near zero.

Then the next video popped up, with a time stamp right there in the image—Paris, June 26, 13:41:44 hours, just a day before Terzian bought a bankroll of Euros and vanished.

<Bingo!> Michelle's fingers formed.

The first thing Michelle saw was Terzian walking out of the frame—no doubt this time that it was him. He was looking over his shoulder at a small crowd of people. There was a dark-haired woman huddled on his arm, her face turned away from the camera. Michelle's heart warmed at the thought of the lonely widow Terzian having an affair in the City of Love.

Then she followed Terzian's gaze to see what had so drawn his attention. A dead man stretched out on the pavement, surrounded by hapless bystanders.

And then, as the scene slowly settled into her astonished mind, the video sang at her in the piping voice of Pan.

Terzian looked at his audience as anger raged in his backbrain. A wooden chair creaked, and the sound spurred Terzian to wonder how long the silence had gone on. Even the Slovenian woman who had been drowsing realized that something had changed, and blinked herself to alertness.

"I'm sorry," he said in French. "But my wife just died, and I don't feel like playing this game anymore."

His silent audience of seven watched as he gathered his papers, put them in his case, and left the lecture room, his feet making sharp, murderous sounds on the wooden floor.

Yet up to that point his paper had been going all right. He'd been uncertain about commenting on Baudrillard in Baudrillard's own country, and in Baudrillard's own language, a cheery compare-and-contrast exercise between Baudrillard's "the self does not exist" and Rorty's "I don't care," the stereotypical French and American answers to modern life. There had been seven in his audience, perched on creaking wooden chairs, and none of them had gone to sleep, or walked out, of condemned him for his audacity.

Yet, as he looked at his audience and read on, Terzian had felt the anger growing, spawned by the sensation of his own uselessness. Here he was, in the City of Lights, its every cobblestone a monument to European civilization, and he was in a dreary lecture hall on the Left Bank, reading to his audience of seven from a paper that was nothing more than a footnote, and a footnote to a footnote at that. To come to the land of *cogito ergo sum* and to answer, *I don't care?*

*I came to Paris for* this? he thought. *To read this* drivel? *I paid* for the privilege of doing this?

I *do* care, he thought as his feet turned toward the Seine. *Desiderio, ergo sum,* if he had his Latin right. I am in pain, and therefore I *do* exist.

He ended in a Norman restaurant on the Île de la Cité, with lunch as his excuse and the thought of getting hopelessly drunk not far from his thoughts. He had absolutely nothing to do until August, after which he would return to the States and collect his belongings from the servants' quarters of the house on Esplanade, and then he would go about looking for a job.

He wasn't certain whether he would be more depressed by finding a job or by not finding one.

*You are alive,* he told himself. *You are alive and in Paris with the whole summer ahead of you, and you're eating the cuisine of Normandy in the Place Dauphine. And if that isn't a command to be joyful, what is?*

It was then that the Peruvian band began to play. Terzian looked up from his plate in weary surprise.

When Terzian had been a child his parents—both university professors—had first taken him to Europe, and he'd seen then that every European city had its own Peruvian or Bolivian street band, Indians in black bowler hats and colorful blankets crouched in some public place, gazing with impassive brown eyes from over their guitars and reed flutes.

Now, a couple decades later, the musicians were still here, though they'd exchanged the blankets and bowler hats for European styles, and their presentation had grown more slick. Now they had amps, and cassettes and CDs for sale. Now they had congregated in the triangular Place Dauphine, overshadowed by the neo-classical mass of the Palais de Justice, and commenced a Latin-flavored medley of old Abba songs.

Maybe, after Terzian finished his veal in calvados sauce, he'd go up to the band and kick in their guitars.

The breeze flapped the canvas overhead. Terzian looked at his empty plate. The food had been excellent, but he could barely remember tasting it.

Anger still roiled beneath his thoughts. And—for God's *sake*—was that band now playing *Oasis*? Those chords were beginning to sound suspiciously like "Wonderwall." "Wonderwall" on Spanish guitars, reed flutes, and a mandolin.

Terzian had nearly decided to call for a bottle of cognac and stay here all afternoon, but not with that noise in the park. He put some euros on the table, anchoring the bills with a saucer against the fresh spring breeze that rattled the green canvas canopy over his head. He was stepping through the restaurant's little wrought-iron gate to the sidewalk when the scuffle caught his attention.

The man falling into the street, his face pinched with pain. The hands of the three men on either side who were, seemingly, unable to keep their friend erect.

*Idiots,* Terzian thought, fury blazing in him.

There was a sudden shrill of tires, of an auto horn.

Papers streamed in the wind as they spilled from a briefcase.

And over it all came the amped sound of pan pipes from the Peruvian band. *Wonderwall.*

Terzian watched in exasperated surprise as the three men sprang after the papers. He took a step toward the fallen man—*someone* had to take charge here. The fallen man's hair had spilled in a shock over his forehead and he'd curled on his side, his face still screwed up in pain.

The pan pipes played on, one distinct hollow shriek after another.

Terzian stopped with one foot still on the sidewalk and looked around at faces that all registered the same sense of shock. Was there a doctor here? he wondered. A *French* doctor? All his French seemed to have just drained from his head. Even such simple questions as *Are you all right?* and *How are you feeling?* seemed beyond him now. The first aid course he'd taken in his Kenpo school was *ages* ago.

Unnaturally pale, the fallen man's face relaxed. The wind floated his shock of thinning dark hair over his face. In the park, Terzian saw a man in a baseball cap panning a video camera, and his anger suddenly blazed up again at the fatuous uselessness of the tourist, the uselessness that mirrored his own.

Suddenly there was a crowd around the casualty, people coming out of stopped cars, off the sidewalk. Down the street, Terzian saw the distinctive flat-topped kepis of a pair of policemen bobbing toward them from the direction of the Palais de Justice, and felt a surge of relief. Someone more capable than this lot would deal with this now.

He began, hesitantly, to step away. And then his arm was seized by a pair of hands and he looked in surprise at the woman who had just huddled her face into his shoulder, cinnamon-dark skin and eyes invisible beneath wraparound shades.

"Please," she said in English a bit too musical to be American. "Take me out of here."

The sound of the reed pipes followed them as they made their escape.

He walked her past the statue of the Vert Galant himself, good old lecherous Henri IV, and onto the Pont Neuf. To the left, across the Seine, the Louvre glowed in mellow colors beyond a screen of plane trees.

Traffic roared by, a stampede of steel unleashed by a green light. Unfocused anger blazed in his mind. He didn't want this woman attached to him, and he suspected she was running some kind of scam. The gym bag she wore on a strap over one shoulder kept banging him on the ass. Surreptitiously he slid his hand into his right front trouser pocket to make sure his money was still there.

*Wonderwall,* he thought. Christ.

He supposed he should offer some kind of civilized comment, just in case the woman was genuinely distressed.

"I suppose he'll be all right," he said, half-barking the words in his annoyance and anger.

The woman's face was still half-buried in his shoulder. "He's dead," she murmured into his jacket. "Couldn't you tell?"

For Terzian death had never occurred under the sky, but shut away, in hospice rooms with crisp sheets and warm colors and the scent of disinfectant. In an explosion of tumors and wasting limbs and endless pain masked only in part by morphia.

He thought of the man's pale face, the sudden relaxation.

Yes, he thought, death came with a sigh.

Reflex kept him talking. "The police were coming," he said. "They'll—they'll call an ambulance or something."

"I only hope they catch the bastards who did it," she said.

Terzian's heart gave a jolt as he recalled the three men who let the man fall, and then dashed through the square for his papers. For some reason all he could remember about them were their black laced boots, with thick soles.

"Who were they?" he asked blankly.

The woman's shades slid down her nose, and Terzian saw startling green eyes narrowed to murderous slits. "I suppose they think of themselves as cops," she said.

Terzian parked his companion in a café near Les Halles, within sight of the dome of the Bourse. She insisted on sitting indoors, not on the sidewalk, and on facing the front door so that she could scan whoever came in. She put her gym bag, with its white Nike swoosh, on the floor between the table legs and the wall, but Terzian noticed she kept its shoulder strap in her lap, as if she might have to bolt at any moment.

Terzian kept his wedding ring within her sight. He wanted her to see it; it might make things simpler.

Her hands were trembling. Terzian ordered coffee for them both. "No," she said suddenly. "I want ice cream."

Terzian studied her as she turned to the waiter and ordered in French. She was around his own age, twenty-nine. There was no question that she was a mixture of races, but *which* races? The flat nose could be African or Asian or Polynesian, and Polynesia was again confirmed by the black, thick brows. Her smooth brown complexion could be from anywhere but Europe, but her pale green eyes were nothing but European. Her broad, sensitive mouth suggested Nubia. The black ringlets yanked into a knot behind her head could be African or East Indian or, for that matter, French. The result was too striking to be beautiful—and also too striking, Terzian thought, to be a successful criminal. Those looks could be too easily identified.

The waiter left. She turned her wide eyes toward Terzian, and seemed faintly surprised that he was still there.

"My name's Jonathan," he said.

"I'm," hesitating, "Stephanie."

"Really?" Terzian let his skepticism show.

"Yes." She nodded, reaching in a pocket for cigarettes. "Why would I lie? It doesn't matter if you know my real name or not."

"Then you'd better give me the whole thing."

She held her cigarette upward, at an angle, and enunciated clearly.

"Stephanie América Pais e Silva."

"America?"

Striking a match. "It's a perfectly ordinary Portuguese name."

He looked at her. "But you're not Portuguese."

"I carry a Portuguese passport."

Terzian bit back the comment, *I'm sure you do.*

Instead he said, "Did you know the man who was killed?"

Stephanie nodded. The drags she took off her cigarette did not ease the tremor in her hands.

"Did you know him well?"

"Not very." She dragged in smoke again, then let the smoke out as she spoke.

"He was a colleague. A biochemist."

Surprise silenced Terzian. Stephanie tipped ash into the Cinzano ashtray, but her nervousness made her miss, and the little tube of ash fell on the tablecloth.

"Shit," she said, and swept the ash to the floor with a nervous movement of her fingers.

"Are you a biochemist, too?" Terzian asked.

"I'm a nurse." She looked at him with her pale eyes. "I work for Santa Croce—it's a—"

"A relief agency." A Catholic one, he remembered. The name meant *Holy Cross.*

She nodded.

"Shouldn't you go to the police?" he asked. And then his skepticism returned. "Oh, that's right—it was the police who did the killing."

"Not the *French* police." She leaned across the table toward him. "This was a different sort of police, the kind who think that killing someone and making an arrest are the same thing. You look at the television news tonight. They'll report the death, but there won't be any arrests. Or any suspects." Her face darkened, and she leaned back in her chair to consider a new thought. "Unless they somehow manage to blame it on me."

Terzian remembered papers flying in the spring wind, men in heavy boots sprinting after. The pinched, pale face of the victim.

"Who, then?"

She gave him a bleak look through a curl of cigarette smoke. "Have you ever heard of Transnistria?"

Terzian hesitated, then decided "No" was the most sensible answer.

"The murderers are Transnistrian." A ragged smile drew itself across Stephanie's face. "They're intellectual property police. They killed Adrian over a copyright."

At that point the waiter brought Terzian's coffee along with Stephanie's order. Hers was colossal, a huge glass goblet filled with pastel-colored ice creams and fruit syrups in bright primary colors, topped by a mountain of cream and a toy pinwheel on a candy-striped stick. Stephanie looked at the creation in shock, her eyes wide.

"I love ice cream," she choked, and then her eyes brimmed with tears and she began to cry.

Stephanie wept for a while, across the table, and between sobs choked down heaping spoonfuls of ice cream, eating in great gulps, and swiping at her lips and tear-stained cheeks with a paper napkin.

The waiter stood quietly in the corner, but from his glare and the set of his jaw it was clear that he blamed Terzian for making the lovely woman cry.

Terzian felt his body surge with the impulse to aid her, but he didn't know what to do. Move around the table and put an arm around her? Take her hand? Call someone to take her off his hands?

The latter, for preference.

He settled for handing her a clean napkin when her own grew sodden.

His skepticism had not survived the mention of the Transnistrian copyright police. This was far too bizarre to be a con—a scam was based on basic human desire, greed or lust, not something as abstract as intellectual property. Unless there was a gang who made a point of targeting academics from the States, luring them with a tantalizing hook about a copyright worth murdering for…

Eventually the storm subsided. Stephanie pushed the half-consumed ice cream away, and reached for another cigarette.

He tapped his wedding ring on the table top, something he did when thinking. "Shouldn't you contact the local police?" he asked. "You know something about this… death." For some reason he was reluctant to use the word *murder*. It was as if using the word would make something true, not the killing itself but his relationship to the killing… to call it murder would grant it some kind of power over him.

She shook her head. "I've got to get out of France before those guys find me. Out of Europe, if I can, but that would be hard. My passport's in my hotel room, and they're probably watching it."

"Because of this copyright."

Her mouth twitched in a half-smile. "That's right."

"It's not a literary copyright, I take it."

She shook her head, the half-smile still on her face.

"Your friend was a biologist." He felt a hum in his nerves, a certainty that he already knew the answer to the next question.

"Is it a weapon?" he asked.

She wasn't surprised by the question. "No," she said. "No, just the opposite." She took a drag on her cigarette and sighed the smoke out. "It's an antidote. An antidote to human folly."

"Listen," Stephanie said. "Just because the Soviet Union fell doesn't mean that *Sovietism* fell with it. Sovietism is still there—the only difference is that its moral justification is gone, and what's left is violence and extortion disguised as law enforcement and taxation. The old empire breaks up, and in the West you think it's great, but more countries just meant more palms to be greased—all throughout the former Soviet empire you've got more 'inspectors' and 'tax collectors,' more 'customs agents' and 'security directorates' than there ever were under the Russians. All these people do is prey off their own populations, because no one else will do business with them unless they've got oil or some other resource that people want."

"Trashcanistans," Terzian said. It was a word he'd heard used of his own ancestral homeland, the former Soviet Republic of Armenia, whose looted economy and paranoid, murderous, despotic Russian puppet regime was supported only by millions of dollars sent to the country by Americans of Armenian descent, who thought that propping up the gang of thugs in power somehow translated into freedom for the fatherland.

Stephanie nodded. "And the worst Trashcanistan of all is Transnistria."

She and Terzian had left the café and taken a taxi back to the Left Bank and Terzian's hotel. He had turned the television to a local station, but muted the sound until the news came on. Until then the station showed a rerun of an American cop show, stolid, businesslike detectives underplaying their latest sordid confrontation with tragedy.

The hotel room hadn't been built for the queen-sized bed it now held, and there was an eighteen-inch clearance around the bed and no room for chairs. Terzian, not wanting Stephanie to think he wanted to get her in the sack, perched uncertainly on a corner of the bed, while Stephanie disposed herself more comfortably, sitting cross-legged in its center.

"Moldova was a Soviet republic put together by Stalin," she said. "It was made up of Bessarabia, which was a part of Romania that Stalin chewed off at the beginning of the Second World War, plus a strip of industrial land on the far side of the Dniester. When the Soviet Union went down, Moldova became 'independent'—" Terzian could hear the quotes in her voice. "But independence had nothing to do with the Moldovan *people*, it was just Romanian-speaking Soviet elites going off on their own account once their own superiors were no longer there to retrain them. And Moldova soon split—first the Turkish Christians..."

"Wait a second," Terzian said. "There are *Christian Turks?*"

The idea of Christian Turks was not a part of his Armenian-American worldview.

Stephanie nodded. "Orthodox Christian Turks, yes. They're called Gagauz, and they now have their own autonomous republic of Gagauzia within Moldova."

Stephanie reached into her pocket for a cigarette and her lighter.

"Uh," Terzian said. "Would you mind smoking in the window?"

Stephanie made a face. "Americans," she said, but she moved to the window and opened it, letting in a blast of cool spring air. She perched on the windowsill, sheltered her cigarette from the wind, and lit up.

"Where was I?" she asked.

"Turkish Christians."

"Right." Blowing smoke into the teeth of the gale. "Gagauzia was only the start—after that a Russian general allied with a bunch of crooks and KGB types created a rebellion in the bit of Moldova that was on the far side of the Dniester—another collection of Soviet elites, representing no one but themselves. Once the Russian-speaking rebels rose against their Romanian-speaking oppressors, the Soviet Fourteenth Army stepped in as 'peacekeepers,' complete with blue helmets, and created a twenty-mile-wide state recognized by no other government. And that meant more military, more border guards, more administrators, more taxes to charge, and customs duties, and uniformed ex-Soviets whose palms needed greasing. And over a hundred thousand refugees who could be put in camps while the administration stole their supplies and rations…

"But—" She jabbed the cigarette like a pointer. "Transnistria had a problem. No other nation recognized their existence, and they were tiny and had no natural resources, barring the underage girls they enslaved by the thousands to export for prostitution. The rest of the population was leaving as fast as they could, restrained only slightly by the fact that they carried passports no other state recognized, and that meant there were fewer people whose productivity the elite could steal to support their predatory post-Soviet lifestyles. All they had was a lot of obsolete Soviet heavy industry geared to produce stuff no one wanted.

"But they still had the *infrastructure.* They had power plants—running off Russian oil they couldn't afford to buy—and they had a transportation system. So the outlaw regime set up to attract other outlaws who needed industrial capacity—the idea was that they'd attract entrepreneurs who were excused from paying most of the local 'taxes' in exchange for making one big payoff to the higher echelon."

"Weapons?" Terzian asked.

"Weapons, sure," Stephanie nodded. "Mostly they're producing cheap knockoffs of other people's guns, but the guns are up to the size of howitzers. They tried banking and data havens, but the authorities couldn't restrain themselves from ripping those off—banks and data run on trust and control of information, and when the regulators are greedy, short-sighted crooks you don't get either one. So what they settled on was, well, *biotech.* They've got companies creating cheap generic pharmaceuticals that evade Western patents..." Her look darkened. "Not that I've got a problem with *that,* not when I've seen thousands dying of diseases they couldn't afford to cure. And they've also got other companies who are ripping off Western genetic research to develop their own products. And as long as they make their payoffs to the elite, these companies remain *completely unregulated.* Nobody, not even the government, knows what they're doing in those factories, and the government gives them security free of charge."

Terzian imagined gene-splicing going on in a rusting Soviet factory, rows and rows of mutant plants with untested, unregulated genetics, all set to be released on an unsuspecting world. Transgenic elements drifting down the Dniester to the Black Sea, growing quietly in its saline environment...

"The news," Stephanie reminded, and pointed at the television.

Terzian reached for the control and hit the mute button, just as the throbbing, anxious music that announced the news began to fade.

The murder on the Île de la Cité was the second item on the broadcast. The victim was described as a "foreign national" who had been fatally stabbed, and no arrests had been made. The motive for the killing was unknown.

Terzian changed the channel in time to catch the same item on another channel. The story was unchanged.

"I told you," Stephanie said. "No suspects. No motive."

"You could tell them."

She made a negative motion with her cigarette. "I couldn't tell them who did it, or how to find them. All I could do is put myself under suspicion."

Terzian turned off the TV. "So what happened exactly? Your friend stole from these people?"

Stephanie swiped her forehead with the back of her wrist. "He stole something that was of no value to them. It's only valuable to poor people, who can't afford to pay. And—" She turned to the window and spun her cigarette into the street below. "I'll take it out of here as soon as I can," she said. "I've got to try to contact some friends." She closed the window, shutting out the spring breeze. "I wish I had my passport. That would change everything."

*I saw a murder this afternoon,* Terzian thought. He closed his eyes and saw the man falling, the white face so completely absorbed in the reality of its own agony.

He was so fucking sick of death.

He opened his eyes. "I can get your passport back," he said.

Anger kept him moving until he saws the killers, across the street from Stephanie's hotel, sitting at an outdoor table in a café-bar. Terzian recognized them immediately—he didn't need to look at the heavy shoes, or the broad faces with their disciplined military mustaches—one glance at the crowd at the café showed the only two in the place who weren't French. That was probably how Stephanie knew to speak to him in English, he just didn't dress or carry himself like a Frenchman, for all that he'd worn an anonymous coat and tie. He tore his gaze away before they saw him gaping at them.

Anger turned very suddenly to fear, and as he continued his stride toward the hotel he told himself that they wouldn't recognize him from the Norman restaurant, that he'd changed into blue jeans and sneaks and a windbreaker, and carried a soft-sided suitcase. Still he felt a gunsight on the back of his neck, and he was so nervous that he nearly ran head-first into the glass lobby door.

Terzian paid for a room with his credit card, took the key from the Vietnamese clerk, and walked up the narrow stair to what the French called the second floor, but what he would have called the third. No one lurked in the stairwell, and he wondered where the third assassin had gone. Looking for Stephanie somewhere else, probably, an airport or train station.

In his room Terzian put his suitcase on the bed—it held only a few token items, plus his shaving kit—and then he took Stephanie's key from his pocket and held it in his hand. The key was simple, attached to a weighted doorknob-shaped ceramic plug.

The jolt of fear and surprise that had so staggered him on first sighting the two men began to shift again into rage.

They were drinking *beer*, there had been half-empty mugs on the table in front of them, and a pair of empties as well.

Drinking on duty. Doing surveillance while drunk

Bastards. Trashcanians. They could kill someone simply through drunkenness.

Perhaps they already had.

He was angry when he left his room and took the stairs to the floor below. No foes kept watch in the hall. He opened Stephanie's room and then closed the door behind him.

He didn't turn on the light. The sun was surprisingly high in the sky for the hour: he had noticed that the sun seemed to set later here than it did at home. Maybe France was very far to the west for its time zone.

Stephanie's didn't have a suitcase, just a kind of nylon duffel, a larger version of the athletic bag she already carried. He took it from the little closet, and enough of Terzian's suspicion remained so that he checked the luggage tag to make certain the name was *Steph. Pais*, and not another.

He opened the duffel, then got her passport and travel documents from the bedside table and tossed them in. He added a jacket and a sweater from the closet, then packed her toothbrush and shaver into her plastic travel bag and put it in the duffel.

The plan was for him to return to his room on the upper floor and stay the night and avoid raising suspicion by leaving a hotel he'd just checked into. In the morning, carrying two bags, he'd check out and rejoin Stephanie in his own hotel, where she had spent the night in his room, and where the air almost would by now reek with her cigarette smoke.

Terzian opened a dresser drawer and scooped out a double handful of Stephanie's t-shirts, underwear, and stockings, and then he remembered that the last time he'd done this was when he cleaned Claire's belongings out of the Esplanade house.

*Shit. Fuck.* He gazed down at the clothing between his hands and let the fury rage like a tempest in his skull.

And then, in the angry silence, he heard a creak in the corridor, and then a stumbling thud.

Thick rubber military soles, he thought. With drunk baboons in them.

Instinct shrieked at him not to be trapped in this room, this dead-end where he could be trapped and killed. He dropped Stephanie's clothes back into the drawer and stepped to the bed and picked up the duffel in one hand. Another step took him to the door, which he opened with one hand while using the other to fling the duffel into the surprised face of the drunken murderer on the other side.

Terzian hadn't been at his Kenpo school in six years, not since he'd left Kansas City, but certain reflexes don't go away after they've been drilled into a person thousands of times—certainly not the front kick that hooked upward under the intruder's breastbone and drove him breathless into the corridor wall opposite.

A primitive element of his mind rejoiced in the fact that he was bigger than these guys. He could really knock them around.

The second Trashcanian tried to draw a pistol but Terzian passed outside the pistol hand and drove the point of an elbow into the man's face. Terzian then grabbed the automatic with both hands, took a further step down the corridor, and spun around, which swung the man around Terzian's hip a full two hundred and seventy degrees and drove him head-first into the corridor wall. When he'd finished falling and opened his eyes he was staring into the barrel of his own gun.

Red rage gave a fangs-bared roar of animal triumph inside Terzian's skull. Perhaps his tongue echoed it. It was all he could do to stop himself from pulling the trigger.

Get Death working for *him* for a change. Why not?

Except the first man hadn't realized that his side had just lost. He had drawn a knife—a glittering chromed single-edged thing that may have already killed once today—and now he took a dangerous step toward Terzian.

Terzian pointed the pistol straight at the knife man and pulled the trigger. Nothing happened.

The intruder stared at the gun as if he'd just realized at just this moment it wasn't his partner who held it.

Terzian pulled the trigger again, and when nothing happened his rage melted into terror and he ran. Behind him he heard the drunken knife man trip over his partner and crash to the floor.

Terzian was at the bottom of the stair before he heard the thick-soled military boots clatter on the risers above him. He dashed through the small lobby—he sensed the Vietnamese night clerk, who was facing away, begin to turn toward him just as he pushed open the glass door and ran into the street.

He kept running. At some point he discovered the gun still in his fist, and he put it in the pocket of his windbreaker.

Some moments later he realized he wasn't being pursued. And he remembered that Stephanie's passport was still in her duffel, which he'd thrown at the knife man and hadn't retrieved.

For a moment rage ran through him, and he thought about taking out the gun and fixing whatever was wrong with it and going back to Stephanie's room and getting the documents one way or another.

But then the anger faded enough for him to see what a foolish course that would be, and he returned to his own hotel.

Terzian had given Stephanie his key, so he knocked on his own door before realizing she was very unlikely to open to a random knock. "It's Jonathan," he said. "It didn't work out."

She snatched the door open from the inside. Her face was taut with anxiety. She held pages in her hand, the text of the paper he'd delivered that morning.

"Sorry," he said. "They were there, outside the hotel. I got into your room, but—"

She took his arm and almost yanked him into the room, then shut the door behind him. "Did they follow you?" she demanded.

"No. They didn't chase me. Maybe they thought I'd figure out how to work the gun." He took the pistol out of his pocket and showed it to her. "I can't believe how stupid I was —"

"*Where did you get that? Where did you get that?*" Her voice was nearly a scream, and she shrank away from him, her eyes wide. Her fist crumpled papers over her heart. To his astonishment he realized that she was afraid of him, that she thought he was *connected*, somehow, with the killers.

He threw the pistol onto the bed and raised his hands in a gesture of surrender. "No really!" he shouted over her cries. "It's not mine! I took it from one of them!"

Stephanie took a deep gasp of air. Her eyes were still wild. "Who the hell are you, then?" she said. "James Bond?"

He gave a disgusted laugh. "James Bond would have known how to shoot."

"I was reading your—your article." She held out the pages toward him. "I was thinking, my God, I was thinking, what have I got this poor guy into. Some professor I was sending to his death." She passed a hand over her forehead. "They probably bugged my room. They would have known right away that someone was in it."

"They were drunk," Terzian said. "Maybe they've been drinking all day. Those assholes really pissed me off."

He sat on the bed and picked up the pistol. It was small and blue steel and surprisingly heavy. In the years since he'd last shot a gun he had forgotten that purposefulness, the way a firearm was designed for a single, clear function. He found the safety where it had been all along, near his right thumb, and flicked it off and then on again.

"There," he said. "That's what I should have done."

Waves of anger shivered through his limbs at the touch of the adrenaline still pouring into his system. A bitter impulse to laugh again rose in him, and he tried to suppress it.

"I guess I was lucky after all," he said. "It wouldn't have done you any good to have to explain a pair of corpses outside your room." He looked up at Stephanie, who was pacing back and forth in the narrow lane between the bed and the wall, and looking as if she badly needed a cigarette. "I'm sorry about your passport. Where were you going to go, anyway?"

"It doesn't so much matter if *I* go," she said. She gave Terzian a quick, nervous glance. "You can fly it out, right?"

"It?" He stared at her. "What do you mean, it?"

"The biotech." Stephanie stopped her pacing and stared at him with those startling green eyes. "Adrian gave it to me. Just before they killed him." Terzian's gaze followed hers to the black bag with the Nike swoosh, the bag that sat at the foot of Terzian's bed.

Terzian's impulse to laugh faded. Unregulated, illegal, stolen biotech, he thought. Right in his own hotel room. Along with a stolen gun and a woman who was probably out of her mind.

Fuck.

The dead man was identified by news files as Adrian Cristea, a citizen of Ukraine and a researcher. He had been stabbed once in the right kidney and bled to death without identifying his assailants. Witnesses reported two or maybe three men leaving the scene immediately after Cristea's death. Michelle set more search spiders to work.

For a moment she considered calling Davout and letting him know that Terzian had probably been a witness to a murder, but decided to wait until she either had some more evidence one way or another.

For the next few hours she did her real work, analyzing the samples she'd taken from Zigzag Lake's sulfide-tainted deeps. It wasn't very physical, and Michelle figured it was only worth a few hundred calories.

A wind floated through the treetops, bringing the scent of night flowers and swaying Michelle's perch beneath her as she peered into her biochemical reader, and she remembered the gentle pressure of Darton against her back, rocking with her as he looked over her shoulder at her results. Suddenly she could remember, with a near perfect clarity, the taste of his skin on her tongue.

She rose from her woven seat and paced along the bough. *Damn it,* she thought, *I watched you die.*

Michelle returned to her deck and discovered that her spiders had located the police file on Cristea's death. A translation program handled the antique French without trouble, even producing modern equivalents of forensic jargon. Cristea was of Romanian descent, had been born in the old USSR, and had acquired Ukrainian citizenship on the breakup of the Soviet Union. The French files themselves had translations of Cristea's Ukrainian travel documents, which included receipts showing that he had paid personal insurance, environmental insurance, and departure taxes from Transnistria, a place of which she'd never heard, as well as similar documents from Moldova, which at least was a province, or country, that sounded familiar.

What kind of places were these, where you had to buy *insurance* at the *border?* And what was environmental insurance anyway?

There were copies of emails between French and Ukrainian authorities, in which the Ukrainians politely declined any knowledge of their citizen beyond the fact that he *was* a citizen. They had no addresses for him.

Cristea apparently lived in Transnistria, but the authorities there echoed the Ukrainians in saying they knew nothing of him.

Cristea's tickets and vouchers showed that he had apparently taken a train to Bucharest, and there he'd got on an airline that took him to Prague, and thence to Paris. He had been in the city less than a day before he was killed. Found in Cristea's hotel room was a curious document certifying that Cristea was carrying medical supplies, specifically a vaccine against hepatitis A. Michelle wondered why he would be carrying a hepatitis vaccine from Transnistria to France. France presumably had all the hepatitis vaccine it needed.

No vaccine had turned up. Apparently Cristea had got into the European Community without having his bags searched, as there was no evidence that the documents relating to the alleged vaccine had ever been examined.

The missing "vaccine"—at some point in the police file the skeptical quotation marks had appeared—had convinced the Paris police that Cristea was a murdered drug courier, and at that point they'd lost interest in the case. It was rarely possible to solve a professional killing in the drug underworld.

Michelle's brief investigation seemed to have come to a dead end. That Terzian might have witnessed a murder would rate maybe half a sentence in Professor Davout's biography.

Then she checked what her spiders had brought her in regard to Terzian, and found something that cheered her.

There he was inside the Basilica di Santa Croce, a tourist still photograph taken before the tomb of Machiavelli. He was only slightly turned away from the camera and the face was unmistakable. Though there was no date on the photograph, only the year, but he wore the same clothes he wore in the video taken outside the church, and the photo caught him in the act of speaking to a companion. She was a tall woman with deep brown skin, but she was turned away from the camera, and a wide-brimmed sun hat made her features indistinguishable.

Humming happily, Michelle deployed her software to determine whether this was the same woman who had been on Terzian's arm on the Place Dauphine. Without facial features or other critical measurements to compare, the software was uncertain, but the proportion of limb and thorax was right, and the software gave an estimate of 41%, which Michelle took to be encouraging.

Another still image of Terzian appeared in an undated photograph taken at a festival in southern France. He wore dark glasses, and he'd grown heavily tanned; he carried a glass of wine in either hand, but the person to whom he was bringing the second glass was out of the frame. Michelle set her software to locating the identity of the church seen in the background, a task the two distinctive belltowers would make easy. She was lucky and got a hit right away: the church was the Eglise St-Michel in Salon-de-Provence, which meant Terzian had attended the Fête des Aires de la Dine in June. Michelle set more search spiders to seeking out photo and video from the festivals. She had no doubt she'd find Terzian there, and perhaps again his companion.

Michelle retired happily to her hammock. The search was going well. Terzian had met a woman in Paris and traveled with her for weeks. The evidence wasn't quite there yet, but Michelle would drag it out of history somehow.

*Romance.* The lonely mermaid was in favor of romance, the kind where you ran away to faraway places to be more intently one with the person you adored.

It was what she herself had done, before everything had gone so wrong, and Michelle had to take steps to re-establish the moral balance of her universe.

Terzian paid for a room for Stephanie for the night, not so much because he was gallant as because he needed to be alone to think. "There's a breakfast buffet downstairs in the morning," he said. "They have hard-boiled eggs and croissants and Nutella. It's a very un-French thing to do. I recommend it."

He wondered if he would ever see her again. She might just vanish, particularly if she read his thoughts, because another reason for wanting privacy was so that he could call the police and bring an end to this insane situation.

He never quite assembled the motivation to make the call. Perhaps Rorty's *I don't care* had rubbed off on him. And he never got a chance to taste the buffet, either. Stephanie banged on his door very early, and he dragged on his jeans and opened the door. She entered, furiously smoking from her new cigarette pack, the athletic bag over her shoulder.

"How did you pay for the room at my hotel?" she asked.

"Credit card," he said, and in the stunned, accusing silence that followed he saw his James Bond fantasies sink slowly beneath the slack, oily surface of a dismal lake.

Because credit cards leave trails. The Transnistrians would have checked the hotel registry, and the credit card impression taken by the hotel, and now they knew who *he* was. And it wouldn't be long before they'd trace him at his hotel.

"Shit, I should have warned you to pay cash." Stephanie stalked to the window and peered out cautiously. "They could be out there right now."

Terzian felt a sudden compulsion to have the gun in his hand. He took it from the bedside table and stood there, feeling stupid and cold and shirtless.

"How much money do you have?" Terzian asked.

"Couple hundred."

"I have less."

"You should max out your credit card and just carry Euros. Use your card now before they cancel it."

"Cancel it? How could they cancel it?"

She gave him a tight-lipped, impatient look. "Jonathan. They may be assholes, but they're still a *government.*"

They took a cab to the American Express near the Opéra and Terzian got ten thousand Euros in cash from some people who were extremely skeptical about the validity of his documents, but who had, in the end, to admit that all was technically correct. Then Stephanie got a cell phone under the name A. Silva, with a bunch of prepaid hours on it, and within a couple hours they were on the TGV, speeding south to Nice at nearly two hundred seventy kilometers per hour, all with a strange absence of sound and vibration that made the French countryside speeding past seem like a strangely unconvincing special effect.

Terzian had put them in first class and he and Stephanie were alone in a group of four seats. Stephanie was twitchy because he hadn't bought seats in a smoking section. He sat uncertain, unhappy about all the cash he was carrying and not knowing what to do with it—he'd made two big rolls and zipped them into the pockets of his windbreaker. He carried the pistol in the front pocket of his jeans and its weight and discomfort was a perpetual reminder of this situation that he'd been dragged into, pursued by killers from Trashcanistan and escorting illegal biotechnology.

He kept mentally rehearsing drawing the pistol and shooting it. Over and over, remembering to thumb off the safety this time. Just in case Trashcanian commandos stormed the train.

"Hurled into life," he muttered. "An object lesson right out of Heidegger."

"Beg pardon?"

He looked at her. "Heidegger said we're hurled into life. Just like I've been hurled into—" He flapped his hands uselessly. "Into whatever this is. The situation exists before you even got here, but here you are anyway, and the whole business is something you inherit and have to live with." He felt his lips draw back in a snarl. "He also said that a fundamental feature of existence is anxiety in the face of death, which would also seem to apply to our situation. And his answer to all of this was to make existence, *dasein* if you want to get technical, an authentic project." He looked at her. "So what's your authentic project, then? And how authentic is it?"

Her brow furrowed. "What?"

Terzian couldn't stop, not that he wanted to. It was just Stephanie's hard luck that he couldn't shoot anybody right now, or break something up with his fists, and was compelled to lecture instead. "Or," he went on, "to put this in a more accessible context, just pretend we're in a Hitchcock film, okay? This is the scene where Grace Kelly tells Cary Grant exactly who she is and what the maguffin is."

Stephanie's face was frozen into a hostile mask. Whether she understood what he was saying or not, the hostility was clear.

"I don't get it," she said.

"*What's in the fucking bag?*" he demanded.

She glared at him for a long moment, then spoke, her own anger plain in her voice. "It's the answer to world hunger," she said. "Is that authentic enough for you?"

Stephanie's father was from Angola and her mother from East Timor, both former Portuguese colonies swamped in the decades since independence by war and massacre. Both parents had with great foresight and intelligence retained Portuguese passports, and had met in Rome, where they worked for UNESCO, and where Stephanie had grown up with a blend both of their genetics and their service ethic.

Stephanie herself had got a degree in administration from the University of Virginia, which accounted for the American lights in her English, then got another degree in nursing and went to work for the Catholic relief agency Santa Croce, which sent her to its every war-wrecked, locust-blighted, warlord-ridden, sandstorm-blasted camp in Africa. And a few that *weren't* in Africa.

"Trashcanistan," Terzian said.

"Moldova," Stephanie said. "For three months, on what was supposed to be my vacation." She shuddered. "I don't mind telling you that it was a frightening thing. I was used to that kind of thing in Africa, but to see it all happening in the developed world… warlords, ethnic hatreds, populations being moved at the point of a gun, whole forested districts being turned to deserts because people suddenly needed firewood…" Her emerald eyes flashed. "It's all politics, okay? Just like in Africa. Famine and camps are all politics now, and have been since before I was born. A whole population starves, and it's because someone, somewhere, sees a profit in it. It's difficult to just kill an ethnic group you don't like, war is expensive and there are questions at the UN and you may end up at The Hague being tried for war crimes. But if you just wait for a bad harvest and then arrange for the whole population to *starve*, it's different—suddenly your enemies are giving you all their money in return for food, you get aid from the UN instead of grief, and you can award yourself a piece of the relief action and collect bribes from all the relief agencies, and your enemies are rounded up into camps and you can get your armed forces into the country without resistance, make sure your enemies disappear, control everything while some deliveries disappear into government warehouses where the food can be sold to the starving or just sold abroad for a profit..." She shrugged. "That's the way of the world, okay? *But no more!*" She grabbed a fistful of the Nike bag and brandished it at him.

What her time in Moldova had done was to leave Stephanie contacts in the area, some in relief agencies, some in industry and government. So that when news of a useful project came up in Transnistria, she was among the first to know.

"So what is it?" Terzian asked. "Some kind of genetically modified food crop?"

"No." She smiled thinly. "What we have here is a genetically modified consumer."

Those Transnistrian companies had mostly been interested in duplicating pharmaceuticals and transgenetic food crops created by other companies, producing them on the cheap and underselling the patent-owners. There were bits and pieces of everything in those labs, DNA human and animal and vegetable. A lot of it had other people's trademarks and patents on it, even the human codes, which US law permitted companies to patent provided they came up with something useful to do with it. And what these semi-outlaw companies were doing was making two things they figured people couldn't do without: drugs and food.

And not just people, since animals need drugs and food, too. Starving, tubercular sheep or pigs aren't worth much at market, so there's as much money in keeping livestock alive as in doing the same for people. So at some point one of the administrators—after a few too many shots of vodka flavored with bison grass—said, "Why should we worry about feeding the animals at all? Why not have them grow their own food, like plants?"

So then began the Green Swine Project, an attempt to make pigs fat and happy by just herding them out into the sun.

"Green swine," Terzian repeated, wondering. "People are getting killed over green swine."

"Well, no." Stephanie waved the idea away with a twitchy swipe of her hand. "The idea never quite got beyond the vaporware stage, because at that point another question was asked—why swine? Adrian said, Why stop at having animals do photosynthesis—why not *people?*"

"No!" Terzian cried, appalled. "You're going to turn people green?"

Stephanie glared at him. "Something wrong with fat, happy green people?" Her hands banged out a furious rhythm on the armrests of her seat. "I'd have skin to match my eyes. Wouldn't that be attractive?"

"I'd have to see it first," Terzian said, the shock still rolling through his bones.

"Adrian was pretty smart," Stephanie said. "The Transnistrians killed themselves a real genius." She shook her head. "He had it all worked out. He wanted to limit the effect to the skin—no green muscle tissue of skeletons—so he started with a virus that has a tropism for the epidermis—papiloma, that's warts, okay?"

*So now we've got green warts,* Terzian thought, but he kept his mouth shut.

"So if you're Adrian, what you do is gut the virus and re-encode it to create chlorophyll. Once a person's infected, exposure to sunlight will cause the virus to replicate and chlorophyll to reproduce in the skin."

Terzian gave Stephanie a skeptical look. "That's not going to be very efficient," he said. "Plants get sugars and oxygen from chlorophyll, okay, but they don't need much food, they stand in place and don't walk around. Add chlorophyll to a person's skin, how many calories do you get each day? Tens? Dozens?"

Stephanie's lips parted in a fierce little smile. "You don't stop with just the chlorophyll. You have to get really efficient electron transport. In a plant that's handled in the chloroplasts, but the human body already has mitochondria to do the same job. You don't have to create these huge support mechanisms for the chlorophyll, you just make use of what's already there. So if you're Adrian, what you do is add trafficking tags to the reaction center proteins so that they'll target the mitochondria, which *already* are loaded with proteins to handle electron transport. The result is that the mitochondria handle transport from the chlorophyll, which is the sort of job they do anyway, and once the virus starts replicating you can get maybe a thousand calories or more just from standing in the sun. It won't provide full nutrition, but it can keep starvation at bay, and it's not as if starving people have much to do besides stand in the sun anyway."

"It's not going to do much good for Icelanders," Terzian said.

She turned severe. "Icelanders aren't starving. It so happens that most of the people in the world who are starving happen to be in hot places."

Terzian flapped his hands. "Fine. I must be a racist. Sue me."

Stephanie's grin broadened, and she leaned toward Terzian. "I didn't tell you about Adrian's most interesting bit of cleverness. When people start getting normal nutrition, there'll have a competition within the mitochondria between normal metabolism and solar-induced electron transport. So the green virus is just a redundant backup system in case normal nutrition isn't available."

A triumphant smile crossed Stephanie's face. "Starvation will no longer be a weapon," she said. "Green skin can keep people active and on their feet long enough to get help. It will keep them healthy enough to fend off the epidemics associated with malnutrition. The point is—" She made fists and shook them at the sky. "*The bad guys don't get to use starvation as a weapon anymore!* Famine *ends!* One of the Four Horsemen of the Apocalypse *dies,* right here, right now, as a result of *what I've got in this bag!*" She picked up the bag and threw it into Terzian's lap, and he jerked on the seat in defensive reflex, knees rising to meet elbows. Her lips skinned back in a snarl, and her tone was mocking.

"I think even that Nazi fuck Heidegger would think my *project* is pretty damn *authentic.* Wouldn't you agree, Herr Doktor Terzian?"

*Got you,* Michelle thought. Here was a still photo of Terzian at the Fête des Aires de la Dine, with the dark-skinned woman. She had the same wide-brimmed straw hat she'd worn in the Florence church, and had the same black bag over her shoulder, but now Michelle had a clear view of a three-quarter profile, and one hand, with its critical alignments, was clearly visible, holding an ice cream cone.

Night insects whirled around the computer display. Michelle batted them away and got busy mapping. The photo was digital and Michelle could enlarge it.

To her surprise she discovered that the woman had green eyes. Black women with green irises—or irises of orange or chartreuse or chrome steel—were not unusual in her own time, but she knew that in Terzian's time they were rare. That would make the search much easier.

"*Michelle...*" The voice came just as Michelle sent her new search spiders into the ether. A shiver ran up her spine.

"*Michelle...*" The voice came again.

It was Darton.

Michelle's heart gave a sickening lurch. She closed her console and put it back in the mesh bag, then crossed the rope bridge between the ironwood tree and the banyan. Her knees were weak, and the swaying bridge seemed to take a couple unexpected pitches. She stepped out onto the banyan's sturdy overhanging limb and gazed out at the water.

*"Michelle…"* To the southwest, in the channel between the mermaid's island and another, she could see a pale light bobbing, the light of a small boat.

*"Michelle, where are you?"*

The voice died away in the silence and surf. Michelle remembered the spike in her hand, the long, agonized trek up the slope above Jellyfish Lake. Darton pale, panting for breath, dying in her arms.

The lake was one of the wonders of the world, but the steep path over the ridge that fenced the lake from the ocean was challenging even for those who were not dying. When Michelle and Darton—at that time apes—came up from their boat that afternoon they didn't climb the steep path, but swung hand-over-hand through the trees overhead, through the hardwood and guava trees, and avoided the poison trees with their bleeding, allergenic black sap. Even though their trip was less exhausting than if they'd gone over the land route, the two were ready for the cool water by the time they arrived at the lake.

Tens of thousands of years in the past the water level was higher, and when it receded the lake was cut off from the Pacific, and with it the *Mastigias* sp. jellyfish, which soon exhausted the supply of small fish that were its food. As the human race did later, the jellies gave up hunting and gathering in exchange for agriculture, and permitted themselves to be farmed by colonies of algae that provided the sugars they needed for life. At night they'd descend to the bottom of the lake, where they fertilized their algae crops in the anoxic, sulfurous waters; at dawn the jellies rose to the surface, and over the course of the day they crossed the lake, following the course of the sun, and allowed the sun's rays to supply the energy necessary for making their daily ration of food.

When Darton and Michelle arrived, there were ten million jellyfish in the lake, from fingertip-sized to jellies the size of a dinner plate, all in one warm throbbing golden-brown mass in the center of the water. The two swam easily on the surface with their long siamang arms, laughing and calling to one another as the jellyfish in their millions caressed them with the most featherlike of touches. The lake was the temperature of their own blood, and it was like a soupy bath, the jellyfish so thick that Michelle felt she could almost walk on the surface. The warm touch wasn't erotic, exactly, but it was sensual in the way that an erotic touch was sensual, a light brush over the skin by the pad of a teasing finger.

Trapped in a lake for thousands of years without suitable prey, the jellyfish had lost most of their ability to sting. Only a small percentage of people were sensitive enough to the toxin to receive a rash or feel a modest burning.

A very few people, though, were more sensitive than that.

Darton and Michelle left at dusk, and by that time Darton was already gasping for breath. He said he'd overexerted himself, that all he needed was to get back to their base for a snack, but as he swung through the trees on the way up the ridge, he lost his hold on a Palauan apple tree and crashed through a thicket of limbs to sprawl, amid a hail of fruit, on the sharp algae-covered limestone of the ridge.

Michelle swung down from the trees, her heart pounding. Darton was nearly colorless and struggling to breathe. They had no way of calling for help unless Michelle took their boat to Koror or to their base camp on another island. She tried to help Darton walk, taking one of his long arms over her shoulder, supporting him up the steep island trail. He collapsed, finally, at the foot of a poison tree, and Michelle bent over him to shield him from the drops of venomous sap until he died.

Her back aflame with the poison sap, she'd whispered her parting words into Darton's ear. She never knew if he heard.

The coroner said it was a million-to-one chance that Darton had been so deathly allergic, and tried to comfort her with the thought that there was nothing she could have done. Torbiong, who had made the arrangements for Darton and Michelle to come in the first place, had been consoling, had offered to let Michelle stay with his family. Michelle had surprised him by asking permission to move her base camp to another island, and to continue her work alone.

She also had herself transformed into a mermaid, and subsequently a romantic local legend.

And now Darton was back, bobbing in a boat in the nearby channel and calling her name, shouting into a bullhorn.

"*Michelle, I love you.*" The words floated clear into the night air. Michelle's mouth was dry. Her fingers formed the sign <go away>.

There was a silence, and then Michelle heard the engine start on Darton's boat. He motored past her position, within five hundred meters or so, and continued on to the northern point of the island.

<go away>…

"*Michelle…*" Again his voice floated out onto the breeze. It was clear he didn't know where she was. She was going to have to be careful about showing lights.

<go away>…

Michelle waited while Darton called out a half-dozen more times, and then Darton started his engine and moved on. She wondered if he would search all three hundred islands in the Rock Island group.

No, she knew he was more organized than that.

She'd have to decide what to do when he finally found her.

While a thousand questions chased each other's tails through his mind, Terzian opened the Nike bag and withdrew the small hard plastic case inside, something like a box for fishing tackle. He popped the locks on the case and opened the lid, and he saw glass vials resting in slots cut into dark grey foam. In them was a liquid with a faint golden cast.

"The papiloma," Stephanie said.

Terzian dropped the lid on the case as he cast a guilty look over his shoulder, not wanting anyone to see him with this stuff. If he were arrested under suspicion of being a drug dealer, the wads of cash and the pistol certainly wouldn't help.

"What do you do with the stuff once you get to where you're going?"

"Brush it on the skin. With exposure to solar energy it replicates as needed."

"Has it been tested?"

"On people? No. Works fine on rhesus monkeys, though."

He tapped his wedding ring on the arm of his seat. "Can it be... caught? I mean, it's a virus, can it go from one person to another?"

"Through skin-to-skin contact."

"I'd say that's a yes. Can mothers pass it on to their children?"

"Adrian didn't think it would cross the placental barrier, but he didn't get a chance to test it. If mothers want to infect their children, they'll probably have to do it deliberately." She shrugged. "Whatever the case, my guess is that mothers won't mind green babies, as long as they're green *healthy* babies." She looked down at the little vials in their secure coffins of foam. "We can infect tens of thousands of people with this amount," she said. "And we can make more very easily."

*If mothers want to infect their children...* Terzian closed the lid of the plastic case and snapped the locks. "You're out of your mind," he said.

Stephanie cocked her head and peered at him, looking as if she'd anticipated his objections and was humoring him. "How so?"

"Where do I start?" Terzian zipped up the bag, then tossed it in Stephanie's lap, pleased to see her defensive reflexes leap in response. "You're planning on unleashing an untested transgenetic virus on Africa—on *Africa* of all places, a continent that doesn't exactly have a happy history with pandemics. And it's a virus that's cooked up by a bunch of illegal pharmacists in a non-country with a murderous secret police, facts that don't give me much confidence that this is going to be anything but a disaster."

Stephanie tapped two fingers on her chin as if she were wishing there were a cigarette between them. "I can put your mind to rest on the last issue. The animal studies worked. Adrian had a family of bright green rhesus in his lab, till the project was canceled and the rhesus were, ah, liquidated."

"So if the project's so terrific, why'd the company pull the plug?"

"Money." Her lips twisted in anger. "Starving people can't afford to pay for the treatments, so they'd have to practically give the stuff away. Plus they'd get reams of endless bad publicity, which is exactly what outlaw biotech companies in outlaw countries don't want. There are millions of people who go ballistic at the very thought of a genetically engineered *vegetable*—you can imagine how people who can't abide the idea of a transgenetic bell pepper would freak at the thought of infecting people with an engineered virus. The company decided it wasn't worth the risk. They closed the project down."

Stephanie looked at the bag in her hands. "But Adrian had been in the camps himself, you see. A displaced person, a refugee from the civil war in Moldova. And he couldn't stand the thought that there was a way to end hunger sitting in his refrigerator in the lab, and that nothing was being done with it. And so..." Her hands outlined the case inside the Nike bag. "He called me. He took some vacation time and booked himself into the Henri IV, on the Place Dauphine. And I guess he must have been careless, because..."

Tears starred in her eyes, and she fell silent. Terzian, strong in the knowledge that he'd shared quite enough of her troubles by now, stared out the window, at the green landscape that was beginning to take on the brilliant colors of Provence. The Hautes-Alpes floated blue and white-capped in the distant east, and nearby were orchards of almonds and olives with shimmering leaves, and hillsides covered with rows of orderly vines. The Rhone ran silver under the westering sun.

"I'm not going to be your bagman," he said. "I'm not going to contaminate the world with your freaky biotech."

"Then they'll catch you and you'll die," Stephanie said. "And it will be for nothing."

"My experience of death," said Terzian, "is that it's *always* for nothing."

She snorted then, angry. "My experience of death," she mocked, "is that it's too often for *profit*. I want to make mass murder an unprofitable venture. I want to crash the market in starvation by *giving away life*." She gave another snort, amused this time. "It's the ultimate anti-capitalist gesture."

Terzian didn't rise to that. Gestures, he thought, were just that. Gestures didn't change the fundamentals. If some jefe couldn't starve his people to death, he'd just use bullets, or deadly genetic technology he bought from outlaw Transnistrian corporations.

The landscape, all blazing green, raced past at over two hundred kilometers per hour. An attendant came by and sold them each a cup of coffee and a sandwich.

"You should use my phone to call your wife," Stephanie said as she peeled the cellophane from her sandwich. "Let her know that your travel plans have changed."

Apparently she'd noticed Terzian's wedding ring.

"My wife is dead," Terzian said.

She looked at him in surprise. "I'm sorry," she said.

"Brain cancer," he said.

Though it was more complicated than that. Claire had first complained of back pain, and there had been an operation, and the tumor removed from her spine. There had been a couple weeks of mad joy and relief, and then it had been revealed that the cancer had spread to the brain and that it was inoperable. Chemotherapy had failed. She died six weeks after her first visit to the doctor.

"Do you have any other family?" Stephanie said.

"My parents are dead, too." Auto accident, aneurism. He didn't mention Claire's uncle Geoff and his partner Luis, who had died of HIV within eight months of each other and left Claire the Victorian house on Esplanade in New Orleans. The house that, a few weeks ago, he had sold for six hundred and fifty thousand dollars, and the furnishings for a further ninety-five thousand, and Uncle Geoff's collection of equestrian art for a further forty-one thousand.

He was disinclined to mention that he had quite a lot of money, enough to float around Europe for years.

Telling Stephanie that might only encourage her.

There was a long silence. Terzian broke it. "I've read spy novels," he said. "And I know that we shouldn't go to the place we've bought tickets for. We shouldn't go anywhere *near* Nice."

She considered this, then said, "We'll get off at Avignon."

They stayed in Provence for nearly two weeks, staying always in unrated hotels, those that didn't even rise to a single star from the Ministry of Tourism, or in *gîtes ruraux,* farmhouses with rooms for rent. Stephanie spent much of her energy trying to call colleagues in Africa on her cell phone and achieved only sporadic success, a frustration that left her in a near-permanent fury. It was never clear just who she was trying to call, or how she thought they were going to get the papiloma off her hands. Terzian wondered how many people were involved in this conspiracy of hers.

They attended some local fêtes, though it was always a struggle to convince Stephanie it was safe to appear in a crowd. She made a point of disguising herself in big hats and shades and ended up looking like a cartoon spy. Terzian tramped rural lanes or fields or village streets, lost some pounds despite the splendid fresh local cuisine, and gained a sun tan. He made a stab at writing several papers on his laptop, and spent time researching them in internet cafés.

He kept thinking he would have enjoyed this trip, if only Claire had been with him.

"What is it you *do*, exactly?" Stephanie asked him once, as he wrote. "I know you teach at university, but…"

"I don't teach anymore," Terzian said. "I didn't get my post-doc renewed. The department and I didn't exactly get along."

"Why not?"

Terzian turned away from the stale, stalled ideas on his display. "I'm too interdisciplinary. There's a place on the academic spectrum where history and politics and philosophy come together—it's called 'political theory' usually—but I throw in economics and a layman's understanding of science as well, and it confuses everybody but me. That's why my MA is in American Studies—nobody in my philosophy or political science department had the nerve to deal with me, and nobody knows what American Studies actually *are*, so I was able to hide out there. And my doctorate is in philosophy, but only because I found one rogue professor emeritus who was willing to chair my committee.

"The problem is that if you're hired by a philosophy department, you're supposed to teach Plato or Hume or whoever, and they don't want you confusing everybody by adding Maynard Keynes and Leo Szilard. And if you teach history, you're supposed to confine yourself to acceptable stories about the past and not toss in ideas about perceptual mechanics and Kant's ideas of the noumenon, and of course you court crucifixion from the laity if you mention Foucault or Nietzsche."

Amusement touched Stephanie's lips. "So where do you find a job?"

"France?" he ventured, and they laughed. "In France, 'thinker' is a job description. It's not necessary to have a degree, it's just something you do." He shrugged. "And if that fails, there's always Burger King."

She seemed amused. "Sounds like burgers in your future."

"Oh, it's not as bad as all that. If I can generate enough interesting, sexy, highly original papers, I might attract attention and a job, in that order."

"And have you done that?"

Terzian looked at his display and sighed. "So far, no."

Stephanie narrowed her eyes and she considered him. "You're not a conventional person. You don't think inside the box, as they say."

"As they say," Terzian repeated.

"Then you should have no objections to radical solutions to world hunger. Particularly ones that don't cost a penny to white liberals throughout the world."

"Hah," Terzian said. "Who says I'm a liberal? I'm an *economist.*"

So Stephanie told him terrible things about Africa. Another famine was brewing across the southern part of the continent. Mozambique was plagued with flood *and* drought, a startling combination. The Horn of Africa was worse. According to her friends, Santa Croce had a food shipment stuck in Mogadishu and before letting it pass the local warlord wanted to renegotiate his bribe. In the meantime people were starving, dying of malnutrition, infection, and dysentery in camps in the dry highlands of Bale and Sidamo. Their own government in Addis Ababa was worse than the Somali warlord, at this stage permitting no aid at all, bribes or no bribes.

And as for the southern Sudan, it didn't bear thinking about.

"What's *your* solution to this?" she demanded of Terzian. "Or do you have one?"

"Test this stuff, this papiloma," he said, "show me that it works, and I'm with you. But there are too many plagues in Africa as it is."

"Confine the papiloma to labs while thousands die? Hand it to governments who can suppress it because of pressure from religious loons and hysterical NGOs? You call *that* an answer?" And Stephanie went back to working her phone while Terzian walked off in anger for another stalk down country lanes.

Terzian walked toward an old ruined castle that shambled down the slope of a nearby hill. And if Stephanie's plant people proved viable? he wondered. All bets were off. A world in which humans could become plants was a world at which none of the old rules applied.

Stephanie had said she wanted to crash the market in starvation. But, Terzian thought, that also meant crashing the market in *food.* If people with no money had all the food they needed, that meant *food itself had no value in the marketplace.* Food would be so cheap that there would be no profit in growing or selling it.

And this was all just *one application* of the technology. Terzian tried to keep up with science: he knew about nanoassemblers. Green people was just the first magic bullet in a long volley of scientific musketry that would change every fundamental rule by which humanity had operated since they'd first stood upright. What happened when *every* basic commodity—food, clothing, shelter, maybe even health—was so cheap that it was free? What then had value?

Even *money* wouldn't have value then. Money only had value if it could be exchanged for something of equivalent worth.

He paused in his walk and looked ahead at the ruined castle, the castle that had once provided justice and security and government for the district, and he wondered if he was looking at the future of *all* government. Providing an orderly framework in which commodities could be exchanged was the basic function of the state, that and providing a secure currency. If people didn't need government to furnish that kind of security and if the currency was worthless, the whole future of government itself was in question. Taxes weren't worth the expense of collecting if the money wasn't any good, anyway, and without taxes government couldn't be paid for.

Terzian paused at the foot of the ruined castle and wondered if he saw the future of the civilized world. Either the castle would be rebuilt by tyrants, or it would fall.

Michelle heard Darton's bullhorn again the next evening, and she wondered why he was keeping fruit-bat hours. Was it because his calls would travel farther at night?

If he were sleeping in the morning, she thought, that would make it easier. She'd finished analyzing some of her samples, but a principle of science was not to do these things alone: she'd have to travel to Koror to mail her samples to other people, and now she knew to do it in the morning, when Darton would be asleep.

The problem for Michelle was that she was a legend. When the lonely mermaid emerged from the sea and walked to the post office in the little foam booties she wore when walking on pavement, she was noticed. People pointed; children followed her on their boards, people in cars waved. She wondered if she could trust them not to contact Darton as soon as they saw her.

She hoped that Darton wasn't starting to get the islanders on his side.

Michelle and Darton had met on a field trip in Borneo, their obligatory government service after graduation. The other field workers were older, paying their taxes or working on their second or third or fourth or fifth careers, and Michelle knew on sight that Darton was no older than she, that he, too, was a child among all these elders. They were pulled to each other as if drawn by some violent natural force, cataloguing snails and terrapins by day and spending their nights wrapped in each other in their own shell, their turtleback tent. The ancients with whom they shared their days treated them with amused condescension, but then that was how they treated everything. Darton and Michelle didn't care. In their youth they stood against all creation.

When the trip came to an end they decided to continue their work together, just a hop across the equator in Belau. Paying their taxes ahead of time. They celebrated by getting new bodies, an exciting experience for Michelle, who had been built by strict parents that wouldn't allow her to have a new body until adulthood, no matter how many of her friends had been transforming from an early age into one newly fashionable shape or another.

Michelle and Darton thought that anthropoid bodies would be suitable for the work, and so they went to the clinic in Delhi and settled themselves on nanobeds and let the little machines turn their bodies, their minds, their memories, their desires and their knowledge and their souls, into long strings of numbers. All of which were fed into their new bodies when they were ready, and reserved as backups to be downloaded as necessary.

Being a siamang was a glorious discovery. They soared through the treetops of their little island, swinging overhand from limb to limb in a frenzy of glory. Michelle took a particular delight in her body hair—she didn't have as much as a real ape, but there was enough on her chest and back to be interesting. They built nests of foliage in trees and lay tangled together, analyzing data or making love or shaving their hair into interesting tribal patterns. Love was far from placid—it was a flame, a fury. An obsession that, against all odds, had been fulfilled, only to build the flame higher.

The fury still burned in Michelle. But now, after Darton's death, it had a different quality, a quality that had nothing to do with life or youth.

Michelle, spooning up blueberries and cream, riffled through the names and faces her spiders had spat out. There were, now she added them up, a preposterous number of pictures of green-eyed women with dark skin whose pictures were somewhere in the net. Nearly all of them had striking good looks. Many of them were unidentified in the old scans, or identified only by a first name. The highest probability the software offered was 43%.

That 43% belonged to a Brasilian named Laura Flor, who research swiftly showed was home in Aracaju during the critical period, among other things having a baby. A video of the delivery was available, but Michelle didn't watch it. The way women delivered babies back then was disgusting.

The next most likely female was another Brasilian seen in some tourist photographs taken in Rio. Not even a name given. A further search based on this woman's physiognomy turned up nothing, not until Michelle broadened the search to a different gender, and discovered the Brasilian was a transvestite. That didn't seem to be Terzian's scene, so she left it alone.

The third was identified only as Stephanie, and posted on a site created by a woman who had done relief work in Africa. Stephanie was shown with a group of other relief workers, posing in front of a tin-roofed, cinderblock building identified as a hospital.

The quality of the photograph wasn't very good, but Michelle mapped the physiognomy anyway, and sent it forth along with the name "Stephanie" to see what might happen.

There was a hit right away, a credit card charge to a Stephanie América Pais e Silva. She had stayed in a hotel in Paris for the three nights before Terzian disappeared.

Michelle's blood surged as the data flashed on her screens. She sent out more spiders and the good news began rolling in.

Stephanie Pais was a dual citizen of Portugal and Angola, and had been educated partly in the States—a quick check showed that her time at university didn't overlap Terzian's. From her graduation she had worked for a relief agency called Santa Croce.

Then a news item turned up, a sensational one. Stephanie Pais had been spectacularly murdered in Venice on the night of July 19, six days before Terzian had delivered the first version of his Cornucopia Theory.

*Two murders…*

One in Paris, one in Venice. And one the woman who seemed to be Terzian's lover.

Michelle's body shivered to a sudden gasping spasm, and she realized that in her suspense she'd been holding her breath. Her head swam. When it cleared, she worked out what time it was in Maryland, where Dr. Davout lived, and then told her deck to page him at once.

Davout was unavailable at first, and by the time he returned her call she had more information about Stephanie Pais. She blurted the story out to him while her fingers jabbed at the keyboard of her deck, sending him copies of her corroborating data.

Davout's startled eyes leaped from the data to Michelle and back. "How much of this…" he began, then gave up. "How did she die?" he managed.

"The news article says stabbed. I'm looking for the police report."

"Is Terzian mentioned?"

<No> she signed. "The police report will have more details."

"Any idea what this is about? There's no history of Terzian *ever* being connected with violence."

"By tomorrow," Michelle said, "I should be able to tell you. But I thought I should send this to you because you might be able to tie this in with other elements of Terzian's life that I don't know anything about."

Davout's fingers formed a mudra that Michelle didn't recognize—an old one, probably. He shook his head. "I have no idea what's happening here. The only thing I have to suggest is that this is some kind of wild coincidence."

"I don't believe in that kind of coincidence," Michelle said.

Davout smiled. "A good attitude for a researcher," he said. "But experience—well," he waved a hand.

*But he loved her,* Michelle insisted inwardly. She knew that in her heart. Stephanie was the woman he loved after Claire died, and then she was killed and Terzian went on to create the intellectual framework on which the world was now built. He had spent his modest fortune building pilot programs in Africa that demonstrated his vision was a practical one. The whole modern world was a monument to Stephanie.

*Everyone* was young then, Michelle thought. Even the seventy-year-olds were young compared to the people now. The world must have been *ablaze* with love and passion. But Davout didn't understand that because he was old and had forgotten all about love.

"Michelle…" Darton's voice came wafting over the waters.

Bastard. Michelle wasn't about to let him spoil this.

Her fingers formed <gotta go>. "I'll send you everything once it comes in," she said. "I think we've got something amazing here."

She picked up her deck and swung it around so that she could be sure that the light from the display couldn't be seen from the ocean. Her bare back against the rough bark of the ironwood, she began flashing through the data as it arrived.

She couldn't find the police report. Michelle went in search of it and discovered that all police records from that period in Venetian history had been wiped out in the Lightspeed War, leaving her only with what had been reported in the media.

"*Where are you? I love you!*" Darton's voice came from farther away. He'd narrowed his search, that was clear, but he still wasn't sure exactly where Michelle had built her nest.

Smiling, Michelle closed her deck and slipped it into its pouch. Her spiders would work for her tirelessly till dawn while she dreamed on in her hammock and let Darton's distant calls lull her to sleep.

They shifted their lodgings every few days. Terzian always arranged for separate bedrooms. Once, as they sat in the evening shade of a farm terrace and watched the setting sun shimmer on the silver leaves of the olives, Terzian found himself looking at her as she sat in an old cane chair, at the profile cutting sharp against the old limestone of the Vaucluse. The blustering wind brought gusts of lavender from the neighboring farm, a scent that made Terzian want to inhale until his lungs creaked against his ribs.

From a quirk of Stephanie's lips Terzian was suddenly aware that she knew he was looking at her. He glanced away.

"You haven't tried to sleep with me," she said.

"No," he agreed.

"But you *look*," she said. "And it's clear you're not a eunuch."

"We fight all the time," Terzian pointed out. "Sometimes we can't stand to be in the same room."

Stephanie smiled. "That wouldn't stop most of the men I've known. Or the women, either."

Terzian looked out over the olives, saw them shimmer in the breeze. "I'm still in love with my wife," he said.

There was a moment of silence. "That's well," she said.

And I'm angry at her, too, Terzian thought. Angry at Claire for deserting him. And he was furious at the universe for killing her and for leaving him alive, and he was angry at God even though he didn't believe in God. The Trashcanians had been good for him, because he could let his rage and his hatred settle there, on people who deserved it.

Those poor drunken bastards, he thought. Whatever they'd expected in that hotel corridor, it hadn't been a berserk grieving American who would just as soon have ripped out their throats with his bare hands.

The question was, could he do that again? It had all occurred without his thinking about it, old reflexes taking over, but he couldn't count on that happening a second time. He'd been trying to remember the Kenpo he'd once learned, particularly all the tricks against weapons. He found himself miming combats on his long country hikes, and he wondered if he'd retained any of his ability to take a punch.

He kept the gun with him, so the Trashcanians wouldn't get it if they searched his room when he was away. When he was alone, walking through the almond orchards or on a hillside fragrant with wild thyme, he practiced drawing it, snicking off the safety, and putting pressure on the trigger... the first time the trigger pull would be hard, but the first shot would cock the pistol automatically and after that the trigger pull would be light.

He wondered if he should buy more ammunition. But he didn't know how to buy ammunition in France and didn't know if a foreigner could get into trouble that way.

"We're both angry," Stephanie said. He looked at her again, her hand raised to her head to keep the gusts from blowing her long ringlets in her face. "We're angry at death. But love must make it more complicated for you."

Her green eyes searched him. "It's not death you're in love with, is it? Because—"

Terzian blew up. She had no right to suggest that he was in a secret alliance with death just because he didn't want to turn a bunch of Africans green. It was their worst argument, and this one ended with both of them stalking away through the fields and orchards while the scent of lavender pursued them on the wind.

When Terzian returned to his room he checked his caches of money, half-hoping that Stephanie had stolen his Euros and run. She hadn't.

He thought of going into her room while she was away, stealing the papiloma and taking a train north, handing it over to the Pasteur Institute or someplace. But he didn't.

In the morning, during breakfast, Stephanie's cell phone rang, and she answered. He watched while her face turned from curiosity to apprehension to utter terror. Adrenaline sang in his blood as he watched, and he leaned forward, feeling the familiar rage rise in him, just where he wanted it. In haste she turned off the phone, then looked at him. "That was one of them. He says he knows where we are, and wants to make a deal."

"If they know where we are," Terzian found himself saying coolly, "why aren't they here?"

"We've got to *go*," she insisted.

So they went. Clean out of France and into the Tuscan hills, with Stephanie's cell phone left behind in a trash can at the train station and a new phone purchased in Siena. The Tuscan countryside was not unlike Provence, with vine-covered hillsides, orchards a-shimmer with the silver-green of olive trees, and walled medieval towns perched on crags; but the slim, tall cypress standing like sentries gave the hills a different profile and there were different types of wine grapes, and many of the vineyards rented rooms where people could stay and sample the local hospitality. Terzian didn't speak the language, and because Spanish was his first foreign language consistently pronounced words like "villa" and "panzanella" as if they were Spanish. But Stephanie had grown up in Italy and spoke the language not only like a native, but like a native Roman.

Florence was only a few hours away, and Terzian couldn't resist visiting one of the great living monuments to civilization. His parents, both university professors, had taken him to Europe several times as a child, but somehow never made it here.

Terzian and Stephanie spent a day wandering the center of town, on occasion taking shelter from one of the pelting rainstorms that shattered the day. At one point, with thunder booming overhead, they found themselves in the Basilica di Santa Croce.

"Holy Cross," Terzian said, translating. "That's your outfit."

"We have nothing to do with this church," Stephanie said. "We don't even have a collection box here."

"A pity," Terzian said as he looked at the soaked swarms of tourists packed in the aisles. "You'd clean up."

Thunder accompanied the camera strobes that flashed against the huge tomb of Galileo like a vast lighting storm. "Nice of them to forget about that Inquisition thing and bury him in a church," Terzian said.

"I expect they just wanted to keep an eye on him."

It was the power of capital, Terzian knew, that had built this church, that had paid for the stained glass and the Giotto frescoes and the tombs and cenotaphs to the great names of Florence: Dante, Michelangelo, Bruni, Alberti, Marconi, Fermi, Rossini, and of course Machiavelli. This structure, with its vaults and chapels and sarcophagi and chanting Franciscans, had been raised by successful bankers, people to whom money was a real, tangible thing, and who had paid for the centuries of labor to build the basilica with caskets of solid, weighty coined silver.

"So what do you think he would make of this?" Terzian asked, nodding at the resting place of Machiavelli, now buried in the city from which he'd been exiled in his lifetime.

Stephanie scowled at the unusually plain sarcophagus with its Latin inscription. "No praise can be high enough," she translated, then turned to him as tourist cameras flashed. "Sounds overrated."

"He was a republican, you know," Terzian said. "You don't get that from just *The Prince*. He wanted Florence to be a republic, defended by citizen soldiers. But when it fell into the hands of a despot, he needed work, and he wrote the manual for despotism. But he looked at despotism a little too clearly, and he didn't get the job." Terzian turned to Stephanie. "He was the founder of modern political theory, and that's what I do. And he based his ideas on the belief that all human beings, at all times, have had the same passions." He turned his eyes deliberately to Stephanie's shoulder bag. "That may be about to end, right? You're going to turn people into plants. That should change the passions if anything would."

"Not *plants*," Stephanie hissed, and glanced left and right at the crowds. "And not *here*." She began to move down the aisle, in the direction of Michelangelo's ornate tomb, with its draped figures who appeared not in mourning, but as if they were trying to puzzle out a difficult engineering problem.

"What happens in your scheme," Terzian said, following, "is that the market in food crashes. But that's not the *real* problem. The real problem is what happens to the market in *labor*."

Tourist cameras flashed. Stephanie turned her head away from the array of Kodaks. She passed out of the basilica and to the portico. The cloudburst had come to an end, but rainwater still drizzled off the structure. They stepped out of the droplets and down the stairs into the piazza.

The piazza was walled on all sides by old palaces, most of which now held restaurants or shops on the ground floor. To the left, one long palazzo was covered with canvas and scaffolding. The sound of pneumatic hammers banged out over the piazza. Terzian waved a hand in the direction of the clatter.

"Just imagine that food is nearly free," he said. "Suppose you and your children can get most of your food from standing in the sunshine. My next question is, *Why in hell would you take a filthy job like standing on a scaffolding and sandblasting some old building?*"

He stuck his hands in his pockets and began walking at Stephanie's side along the piazza. "Down at the bottom of the labor market, there are a lot of people whose labor goes almost entirely for the necessities. Millions of them cross borders illegally in order to send enough money back home to support their children."

"You think I don't know that?"

"The only reason that there's a market in illegal immigrants is that *there are jobs that well-off people won't do.* Dig ditches. Lay roads. Clean sewers. Restore old buildings. Build *new* buildings. The well-off might serve in the military or police, because there's a certain status involved and an attractive uniform, but we won't guard prisons no matter how pretty the uniform is. That's strictly a job for the laboring classes, and if the laboring classes are too well-off to labor, who guards the prisons?"

She rounded on him, her lips set in an angry line. "So I'm supposed to be afraid of people having more choice in where they work?"

"No," Terzian said, "you should be afraid of people having *no choice at all.* What happens when markets collapse is *intervention*—and that's state intervention, if the market's critical enough, and you can bet the labor market's critical. And because the state depends on ditch-diggers and prison guards and janitors and road-builders for its very being, then if these classes of people are no longer available, and the very survival of civil society depends on their existence, in the end the state will just *take* them.

"You think our friends in Transnistria will have any qualms about rounding up people at gunpoint and forcing them to do labor? The powerful are going to want their palaces kept nice and shiny. The liberal democracies will try volunteerism or lotteries or whatever, but you can bet that we're going to want our sewers to work, and somebody to carry our grandparents' bedpans, and the trucks to the supermarkets to run on time. And what *I'm* afraid of is that when things get desperate, we're not going to be any nicer about getting our way than those Sovietists of yours. We're going to make sure that the lower orders do their jobs, even if we have to kill half of them to convince the other half that we mean business. And the technical term for that is *slavery.* And if someone of African descent isn't sensitive to *that* potential problem, then I am very surprised."

The fury in Stephanie's eyes was visible even through her shades, and he could see the pulse pounding in her throat. Then she said, "I'll save the *people,* that's what I'm good at. You save the rest of the world, *if* you can." She began to turn away, then swung back to him. "And by the way," she added, "fuck you!" turned, and marched away.

"Slavery or anarchy, Stephanie!" Terzian called, taking a step after. "That's the choice you're forcing on people!"

He really felt he had the rhetorical momentum now, and he wanted to enlarge the point by saying that he knew some people thought anarchy was a good thing, but no anarchist he'd ever met had ever even *seen* a real anarchy, or been in one, whereas Stephanie had—drop your anarchist out of a helicopter into the eastern Congo, say, with all his theories and with whatever he could carry on his back, and see how well he prospered…

But Terzian never got to say any of these things, because Stephanie was gone, receding into the vanishing point of a busy street, the shoulder bag swinging back and forth across her butt like a pendulum powered by the force of her convictions.

Terzian thought that perhaps he'd never see her again, that he'd finally provoked her into abandoning him and continuing on her quest alone, but when he stepped off the bus in Montespèrtoli that night, he saw her across the street, shouting into her cell phone.

The next day, as with frozen civility they drank their morning coffee, she said she was going to Rome the next day. "They might be looking for me there," she said, "because my parents live there. But I won't go near the family, I'll meet Odile at the airport and give her the papiloma."

*Odile?* Terzian thought. "I should go along," he said.

"What are you going to do?" she said. "Carry that gun into an *airport?*"

"I don't have to take the gun. I'll leave it in the hotel room in Rome."

She considered. "Very well."

Again, that night, Terzian found the tumbled castle in Provence haunting his thoughts, that ruined relic of a bygone order, and once more considered stealing the papiloma and running. And again, he didn't.

They didn't get any farther than Florence, because Stephanie's cell phone rang as they waited in the train station. Odile was in Venice. *"Venezia?"* Stephanie shrieked in anger. She clenched her fists. There had been a cache of weapons found at the Fiumicino airport in Rome, and all planes had been diverted, Odile's to Marco Polo outside Venice. Frenzied booking agents had somehow found rooms for her despite the height of the tourist season.

Fiumicino hadn't been reopened, and Odile didn't know how she was going to get to Rome. "Don't try!" Stephanie shouted. "I'll come to *you.*"

This meant changing their tickets to Rome for tickets to Venice. Despite

Stephanie's excellent Italian the ticket seller clearly wished the crazy tourists would make up their mind which monuments of civilization they really wanted to see.

Strange—Terzian had actually *planned* to go to Venice in five days or so. He was scheduled to deliver a paper at the Conference of Classical and Modern Thought.

Maybe, if this whole thing was over by then, he'd read the paper after all. It wasn't a prospect he coveted: he would just be developing another footnote to a footnote.

The hills of Tuscany soon began to pour across the landscape like a green flood. The train slowed at one point—there was work going on on the tracks, men with bronze arms and hard hats—and Terzian wondered how, in the Plant People Future, in the land of Cockaigne, the tracks would ever get fixed, particularly in this heat. He supposed there were people who were meant by nature to fix tracks, who would repair tracks as an avocation or out of boredom regardless of whether they got paid for their time or not, but he suspected there wouldn't be many of them.

You could build machines, he supposed, robots or something. But they had their own problems, they'd cause pollution and absorb resources and on top of everything they'd break down and have to be repaired. And who would do *that?*

If you can't employ the carrot, Terzian thought, if you can't reward people for doing necessary labor, then you have to use the stick. You march people out of the cities at gunpoint, like Pol Pot, because there's work that needs to be done.

He tapped his wedding ring on the arm of his chair and wondered what jobs would still have value. Education, he supposed; he'd made a good choice there. Some sorts of administration were necessary. There were people who were natural artists or bureaucrats or salesmen and who would do that job whether they were paid or not.

A woman came by with a cart and sold Terzian some coffee and a nutty snack product that he wasn't quite able to identify. And then he thought, *labor.*

"Labor," he said. In a world in which all basic commodities were provided, the thing that had most value was actual labor. Not the stuff that labor bought, but the work itself.

"Okay," he said, "it's labor that's rare and valuable, because people don't *have* to do it anymore. The currency has to be based on some kind of labor exchange—you purchase $x$ hours with $y$ dollars. Labor is the thing you use to pay taxes."

Stephanie gave Terzian a suspicious look. "What's the difference between that and slavery?"

"Have you been reading Nozick?" Terzian scolded. "The difference is the same as the difference between *paying taxes* and *being a slave*. All the time you don't spend paying your taxes is your own." He barked a laugh. "I'm resurrecting Labor Value Theory!" he said. "Adam Smith and Karl Marx are dancing a jig on their tombstones! In Plant People Land the value is the *labor itself!* The *calories!*" He laughed again, and almost spilled coffee down his chest.

"You budget the whole thing in calories! The government promises to pay you a dollar's worth of calories in exchange for their currency! In order to keep the roads and the sewer lines going, a citizen owes the government a certain number of calories per year—he can either pay in person or hire someone else to do the job. And jobs can be budgeted in calories-per-hour, so that if you do hard physical labor, you owe fewer hours than someone with a desk job—that should keep the young, fit, impatient people doing the nasty jobs, so that they have more free time for their other pursuits." He chortled. "Oh, the intellectuals are going to just hate this! They're used to valuing their brain power over manual labor—I'm going to reverse their whole scale of values!"

Stephanie made a pffing sound. "The people I care about have no money to pay taxes at all."

"They have bodies. They can still be enslaved." Terzian got out his laptop. "Let me put my ideas together."

Terzian's frenetic two-fingered typing went on for the rest of the journey, all the way across the causeway that led into Venice. Stephanie gazed out the window at the lagoon soaring by, the soaring water birds and the dirt and stink of industry. She kept the Nike bag in her lap until the train pulled into the Stazione Ferrovie dello Stato Santa Lucia at the end of its long journey.

Odile's hotel was in Cannaregio, which according to the map purchased in the station gift shop was the district of the city nearest the station and away from most of the tourist sites. A brisk wind almost tore the map from their fingers as they left the station, and their vaporetto bucked a steep chop on the greygreen Grand Canal as it took them to the Ca' d'Oro, the fanciful white High Gothic palazzo that loomed like a frantic wedding cake above a swarm of bobbing gondolas and motorboats.

Stephanie puffed cigarettes at first with ferocity, then with satisfaction. Once they got away from the Grand Canal and into Cannaregio itself they quickly became lost. The twisted medieval streets were broken on occasion by still, silent canals, but the canals didn't seem to lead anywhere in particular. Cooking smells demonstrated that it was dinnertime, and there were few people about, and no tourists. Terzian's stomach rumbled. Sometimes the streets deteriorated into mere passages. Stephanie and Terzian were in such a passage, holding their map open against the wind and shouting directions at each other when someone slugged Terzian from behind.

He went down on one knee with his head ringing and the taste of blood in his mouth, and then two people rather unexpectedly picked him up again, only to slam him against the passage wall. Through some miracle he managed not to hit his head on the brickwork and knock himself out. He could smell garlic on the breath of one of the attackers. Air went out of him as he felt an elbow to his ribs.

It was the scream from Stephanie that fortified his attention. There was violent motion in front of him, and he saw the Nike swoosh and remembered that he was dealing with killers and that he had a gun.

In an instant Terzian had his rage back. He felt his lungs fill with the fury that spread through his body like a river of scalding blood. He planted his feet and twisted abruptly to his left, letting the strength come up his legs from the earth itself, and the man attached to his right arm gave a grunt of surprise and swung counterclockwise. Terzian twisted the other way, which budged the other man only a little, but which freed his right arm to claw into his right pants pocket.

And from this point on it was just the movement that he rehearsed. Draw, thumb the safety, pull the trigger hard. He shot the man on his right and hit him in the groin. For a brief second Terzian saw his pinched face, the face that reflected such pain that it folded in on itself, and he remembered Adrian falling in the Place Dauphine with just that look. Then he stuck the pistol in the ribs of the man on his left and fired twice. The arms that grappled him relaxed and fell away.

There were two more men grappling with Stephanie. That made four altogether, and Terzian reasoned dully that after the first three fucked up in Paris, the home office had sent a supervisor. One was trying to tug the Nike bag away, and Terzian lunged toward him and fired at a range of two meters, too close to miss, and the man dropped to the ground with a whuff of pain.

The last man had ahold of Stephanie and swung her around, keeping her between himself and the pistol. Terzian could see the knife in his hand and recognized it as one he'd seen before. Her dark glasses were cockeyed on her face and Terzian caught a flash of her angry green eyes. He pointed the pistol at the knife man's face. He didn't dare shoot.

"*Police!*" he shrieked into the wind. "*Policia!*" He used the Spanish word. Bloody spittle spattered the cobblestones as he screamed.

In the Trashcanian's eyes he saw fear, bafflement, rage.

"*Polizia!*" He got the pronunciation right this time. He saw the rage in Stephanie's eyes, the fury that mirrored his own, and he saw her struggle against the man who held her.

"No!" he called. Too late. The knife man had too many decisions to make all at once, and Terzian figured he wasn't very bright to begin with. *Kill the hostages* was probably something he'd been taught on his first day at Goon School.

As Stephanie fell, Terzian fired, and kept firing as the man ran away. The killer broke out of the passageway into a little square, and then just fell down.

The slide of the automatic locked back as Terzian ran out of ammunition, and then he staggered forward to where Stephanie was bleeding to death on the cobbles.

Her throat had been cut and she couldn't speak. She gripped his arm as if she could drive her urgent message through the skin, with her nails. In her eyes he saw frustrated rage, the rage he knew well, until at length he saw there nothing at all, a nothing he knew better than any other thing in the world.

He shouldered the Nike bag and staggered out of the passageway into the tiny Venetian square with its covered well. He took a street at random, and there was Odile's hotel. Of course: the Trashcanians had been staking it out.

It wasn't much of a hotel, and the scent of spice and garlic in the lobby suggested the desk clerk was eating his dinner. Terzian went up the stair to Odile's room and knocked on the door. When she opened—she was a plump girl with big hips and a suntan—he tossed the Nike bag on the bed.

"You need to get back to Mogadishu right away," he said. "Stephanie just died for that."

Her eyes widened. Terzian stepped to the wash basin to clean the blood off as best he could. It was all he could do not to shriek with grief and anger.

"You take care of the starving," he said finally, "and I'll save the rest of the world."

Michelle rose from the sea near Torbiong's boat, having done thirty-six-hundred calories' worth of research and caught a honeycomb grouper into the bargain. She traded the fish for the supplies he brought. "Any more blueberries?" she asked.

"Not this time." He peered down at her, narrowing his eyes against the bright shimmer of sun on the water. "That young man of yours is being quite a nuisance. He's keeping the turtles awake and scaring the fish."

The mermaid tucked away her wings and arranged herself in her rope sling. "Why don't you throw him off the island?"

"My authority doesn't run that far." He scratched his jaw. "He's interviewing people. Adding up all the places you've been seen. He'll find you pretty soon, I think."

"Not if I don't want to be found. He can yell all he likes, but I don't have to answer."

"Well, maybe." Torbiong shook his head. "Thanks for the fish."

Michelle did some preliminary work with her new samples and then abandoned them for anything new that her search spiders had discovered. She had a feeling she was on the verge of something colossal.

She carried her deck to her overhanging limb and let her legs dangle over the water while she looked through the new data. While paging through the new information, she ate something called a Raspberry Dynamo Bar that Torbiong had thrown in with her supplies. The old man must have included it as a joke: it was over-sweet and sticky with marshmallow and strangely flavored. She chucked it in the water and hoped it wouldn't poison any fish.

Stephanie Pais had been killed in what the news reports called a "street fight" among a group of foreign visitors. Since the authorities couldn't connect the foreigners to Pais, they had to assume she was an innocent bystander caught up in the violence. The papers didn't mention Terzian at all.

Michelle looked through pages of follow-up. The gun that had shot the four men had never been found, though nearby canals were dragged. Two of the foreigners had survived the fight, though one died eight weeks later from complications of an operation. The survivor maintained his innocence and claimed that a complete stranger had opened fire on him and his friends, but the judges hadn't believed him and sent him to prison. He lived a great many years and died in the Lightspeed War, along with most people caught in prisons during that deadly time.

One of the four men was Belorussian. Another Ukrainian. Another two Moldovan. All had served in the Soviet military in the past, in the Fourteenth Army in Transnistria. It frustrated Michelle that she couldn't shout back in time to tell the Italians to connect these four to the murder of another ex-Soviet, seven weeks earlier, in Paris.

What the hell had Pais and Terzian been up to? Why were all these people with Transnistrian connections killing each other, and Pais?

Maybe it was Pais they'd been after all along. Her records at Santa Croce were missing, which was odd because other personnel records from the time had survived. Perhaps someone was arranging that certain things not be known.

She tried a search on Santa Croce itself, and slogged through descriptions and mentions of a whole lot of Italian churches, including the famous one in Florence where Terzian and Pais had been seen at Machiavelli's tomb. She refined the search to the Santa Croce relief organization, and found immediately the fact that let it all fall into place.

Santa Croce had maintained a refugee camp in Moldova during the civil war following the establishment of Transnistria. Michelle was willing to bet that Stephanie Pais had served in that camp. She wondered if any of the other players had been residents there.

She looked at the list of other camps that Santa Croce had maintained in that period, which seemed to have been a busy one for them. One name struck her as familiar, and she had to think for a moment before she remembered why she didn't know it. It was at a Santa Croce camp in the Sidamo province of Ethiopia where the Green Leopard Plague had first broken out, the first transgenetic epidemic.

It had been the first real attempt to modify the human body at the cellular level, to help marginal populations synthesize their own food, and it had been primitive compared to the more successful mods that came later. The ideal design for the efficient use of chlorophyll was a leaf, not the Homo sapiens—the designer would have been better advised to create a plague that made its victims leafy, and later designers, aiming for the same effect, did exactly that. And Green Leopard's designer had forgotten that the epidermis already contains a solar-activated enzyme: melanin. The result on the African subjects was green skin mottled with dark splotches, like the black spots on an implausibly verdant leopard.

The Green Leopard Plague broke out in the Sidamo camp, then at other camps in the Horn of Africa. Then it leaped clean across the continent to Mozambique, where it first appeared at an Oxfam camp in the flood zone, then spread rapidly across the continent, then leaped across oceans. It had been a generation before anyone found a way to disable it, and by then other transgenetic modifiers had been released into the population, and there was no going back.

The world had entered Terzian's future, the one he had proclaimed at the Conference of Classical and Modern Thought.

What, Michelle thought excitedly, if Terzian had known about Green Leopard ahead of time? His Cornucopia Theory had seemed prescient precisely because Green Leopard appeared just a few weeks after he'd delivered his paper. But if those Eastern Bloc thugs had been involved somehow in the plague's transmission, or were attempting to prevent Pais and Terzian from sneaking the modified virus to the camps....

*Yes!* Michelle thought exultantly. That had to be it. No one had ever worked out where Green Leopard originated, but there had always been suspicion directed toward several semi-covert labs in the former Soviet empire. This was *it*. The only question was how Terzian, that American in Paris, had got involved....

It had to be Stephanie, she thought. Stephanie, who Terzian had loved and who had loved him, and who had involved him in the desperate attempt to aid refugee populations.

For a moment Michelle bathed in the beauty of the idea. Stephanie, dedicated and in love, had been murdered for her beliefs—realdeath!—and Terzian, broken-hearted, had carried on and brought the future—Michelle's present—into being. A *wonderful* story. And no one had known it till *now*, no one had understood Stephanie's sacrifice, or Terzian's grief... not until the lonely mermaid, working in isolation on her rock, had puzzled it out.

"Hello, Michelle," Darton said.

Michelle gave a cry of frustration and glared in fury down at her lover. He was in a yellow plastic kayak—kayaking was popular here, particularly in the Rock Islands—and Darton had slipped his electric-powered boat along the margin of the island, moving in near-silence. He looked grimly up at her from below the pitcher plant that dangled below the overhang.

They had rebuilt him, of course, after his death. All the data was available in backup, in Delhi where he'd been taken apart, recorded, and rebuilt as an ape. He was back in a conventional male body, with the broad shoulders and white smile and short hairy bandy legs she remembered.

Michelle knew he hadn't made any backups during their time in Belau. He had his memories up to the point where he'd lain down on the nanobed in Delhi. That had been the moment when his love of Michelle had been burning its hottest, when he had just made the commitment to live with Michelle as an ape in the Rock Islands.

That burning love had been consuming him in the weeks since his resurrection, and Michelle was glad of it, had been rejoicing in every desperate, unanswered message that Darton sent sizzling through the ether.

"Damn it," Michelle said, "I'm working."

<Talk to me> Darton's fingers formed. Michelle's fingers made a ruder reply.

"I don't understand," Darton said. "We were in love. We were going to be together."

"I'm not talking to you," Michelle said. She tried to concentrate on her video display.

"We were still together when the accident happened," Darton said. "I don't understand why we can't be together now."

"I'm not listening, either," said Michelle.

*"I'm not leaving, Michelle!"* Darton screamed. *"I'm not leaving till you*

*talk to me!"*

White cockatoos shrieked in answer. Michelle quietly picked up her deck, rose to her feet, and headed inland. The voice that followed her was amplified, and she realized Darton had brought his bullhorn.

*"You can't get away, Michelle! You've got to tell me what happened!"*

*I'll tell you about Lisa Lee,* she thought, *so you can send her desperate messages, too.*

Michelle had been deliriously happy for her first month in Belau, living in arboreal nests with Darton and spending the warm days describing their island's unique biology. It was their first vacation, in Prague, that had torn Michelle's happiness apart. It was there that they'd met Lisa Lee Baxter, the American tourist who thought apes were cute, and who wondered what these shaggy kids were doing so far from an arboreal habitat.

It wasn't long before Michelle realized that Lisa Lee was at least two hundred years old, and that behind her diamond-blue eyes was the withered, mummified soul that had drifted into Prague from some waterless desert of the spirit, a soul that required for its continued existence the blood and vitality of the young. Despite her age and presumed experience Lisa Lee's ploys seemed to Michelle to be so *obvious,* so *blatant.* Darton fell for them all.

It was only because Lisa Lee had finally tired of him that Darton returned to Belau, chastened and solemn and desperate to be in love with Michelle again. But by then it was Michelle who was tired. And who had access to Darton's medical records from the downloads in Delhi.

*"You can't get away, Michelle!"*

Well, maybe not. Michelle paused with one hand on the banyan's trunk. She closed her deck's display and stashed it in a mesh bag with some of her other stuff, then walked again out on the overhanging limb.

"I'm not going to talk to you like this," she said. "And you can't get onto the island from that side, the overhang's too acute."

"Fine," Darton said. The shouting had made him hoarse. "Come down here, then."

She rocked forward and dived off the limb. The saltwater world exploded in her senses. She extended her wings and fluttered close to Darton's kayak, rose, and shook seawater from her eyes.

"There's a tunnel," she said. "It starts at about two meters and exits into the lake. You can swim it easily if you hold your breath."

"All right," he said. "Where is it?"

"Give me your anchor."

She took his anchor, floated to the bottom, and set it where it wouldn't damage the live coral.

She remembered the needle she'd taken to Jellyfish Lake, the needle she'd loaded with the mango extract to which Darton was violently allergic. Once in the midst of the jellyfish swarm, it had been easy to jab the needle into Darton's calf, then let it drop to the anoxic depths of the lake.

He probably thought she'd given him a playful pinch.

Michelle had exulted in Darton's death, the pallor, the labored breathing, the desperate pleading in the eyes.

It wasn't murder, after all, not really, just a fourth-degree felony. They'd build a new Darton in a matter of days. What was the value of a human life, when it could be infinitely duplicated, and cheaply? As far as Michelle was concerned, Darton had amusement value only.

The rebuilt Darton still loved her, and Michelle enjoyed that as well, enjoyed the fact she caused him anguish, that he would pay for ages for his betrayal of her love.

Linda Lee Baxter could take a few lessons from the mermaid, Michelle thought.

Michelle surfaced near the tunnel and raised a hand with the fingers set at <follow me>. Darton rolled off the kayak, still in his clothes, and splashed clumsily toward her.

"Are you sure about this?" he asked.

"Oh yes," Michelle replied. "You go first, I'll follow and pull you out if you get in trouble."

He loved her, of course. That was why he panted a few times for breath, filled his lungs, and dove.

Michelle had not, of course, bothered to mention the tunnel was fifteen meters long, quite far to go on a single breath. She followed him, very interested in how this would turn out, and when Darton got into trouble in one of the narrow places and tried to back out, she grabbed his shoes and held him right where he was.

He fought hard but none of his kicks struck her. She would remember the look in his wide eyes for a long time, the thunderstruck disbelief in the instant before his breath exploded from his lungs and he died.

She wished she could speak again the parting words she'd whispered into Darton's ear when he lay dying on the ridge above Jellyfish Lake. *"I've just killed you. And I'm going to do it again."*

But even if she could have spoken the words underwater, they would have been untrue. Michelle supposed this was the last time she could kill him. Twice was dangerous, but a third time would be too clear a pattern. She could end up in jail for a while, though of course you only did severe prison time for realdeath.

She supposed she would have to discover his body at some point, but if she cast the kayak adrift it wouldn't have to be for a while. And then she'd be thunderstruck and grief-stricken that he'd thrown away his life on this desperate attempt to pursue her after she'd turned her back on him and gone inland, away from the sound of his voice.

Michelle looked forward to playing that part.

She pulled up the kayak's anchor and let it coast away on the six-knot tide, then folded away her wings and returned to her nest in the banyan tree. She let the breeze dry her skin and got her deck from its bag and contemplated the data about Terzian and Stephanie Pais and the outbreak of the Green Leopard Plague.

Stephanie had died for what she believed in, murdered by the agents of an obscure, murderous regime. It had been Terzian who had shot those four men in her defense, that was clear to her now. And Terzian, who lived a long time and then died in the Lightspeed War along with a few billion other people, had loved Stephanie and kept her secret till his death, a secret shared with the others who loved Stephanie and spread the plague among the refugee populations of the world.

It was realdeath that people suffered then, the death that couldn't be corrected. Michelle knew that she understood that kind of death only as an intellectual abstract, not as something she would ever have to face or live with. To lose someone *permanently...* That was something she couldn't grasp. Even the ancients, who faced realdeath every day, hadn't been able to accept it, that's why they'd invented the myth of Heaven.

Michelle thought about Stephanie's death, the death that must have broken Terzian's heart, and she contemplated the secret Terzian had kept all those years, and she decided that she was not inclined to reveal it.

Oh, she'd give Davout the facts, that was what he paid her for. She'd tell him what she could find out about Stephanie and the Transnistrians. But she wouldn't mention the camps that Santa Croce had built across the starvation-scarred world, she wouldn't point him at Sidamo and Green Leopard. If he drew those conclusions himself, then obviously the secret was destined to be revealed. But she suspected he wouldn't—he was too old to connect those dots, not when obscure ex-Soviet entities and relief camps in the Horn of Africa were so far out of his reference.

Michelle would respect Terzian's love, and Stephanie's secret. She had some secrets of her own, after all.

The lonely mermaid finished her work for the day and sat on her overhanging limb to gaze down at the sea, and she wondered how long it would be before Darton called her again, and how she would torture him when he did.

—*With thanks to Dr. Stephen C. Lee.*

## AFTERWORD: THE GREEN LEOPARD PLAGUE

*I was thinking of calling this one "The Pitcher Plant," but editor Gardner Dozois said he wanted a title that was more science fiction-y. I thought about calling it "Sex Kings of Mars," but decided to settle for "The Green Leopard Plague" instead.*

*Astute readers will note that this takes place in the same future as "Lethe," and features some of the same characters. I decided, some years after the first story, that in "Lethe" I had created a rich future that deserved further exploration, and decided to write another story in what I subsequently decided to call the College of Mystery sequence.*

*These same astute readers will have also noticed that this story, like "Lethe," involves death, the point being to contrast our own present-day attitudes toward death with those of a society in which death is little more than an inconvenience.*

*I was also interested in how a young person would fit into a world where practically everyone else had lived for many decades, if not centuries.*

*I had also got interested in the economics of a world of abundance. In a society where death is impossible, death becomes the rarest thing of all—that was the thought that had prompted "Lethe." But in a world of abundance, what else is rare, and how is it valued?*

*Labor seemed an obvious answer.*

*Terzian's fear that the collapse of the markets for food and labor would lead to state intervention amounting to slavery was an insight that I was very proud of. It was only after I'd written the story that I learned that my stunningly original idea had first been explicated by Fred Pohl in his 1965 story "The Anything Box."*

*Another crucial idea—that of the rise of the Trashcanistans—was borrowed from an article by Stephen Kotkin in a 2002 issue of The New Republic.*

*The descriptions of Michelle's environment were inspired by a diving trip to the island chain of Palau in 2001. The Rock Islands, Jellyfish Lake, and the other marine lakes are real locations, and my swim in the midst of a swarm of millions of jellyfish remains one of the highlights of the trip.*

*After I first drafted the story, I submitted it to the Rio Hondo* workshop, where Ted Chiang subjected it to a memorable critique. Employing "back-of-the-envelope" calculations (always the best kind), he demolished my original scientific justification for the Green Leopard Plague. Fortunately I was able to call on Dr. Stephen C. Lee, a genuine specialist in nanotechnology, to provide a far more plausible explanation.

The story was awarded the Nebula Award by the Science Fiction and Fantasy Writers of America in 2005. I was recovering from a ruptured appendix and was heavily medicated when the call came from the awards banquet, and at first I was totally confused: I had forgotten all about the story and its nomination.

I celebrated with some champagne, but it didn't agree with the painkillers I was taking, and I had a wretched time.

# THE TANG
# DYNASTY
# UNDERWATER
# PYRAMID

What we might call the Tang Dynasty Underwater Pyramid Situation began in the Staré Město on a windy spring day. We were clumped beneath the statue of Jan Hus and in the midst of our medley of South American Tunes Made Famous by North American Pop Singers. The segue from "Cielito Lindo" to "El Condor Pasa" required some complicated fingering, and when I glanced up from my *guitarra* I saw our contact standing in the crowd, smoking a cigarette and making a bad show of pretending he had nothing better to do but stand in Prague's Old Town and listen to a family of nine Aymara Indians deconstruct Simon and Garfunkel.

My uncle Iago had described the man who was planning to hire us, and this man matched the description: a youngish Taiwanese with a fashionable razor cut, stylish shades, a Burberry worn over a cashmere suit made by Pakistani tailors in Hong Kong, a silk tie, and glossy handmade Italian shoes.

He just didn't look like a folk music fan to me.

After the medley was over, I called for a break, and my cousin Rosalinda passed the derby among the old hippies hanging around the statue while my other cousin, Jorge, tried to interest the crowd in buying our CDs. I ambled up to our contact and bummed a smoke and a light.

"You're Ernesto?" he asked in Oxford-accented English.

"Ernesto, that's me," I said.

"Your uncle Iago suggested I contact you," he said. "You can call me Jesse."

His name wasn't Jesse any more than mine was really Ernesto, this being the moniker the priest gave me when the family finally got around to having me baptized. I'd been born on an artificial reed island drifting around Lake Titicaca, a place where opportunities for mainstream religious

167

ceremony were few.

My real name is Cari, just in case you wondered.

"Can we go somewhere a little more private?" Jesse asked.

"Yeah, sure. This way."

He ground out his cigarette beneath one of his wingtips and followed me into the Church of St. Nicholas while I wondered if there was any chance that we were really under surveillance, or whether Jesse was just being unreasonably paranoid.

Either way, I thought, it would affect my price.

The baroque glories of the church burst onto my retinas as I entered—marble statues and bravura frescos and improbable amounts of gold leaf. Strangely enough, the church belonged to the Hussites, who you don't normally associate with that sort of thing.

Booms and bleats echoed through the church. The organist was tuning for his concert later in the day, useful interference in the event anyone was actually pointing an audio pickup at us.

Jesse didn't spare a glance for the extravagant ornamentation that blazed all around him, just removed his shades as he glanced left and right to see if anyone was within listening distance.

"Did Iago tell you anything about me?" Jesse asked.

"Just that he'd worked for you before, and that you paid."

Iago and his branch of the family were in Sofia doing surveillance on an ex-Montenegrin secret policeman who was involved in selling Russian air-to-surface ATASM missiles from Transnistria through the Bosporus to the John the Baptist Liberation Army, Iraqi Mandaean separatists who operated out of Cyprus. Lord alone knew what the Mandaeans were going to do with the missiles, as they didn't have any aircraft to fire them *from*—or at least we can only hope they don't. Probably they were just middlemen for the party who really wanted the missiles.

I'd been holding my group ready to fly to Cyprus if needed, but otherwise the Iraqi Mandaeans were none of my concern. Reflecting on this, I wondered if the world had always been this complicated, or if this was some kind of twenty-first-century thing.

"We need you to do a retrieval," Jesse said.

"What are we retrieving?"

His mouth gave an impatient twitch. "You don't need to know that."

He was beginning to irritate me. "Is it bigger than a breadbox?" I asked. "I need to know if I'll need a crane or truck or…"

"A boat," Jesse said. "And diving gear."

The organist played a snatch of Bach—the D Minor, I thought, and too fast.

If you hang out in European churches, you hear the D Minor a lot. Over the years I had become a connoisseur in these matters.

"Diving gear," I said cautiously. "That's interesting."

"Three days ago," Jesse said, "the five-thousand-ton freighter *Goldfish Fairy* sank in a storm in the Pearl River Delta off Hong Kong. Our cargo was in the hold. After the Admiralty Court holds its investigation, salvage rights will go on offer. We need you to retrieve our cargo before salvage companies get to the scene."

I thought about this while organ pipes bleated above my head. "Five thousand tons," I said, "that's a little coaster, not a real ship at all. How do you know it didn't break up when it went down?"

"When the pumps stopped working, the *Goldfish Fairy* filled and sank. The crew got away to the boats and saw it sink on an even keel."

"Do you know where?"

"The captain got a satellite fix."

"How deep did it sink?"

"Sixty meters."

I let out a slow breath. A depth of sixty meters required technical diving skills I didn't possess.

"The Pearl River Delta is one of the busiest sea lanes in the world," I said. "How are we going to conduct an unauthorized salvage operation without being noticed?"

There was a moment's hesitation, and then Jesse said, "That's your department."

I contemplated this bleak picture for a moment, then said, "How big is your cargo again?"

"We were shipping several crates—mainly research equipment. But only one crate matters, and it's about two meters long by eighty centimeters wide. The captain said they were stored on top of the hold, so all you have to do is open the hold and raise the box."

That seemed to simplify matters. "Right," I said. "We'll take the job."

"For how much?"

I let the organist blat a few times while I considered, and then I named a sum. Jesse turned stern.

"That's a lot of money," he said.

"Firstly," I said, "I'm going to have to bribe some people to get hernias, and that's never fun. Then I've got to subcontract part of the job, and the ones I have in mind are notoriously difficult."

He gave me a look. "Why don't I hire the subcontractors myself, then?"

"You can try. But they won't know who needs to get hernias, and besides, they can't do the *other* things my group can do. We can give you *worldwide coverage*, man!"

He brooded a bit behind his eyelids, then nodded. "Very well," he said.

I knew that he would concede in the end. If he was moving important cargo in a little Chinese coaster instead of by Federal Express, then that meant he was moving it illegally—smuggling, to use the term that would be employed by the Admiralty Court were Jesse ever caught. He had to get his job done quickly and discreetly, and for speed and discretion he had to pay.

I told him which bank account to wire the money to, and he wrote it down with a gold-plated pen. I began to wonder if I had undercharged him.

We left the church and made our way back to the square, where Jan Hus stood bleakly amid a sea of iron-grey martyrs to his cause. The band had begun playing without me—our Latin-Flavored Beatle Medley. "You'll want to check this out," I told Jesse. "My brother Sancho does an *amaaazing* solo on 'Twist and Shout' with his *malta*—that's the medium-sized panpipe."

"Is pop tunes all you do?" Jesse asked, his expression petulant. "I thought you were an authentic folk band."

I must admit that Jesse's comment got under my skin. Just because he'd bought our services didn't mean we'd *sold out*.

Besides, "El Condor Pasa" *was* an authentic folk tune.

"We play what the public will pay for," I said. "And there are relatively few Latin folk fans in Prague, believe it or not." I took off my fedora and held it out to him. "But I didn't realize you were an *aficionado*. If it's authentic folk music you want, then it's what you'll get."

Jesse gave an amused little grin, reached into his Burberry, and produced a wad of notes that he dropped into my hat.

"*Gracias*," I said, and put the hat on my head. I didn't realize till later that he'd stuck me with Bulgarian currency.

I returned to my chair and took my *guitarra* in hand. Jesse hung around on the fringes of the crowd and talked on his cell phone. When the medley was over, I led the band into "Llaqui Runa," which is about as authentic folk music as you can get.

Jesse put away his cell phone, put on his shades, and sauntered away.

But that wasn't what put me in a bad mood.

What had me in bad temper was the fact that I'd have to deal with the water ballet guys.

Three beautifully manicured pairs of hands rose from the water, the fingers undulating in wavelike motions. The hands rose further, revealing arms, each pair arced to form an *O*. Blue and scarlet smoke billowed behind them. The owners of these arms then appeared above the wavetops and were revealed to be mermaids, scales glinting green and gold, each smiling with cupid's-bow lips.

The mermaids began to rotate as they rose, free of the water now, water streaming from their emerald hair, each supported by a pair of powerful male hands. As the figures continued to rise, the male hands were revealed to belong to three tanned, muscular Apollos with sun-bleached hair and brilliant white smiles.

The figures continued to rotate, and then the brilliant clouds behind billowed and parted as three more figures dived through the smoke, arrowing through the circles of the mermaids' arms to part the water with barely a splash.

The Apollos leaned mightily to one side, allowing the mermaids to slip from their embrace and fall into the water. Then the Apollos themselves poised their arms over their heads and leaned back to drop beneath the waves.

For a moment the water was empty save for the curls of red and blue smoke that licked the tops of the waves, and then all nine figures rose as one, inverted, arms moving in unison, after which they lay on their sides, linked themselves with legs and arms, and formed an unmistakable Leaping Dolphin.

The Leaping Dolphin was followed by Triton in His Chariot, the Anemone, the Tiger Shark, the Water Sprite, the Sea Serpent, and a Salute to the Beach Boys, which featured the California Girl, the Deuce Coupe, and climaxed with Good Vibrations. The finale featured more smoke, each of the mermaids rising from the water wearing a crown of sparklers while the six men held aloft billowing, colorful flares.

"Magnificent!" I applauded. "I've never seen anything like it! You've outdone yourselves!"

One of the Apollos swam to the edge of the pool and looked up at me, his brow furrowed with a modesty that was charming, boyish, and completely specious.

"You don't think the Deuce Coupe was a little murky?" he said.

"Not at all. I've never seen a Deuce Coupe in my life, and I recognized it at once!"

I was in California, while the rest of my band was on their way to Hong Kong, where they could expedite their visas to the mainland. I myself was traveling on a U.S. visa belonging to my cousin Pedrito, who was in Sofia and not using it, and who looked enough like me—at least to a U.S. Customs agent—for me to pass.

Laszlo deVign—of Laszlo deVign's Outrageous Water Ballet of Malibu—vaulted gracefully from the pool and reached for a towel, making sure as he did so that I had a chance to appreciate the definition of his lats and the extension of arm and body. "So, you have some kind of job for us?" he said.

"Recovery of a coffin-sized box from the hold of a sunken ship lying on an even keel in sixty meters of water."

He straightened, sucked in his tummy just a little to better define the floating ribs, and narrowed his blue eyes. "Sixty meters? What's that in feet?"

I ran an algorithm through my head. "Just under two hundred, I think."

"Oh." He shrugged. "That should be easy enough."

I explained how the whole operation had to be conducted on the q.t., with no one finding out.

He paused and looked thoughtful again.

"How do you plan to do that?"

I explained. Laszlo nodded. "Ingenious," he said.

"You've got to get over to Hong Kong right away," I said. "And bring your gear and cylinders of whatever exotic gasses you're going to need to stay at depth. The ship will give you air or Nitrox fills, but they're not going to have helium or whatever else you're going to need."

"Wait a minute," Laszlo said. He struck a pose of belligerence, and in so doing made certain I got a clear view of his profile. "We haven't talked about money."

"Here's what I'm offering," I said, and told him the terms.

He argued, but I held firm. I happened to know he'd blown his last gig in Vegas because of an argument with the stage manager over sound cues, and I knew he needed the cash.

"Plus," I pointed out, "they'll love you over there. They'll never have seen anything like what you do. You're going to hit popular taste smack between the eyes."

He looked firm. "There's one thing I'm going to insist on, though."

I sighed. We'd reached the moment I'd been dreading for the last two days.

"What's that?" I asked, knowing the answer..

He brandished a finger in the air, and his blue eyes glowed with an inner flame "I must," he said, "I absolutely *must* have *total artistic control!*"

Six days later we found ourselves in Shanghai, boarding the *Tang Dynasty*. It had taken that long for me to bribe two key members of the Acrobat Troupe of Xi'an into having hernias, thus leaving the Long Peace Lounge without an opening act for the Bloodthirsty Hopping Vampire Show. Fortunately I'd been in a position to contact the ship's entertainment director—who was underpaid, as was most of the ship's crew—and I was able to solve both his problems, the absence of an opening act and his lack of a decent salary. That he could have a genuine California water ballet, complete with Deuce Coupe, for a token sum was just a fraction of the good luck I bestowed upon him.

The *Tang Dynasty* was a themed cruise ship that did the Shanghai–Hong Kong–Macau route twice a week. The bulbous hull was more or less hull-like, though it was entwined with fiberglass dragons; but the superstructure looked like a series of palaces from the Forbidden City, each with the up-turned eaves common in China and with the ridgepoles ornamented with the "fish tail" standard in Tang Dynasty architecture—a protection against fire, I was told, as in the event of a blaze the tail was supposed to slap the water and drown the conflagration. The buildings were covered with orna-ment, slathered with gold and vermilion, crowned with phoenixes, twined with dragons, fronted with lions.

To say nothing of the audioanimatronic unicorns.

The interior carried on the theme. The staterooms, swathed with silks and embroidery, gave every impression of being rooms of state in a thousand-year-old palace. At any time of the day, passengers could dine at the Peaches of Heaven Buffet, have a reading from any one of four fortune-tellers (Tao-ist, Buddhist, Animist, and an alcoholic Gypsy imported from Romania), get a pedicure at the Empress Wu Pavilion of Beauty, light incense at the Temple of Tin Hau, Goddess of the Sea, or defy the odds in the Lucky Boy Casino (international waters and Macau SAR only).

The crew were dressed in Tang Dynasty costumes, with the captain garbed as the Emperor, in yellow robes covered with the five-toed dragons reserved for the Son of Heaven. Those of us who played in the lounges were not required to dress as Chinese entertainers, except of course unless they *were* Chinese entertainers.

The water ballet guys favored Speedos whether they were in the water or not, and spent a lot of time in the ship's gym, pumping iron and admiring themselves in the mirrors. The troupe's three women kept to themselves except when they went for a smoke on the fantail. I and my band, when performing, abandoned the contemporary look we'd adopted in Europe and did so in our traditional alpaca-wool ponchos.

Our first performance, as the *Tang Dynasty* sped south through the night toward Hong Kong, was received fairly well, especially considering that we performed in a language that no one else on the ship actually spoke, and that the audience had come to see the Hopping Vampires anyway.

All but one. Right in the front row, where I could scarcely miss him, was a man in a red poncho and a derby hat. He spent the entire concert grinning from ear to ear and bobbing his head in time with my nephew Esteban's electric bass. I could have understood this behavior if the head under the derby had been from the Andean highlands, but the face that grinned at me so blindingly was plump and bespectacled and Asian.

The man in the poncho gave us a standing ovation and generated enough enthusiasm in the audience to enable us to perform a second encore. Afterwards, he approached.

"Mucho fantastico!" he said, in what was probably supposed to be Spanish. "Muy bien!"

"Thanks," I said.

"I'm a huge fan," he said, dropping into something like English. "That was a terrific rendition of 'Urupampa,' by the way."

"I noticed you were singing along."

I soon understood that he was a Japanese businessman named Tobe Oharu, and that he belonged to a club devoted to Andean folk music. He and a group of fellow enthusiasts met weekly at a bar dressed in ponchos and derbies, listened to recordings, and studied Spanish from books.

He was so enthusiastic that I never had the heart to tell him that in our culture it's the women who wear the derby hats, whereas the men wear knit caps, or in my case a fedora.

"I had no idea you were performing here till I looked on the *Tang Dynasty* website the night before I left!" he said. "My friends are going to be so jealous!"

I tried this story on for size and decided that the odds were that it was too bizarre not to be true. Besides, I knew that Japanese hobbyists were very particular about wearing the right uniform, dressing up for instance as cowboys while listening to country and western.

"How did you happen to become a fan of Andean music?" I asked.

"Pure accident. I was on a business trip to Brussels, and I heard a group playing at the central station. I fell in love with the music at once! How could I help it, when it was Fernando Catacachi I heard on the *kena*."

Since Fernando happened to be my uncle, I agreed at once that he was the best, though personally I've always had a soft spot for the playing of another uncle of mine, Arturo.

Oharu's eyes glittered behind his spectacles. "And of course," he said, "Fidel Perugachi is supreme on the *secus*."

There I had to disagree. "His playing is full of showy moves and cheap, audience-pleasing tricks," I said. "Compared to my brother Sancho, Perugachi is an alpaca herder."

Oharu seemed a little taken aback. "Do you think so?"

"Absolutely. It's a pity we're playing only traditional music, and you can't hear Sancho on 'Twist and Shout.'"

Oharu considered this. "Perhaps this could be an encore tune tomorrow night?"

I had to credit Oharu for being a man of sound ideas. "Good plan," I said.

He offered to stand us all a round of drinks, but I begged off, pleading jet lag. I had to meet with Jesse and with the water ballet guys between the first and second show and get involved in some serious plotting.

I did stick around for the opening of the Bloodthirsty Hopping Vampire Show, however. The title was irresistible, after all. I'd tried to chat with the performers during the interlude, but with no success. Apparently the actors all spoke a Chinese dialect shared by no one else on the ship: they were just told the time they had to show up, and went on from there.

The massed vampires, with their slow, synchronous hops, achieved a genuine eerie quality, and the young hero and his girlfriend were clearly in jeopardy, and were rapidly depleting their considerable store of flashy kung fu moves when I had to drag myself away for the meeting with Laszlo.

Next morning, after breakfast, *Tang Dynasty*'s tourists swarmed from the ship for their encounters with the boutiques of Tsim Sha Tsui and the bustle of Stanley Market. From the other side of the ship, unobserved by the majority of the passengers, I and the entire Water Ballet of Malibu motored off on one of the ship's launches for our top-secret rendezvous with the *Goldfish Fairy*.

Laszlo had told everyone we were going, and he'd told everyone about the top-secret part too—except he'd made out it was a top-secret rehearsal of new water ballet moves, moves that he wished to conceal from the eyes of jealous rivals. His supercilious character and his obsession with artistic control helped to make this story more plausible, but even so I'm not sure we would have been given a boat if we hadn't greased a few palms among the crew.

It hadn't taken me long to work out that there was no way to conceal the fact of our presence in the Pearl River Delta, and secret water ballet rehearsals was the best cover story I could work out on short notice. It was bizarre, I knew, but it was bizarre enough to be true, and Laszlo and his crew were going to make it truer by conducting some genuine training.

The day was warm and humid, with shifting mists at dawn that had burned off by midmorning. We roared south out of Hong Kong's harbor, with bronzed Apollos striking poses on the gunwales like figureheads on the USS *Muscle Beach*. The posing wasn't entirely affected, as with all the diving gear stowed in the boat there was scant room for people; and the women of the troupe, with cigarettes in their sunscreen-slathered lips, draped themselves disdainfully on the bags that held the towels and the softer bits of scuba gear, and declined to speak to anyone.

About an hour after leaving port, our satellite locators told us we had reached our destination, and we sent our anchor down, shortly followed by Laszlo, one of the Apollos, and my own highly reluctant person.

I had decided that, as the person in charge, I should inspect the *Goldfish Fairy* myself. Though I had acquired diving skills for a task that involved retrieving documents from the cabin of a Tupolev aircraft that had made the mistake of crashing into the Black Sea, the Tupolev had been at a mere twenty-five meters, and the *Goldfish Fairy* was at sixty, well below the depth at which it was safe for sport divers such as myself to venture. But Laszlo and his crew—who by the way all had names like Deszmond and Szimon—had instructed me in the various skills required in staying alive at two hundred feet, and they would be on hand to look after me if I had a misadventure. I decided that the risk was worth taking.

I was carrying a ton of weight as I went over the side, not only the two cylinders on my back but another pair that would be clipped onto the anchor line at certain depths so that they could aid our decompression stops. Out of deference to me, I suspect, we were all breathing air, instead of the nitrogen-oxygen-helium mixture usually employed at depth—I had no experience with "Trimix," as it's known, and Laszlo had decided to save the exotic mixtures for when the water ballet guys actually had to stay down for a while and work. This would be a fast reconnaissance, it was thought. Fast down, and slowly but surely up again. There was no need to worry.

It was nevertheless one highly nervous Injun that flopped backward off the side of the boat into the Pearl River Delta and descended with the others into the murky water in search of Jesse's lost cargo.

In any event, I needn't have been so worried. From the forty-meter mark, I spent the entire dive in a state of complete hilarity.

I chortled. I laughed. I giggled. I found the fish in my vicinity a source of mirth and tried to point out the more amusing aspects of their anatomy to my fellow divers. Eventually I became so helpless with laughter that Laszlo, wearing an expression of even greater disgust than was normal for him, grabbed me by one of the shoulder straps of my buoyancy compensator, or B.C., and simply hauled me around like a package.

I had become prey to nitrogen narcosis, more colorfully known as "rapture of the deep."

When we got within sight of the muddy bottom, it was clear that the *Goldfish Fairy* was not to be seen. The captain appeared to be a little off on his calculations. So, still a good fifteen or so meters off the bottom, Laszlo checked his compass and we began searching the bottom, so many kicks in one direction followed by a ninety-degree turn and so many kicks in the next, the whole creating a kind of squarish, outwardly expanding spiral.

We found the *Goldfish Fairy* within moments, the bow section looming suddenly out of the murk like that of the *Titanic* in, well, the film *Titanic*. Bibbling with laughter, I tried to point out this similarity to Laszlo, who simply jerked me in the direction of the sunken ship and yanked me over the bows to begin his inspection of the vessel.

The bow section was a little crumpled, having struck first, but the rest of the little ship was more or less intact. The hatches were still secure. These would present very little trouble, but the fly in the ointment was the ship's mast, which had fallen over both hatches and which presented a nasty snarl of wire designed as if on purpose to entangle divers.

Laszlo grimly dragged me around the ship as he made his survey, and I spat my air supply from my mouth and tried to explain to a school of nearby fish the finer points of playing the *charango*, which is the little ten-string guitar with its body made from the shell of an armadillo. Eventually Laszlo had to look at me very severely and wrote a message on the underwater slate he kept clipped to his B.C.

*I think you should breathe now*, I read, and I flashed him the okay sign and returned the regulator to my mouth.

Our survey complete, Laszlo tied a buoy to the stern rail of the ship so that we could find it again, inflated the buoy from his air supply, and then led us in stages to the surface, breathing during our decompression stops from the cylinders we'd attached to the anchor line. As soon as we passed the forty-meter mark, I became cold sober. The transition was instantaneous, and I wanted to dive down a bit and see if I could trigger the narcosis once more—just as an experiment—but Laszlo wasn't about to permit this, so we continued to rise until we saw from below the remaining members of the water ballet practicing their moves. The women were wearing their mermaid tails, the better to convince any prying eyes that their reasons for being here had nothing to do with any hypothetical wrecks lying on the bottom sixty meters below, while the men swam in formation and flexed their muscles in synchrony.

"Just sit in the boat and *don't do anything*," Laszlo hissed to me after we were back in the launch and had got our gear off. "And don't *say* anything either," he added as he saw me about to speak, even though I had only opened my mouth to apologize.

A pair of Apollos went down next, breathing the gas mixtures that would enable them to stay longer at depth. They were to enter the hold through one of the crew passages that led down through the deck, and in order to find their way back, carried a reel with a long line on it, one end of which they attached to the launch and the rest of which, like Theseus in the Labyrinth, they payed out behind them as they swam.

"That approach won't work, I'm afraid," Laszlo explained to Jesse later. "When the ship hit the bottom, it threw everything in the hold forward against the bulkhead. We can't shift it from down there, so we'll have to open the hold and go in that way."

"It should be an easy enough job." We were sipping drinks in Jesse's palatial *Tang Dynasty* lodgings. He had, of course, acquired a suite, complete with a little Taoist shrine all in scarlet and gold. The Taoist god, with pendulous earlobes the size of fists, gazed at us with a benign smile from his niche as we plotted our retrieval.

"Clearing the wire is going to be the most dangerous part of it," Laszlo continued. "Afterward we'll have to use jacks to get the mast off the cargo hatch. Actually opening the hatch and retrieving the target will be the easiest part of all."

"Do you have all the gear you need?" Jesse asked.

"We'll have it flown to Macau to meet us," Laszlo said. "It's just a matter of your giving us your credit card number."

"There isn't a cheaper or quicker way to do this?" Jesse asked.

"Total. Artistic. Control," said Laszlo, which settled it as far as he was concerned.

As for myself, I planted some sandalwood incense in Jesse's shrine and set it alight along with a prayer for success and safety. It seemed only sensible to try to get the local *numina* on my side.

Happy with a drink in my hand and my feet upon a cushion, I was inclined to loiter in Jesse's sumptuous suite as long as I could. The passengers lived in a Forbidden City of pleasures and delights, but the crew and entertainers were stuck in little bare cabins below the water line, with no natural light, precious little ventilation, and with adjacent compressors, generators, and maneuvering thrusters screaming out in the small hours of the night.

Eventually, though, Jesse grew weary of our company, and I wandered out to the Peaches of Heaven Buffet for a snack. I got some dumplings and a bottle of beer, and who should I encounter but folk music fan Tobe Oharu, fresh from bargain-hunting at the Stanley Market, who plunked down opposite me with some ox-tendon soup and a bottle of beer.

"I got some pashmina shawls for my mother," he said with great enthusiasm, "and some silk scarves and ties for presents, and some more ties and some cashmere sweaters for myself."

"Very nice," I said.

"How did you spend your day?"

"I went out for a swim," I said, "but I didn't have a good time." I was still embarrassed that I had so completely flaked out at the forty-meter mark.

"That's a shame," Oharu said. "Was the beach too crowded?"

"The company *did* leave something to be desired," I said, after which he opened what proved to be a highly informed discussion of Andean music.

The audiences for our shows that night were modest, because most of the passengers were still enjoying the fleshpots of Hong Kong, but Oharu was there, right in front as before, wearing his poncho and derby and leading the audience in applause. We tried "Twist and Shout" as an encore number, and it was a hit, getting us a second encore, which meant that the band took Oharu to the bar for several rounds of thank-you drinks.

After the second show, I stuck around for the entire Hopping Vampire Show and had a splendid time watching Chinese demons chomp ingenues while combating a Taoist magician, who repelled them with glutinous rice, which enabled him to dodge attacks long enough to control the vampires with yellow-paper magic, in which a sutra or spell was written on yellow paper with vermilion ink, then stuck on the vampire's forehead like a spiritual Post-It note.

I made a note to remember this trick in case I ever encountered a Hopping Vampire myself.

After the second show, the *Tang Dynasty* got under way for its short run to Macau, and I knew that I wouldn't be able to sleep with the maneuvering thrusters shrieking and the anchor chain clattering inboard, so I took a turn on deck. The ship lay in a pool of mist, an even cloud lightened only slightly by the distant moon. The ship was picking up speed as it swung onto a new heading… and then suddenly the air was full of the scent of sandalwood. It was as if we were no longer in fog, but in the smoke produced by an entire sandalwood grove going up in flames.

I had scant time to marvel at this when I heard, magnified by the fog, the sound of a *toyo*, the largest of the Andean panpipes. The sound was loud and flamboyant and showy, featuring triple-stopping and double-tonguing slick as the pomade on Elvis' hair, and it was followed by a roar of applause.

"Damn it!" I shouted into the mist. "It's *Fidel Perugachi!*"

And then I ran for the nearest companionway.

While I was banging on Jesse's cabin door—and simultaneously trying to reach him on his cell phone—I was interrupted by my cousin Jorge and my brother Sancho, who were strolling down the corridor with their fan Oharu, who carried an umbrella drink in one hand, had an inebriated smile on his face, and was still wearing his poncho and derby.

"What's up, bro?" Jorge asked.

I replied in Aymara. "The Ayancas have turned up. Get rid of our friend here as soon as you can and get back here." When I spoke to Oharu, I switched back to English. "I'm trying to collect some gambling winnings."

"Ah," he nodded. "Good luck." He raised a pudgy fist. "You want me to bash him on the head?"

"Ah," I said, "I don't think that will be necessary."

Jesse opened the door and answered his cell phone simultaneously, blinking in the corridor light. "What's happening?"

"We need to talk," I said, and shoved my way into his room.

"The Ayancas are here!" I said while Jesse put on a dressing gown. "They're out in the fog, taunting us with flute music! We've got to do something!"

"Like what?" Jesse, still not exactly *compos*, groped on the lacquered side table for a cigarette.

"Get some machine guns! Mortars! Rocket launchers! Those guys are *evil!*"

Jesse lit his coffin nail and inhaled. "Perhaps you had better tell me who these Ayancas are, exactly."

It was difficult to condense the last thousand years of Andean history into a few minutes, but I did my best. It was only the last forty years that mattered anyway, because that's when my uncle Iago, returning from a trip to Europe (to buy a shipment of derby hats, believe it or not), saw his first James Bond movie and decided to form his own private intelligence service, and subsequently sent his young relatives (like me) to an elite Swiss prep school, while the rest formed into bands of street musicians who could wander the streets, not unobtrusive but at least unsuspected as they went about their secret work.

"Fidel Perugachi is a traitor and a copycat cheat!" I said. "He formed his own outfit and went into competition with us." I shook a fist. "Perugachi's nothing but llama spit!"

"So there are competing secret organizations of Andean street musicians?" Jesse said, slow apparently to wrap his mind around this concept.

"All the musicians belong to one group or the other," I said. "But the Ayancas lack our heritage. They're sort-of cousins to the Urinsaya moiety, but *we're* the Hanansaya moiety! *Our* ancestors were the Alasaa, and were buried in stone towers!"

Jesse blinked. "Good for them," he said. "But do you really think the Ayancas are here for the *Goldfish Fairy?*"

"Why else would they be in Hong Kong at this moment?" I demanded. "You were *right* in Prague when you worried that you were being shadowed.

Your opposition found out you were hiring us, so they countered by hiring the Ayancas. Why else would Fidel Perugachi be off playing his *toyo* in the fog and the clouds of sandalwood smoke?"

"Sandalwood?" he said, puzzled.

"Like your incense," I said, and pointed to his little shrine. "There were great gusts of sandalwood smoke coming over the rail along with Perugachi's music."

Jesse puffed on his cigarette while considering this, and then he slammed his hand on the arm of his chair. "*Thunderbolt Sow!*" he said.

I looked at him. "Beg pardon?"

"The Thunderbolt Sow is a holy figure in Buddhism. But *Thunderbolt Sow* is also the name of another cruise ship—Buddhist-themed, with a huge temple to Buddha on the stern, and several very well-regarded vegetarian restaurants. I bet that temple pours out a lot of sandalwood incense."

"At this time of night?"

"Do you know about the smoke towers? Those coils of incense that hang from the roofs of the temples? They burn twenty-four hours per day—some of them are big enough to burn for weeks."

"So Perugachi wasn't taunting us," I said. "He got a job like ours, on a cruise ship, and he was finishing his second show as the ship came into harbor." I thought about this and snarled. "Copycat! What did I tell you!"

"The question is," Jesse said, "what kind of menace is this, and what are we going to do?"

So we had an early-morning conference, with the water ballet guys and Jesse and the members of my band. Jesse connected with the Internet through the cellular modem on his notebook, and we found that *Thunderbolt Sow* belonged to the same cruise line as *Tang Dynasty*, and followed the same schedule, only a day later.

"We'll be anchoring in Macau in an hour or so," Laszlo said from beneath the avocado green beauty mask he hadn't bothered to wash off. "But we won't be able to get our salvage gear till midmorning at the earliest." He considered. "We'll spend tomorrow clearing off that tangle of cable, and maybe get a start on shifting the mast. The day following, *Tang Dynasty* discharges most of its passengers, takes on new ones, and heads for Shanghai to start the circuit all over again, so we won't be able to dive."

"But the Ayancas *can*," I pointed out. "They can take advantage of all the preparatory work you've done and lift the package while we're on our way to Shanghai and back."

"In that case," Jesse said, "don't do anything tomorrow. Just sit on the site to keep the Ayancas from pillaging it, and let *them* deal with the cable and the mast."

"We can spend the day rehearsing!" Laszlo said brightly, and the members of his troupe rolled their eyes.

I rubbed my chin and gave this some thought. Jesse's idea was good enough, but it lacked savor somehow. I felt it was insufficient in terms of dealing with the Ayancas. With Fidel Perugachi and his clique, I prefer instead to employ the more decisive element of diabolical vengeance.

"Instead," I suggested calmly, "why don't we mislead the Ayancas and drive them mad?"

Jesse seemed a little taken aback by this suggestion.

"How?" he asked.

"Let's give them the Goldfish Fairy, but give them a Goldfish Fairy that will drive them insane!"

"You mean sabotage the ship?" Jesse blinked. "So that they dive down there and get killed?"

"It's not that murdering the Ayancas wouldn't be satisfying," I said, "but practically speaking it would only motivate them toward reprisal. No, I mean simply give them a day of complete frustration, preferably one that will cause them in the end to realize that we were the cause of their difficulties."

I turned to Laszlo. "For example," I said, "this morning you attached a buoy to the Goldfish Fairy that would make it easier to find. Suppose that tomorrow you move that buoy about five hundred meters into deeper water. They'll waste at least one dive, possibly more, finding the ship again."

Laszlo grinned, his white teeth a frightening contrast to his green mask.

"You can only dive that deep a certain number of times each day," Laszlo explained to Jesse. "If we waste their dives, we use up their available bottom time."

"And," I added, "suppose you clear the wire only from the *front* half of the ship. You use the jacks to move the mast partly off the fore hatch. This will suggest to them that their target is in the forward hold, not in the after hold."

Lazslo's grin broadened. He looked like a bloodthirsty idol contemplating an upcoming sacrifice.

"They'll spend all day getting into the forward hold and find *nothing!*" he said. "Brilliant!" He nodded at me and gave his highest accolade.

"Ernesto," he said, "you're an *artist!*"

I spent the next day on the launch at the dive site, but I didn't so much as put a foot into the water. Instead I watched the horizon for signs of the Ayancas—and there was a boat that seemed to be lurking between us and Hong Kong—while the mermaids and the off-duty Apollos swam about the boat and practiced their moves. The mermaids were even more list-less, if possible, than the day before, and Laszlo felt obliged to offer them several sharp reproofs.

When Laszlo and a colleague made their second dive to the wreck, the others happily called a lunch break. Someone turned a radio to a station filled with bouncy Cantonese pop music. The Apollos sat in the stern slathering on sun oil, performing dynamic-tension exercises, and quaff-ing drinks into which, to aid in building muscle, vast arrays of steaks and potatoes seemed to have been scientifically crammed. Since no one else seemed inclined to pay attention to the ladies, I perched on the forward gunwales with the mermaids and helped them devour some excellent dim sum that we'd filched from the kitchens of the Grand Dynasty Restaurant that morning.

"So, how do you find the water ballet business?" I asked one of the mer-maids, a nymph from Colorado named Leila.

She took her time about lighting up a cigarette. "After Felicia and I came in sixth in the Olympics, we turned pro," she said. "I'm not sure what I expected, but it certainly wasn't this. *You* try cramming your lower half into one of those rubber fish tails for an hour a day."

"Yet here you are in the Pacific, on a beautiful sunny day, on a grand adventure and with the whole of Asia before you."

She flicked cigarette ash in the direction of the Apollos. "*That's* not what I'd call the whole of Asia."

"You're not fond of your co-workers?" I asked. For it was obvious that the mermaids kept very much to themselves, and I'd wondered why.

"Let's just say that they and I have a different idea of what constitutes an object of desire."

"Surely they can't *all* be gay," I said, misunderstanding.

"They aren't," Leila said. "But they are all narcissists. When I cuddle on a couch with a guy, I want him to be looking at *me*, not at his own reflec-tion in a mirror."

"I take your point. Perhaps you ought to confine yourself to homely men."

She looked at me. "*You're* homely," she pointed out.

"As homely as they come," I agreed, and shifted a bit closer to her on the gunwale.

These pleasantries continued until Laszlo finished his dive and demanded more rehearsals. Since he had Total Artistic Control, there was little I could say on the matter.

By the time the water ballet guys had finished all the dives safety proce-dures would allow, they'd prepared *Goldfish Fairy* to a fare-thee-well. The wire tangle had been shifted aft and, according to Laszlo, looked awful but would be relatively easy to clear when the time came. The mast had been partially shifted off the forward hatch, with the marks of the jacks plain to see, but the jacks themselves had been removed—if the Ayancas didn't bring their own, they were out of luck.

In a final bit of mischief, we shifted the buoy half a kilometer, then raced back to the *Tang Dynasty* just in time for our first show. Leila and I made plans to meet after the second show. Among other things, I wanted to hear her memories of the Olympics—I'd actually been to an Olympics once, but I'd been too busy dodging homicidal Gamsakhurdians to pay much attention to the games.

We'd barely got into the general wretchedness of the judging at synchronized swimming events when my cell played a bit of Mozart, and I answered to hear the strained tones of the ship's entertainment director.

"I thought you should know that there's a problem," he said, "a problem with your friend, the one in Emperor Class."

"What sort of problem?" I asked as my heart foundered. The tone of his voice was answer enough to my question.

"I'm afraid he's been killed."

"Where?"

"In his room."

"I'll meet you there."

I told Leila to go to Laszlo's room, and after she yelped in protest I told her that she had to contact everyone in the troupe and insist that no one was to be alone for the rest of the trip. Apparently my words burned with conviction, because her eyes grew wide and she left the room fast.

I sprinted to Jesse's room and called Jorge, who was our forensics guy, and Sancho, who was the strongest, just in case we needed to rearrange something.

The entertainment director stood in front of Jesse's door, literally wringing his hands.

"The cabin steward brought him a bottle of cognac he'd ordered," he said, "and found him, ah…" His voice trailed away, along with his sanguinary complexion.

"I'll have to call the police soon," he said faintly. "Not to mention the captain. It's lucky I was on watch, and not someone else."

I was so utterly glad that I'd bribed the man. There's nothing you can trust like corruption and dishonesty, and I made a mental note to slip the entertainment director a few extra hundred at the end of the voyage.

"Where's the steward?"

"I told him to stay in my office."

Sancho and Jorge arrived—Jorge with a box of medical gloves that he shared with us—and our confidant opened the cabin door with his pass-key.

"I won't go in again, if you don't mind," he said, swallowing hard, and stepped well away.

I put on gloves and pushed the door open. We entered and closed the door behind us.

"Well," Jorge said, "I can tell you right away that it's not a subtle Oriental poison."

Nor was it. Jesse lay on his back in the center of his suite, his throat laid open, his arms thrown out wide, and an expression of undiluted horror on his face. There was a huge splash of blood on the wall hangings and more under the body.

"Don't step in it," I said.

Jorge gingerly knelt by the body and examined the wound. "You're not going to like this," he said.

"I *already* don't like it," I said.

"You're going to like it less when I tell you that his throat appears to have been torn open by the fangs of an enormous beast."

There was a moment of silence.

"Maybe we should talk to the Hopping Vampires," Sancho said.

"Nobody *can* talk to them," I said. "They don't speak anybody's language."

"So they claim," Sancho said darkly.

"Never mind that now," I decided. "Search the room."

I found Jesse's wallet and card case, from which I learned that his name was actually Jiu Lu, and that he was the head of the microbiology department at Pacific Century Corporation.

Well. Who knew?

I also found his cell phone, with all the numbers he'd set on speed dial.

"Where's his notebook computer?" I asked.

We couldn't find it, or the briefcase he'd carried it in, or any notes that may have been in the briefcase.

"Let's hope he kept everything on that machine encrypted," Jorge said.

We left the wallet where we found it, but took the cell phone and one of Jesse's business cards. When we slipped out of the room, the entertainment director almost fainted with relief.

"Go ahead and call the cops," I told him.

"Macanese police." His eyes were hollow with tragedy. "You have no idea."

With Sancho guarding my back, I went on the fantail and called every number that Jesse had set on his speed dial. For the most part I got answering machines of one sort or another, and any actual human beings answered in an irate brand of Mandarin that discouraged communication from the start. I tried to inquire about "Jiu Lu," but I must not have got any of the tones right, because no one understood me.

In the morning I would call again, with the entertainment director as interpreter.

Most of the ship's passengers disembarked that morning, all those who weren't making the round trip to Shanghai and who preferred to remain in the languid, mildly debauched atmosphere of Macau, or who were heading by hydrofoil ferry back to the hustle of Hong Kong.

Whatever the Macanese police were doing by way of investigation, they weren't interfering with the wheels of commerce as represented by the cruise ship company.

"There goes Jesse's killer," Jorge said glumly as, from the rail, we watched the boats fill with cheerful, sunburned tourists.

Rosalinda, who gloomed at my other elbow, flicked her cigar ash into the breeze. "This afternoon the boats will come back with his replacement."

"Unless the killer is a Hopping Vampire who's sleeping in his coffin at this very moment," Sancho added from over my shoulder.

Most of those who came aboard that afternoon were people who had come to Macau on *Tang Dynasty*'s previous journey and were returning home by way of Shanghai. Only two actually made Macau their point of initial departure, and when we got ahold of a passenger manifest we made these the objects of particular scrutiny. One of them was an elderly man who trailed an oxygen bottle behind him on a cart. He went straight to the casino and began to bet heavily on roulette while lighting up one cigarette after another, which certainly explained the oxygen bottle. The other was his nurse.

Given that I hailed from a family of Aymara street musicians who also formed a private intelligence-gathering agency, at the moment operating in tandem with a water ballet company aboard a passenger ship disguised as a Tang Dynasty palace, I was not about to discount the less unlikely possibility that the old gambler and his nurse were a pair of assassins, so I slipped the entertainment director a few hundred Hong Kong dollars for the key to the old man's room and gave it a most professional going-over.

No throat-ripping gear was discovered, or anything the least bit suspicious.

Sancho and a couple of cousins also tossed the Hopping Vampires' cabin, and they found throat-ripping gear aplenty, but nothing that couldn't be explained with reference to their profession.

The entertainment director had got through to the people on Jesse's speed dial who he believed were Jesse's employers, but he was Cantonese and his Mandarin was very shaky, and he wasn't certain.

Because of the smallish crowd on board, and consequent low demand, we were scheduled for only one show that night, and I confess that it wasn't one of our best. The band as a whole lacked spirit. Our dejection transmitted itself to our music. Even the presence of our mascot Oharu in his poncho and derby hat failed to put heart into us.

After the show, Jorge and Sancho carried Oharu off to the Western Paradise Bar while I visited the entertainment director and again borrowed his passkey.

I found a yellow Post-It note and wrote a single word on it with a crimson pen.

And when Oharu stepped into his cabin with Jorge and Sancho behind him, I lunged from concealment and slapped the note on his forehead, just as the Taoist Sorcerer slapped his yellow paper magic on the foreheads of the Bloodthirsty Hopping Vampires in their stage show.

Oharu looked at me in dazed surprise.

"What's this about?" he asked.

"Read it," I said.

He peeled the note off his forehead and read the single scarlet word, "Confess."

"You should have got off at Macau," I told him. "You would have got clean away." I held up the bloodstained ninja gear I'd found in his room, the leather palm with the lethal steel hooks that could tear open a throat with a single slap.

At that point Oharu fought, of course, but his responses were disorganized by the alcohol that Sancho and Jorge had been pouring down his throat for the last hour, and of course Sancho was a burly slab of solid muscle and started the fight by socking Oharu in the kidney with a fist as hard as hickory. It wasn't very long before we had Oharu stretched out on his bed with his arms and legs duct-taped together and I was booting up Jesse's computer, which I had found in Oharu's desk drawer.

"Our next stop," I told Oharu, "is Shanghai, and Shanghai's in the People's Republic, not a Special Administrative Region like Hong Kong or Macau. If we turn you in, you get shot in the back of the head and your family gets a bill for the bullet."

Oharu spat out a blood clot and spoke through mashed lips. "I'll tell them all about *you*."

I shrugged. "So? Nothing *we're* doing is illegal. All we're doing is recovering an item on behalf of its legitimate owners."

"That's debatable. I could still make trouble for you."

I considered this. "If that's the case," I said, "maybe we ought not to keep you around long enough to say *anything* to the authorities."

He glowered. "You wouldn't dare kill me."

Again I shrugged. "*We* won't kill you. It'll be the *ocean* that'll do that."

Sancho slapped a hand over Oharu's mouth just as he inhaled to scream. In short order we taped his mouth shut, hoisted him up, and thrust him through his cabin porthole. There he dangled, with Sancho hanging onto one ankle and Jorge the other.

I took off his right shoe and sock.

"Clench your toes three times," I said, "when you want to talk. But make it quick, because you're overweight and Jorge is getting tired."

Jorge deliberately slackened his grip and let Oharu drop a few centimeters. There was a muffled yelp and a thrash of feet.

The toe-clenching came a few seconds later. We hauled Oharu in and dropped him onto his chair.

"So tell us," I began, "who hired you."

A Mr. Lau, Oharu said, of Shining Spectrum Industries in the Guangzhong Economic Region. He went on to explain that Dr. Jiu Lu, or Jesse as we'd known him, had worked for Shining Spectrum before jumping suddenly to Pacific Century. Magnum had suspected Jesse of taking Shining Spectrum assets with him, in the form of a project he was developing, and made an effort to get it back.

"This got Jiu scared," Oharu said, "so he tried to smuggle the project out of Guangzhou to Taiwan, but his ship went down in a storm. You know everything else."

"Not quite," I said. "What *is* the project?"

"I wasn't told that," Oharu said. "All I know is that it's biotechnology and that it's illegal, otherwise Jiu wouldn't have had to smuggle it out."

A warning hummed in my nerves. "Some kind of weapon?"

Oharu hesitated. "I don't think so," he said. "This operation doesn't have that kind of vibe."

I took that under advisement while I paged through the directory on Jesse's computer. Everything was in Chinese, and I didn't have a clue. I tried opening some of the files, but the computer demanded a password.

"Where did you send the data?" I asked.

"I never sent it anywhere," Oharu said. "I was just going to turn it over to Mr. Lau when I got off the boat tomorrow."

"You have a meeting set?" I asked.

A wary look entered his eyes. "He was going to call."

"Uh-huh." I grinned. "Too bad for Mr. Lau that you didn't get off in Macau and fly to Shanghai to meet him."

He looked disconsolate. "I really *am* an Andean folk music fan," he said. "That part I didn't make up. I wanted to catch your last show."

Somehow I failed to be touched.

I shut down the computer and looked through the papers that Oharu had got out of Jesse's briefcase. They were also in Chinese, and likewise incomprehensible. I put them aside and considered Oharu's situation.

He had murdered my employer, and besides that cut into my action with Leila, and I wasn't inclined to be merciful. On the other hand, I wasn't an assassin, and cold-bloodedly shoving him out the porthole wasn't my style.

On the third hand, I could see that he was turned over to the authorities once the ship reached Shanghai and let justice take its course. Getting shot in the neck by Chinese prison guards was too good for him.

But on the fourth hand, he *could* make trouble for us. The knowledge that there was illegal biotechnology being shipped to Taiwan was enough to make the Chinese authorities sit up and take notice.

"Right," I said, "this is what's going to happen." I pointed to the ninja gear I'd laid out on the bed. "In the morning, the cabin steward is going to find your murder implements laid out, and it will be obvious that you killed our employer."

He glared at me. "I'll tell the police all about you," he said. "They're not going to appreciate Western spies in their country."

"You're not going to get a chance to talk to the police," I said. "Because by then you'll have gone out the porthole."

He filled his lungs to scream again, but Sancho stifled him with a pillow.

"*However,*" I said, raising my voice a little to make sure he was paying attention as he flopped around on the bed, "we'll wait till we make Shanghai before you go into the drink, and we'll untie you first."

Oharu calmed somewhat. Once I had his attention, I continued. "You won't go to your Mr. Lau for help, because once your employers realize you're a wanted man, they'll cut your throat themselves."

He glared at me from over the top of the pillow. I signaled Sancho to lift the pillow off his face.

"Where does that leave me?" he asked. "Stuck in Shanghai in the early morning, having swum ashore soaking wet?"

"You're the ninja," I said. "Deal with it."

The plan went off without complications, which did my morale some good. *Tang Dynasty* made Shanghai about four in the morning and pulled into its pier. Oharu's porthole faced away from the pier, and out into the drink he went.

I suppose he made it to shore, though I won't mourn if it turned out otherwise. All I know is that I never saw him again.

The cabin steward went into the room about seven o'clock with Oharu's breakfast tea and was horrified to discover the murder gear lying in plain sight. The alarm was raised. I was asleep in my cabin by then, with Jesse's computer under my pillow.

*Tang Dynasty* discharged its passengers, then the crew spent the day scrubbing the ship from top to bottom. The entertainment had the day off, and the band took advantage to see a few of the sights of Shanghai, although we went in pairs, just in case enemy ninjas were lurking somewhere in the crowds. We wore our everyday clothes, not our traditional ponchos, and the locals probably thought we were Uighurs or something.

Laszlo and the guys went off to refill their helium cylinders. I don't think Leila and the mermaids left their cabin. I tried to tell her through the door that she was the least likely of any of us to be murdered, but I don't think I succeeded in reassuring her.

In the course of the night, *Thunderbolt Sow* pulled into the next berth in a cloud of sandalwood incense. I kept an eye on the ship, and an ear too, but I neither saw nor heard the evil-eyed Perugachi or his minions.

That day Jesse's replacements turned up, a white-haired Dr. Pan and his assistant, a round-faced, bespectacled Dr. Chun, who radiated enough anxiety for both of them. Each of them had bodyguards, slablike Westerners with identical ponytails—I won't swear to it, but I believe the language they used among themselves was Albanian.

"Another three dives," Laszlo said, "maybe four. The first to clear the wire away and get started on moving the mast. The second to finish with the mast, then another to open the hatch. If cargo's shifted on top of your box, we might need another dive to clear that away. But we should be finished tomorrow."

Dr. Pan gave a smooth smile and said that was good, then lit one of his little cigars. Dr. Chun didn't look any less anxious than he had at the start of the meeting.

That night our shows went off as per normal, if you consider scoping the audience for potential assassins to be normal, which for us it all too often was. We'd been over the passenger manifest, and the only last-minute additions had been Dr. Pan and his party, so I thought we were reasonably safe.

When we awakened next morning we were anchored off Hong Kong Island, and I joined the water ballet guys in their launch with a box of dim sum I'd nicked from the kitchens. To my disappointment, I found that the mermaids were not going along.

"It's so *unprofessional,*" Laszlo complained. "They think someone's going to come along and rip their throats out."

"You could offer them hazardous duty pay," I suggested hopefully.

"But it's not hazardous!" he said. "Diving to seven atmospheres breathing exotic gasses is *hazardous*—but do I hold you up for extra money?"

I shrugged—he'd *tried,* after all—and resigned myself to a heavy lunch of dim sum.

In short order we were bobbing in the swell over the wreck, and Laszlo and one of the guys went down on the first dive of the day. As the dive plan called for Laszlo to stay under the water for over two hours, I was surprised to see him break the surface ninety minutes early.

"What's wrong?" I asked as I helped him over the gunwale.

His face was grim. "You've got to go down and look at it yourself."

"What is it? Did Perugachi get the cargo?"

"Maybe the cargo got *him,*" he said, and he turned to one of the Apollos. "Sztephen," he said, "take Ernesto down to the wreck, show him around, and make sure he doesn't die."

Sztephen gave me a dubious look while he struck a pose that emphasized his triceps development. I gave him what was meant to be a reassuring grin and reached for my wet suit.

Because I'd been so thoroughly narked on my last trip, Laszlo insisted that I make this one on Trimix, which involved two extra-heavy cylinders on my back and a mixture that was fifty percent helium, fifteen percent oxygen, and the rest nitrogen. We also carried stage cylinders on our chests, for use in decompression, which we were to rig to our descent line as we went down.

It was all unfamiliar enough to have my nerves in a jangle by the time I splashed into the briny lamenting the fact that while I breathed Trimix instead of air the consolations of nitrogen narcosis were beyond my reach. Still, the descent went well enough, and the great stillness and silence and darkness helped to calm my throbbing heart.

Which was a pity, because my heart slammed into overdrive again once I saw *Goldfish Fairy.* The wreck lay with a black cavern just behind the bows, where the covers to the fore hatch had been thrown off. Much of the cargo had also been lifted from the hold and thrown over the side, where it lay in piles. Such of the cargo as I saw seemed to consist of T-shirts with the Pocari Sweat logo on them.

But Pocari Sweat was not long in my thoughts, because I observed something pale and geometric protruding from the after hatch, and when I kicked toward the object, I discovered that it was a brilliant white pyramid.

No, I corrected on further inspection, not a pyramid—a tetrahedron, a four-sided figure with each side making an equilateral triangle. It had broken out of the hatch, and its colorless tip had shoved aside the mast and was reaching for the surface, sixty meters above. The brilliant whiteness of the tetrahedron was so striking that it looked like a belated iceberg turned up too late for the sinking.

So fascinated was I by this object that I let myself drift toward it, only to be checked by Sztephen, who seized my arm and drew me back. There was an expression of horror on his face.

I decided that Sztephen had a point. Whatever this thing was, it wasn't in our dive plan, and it might be in some way hostile.

It occurred to me to wonder whether it was a surprise that Fidel Perugachi had left for us.

I made a careful circuit of the after hatch to judge the object's size—a proper estimate was difficult, as the tetrahedron's base was in the darkness of the hold, but it seemed about eight or nine meters per side. Then my heart lurched as I saw another, tiny tetrahedron—about the size of my palm—on the deck near the rail. I drifted downward to get a look at it, and this time saw a number of even smaller pyramids on the ship's hull, leading down to a cluster of them on the muddy bottom, none of them larger than my fingernail.

I began to have a feeling that all of them would be Giza-sized, given time.

I made a circuit of *Goldfish Fairy* in order to see how far the pyramid plague had spread and found a smaller number of the four-sided items on the other side of the barge. I checked the forward hold, and there I saw the cause of it all. Fidel Perugachi's crew, when they realized that the forehold didn't have what they were looking for, and that they didn't have time to open the rear hold, had tried to break into the after hold through a hatch high in the bulkhead. But the hatch hadn't opened because the cargo in the aft hold had been thrown forward when the *Goldfish Fairy* hit the bottom, and Perugachi's raiders had tried to force it open with the jacks they'd brought to shift the fallen mast.

They'd ended up opening more than the hatch, I thought. Their attempt to shove the hatch open had broken whatever contained Jesse's biotech.

It wasn't Fidel Perugachi who had created these objects. These pyramids now growing silently beneath the sea were what we'd been hired to *prevent*.

I reckoned I'd seen enough, so I signaled to Sztephen that it was time to head for the surface, and he agreed with wide-eyed relief.

It took some time to rise, as we had to pause every three meters or so for a decompression stop, and at certain intervals we had to shift to a different gas mixture, first to Nitrox 36 and then to $O^2$, making use of the cylinders we'd tethered to our line. Sztephen assisted with the unfamiliar procedures, and I managed them without trouble.

We were at a depth of twenty meters, hovering at our decompression stop while juggling a formidable number of depleted cylinders, when we heard the rumble of a boat approaching and looked up to see the twin hulls of a catamaran cutting the water toward our launch.

My overtaxed nerves gave a sustained quaver as the jet-powered catamaran cut its impellers and drifted up to the launch. I could only imagine what was happening on the surface—Pearl River pirates slitting the throats of everyone aboard; water police from the People's Republic putting everyone under arrest for disturbing the wreck; Fidel Perugachi sneering as he brandished automatic weapons at the hapless Apollos of the water ballet; ninjas feathering everyone aboard with blowgun darts…

Whatever was happening, I wasn't going to be a part of it. I probably wouldn't actually *die* if I bolted to the surface from a depth of twenty meters, but ere long I'd be damned sick with a case of the bends, and hardly in a condition to aid my cause.

So Sztephen and I sat in the heavy silence, both our imaginations and our nerves running amok, while we made our regulation number of decompression stops, the last being at ten meters. A myriad of schemes whirled through my mind, all of them useless until I actually knew what was going on above our heads.

The last seconds of our decompression stop ticked away. While Sztephen watched with puzzled interest, I reached for one of the Nitrox cylinders and removed the first-stage regulator, the device through which a diver actually breathes the contents of the cylinder. I then turned the valve to crack open the cylinder slightly and produced a satisfying stream of bubbles that rose unbroken to the surface. Then I did the same to another cylinder.

Anyone on the surface, looking for divers, would be able to track us simply by observing our exhaust bubbles rising. I had now given them a false bubble trail to watch.

Gesturing for Sztephen to follow, I kicked off from our line, positioned myself beneath the catamaran, and at slow, deliberate speed rose to the surface, my head breaking water between the twin hulls. Once there, I dropped my weight belt to the ocean bottom, then climbed out of my scuba gear, leaving myself just the mask, flippers, and snorkel.

And my dive knife, which was strapped to my leg. Many divers—usually the beginners—buy knives the length of their forearm, formidable enough to fight the U.S. Marines singlehanded.

Unfortunately for my current dilemma, I had developed a more realistic appraisal of the circumstances under which I might need a knife underwater, and my own blade was about the length of my little finger. It was unlikely to stop a sufficiently determined Pekingese, let alone the U.S. Marines. I whispered a query to Sztephen, and like a true professional he produced one no larger than my own.

I sighed inwardly and explained my plan, such as it was. Sztephen, who liked my plan no more than I did but couldn't think of a better, likewise climbed out of his gear. We then inflated the B.C.s just enough to float and tied them together with B.C. straps. It was unlikely we'd need the gear again, but it didn't seem right to sink it.

I listened carefully all the while, but all I heard was the rumble of the idling engines and the surge and slap of waves against the white fiberglass hull—no screams, no shots, no maniacal cackling from a sadistic enemy.

It was time to do it, whatever it was. Those bubbles rising from the decoy cylinders wouldn't last forever.

The catamaran's port hull was moored to our launch, so I swam to the starboard hull, took a breath, and swam beneath the hull to surface cautiously on the other side. No one seemed to be looking for me, and by this point I was hearing nothing but the throbbing of my own heart. The ocean chop lifted me most of the way up the hull, and with a strong kick with my flippers I managed to get a hand around a chrome stanchion used to support the double safety line that ran around the fore part of the boat. The stanchion was strong enough to support my weight, and I pulled myself up, crawled under the safety line, and lay on the deck for a moment gathering my wits and my breath.

I was lying against the pilothouse of what clearly was a dedicated dive boat. The wide platform between the two hulls was ideal for moving gear around, and divers could simply jump off the back when they wanted to enter the sea. Cylinders were set in racks aft of me, and when I blinked up against the bright sun, I could see the silhouette of a crane intended to raise salvage from the depths.

I pulled my mask down around my neck and worked my flippers off my feet. At this point Sztephen's sun-bleached head appeared above the deck, looking at me wide-eyed: I'd told him to wait a moment or two before following me, and wait to hear if there was gunfire. Apparently this warning had made an impression on him.

I helped him aboard, hoping he wouldn't make too much noise, and he was about as silent as the situation permitted. While he stripped off his flippers, I rose to a crouch and chanced a look through the open door into the boat's pilothouse. No one was visible, so I crept inside, and then froze.

Two figures were visible, and though I hadn't met either one I recognized them from photographs that my uncle Iago had made me memorize. They were both members of Fidel Perugachi's band, the bass player and the *bombo* player to be exact. It appeared that Perugachi had brought his whole rhythm section. One crouched in a wet suit on the afterdeck, working with some cylinders and a B.C., readying the outfit for a dive. Every few seconds he'd glance aft, to make certain that bubbles were still rising from our decoy cylinder. The other Ayanca, in shorts, baseball cap, and a Pocari Sweat T-shirt he must have stolen from the wreck, stood forward of the pilothouse by the port rail, watching whatever was going on in the launch.

A pistol was stuck casually into his shorts at the small of his back, and I recognized the distinctive toggle of a German Luger. The century-old Luger had been the standard sidearm of the P.R.C. police until recently, and when it was replaced by another weapon, the thrifty Chinese had sold tens of thousands of Lugers all at once. Perugachi must have picked up this one in the Hong Kong or Macau black market.

At least Fidel Perugachi hadn't been able to bring his own weaponry into China with him, and this gave me hope that his resources were fairly limited.

If I attacked the man with the Luger, it would be in full view of everyone on the launch; whereas the *bombo* player in the stern was crouched down out of sight. I gestured for Sztephen to be quiet, then slipped further into the cabin in search of a weapon. I suppose I could have slit the drummer's throat with my little knife, but that seemed drastic, and I hated to set that kind of precedent unless I needed to.

I was considering one of the five-pound lead divers' weights when I noticed that the drummer had his tool box open. Two crouching steps took me to the box, where I found a large wrench laid out neatly in its own compartment. Another two steps took me to the *bombo* player, who I promptly whanged behind the ear.

I probably hit him much harder than I intended to, as he only began to wake a couple hours later. Blame an excess of adrenaline if you will.

After checking my victim to see if he was still alive, I slipped to the rear corner of the boat, where a line had been tied holding the catamaran to the launch. I slipped the line off the cleat, then moved forward again, back to the pilothouse, where I had a quick whispered conversation with Sztephen about whether he felt he could steer the boat. He gave a quick scan of the instrument board and said that he could. The engines were idling, and all he had to do was put them in gear and shove the throttles forward.

As we hadn't heard any shouts or complaints that we were drifting away from the launch, I surmised that there was another mooring line, and that this one was forward and under the supervision of the bass player.

I told Sztephen to shove the throttles forward when I yelled, then slipped out of the pilothouse on the port side, the side away from the launch. I intended to use the pilothouse for cover on the approach, come up behind the bass player, then pull his own pistol and stick it in his back. If Perugachi's crew saw me at that point it wouldn't matter, as I'd have a ready-made hostage.

It didn't work out that way. I crept around the pilothouse and approached my target, using as cover a big galvanized storage compartment. I looked around the corner of the compartment and saw the bass player a few paces away. His back was to me, and he was chatting in Aymara with a man in the launch.

My heart gave a sudden thud against my ribs as I realized that this second man was Fidel Perugachi himself, and then another great knock as I saw Perugachi's heavy-lidded demonic eyes drop from his bass player to look straight at me. I suddenly realized how hot it was inside my wet suit, and how odd that was considering it was still full of seawater.

Before the loathsome offspring of the Ayanca moiety could cry a warning, I crossed the deck in three strides and kicked the bass player with both feet in the small of the back. This catapulted him over the safety line and—the most satisfying part—on top of Perugachi himself. Then, yelling demented abuse at the Ayancas in our native language, I sprawled forward on the deck to reach for the remaining mooring line.

"*Allu!*" I yelled. "*Umata urqu!*"

Taking my invective as his cue, Sztephen threw the catamaran into gear and shoved the throttles forward. Impellers screamed, jets boiled, and the craft lunged into the next wave, taking the launch with it.

This was fortunate, as it turns out, because the Ayancas were in the process of organizing a response just as the sudden acceleration jerked them off their feet. I untied the mooring line and let it fly through the chrome-plated cleat and off the boat.

Luger bullets flew wild as the launch, checked by its anchor, came to an abrupt halt astern, and everyone on the boat took another tumble.

I rose and shook a fist. "*Jallpiña chinqi,* you *lunthata llujchi!*" I shouted.

It was only then that I noticed the dive boat had another passenger. Leila was crouched in the shadow of the pilothouse, where I hadn't been able to see her, and was looking in alarm at the Ayancas, all of whose arms were suddenly waving weapons.

I got to my feet and ran to the pilothouse, where Sztephen was crouched down in cover, steering the boat with a wild expression on his face.

"Good work," I said and took the controls.

Fidel Perugachi still had the launch, which had a powerful motor and could quite possibly outspeed the heavily laden catamaran once they got the anchor up.

I swung the boat into a wide circle, aimed straight at the launch, and let the boat build speed. There was a fusillade of shots from the Ayancas—I had to wonder what possible good they thought it would do—and then the white splashes of five bronzed Apollos making perfect entries into the water. The Ayancas stared at the twin-hulled doom approaching at flank speed, and then most of them followed the Apollos.

Fidel Perugachi was made of sterner stuff. He stood on the boat's thwart, arms folded in an attitude of defiance, glaring at me with his ferocious eyes until the catamaran thundered right over him.

Showy, flamboyant, and self-dramatizing. What did I tell you? Just like his flute-playing.

I didn't want to cut the launch in half, so I struck it a glancing blow with the left hull, which was strong enough to roll the craft under. It came bobbing up astern—it was a tough boat, stuffed with foam to make it unsinkable and suitable for use as a lifeboat—but we lost most of our diving gear.

I slowed and began to circle. That provided me an opportunity to step out of the pilothouse and glare at Leila, who was still crouched against the pilothouse, paralyzed with shock at the bullets her erstwhile allies had been volleying in her direction. She seemed otherwise unharmed.

"Young lady," I said, shaking a finger, "I'm very disappointed in you."

She looked up at me. "Fidel met my price," she said. "We needed money to start the Fabulous Femmes Water Ballet of Zuma."

My indignation at her being on a first-name basis with Perugachi only heightened my disapproval. "You'll get nowhere through this kind of imitation," I said. "Look at where it got the Ayancas."

We picked up the Apollos first, and they sat wet and bedraggled on the stern deck—I believe it was the only time in our acquaintance when at least some of them weren't posing—and then we brought aboard the Ayancas, one by one. They hadn't hung onto their weapons, but we patted them down just in case and tied them on the afterdeck and put them under guard of the Apollos, who soon regained their swagger.

Fidel Perugachi came aboard last, having survived the collision intact save for a dramatic and bloody cut on his forehead. He glared at me as we tied him and dropped him like a sack on the deck, and I flashed him a grim smile.

"Serves you right for killing my employer," I said.

"That wasn't my idea," he said, "and I didn't do it. I advised against it, in fact. I knew it would only piss you off."

"So who's idea *was* it?" I asked. I didn't expect him to reply, and he didn't.

We took the waterlogged launch in tow and headed for the People's Republic, where we dropped the Ayancas on a deserted rocky shore after making them bail out the launch. We also took their clothing.

Stranding them naked in a deserted corner of China, with no papers for crossing back into Hong Kong and no way of communicating with their employers, seemed likely to keep the Ayancas out of our hair for a while.

We also stranded the Fabulous Femme of Zuma, though we left her a towel for modesty's sake.

Leila was sullen and tried to bum a cigarette, but Perugachi did not take it well. He waded into the sea after us and shook his fist, filling the air with colorful Aymara oaths.

"*Allu!*" he called. "*Jama!*"

"Don't mess with the Hanansaya moiety!" I shouted back at him. "Our ancestors were *kings!*"

Which in our democratic age may seem a bit of aristocratic pretension, but quite frankly I thought it was time that Fidel Perugachi was put in his place.

"A pyramid," murmured Dr. Pan. "A white pyramid."

"Tetrahedron," I corrected helpfully.

His assistant Chun ignored me and gave Pan a desperate, hollow-eyed look. "The culture wasn't supposed to be able to survive in nature," he said.

"Didn't test it in the nutrient-rich effluent of the Pearl River, now, did you?" I asked.

Again Chun ignored me. "I can't understand the part about the pyramids. That's not supposed to happen at all."

"Tetrahedrons," I said again, "and *what* culture?" I focused on him a glower that would do Fidel Perugachi proud. "I was exposed to it, after all. If I'm about to turn into a four-sided polygon, I have the right to know."

We were in Pan's luxurious suite aboard *Tang Dynasty*, all silk hangings and rich furniture inlaid with mother-of-pearl, and air thick with tobacco smoke from Chun's pipe and Pan's disgusting little cigars. Those of us who had returned from the *Goldfish Fairy*—minus Deszmond, who had been assigned to run the catamaran hard aground in Aberdeen harbor and then take the bus back—had decided it was time to confront Dr. Pan and find out just what our little mission was all about.

Pan caved in without resistance. "Our colleague, Dr. Jiu," he said, referring to Jesse, "was working with a type of diatom. These are small one-celled algae that live in colonies and create crystalline structures."

"Divers know about diatoms," Laszlo said.

Pan nodded. "What Dr. Jiu managed to create was a diatom modified to excrete polycarbon plastic instead of a silicate. Since our current lines of plastics are created from fossil fuels, our company was quick to see the economic advantages of a far cheaper plastic that was created from, well, nothing, and we acquired both Dr. Jiu and his, ah, creation."

"And now the sea's got it," I said.

"The plastic structure is itself organic," Chun added hopefully. "Sooner or later, other microorganisms will eat it. And in the meantime it's a very nice sink for carbon dioxide."

I looked at them. "Is that before or after the white tetrahedron breaks surface in the shipping lanes?"

Sometimes it is necessary to be blunt in order to shock some of these more cerebral types back to reality. Both Pan and Chun winced.

Pan combed his distinguished white hair with his fingers and looked at Laszlo. "What is normally done to stop an underwater contamination?"

Laszlo stared at his right biceps while absentmindedly flexing it. "Well," he said, "in cases of seaweed, like that *Caulerpa taxifolia* that can infest whole ecosystems, you cover the infected area with plastic, then pump in something that will kill it, like chlorine. You have to keep coming back at regular intervals to make certain it hasn't come back." He shrugged. "But how you deal with a *diatom*, I don't know. Wouldn't the little critters be carried off by the current? Shouldn't it be all over the South China Sea by now?"

Sometimes it's possible to be *too* blunt: Chun looked as if he were about to cry, and Pan seemed profoundly cast down and gave a deep sigh.

"We are dealing with a specific diatom," Pan said, "a bilaterally symmetrical organism that reproduces sexually through the fusion of protoplasts. It won't survive long on its own, but will do well in its colony." He looked at Chun for reassurance. "We don't think the organism will spread far."

"How much plastic sheeting can you get on short notice?" Laszlo asked them.

They looked dubious.

"Oh come on," he urged. "You're in the plastic *business*."

"That would involve contacting another division of the company," Pan murmured in a subdued voice.

"It would involve *explanation*," Chun murmured back.

Pan gave another profound sigh. "So very awkward," he said.

"Awkward," Chun agreed.

I began to suspect that huge sheets of plastic were not in our future.

Which was how, two days later, I found myself the skipper of the ten-thousand-ton freighter *Twice-Locked Mountain,* a rusting hulk that had been thumping around the bywaters of Asia for the better part of the last century, so ancient and decrepit that it could only have been kept from the breakers' yards in the hope it might successfully be involved in some kind of insurance fraud.

I swung the wheel, steadied onto my new course, took dead aim at the anchored freighter *Green Snake,* and rang Jorge in the engine room for more turns.

The old reciprocating engines thumped and banged, the propeller flailed water, and a shudder ran along the old ship, shaking off a few hundred pounds of rust flakes. I hoped she would hold together just a few more minutes. It would be embarrassing to sink her prematurely.

"Hurry up," came Laszlo's voice on the radio. "We've got to be in Shanghai by tomorrow night."

"I'm doing the best I can," I said, and reached for the controls of the ship's siren to signal *brace for collision.*

We were probably doing all of ten knots when we hit *Green Snake* dead abeam in a crash of tormented iron, venting steam, and gurgling water. Since *Green Snake* was at least as old a ship as *Twice-Locked Mountain,* and in even worse condition, I half expected us to slice our target in two, but instead we stayed locked together, which wasn't in the plan, either.

"Get everyone on deck," I told Laszlo. "You're about to go down fast."

I reached for the engine room telegraph and rang for *full astern,* which is exactly what you're not supposed to do when your ship has just collided with another. *Twice-Locked Mountain* backed out of the hole it had torn in *Green Snake* with another shriek of dying metal, and the sea flooded in. In mere moments the *Green Snake* was listing, and the water ballet guys, pausing every so often to flex, began piling into their lifeboat.

Our bow had been caved in, but I wasn't sure how much water was coming in through the bulkhead that we had so carefully punched full of holes, and I called Rosalinda on her cell to find out. The intake seemed insufficient, so I ordered the seacocks opened, and then we began to settle fast. I managed some last maneuvering with the aid of my satnav, then signaled Sancho on the foredeck to trip the anchor, which ran out with a roar and clatter and a splash.

I blew the siren that ordered everyone to assemble amidships, and we watched in some fascination as *Green Snake* rolled over, then plunged to the bottom amid a roil of water and the thunder of collapsing bulkheads. We transferred to our own boats in some haste, as we wanted to get out of the area before the sea turned to poison.

In our own lifeboat we followed the Outrageous Water Ballet of Malibu toward Hong Kong, while I got busy on the radio and, in the voice of one Captain Nicholas Turgachev of the *Green Snake,* called in an SOS and issued the first of several environmental warnings, the second followed by the equally fictional Captain Bellerophos Kallikanzaros of the *Twice-Locked Mountain.*

The environmental warning was the only genuine part, as both ships had been loaded with sacks of arsenic originally intended to poison China's substantial population of rats. We had carefully anchored the wrecks so that they would bracket *Goldfish Fairy* when they went down. The arsenic would kill anything: man, woman, fish, plant, or mutated diatom, and the heavy metal would be leaking out of the wrecks and drifting over the site for weeks.

In the normal course of events, this would be considered an environmental catastrophe. In fact, it *was* an environmental catastrophe.

What I hoped was that it would be preferable to white tetrahedrons growing on the ocean floor from here to Panama, a bleak eerie forest like the setting of some early work by J. G. Ballard.

Soon Sancho, impersonating yet another fictional captain (this one a Filipino named Suarez), got on the radio to inform the authorities that he'd taken the survivors aboard the freighter *Ode to Constancy,* heading for Taipei, where they would be made available for questioning as soon as the ship docked. Of course the ship would never dock there, and the crews would never be found, and neither would the owners of all the vessels involved. Over the years the Chinese had become very good at obscuring ship registries, and I was inclined to trust them.

Questions rattled over the radio, but Turgachev and Kallikanzaros and Suarez managed not to find a language in common with the authorities, just scattered words here and there. An emergency helicopter scrambled from Hong Kong got to the wreck site just in time to see *Twice-Locked Mountain* make its final dive.

I, my band, and the water ballet were on our way to Hong Kong, where we'd get a Dragon Air flight to Shanghai to rejoin *Tang Dynasty.*

It was the only gig we had left, after all. Doctors Pan and Chun would soon be on their way back to Taiwan, where they would attempt to reconstruct Jesse's work from his notes. Even without their female contingent, the water ballet guys had found a new audience here, one that might keep them in Asia for quite some time. Every so often, suitably armored against the arsenic, they might make a dive down to the wreck to make certain that the diatoms weren't making a comeback.

We Hanansayas had become redundant. We were reduced to playing our music and flogging our CDs till the next emergency rose.

Or until the tetrahedrons rose from the sea. One way or the other.

# AFTERWORD: THE TANG DYNASTY

# UNDERWATER PYRAMID

*Sometimes I'm just out to have a good time.*

*This story was inspired by a trip to China—the cruise ship on which the crew dress as Tang Dynasty mandarins is a real vessel, though it sails the Yangtze and not the Pacific. (And no, I haven't actually been a passenger on it.)*

*I was also inspired by a dream in which I was some kind of secret agent trying to salvage some highly valued sunken object, with the help of the Water Ballet Guys I had recruited and placed on a cruise ship. As I remember, the dream took place on the Gulf Coast rather than the Pearl River Delta, but in the dream I was much vexed by the Ballet Guys' demands for Total Artistic Control.*

*Another inspiration came from a trip to Europe by some friends. They had enjoyed an Andean band in Paris, playing across the street from their hotel; but then when they later flew to Rome, the very same band arrived to play near their new hotel.*

*"That band was following us," one of them said.*

*I began to wonder if the band was following them. And why. And whether all the bands of Andean street musicians in Europe are somehow linked into one vast conspiracy.*

*And, for the purposes of the story, I decided they were.*

*Whether it's Ernesto's group that's playing the Place Dauphine in the opening scenes of "The Green Leopard Plague," I will leave it to the reader to decide.*

# INCARNATION DAY

It's your understanding and wisdom that makes me want to talk to you, Doctor Sam. About how Fritz met the Blue Lady, and what happened with Janis, and why her mother decided to kill her, and what became of all that. I need to get it sorted out, and for that I need a real friend. Which is you.

Janis is always making fun of me because I talk to an imaginary person. She makes even more fun of me because my imaginary friend is an English guy who died hundreds of years ago.

"You're wrong," I pointed out to her, "Doctor Samuel Johnson was a real person, so he's not imaginary. It's just my *conversations* with him that are imaginary."

I don't think Janis understands the distinction I'm trying to make.

But I know that *you* understand, Doctor Sam. You've understood me ever since we met in that Age of Reason class, and I realized that you not only said and did things that made you immortal, but that you said and did them while you were hanging around in taverns with actors and poets.

Which is about the perfect life, if you ask me.

In my opinion Janis could do with a Doctor Sam to talk to. She might be a lot less frustrated as an individual.

I mean, when I am totally stressed trying to comprehend the equations for electron paramagnetic resonance or something, so I just can't stand cramming another ounce of knowledge into my brain, I can always imagine my Doctor Sam—a big fat man (though I think the word they used back then was "corpulent")—a fat man with a silly wig on his head, who makes a magnificent gesture with one hand and says, with perfect wisdom and gravity, *All intellectual improvement, Miss Alison, arises from leisure.*

Who could put it better than that? Who else could be as sensible and wise? Who could understand me as well?

Certainly nobody *I* know.

(And have I mentioned how much I like the way you call me *Miss Alison?*)

We might as well begin with Fahd's Incarnation Day on Titan. It was the first incarnation among the Cadre of Glorious Destiny, so of course we were all present.

The celebration had been carefully planned to showcase the delights of Saturn's largest moon. First we were to be downloaded onto *Cassini Ranger*, the ship parked in Saturn orbit to service all the settlements on the various moons. Then we would be packed into individual descent pods and dropped into Titan's thick atmosphere. We'd be able to stunt through the air, dodging in and out of methane clouds as we chased each other across Titan's cloudy, photochemical sky. After that would be skiing on the Tomasko Glacier, Fahd's dinner, and then skating on frozen methane ice.

We would all be wearing bodies suitable for Titan's low gravity and high-pressure atmosphere—sturdy, low to the ground, and furry, with six legs and a domelike head stuck onto the front between a pair of arms.

But my body would be one borrowed for the occasion, a body the resort kept for tourists. For Fahd it would be different. He would spend the next five or six years in orbit around Saturn, after which he would have the opportunity to move on to something else.

The six-legged body he inhabited would be his own, his first. He would be incarnated—a legal adult, and legally human despite his six legs and furry body. He would have his own money and possessions, a job, and a full set of human rights.

Unlike the rest of us.

After the dinner, where Fahd would be formally invested with adulthood and his citizenship, we would all go out for skating on the methane lake below the glacier. Then we'd be uploaded and head for home.

All of us but Fahd, who would begin his new life. The Cadre of Glorious Destiny would have given its first member to interplanetary civilization.

I envied Fahd his incarnation—his furry six-legged body, his independence, and even his job, which wasn't all that stellar if you ask me. After fourteen years of being a bunch of electrons buzzing around in a quantum matrix, I wanted a real life even if it meant having twelve dozen legs.

I suppose I should explain, because you were born in an era when electricity came from kites, that at the time of Fahd's Incarnation Day party I was not exactly a human being. Not legally, and especially not physically.

Back in the old days—back when people were establishing the first settlements beyond Mars, in the asteroid belt and on the moons of Jupiter and then Saturn—resources were scarce. Basics such as water and air had to be shipped in from other places, and that was very expensive. And of course the environment was extremely hazardous—the death rate in those early years was phenomenal.

It's lucky that people are basically stupid, otherwise no one would have gone.

Yet the settlements had to grow. They had to achieve self-sufficiency from the home worlds of Earth and Luna and Mars, which sooner or later were going to get tired of shipping resources to them, not to mention shipping replacements for all the people who died in stupid accidents. And a part of independence involved establishing growing, or at least stable, populations, and that meant having children.

But children suck up a lot of resources, which like I said were scarce. So the early settlers had to make do with virtual children.

It was probably hard in the beginning. If you were a parent you had to put on a headset and gloves and a body suit in order to cuddle your infant, whose objective existence consisted of about a skazillion lines of computer code anyway… well, let's just say you had to want that kid *really badly*.

Especially since you couldn't touch him in the flesh till he was grown up, when he would be downloaded into a body grown in a vat just for him. The theory being that there was no point in having anyone in your settlement who couldn't contribute to the economy and help pay for those scarce resources, so you'd only incarnate your offspring when he was already grown up and could get a job and help to pay for all that oxygen.

You might figure from this that it was a hard life, out there on the frontier.

Now it's a lot easier. People can move in and out of virtual worlds with nothing more than a click of a mental switch. You get detailed sensory input through various nanoscale computers implanted in your brain, so you don't have to put on oven mitts to feel your kid. You can dandle your offspring, and play with him, and teach him to talk, and feed him even. Life in the virtual realms claims to be 100% realistic, though in my opinion it's more like 95%, and only in the realms that *intend* to mimic reality, since some of them don't.

Certain elements of reality were left out, and there are advantages—at least if you're a parent. No drool, no messy diapers, no vomit. When the child trips and falls down, he'll feel pain—you *do* want to teach him not to fall down, or to bang his head on things—but on the other hand there won't be any concussions or broken bones. There won't be any fatal accidents involving fuel spills or vacuum.

There are other accidents that the parents have made certain we won't have to deal with. Accidental pregnancy, accidental drunkenness, accidental drug use.

Accidental gambling. Accidental vandalism. Accidental suicide. Accidentally acquiring someone else's property. Accidentally stealing someone's extra-vehicular unit and going for a joy ride among the asteroids.

Accidentally having fun. Because believe me, the way the adults arrange it here, all the fun is *planned ahead of time.*

Yep, Doctor Sam, life is pretty good if you're a grownup. Your kids are healthy and smart and extremely well-educated. They live in a safe, organized world filled with exciting educational opportunities, healthy team sports, family entertainment, and games that reward group effort, cooperation, and good citizenship.

It all makes me want to puke. If I *could* puke, that is, because I can't. (Did I mention there was no accidental bulimia, either?)

*Thy body is all vice, Miss Alison, and thy mind all virtue.*

Exactly, Doctor Sam. And it's the vice I'm hoping to find out about. Once I get a body, that is.

We knew that we weren't going to enjoy much vice on Fahd's Incarnation Day, but still everyone in the Cadre of Glorious Destiny was excited, and maybe a little jealous, about his finally getting to be an adult, and incarnating into the real world and having some real world fun for a change. Never mind that he'd got stuck in a dismal job as an electrical engineer on a frozen moon.

All jobs are pretty dismal from what I can tell, so he isn't any worse off than anyone else really.

For days before the party I had been sort of avoiding Fritz. Since we're electronic we can avoid each other easily, simply by not letting yourself be visible to the other person, and not answering any queries he sends to you, but I didn't want to be rude.

Fritz was cadre, after all.

So I tried to make sure I was too busy to deal with Fritz—too busy at school, or with my job for Dane, or working with one of the other cadre members on a project. But a few hours before our departure for Titan, when I was in a conference room with Bartolomeo and Parminder working on an assignment for our Artificial Intelligence class, Fritz knocked on our door, and Bartolomeo granted him access before Parminder and I could signal him not to.

So in comes Fritz. Since we're electronic we can appear to one another as whatever we like, for instance Mary Queen of Scots or a bunch of snowflakes or even *you*, Doctor Sam. We all experiment with what we look like. Right now I mostly use an avatar of a sort-of Picasso woman—he used to distort people in his paintings so that you had a kind of 360-degree view of them, or parts of them, and I think that's kind of interesting, because my whole aspect changes depending on what angle of me you're viewing.

For an avatar Fritz used the image of a second-rate action star named Norman Isfahan. Who looks okay, at least if you can forget his lame videos, except that Fritz added an individual touch in the form of a balloon-shaped red hat. Which he thought made him look cool, but which only seemed ludicrous and a little sad.

Fritz stared at me for a moment, with a big goofy grin on his face, and Parminder sends me a little private electronic note of sympathy. In the last few months Fritz had become my pet, and he followed me around whenever he got the chance. Sometimes he'd be with me for hours without saying a word, sometimes he'd talk the entire time and not let me get a single word in.

I did my best with him, but I had a life to lead, too. And friends. And family. And I didn't want this person with me every minute, because even though I was sorry for him he was also very frustrating to be around.

*Friendship is not always the sequel of obligation.*

Alas, Doctor J., too true.

Fritz was the one member of our cadre who came out, well, wrong. They build us—us software—by reasoning backwards from reality, from our parents' DNA. They find a good mix of our parents' genes, and that implies certain things about *us*, and the sociologists get their say about what sort of person might be needful in the next generation, and everything's thrown together by a really smart artificial intelligence, and in the end you get a virtual child.

But sometimes despite all the intelligence of everyone and everything involved, mistakes are made. Fritz was one of these. He wasn't stupid exactly—he was as smart as anyone—but his mental reflexes just weren't in the right plane. When he was very young he would spend hours without talking or interacting with any of us. Fritz's parents, Jack and Hans, were both software engineers, and they were convinced the problem was fixable. So they complained and they or the AIs or somebody came up with a software patch, one that was supposed to fix his problem—and suddenly Fritz was active and angry, and he'd get into fights with people and sometimes he'd just scream for no reason at all and go on screaming for hours.

So Hans and Jack went to work with the code again, and there was a new software patch, and now Fritz was stealing things, except you can't really steal anything in sims, because the owner can find any virtual object just by sending it a little electronic ping.

That ended with Fritz getting fixed yet *again*, and this went on for years. So while it was true that none of us were exactly a person, Fritz was less a person than any of us.

We all did our best to help. We were cadre, after all, and cadres look after their own. But there was a limit to what any of us could do. We heard about unanticipated feedback loops and subsystem crashes and weird quantum transfers leading to fugue states. I think that the experts had no real idea what was going on. Neither did we.

There was a lot of question as to what would happen when Fritz incarnated. If his problems were all software glitches, would they disappear once he was meat and no longer software? Or would they short-circuit his brain?

A check on the histories of those with similar problems did not produce encouraging answers to these questions.

And then Fritz became *my* problem because he got really attached to me, and he followed me around.

"Hi, Alison," he said.

"Hi, Fritz."

I tried to look very busy with what I was doing, which is difficult to do if you're being Picasso Woman and rather abstract-looking to begin with.

"We're going to Titan in a little while," Fritz said.

"Uh-huh," I said.

"Would you like to play the shadowing game with me?" he asked.

Right then I was glad I was Picasso Woman and not incarnated, because I knew that if I had a real body I'd be blushing.

"Sure," I said. "If our capsules are anywhere near each other when we hit the atmosphere. We might be separated, though."

"I've been practicing in the simulations," Fritz said. "And I'm getting pretty good at the shadowing game."

"Fritz," Parminder said. "We're working on our AI project now, okay? Can we talk to you later, on Titan?"

"Sure."

And I sent a note of gratitude to Parminder, who was in on the scheme with me and Janis, and who knew that Fritz couldn't be a part of it.

Shortly thereafter my electronic being was transmitted from Ceres by high-powered communications lasers and downloaded into an actual body, even if it was a body that had six legs and that didn't belong to me. The body was already in its vacuum suit, which was packed into the descent capsule—I mean nobody wanted us floating around in the *Cassini Ranger* in zero gravity in bodies we weren't used to—so there wasn't a lot I could do for entertainment.

Which was fine. It was the first time I'd been in a body, and I was absorbed in trying to work out all the little differences between reality and the sims I'd grown up in.

In reality, I thought, things seem a little quieter. In simulations there are always things competing for your attention, but right now there was nothing to do but listen to myself breathe.

And then there was a bang and a big shove, easily absorbed by foam padding, and I was launched into space, aimed at the orange ball that was Titan, and behind it the giant pale sphere of Saturn.

The view was sort of disappointing. Normally you see Saturn as an image with the colors electronically altered so as to heighten the subtle differences in detail. The reality of Saturn was more of a pasty blob, with faint brown stripes and a little red jagged scrawl of a storm in the southern hemisphere.

Unfortunately I couldn't get a very good view of the rings, because they were edge-on, like a straight silver knife-slash right across a painted canvas.

Besides Titan I could see at least a couple dozen moons. I could recognize Dione and Rhea, and Enceladus because it was so bright. Iapetus was obvious because it was half light and half dark. There were a lot of tiny lights that could have been Atlas or Pan or Prometheus or Pandora or maybe a score of others.

I didn't have enough time to puzzle out the identity of the other moons, because Titan kept getting bigger and bigger. It was a dull orange color, except on the very edge where the haze scatters blue light. Other than that arc of blue, Titan is orange the same way Mars is red, which is to say that it's orange all the way down, and when you get to the bottom there's still more orange.

It seemed like a pretty boring place for Fahd to spend his first years of adulthood.

I realized that if I were doing this trip in a sim, I'd fast-forward through this part. It would be just my luck if all reality turned out to be this dull.

Things livened up in a hurry when the capsule hit the atmosphere. There was a lot of noise, and the capsule rattled and jounced, and bright flames of ionizing radiation shot up past the view port. I could feel my heart speeding up, and my breath going fast. It was *my* body that was being bounced around, with *my* nerve impulses running along *my* spine. *This* was much more interesting. *This* was the difference between reality and a sim, even though I couldn't explain exactly what the difference was.

*It is the distinction, Miss Alison, between the undomesticated awe which one might feel at the sight of a noble wild prospect discovered in nature; and that which is produced by a vain tragedian on the stage, puffing and blowing in a transport of dismal fury as he tries to describe the same vision.*

Thank you, Doctor Sam.

*We that live to please must please to live.*

I could see nothing but fire for a while, and then there was a jolt and a *CrashBang* as the braking chute deployed, and I was left swaying frantically in the sudden silence, my heart beating fast as high-atmosphere winds fought for possession of the capsule. Far above I could just see the ionized streaks of some of the other cadre members heading my way.

It was then, after all I could see was the orange fog, that I remembered that I'd been so overwhelmed by the awe of what I'd been seeing that I forgot to *observe*. So I began to kick myself over that.

It isn't enough to stare when you want to be a visual artist, which is what I want more than anything. A noble wild prospect (as you'd call it, Doctor Sam) isn't simply a gorgeous scene, it's also a series of technical problems. Ratios, colors, textures. Media. Ideas. Frames. *Decisions*. I hadn't thought about any of that when I had the chance, and now it was too late.

I decided to start paying better attention, but there was nothing happening outside but acetylene sleet cooking off the hot exterior of the capsule. I checked my tracking display and my onboard map of Titan's surface. So I was prepared when a private message came from Janis.

"Alison. You ready to roll?"

"Sure. You bet."

"This is going to be *brilliant*."

I hoped so. But somewhere in my mind I kept hearing Doctor Sam's voice:

*Remember that all tricks are either knavish or childish.*

The trick I played on Fritz was both.

I had been doing some outside work for Dane, who was a communications tech, because outside work paid in real money, not the Citizenship Points we get paid in the sims. And Dane let me do some of the work on Fahd's Incarnation Day, so I was able to arrange which capsules everyone was going to be put into.

I put Fritz into the last capsule to be fired at Titan. And those of us involved in Janis' scheme—Janis, Parminder, Andy, and I—were fired first.

This basically meant that we were going to be on Titan five or six minutes ahead of Fritz, which meant it was unlikely that he'd be able to catch up to us. He would be someone else's problem for a while.

I promised myself that I'd be extra nice to him later, but it didn't stop me from feeling knavish and childish.

After we crashed into Titan's atmosphere, and after a certain amount of spinning and swaying we came to a break in the cloud, and I could finally look down at Titan's broken surface. Stark mountains, drifts of methane snow, shiny orange ethane lakes, the occasional crater. In the far distance, in the valley between a pair of lumpy mountains, was the smooth toboggan slide of the Tomasko Glacier. And over to one side, on a plateau, were the blinking lights that marked our landing area.

And directly below was an ethane cloud, into which the capsule soon vanished. It was there that the chute let go, and there was a stomach-lurching drop before the airfoils deployed. I was not used to having my stomach lurch—recall if you will my earlier remarks on puking—so it was a few seconds before I was able to recover and take control of what was now a large and agile glider.

No, I hadn't piloted a glider before. But I'd spent the last several weeks working with simulations, and the technology was fail-safed anyway. Both I and the onboard computer would have to screw up royally before I could damage myself or anyone else. I took command of the pod and headed for Janis' secret rendezvous.

There are various sorts of games you can play with the pods as they're dropping through the atmosphere. You can stack your airfoils in appealing and intricate formations. (I think this one's really stupid if you're trying to do it in the middle of thick clouds.) There's the game called "shadowing," the one that Fritz wanted to play with me, where you try to get right on top of another pod, above the airfoils where they can't see you, and you have to match every maneuver of the pod that's below you, which is both trying to evade you and to maneuver so as to get above you. There are races, where you try to reach some theoretical point in the sky ahead of the other person. And there's just swooping and dashing around the sky, which is probably as fun as anything.

But Janis had other plans. And Parminder and Andy and I, who were Janis' usual companions in her adventures, had elected to be a part of her scheme, as was our wont. (Do you like my use of the word "wont," Doctor Sam?) And a couple other members of the cadre, Mei and Bartolomeo, joined our group without knowing our secret purpose.

We disguised our plan as a game of shadowing, which I turned out to be very good at. It's not simply a game of flying, it's a game of spacial relationships, and that's what visual artists have to be good at understanding. I spent more time on top of one or more of the players than anyone else.

Though perhaps the others weren't concentrating on the game. Because although we were performing the intricate spiraling maneuvers of shadowing as a part of our cover, we were also paying very close attention to the way the winds were blowing at different altitudes—we had cloud-penetrating lasers for that, in addition to constant meteorological data from the ground—and we were using available winds as well as our maneuvers to slowly edge away from our assigned landing field, and toward our destined target.

I kept expecting to hear from Fritz, wanting to join our game. But I didn't. I supposed he had found his fun somewhere else.

All the while we were stunting around, Janis was sending us course and altitude corrections, and thanks to her navigation we caught the edge of a low pressure area that boosted us toward our objective at nearly two hundred kilometers per hour. It was then that Mei swung her capsule around and began a descent toward the landing field.

"I just got the warning that we're on the edge of our flight zone," she reported.

"Roger," I said.

"Yeah," said Janis. "We know."

Mei swooped away, followed by Bartolomeo. The rest of us continued soaring along in the furious wind. We made little pretense by this point that we were still playing shadow, but instead tried for distance.

Ground Control on the landing area took longer to try to contact us than we'd expected.

"Capsules six, twenty-one, thirty," said a ground controller. She had one of those smooth, controlled voices that people use when trying to coax small children away from the candy and toward the spinach.

"You have exceeded the safe range from the landing zone. Turn at once to follow the landing beacon."

I waited for Janis to answer.

"It's easier to reach Tomasko from where we are," she said. "We'll just head for the glacier and meet the rest of you there."

"The flight plan prescribes a landing on Lake Southwood," the voice said. "Please lock on the landing beacon at once and engage your autopilots."

Janis' voice rose with impatience. "Check the flight plan I'm sending you! It's easier and quicker to reach Tomasko! We've got a wind shoving us along at a hundred eighty clicks!"

There was another two or three minutes of silence. When the voice came back, it was grudging.

"Permission granted to change flight plan."

I sagged with relief in my vac suit, because now I was spared a moral crisis. We had all sworn that we'd follow Janis' flight plan whether or not we got permission from Ground Control, but that didn't necessarily mean that we would have. Janis would have gone, of course, but I for one might have had second thoughts. I would have had an excuse if Fritz had been along, because I could have taken him to the assigned landing field—we didn't want him with us, because he might not have been able to handle the landing if it wasn't on an absolutely flat area.

I'd like to think I would have followed Janis, though. It isn't as if I hadn't before.

And honestly, that was about it. If this had been one of the adult-approved video dramas we grew up watching, something would have gone terribly wrong and there would have been a horrible crash. Parminder would have died, and Andy and I would have been trapped in a crevasse or buried under tons of methane ice, and Janis would have had to go to incredible, heroic efforts in order to rescue us. At the end Janis would have Learned an Important Life Lesson, about how following the Guidance of our Wise, Experienced Elders is preferable to staging wild, disobedient stunts.

By comparison what actually happened was fairly uneventful. We let the front push us along till we were nearly at the glacier, and then we dove down into calmer weather. We spiraled to a soft landing in clean snow at the top of Tomasko Glacier. The airfoils neatly folded themselves, atmospheric pressure inside the capsules equalized with that of the moon, and the hatches opened so we could walk in our vac suits onto the top of Titan.

I was flushed with joy. I had never set an actual foot on an actual world before, and as I bounded in sheer delight through the snow I rejoiced in all the little details I felt all around me.

The crunch of the frozen methane under my boots. The way the wind picked up long streamers of snow that made little spattering noises when they hit my windscreen. The suit heaters that failed to heat my body evenly, so that some parts were cool and others uncomfortably warm.

None of it had the immediacy of the simulations, but I didn't remember this level of detail either. Even the polyamide scent of the suit seals was sharper than the generic stuffy suit smell they put in the sim.

This was all real, and it was wonderful, and even if my body was borrowed I was already having the best time I'd ever had in my life.

I scuttled over to Janis on my six legs and crashed into her with affectionate joy. (Hugging wasn't easy with the vac suits on.) Then Parminder ran over and crashed into her from the other side.

"We're finally out of Plato's Cave!" she said, which is the sort of obscure reference you always get out of Parminder. (I looked it up, though, and she had a good point.)

The outfitters at the top of the glacier hadn't been expecting us for some time, so we had some free time to indulge in a snowball fight. I suppose snowball fights aren't that exciting if you're wearing full-body pressure suits, but this was the first real snowball fight any of us had ever had, so it was fun on that account anyway.

By the time we got our skis on, the shuttle holding the rest of the cadre and their pods was just arriving. We could see them looking at us from the yellow windows of the shuttle, and we just gave them a wave and zoomed off down the glacier, along with a grownup who decided to accompany us in case we tried anything else that wasn't in the regulation playbook.

Skiing isn't a terribly hazardous sport if you've got six legs on a body slung low to the ground. The skis are short, not much longer than skates, so they don't get tangled; and it's really hard to fall over—the worst that happens is that you go into a spin that might take some time to get out of. And we'd all been practicing on the simulators and nothing bad happened.

The most interesting part was the jumps that had been molded at intervals onto the glacier. Titan's low gravity meant that when you went off a jump, you went very high and you stayed in the air for a long time. And Titan's heavy atmosphere meant that if you spread your limbs apart like a skydiver, you could catch enough of that thick air almost to hover, particularly if the wind was cooperating and blowing uphill. That was wild and thrilling, hanging in the air with the wind whistling around the joints of your suit, the glossy orange snow coming up to meet you, and the sound of your own joyful whoops echoing in your ears.

*I am a great friend to public amusements, because they keep people from vice.*

Well. Maybe. We'll see.

The best part of the skiing was that this time I didn't get so carried away that I'd forgot to *observe*. I thought about ways to render the dull orange sheen of the glacier, the wild scrawls made in the snow by six skis spinning out of control beneath a single squat body, the little crusty waves on the surface generated by the constant wind.

Neither the glacier nor the lake is always solid. Sometimes Titan generates a warm front that liquifies the topmost layer of the glacier, and the liquid methane pours down the mountain to form the lake. When that happens, the modular resort breaks apart and creeps away on its treads. But sooner or later everything freezes over again, and the resort returns.

We were able to ski through a broad orange glassy chute right onto the lake, and from there we could see the lights of the resort in the distance. We skied into a big ballooning pressurized hangar made out of some kind of durable fabric, where the crew removed our pressure suits and gave us little felt booties to wear. I'd had an exhilarating time, but hours had passed and I was tired. The Incarnation Day banquet was just what I needed.

Babbling and laughing, we clustered around the snack tables, tasting a good many things I'd never got in a simulation. (They make us eat in the sims, to get us used to the idea so we don't accidentally starve ourselves once we're incarnated, and to teach us table manners, but the tastes tend to be a bit monotonous.)

"Great stuff!" Janis said, gobbling some kind of crunchy vat-grown treat that I'd sampled earlier and found disgusting. She held the bowl out to the rest of us. "Try this! You'll like it!"

I declined.

"Well," Janis said, "if you're afraid of new things…"

That was Janis for you—she insisted on sharing her existence with everyone around her, and got angry if you didn't find her life as exciting as she did.

About that time Andy and Parminder began to gag on the stuff Janis had made them eat, and Janis laughed again.

The other members of the cadre trailed in about an hour later, and the feast proper began. I looked around the long table—the forty-odd members of the Cadre of Glorious Destiny, all with their little heads on their furry multipede bodies, all crowded around the table cramming in the first real food they've tasted in their lives. In the old days, this would have been a scene from some kind of horror movie. Now it's just a slice of posthumanity, Earth's descendants partying on some frozen rock far from home.

But since all but Fahd were in borrowed bodies I'd never seen before, I couldn't tell one from the other. I had to ping a query off their implant communications units just to find out who I was talking to.

Fahd sat at the place of honor at the head of the table. The hair on his furry body was ash-blond, and he had a sort of widow's peak that gave his head a kind of geometrical look.

I liked Fahd. He was the one I had sex with, that time that Janis persuaded me to steal a sex sim from Dane, the guy I do outside programming for. (I should point out, Doctor Sam, that our simulated bodies have all the appropriate organs, it's just that the adults have made sure we can't actually use them for sex.)

I think there was something wrong with the simulation. What Fahd and I did wasn't wonderful, it wasn't ecstatic, it was just… strange. After a while we gave up and found something else to do.

Janis, of course, insisted she'd had a glorious time. She was our leader, and everything she did had to be totally fabulous. It was just like that horrid vat-grown snack food product she'd tried—not only was it the best food she'd ever tasted, it was the best food *ever*, and we all had to share it with her.

I hope Janis actually *did* enjoy the sex sim, because she was the one caught with the program in her buffer—and after I *told* her to erase it. Sometimes I think she just wants to be found out.

During dinner those whose parents permitted it were allowed two measured doses of liquor to toast Fahd—something called Ring Ice, brewed locally. I think it gave my esophagus blisters.

After the Ring Ice, things got louder and more lively. There was a lot more noise and hilarity when the resort crew discovered that several of the cadre had slipped off to a back room to find out what sex was like, now they had real bodies. It was when I was laughing over this that I looked at Janis and saw that she was quiet, her body motionless. She's normally louder and more demonstrative than anyone else, so I knew something was badly wrong. I sent her a private query through my implant. She sent a single-word reply.

*Mom...*

I sent her a glyph of sympathy while I wondered how Janis' mom had found out about our little adventure so quickly. There was barely time for a lightspeed signal to bounce to Ceres and back.

Ground Control must have really been annoyed. Or maybe she, like Janis' mom, was a Constant Soldier in the Five Principles Movement and was busy spying on everyone else—all for the greater good, of course.

Whatever the message was, Janis bounced back pretty quickly. Next thing I knew she was sidling up to me saying, "Look, you can loan me your vac suit, right?"

Something about the glint in her huge platter eyes made me cautious.

"Why would I want to do that?" I asked.

"Mom says I'm grounded. I'm not allowed to go skating with the rest of you. But nobody can tell these bodies apart—I figured if we switched places we could show her who's boss."

"And leave me stuck here by myself?"

"You'll be with the waiters—and some of them are kinda cute, if you like them hairy." Her tone turned serious. "It's solidarity time, Alison. We can't let Mom win this one."

I thought about it for a moment, then said, "Maybe you'd better ask someone else."

Anger flashed in her huge eyes. "I knew you'd say that! You've always been afraid to stand up to the grownups!"

"Janis," I sighed. "Think about it. Do you think your mom was the only one that got a signal from Ground Control? My parents are going to be looking into the records of this event *very closely*. So I think you should talk someone else into your scheme—and not Parminder or Andy, either."

Her whole hairy body sulked. I almost laughed.

"I guess you're right," she conceded.

"You know your mom is going to give you a big lecture when we get back."

"Oh yeah. I'm sure she's writing her speech right now, making sure she doesn't miss a single point."

"Maybe you'd better let me eavesdrop," I said. "Make sure you don't lose your cool."

She looked even more sulky. "Maybe you'd better."

We do this because we're cadre. Back in the old days, when the first poor kids were being raised in virtual, a lot of them cracked up once they got incarnated. They went crazy, or developed a lot of weird obsessions, or tried to kill themselves, or turned out to have a kind of autism where they could only relate to things through a computer interface.

So now parents don't raise their children by themselves. Most kids still have two parents, because it takes two to pay the citizenship points and taxes it takes to raise a kid, and sometimes if there aren't enough points to go around there are three parents, or four or five. Once the points are paid the poor moms and dads have to wait until there are enough applicants to fill a cadre. A whole bunch of virtual children are raised in one group, sharing their upbringing with their parents and crèche staff. Older cadres often join their juniors and take part in their education, also.

The main point of the cadre is for us all to keep an eye on each other. Nobody's allowed to withdraw into their own little world. If anyone shows sign of going around the bend, we unite in our efforts to retrieve them.

Our parents created the little hell that we live in. It's our job to help each other survive it.

*A person used to vicissitudes is not easily dejected.*

Certainly Janis isn't, though despite cadre solidarity she never managed to talk anyone else into changing places with her. I felt only moderately sorry for her—she'd already had her triumph, after all—and I forgot all about her problems once I got back into my pressure suit and out onto the ice.

Skating isn't as thrilling as skiing, I suppose, but we still had fun. Playing crack-the-whip in the light gravity, the person on the end of the line could be fired a couple kilometers over the smooth methane ice.

After which it was time to return to the resort. We all showered while the resort crew cleaned and did maintenance on our suits, and then we got back in the suits so that the next set of tourists would find their rental bodies already armored up and ready for sport.

We popped open our helmets so that the scanners could be put on our heads. Quantum superconducting devices tickled our brain cells and re-covered everything they found, and then our brains—our essences—were dumped into a buffer, then fired by communication laser back to Ceres and the sim in which we all lived.

The simulation seemed inadequate compared to the reality of Titan. But I didn't have time to work out the degree of difference, because I had to save Janis' butt.

That's us. That's the cadre. All for one and one for all.

And besides, Janis has been my best friend for practically ever.

Anna-Lee, Janis' mom, was of course waiting for her, sitting in the little common room outside Janis' bedroom. (Did I mention that we sleep, Doctor Sam? We don't sleep as long as incarnated people do, just a few hours, but our parents want us to get used to the idea so that when we're incarnated we know to sleep when we get tired instead of ignoring it and then passing out while doing something dangerous or important.

(The only difference between our sleep and yours is that we don't dream. I mean, what's the point, we're stuck in our parents' dream anyway.)

So I've no sooner arrived in my own simulated body in my own simulated bedroom when Janis is screaming on the private channel.

"Mom is here! I need you *now!*"

So I press a few switches in my brain and there I am, right in Janis' head, getting much of the same sensor feed that she's receiving herself. And I look at her and I say, "Hey, you can't talk to Anna-Lee looking like *this.*"

Janis is wearing her current avatar, which is something like a crazy person might draw with crayons. Stick-figure body, huge yellow shoes, round bobble head with crinkly red hair like wires.

"Get your quadbod on!" I tell her. "Now!"

So she switches, and now her avatar has four arms, two in the shoulders, two in the hip sockets. The hair is still bright red. Whatever her avatar looks like, Janis always keeps the red hair.

"Good," I say. "That's normal."

Which it is, for Ceres. Which is an asteroid without much gravity, so there really isn't a lot of point in having legs. In microgravity legs just drag around behind you and bump into things and get bruises and cuts. Whereas everyone can use an extra pair of arms, right? So most people who live in low- or zero-gravity environments use quadbods, which are more practical than the two-legged model.

So Janis pushes off with her left set of arms and floats through the door into the lounge where her mom awaits. Anna-Lee wears a quadbod, too, except that hers isn't an avatar, but a three-dimensional holographic scan of her real body. And you can tell that she's really pissed—she's got tight lips and tight eyelids and a tight face, and both sets of arms are folded across her midsection with her fingers digging into her forearms as if she's repressing the urge to grab Janis and shake her.

"Hi, Mom," Janis said.

"You not only endangered yourself," Anna-Lee said, "but you chose to endanger others, too."

"Sit down before you answer," I murmured in Janis' inward ear. "Take your time."

I was faintly surprised that Janis actually followed my advice. She drifted into a chair, used her lower limbs to settle herself into it, and then spoke.

"Nobody was endangered," she said, quite reasonably.

Anna-Lee's nostrils narrowed.

"You diverted from the flight plan that was devised for your safety," she said.

"I made a new flight plan," Janis pointed out. "Ground Control accepted it. If it was dangerous, she wouldn't have done that."

Anna-Lee's voice got that flat quality that it gets when she's following her own internal logic. Sometimes I think she's the program, not us.

"You are not authorized to file flight plans!" she snapped.

"Ground Control accepted it," Janis repeated. Her voice had grown a little sharp, and I whispered at her to keep cool.

"And Ground Control immediately informed *me!* They were right on the edge of calling out a rescue shuttle!"

"But they didn't, because there was no problem!" Janis snapped out, and then there was a pause while I told her to lower her voice.

"Ground Control accepted my revised plan," she said. "I landed according to the plan, and nobody was hurt."

"You planned this from the beginning!" All in that flat voice of hers. "This was a deliberate act of defiance!"

Which was true, of course.

"What harm did I do?" Janis asked.

("Look," I told Janis. "Just tell her that she's right and you were wrong and you'll never do it again."

("I'm not going to lie!" Janis sent back on our private channel. "Whatever Mom does, she's never going to make me lie!")

All this while Anna-Lee was saying, "We must all work together for the greater good! Your act of defiance did nothing but divert people from their proper tasks! Titan Ground Control has better things to do than worry about you!"

There was no holding Janis back now. "You *wanted* me to learn navigation! So I learned it—because *you* wanted it! And now that I've proved that I can use it, and you're angry about it!" She was waving her arms so furiously that she bounced up from her chair and began to sort of jerk around the room.

"And do you know why that is, Mom?" she demanded.

"*For God's sake shut up!*" I shouted at her. I knew where this was leading, but Janis was too far gone in her rage to listen to me now.

"It's because you're second-rate!" Janis shouted at her mother. "Dad went off to Barnard's Star, but *you* didn't make the cut! And I can do all the things you wanted to do, and do them better, and *you can't stand it!*"

"*Will you be quiet!*" I tell Janis. "Remember that *she owns you!*"

"I accepted the decision of the committee!" Anna-Lee was shouting. "I am a Constant Soldier and I live a productive life, and I will *not* be responsible for producing a child who is a *burden* and a *drain on resources!*"

"Who says I'm going to be a burden?" Janis demanded. "*You're* the only person who says that! If I incarnated tomorrow I could get a good job in ten minutes!"

"Not if you get a reputation for disobedience and anarchy!"

By this point it was clear that since Janis wasn't listening to me, and Anna-Lee *couldn't* listen, there was no longer any point in my involving myself in what had become a very predictable argument. So I closed the link and prepared my own excuses for my own inevitable meeting with my parents.

I changed from Picasso Woman to my own quadbod, which is what I use when I talk to my parents, at least when I want something from them. My quadbod avatar is a girl just a couple years younger than my actual age, wearing a school uniform with a Peter Pan collar and a white bow in her—my—hair. And my beautiful brown eyes are just slightly larger than eyes are in reality, because that's something called "neoteny," which means you look more like a baby and babies are designed to be irresistible to grownups.

Let me tell you that it works. Sometimes I can blink those big eyes and get away with anything.

And at that point my father called, and told me that he and my mom wanted to talk to me about my adventures on Titan, so I popped over to my parents' place, where I appeared in holographic form in their living room.

My parents are pretty reasonable people. Of course I take care to *keep* them reasonable, insofar as I can. *Let me smile with the wise,* as Doctor Sam says, *and feed with the rich.* I will keep my opinions to myself, and try my best to avoid upsetting the people who have power over me.

Why did I soar off with Janis on her flight plan? my father wanted to know.

"Because I didn't think she should go alone," I said.

Didn't you try to talk her out of it? my mother asked.

"You can't talk Janis out of anything," I replied. Which, my parents knowing Janis, was an answer they understood.

So my parents told me to be careful, and that was more or less the whole conversation.

Which shows you that not all parents up here are crazy.

Mine are more sensible than most. I don't think many parents would think much of my ambition to get involved in the fine arts. That's just not *done* up here, let alone the sort of thing *I* want to do, which is to incarnate on Earth and apprentice myself to an actual painter, or maybe a sculptor. Up here they just use cameras, and their idea of original art is to take camera pictures or alter camera pictures or combine camera pictures with one another or process the camera pictures in some way.

I want to do it from scratch, with paint on canvas. And not with a computer-programmed spray gun either, but with a real brush and blobs of paint. Because if you ask me the *texture* of the thing is important, which is why I like oils. Or rather the *idea* of oils, because I've never actually had a chance to work with the real thing.

And besides, as Doctor Sam says, *A man who has not been in Italy, is always conscious of an inferiority, from his not having seen what is expected a man should see. The grand object of traveling is to see the shores of the Mediterranean.*

So when I told my parents what I wanted to do, they just sort of shrugged and made me promise to learn another skill as well, one just a little bit more practical. So while I minor in art I'm majoring in computer design and function and programming, which is pretty interesting because all our really complex programs are written by artificial intelligences who are smarter than we are, so getting them to do what you want is as much like voodoo as science.

So my parents and I worked out a compromise that suited everybody, which is why I think my parents are pretty neat actually.

About twenty minutes after my talk with my parents, Janis knocked on my door, and I made the door go away, and she walked in, and then I put the door back. (Handy things, sims.)

"Guess that didn't work out so good, huh?" she said.

"On your family's civility scale," I said, "I think that was about average."

Her eyes narrowed (she was so upset that she forgot to change out of her quadbod, which is why she had the sort of eyes that could narrow).

"I'm going to get her," she said.

"I don't think that's very smart," I said.

Janis was smacking her fists into my walls, floor, and ceiling and shooting around the room, which was annoying even though the walls were virtual and she couldn't damage them or get fingerprints on them.

"Listen," I said. "All you have to do is keep the peace with your mom until you've finished your thesis, and then you'll be incarnated and she can't touch you. It's just *months*, Janis."

"My *thesis!*" A glorious grin of discovery spread across Janis' face. "I'm going to use my *thesis!* I'm going to stick it to Mom right where it hurts!"

I reached out and grabbed her and steadied her in front of me with all four arms.

"Look," I said. "You can't keep calling her bluff."

Her voice rang with triumph. "Just watch me."

"Please," I said. "I'm begging you. *Don't do anything till you're incarnated!*"

I could see the visions of glory dancing before her eyes. She wasn't seeing or hearing me at all.

"She's going to have to admit that I am right and that she is wrong," she said. "I'm going to nail my thesis to her forehead like Karl Marx on the church door."

"That was Martin Luther actually." (Sometimes I can't help these things.)

She snorted. "Who cares?"

"I do." Changing the subject. "*Because I don't want you to die.*"

Janis snorted. "I'm not going to bow to her. I'm going to *crush her*. I'm going to show her how stupid and futile and second-rate she is."

And at that moment there was a signal at my door. I ignored it.

"The power of punishment is to silence, not to confute," I said.

Her face wrinkled as if she'd bit into something sour. "I can't *believe* you're quoting that old dead guy again."

*I have found you an argument,* I wanted to say with Doctor Sam, *but I am not obliged to find you an understanding.*

The signal at my door repeated, and this time it was attached to an electronic signal that meant *Emergency!* Out of sheer surprise I dissolved the door.

Mei was there in her quadbod, an expression of anger on her face.

"If you two are finished congratulating each other on your brilliant little prank," she said, "you might take time to notice that Fritz is missing."

"Missing?" I didn't understand how someone could be missing. "Didn't his program come back from Titan?"

If something happened to the transmission, they could reload Fritz from a backup.

Mei's expression was unreadable. "He never went. He met the Blue Lady."

And then she pushed off with two of her hands and drifted away, leaving us in a sudden, vast, terrible silence.

We didn't speak, but followed Mei into the common room. The other cadre members were all there, and they all watched us as we floated in.

When you're little, you first hear about the Blue Lady from the other kids in your cadre. Nobody knows for sure how we *all* find out about the Blue Lady—not just the cadres on Ceres, but the ones on Vesta, and Ganymede, and *everywhere.*

And we all know that sometimes you might see her, a kind smiling woman in a blue robe, and she'll reach out to you, and she seems so nice you'll let her take your hand.

Only then, when it's too late, you'll see that she has no eyes, but only an empty blackness filled with stars.

She'll take you away and your friends will never see you again.

And of course it's your parents who send the Blue Lady to find you when you're bad.

We all know that the Blue Lady doesn't truly exist, it's ordinary techs in ordinary rooms who give the orders to zero out your program along with all its backups, but we all believe in the Blue Lady really, and not just when we're little.

Which brings me to the point I made about incarnation earlier. Once you're incarnated, you are considered a human being, and you have human rights.

But *not until then.* Until you're incarnated, you're just a computer program that belongs to your parents, and if your parents think the program is flawed or corrupted and simply too awkward to deal with, they can have you zeroed.

Zeroed. Not killed. The grownups insist that there's a difference, but I don't see it myself.

Because the Blue Lady really comes for some people, as she came for Fritz when Jack and Hans finally gave up trying to fix him. Most cadres get by without a visit. Some have more than one. There was a cadre on Vesta who lost eight, and then there were suicides among the survivors once they incarnated, and it was a big scandal that all the grownups agreed never to talk about.

I have never for an instant believed that my parents would ever send the Blue Lady after me, but still it's always there in the back of my mind, which is why I think that the current situation is so horrible. It gives parents a power they should never have, and it breeds a fundamental distrust between kids and their parents.

The grownups' chief complaint about the cadre system is that their children bond with their peers and not their parents. Maybe it's because their peers can't kill them.

Everyone in the cadre got the official message about Fritz, that he was basically irreparable and that the chance of his making a successful incarnation was essentially zero. The message said that none of us were at fault for what had happened, and that everyone knew that we'd done our best for him.

This was in the same message queue as a message to me from Fritz, made just before he got zeroed out. There he was with his stupid hat, smiling at me.

"Thank you for saying you'd play the shadowing game with me," he said. "I really think you're wonderful." He laughed. "See you soon, on Titan!"

So then I cried a lot, and I erased the message so that I'd never be tempted to look at it again.

We all felt failure. It was our job to make Fritz right, and we hadn't done it. We had all grown up with him, and even though he was a trial he was a part of our world. I had spent the last few days avoiding him, and I felt horrible about it; but everyone else had done the same thing at one time or another.

We all missed him.

The cadre decided to wear mourning, and we got stuck in a stupid argument about whether to wear white, which is the traditional mourning color in Asia, or black, which is the color in old Europe.

"Wear blue," Janis said. So we did. Whatever avatars we wore from that point on had blue clothing, or used blue as a principal color somewhere in their composition.

If any of the parents noticed, or talked about it, or complained, I never heard it.

I started thinking a lot about how I related to incarnated people, and I thought that maybe I'm just a little more compliant and adorable and sweet-natured than I'd otherwise be, because I want to avoid the consequences of being otherwise. And Janis is perhaps more defiant than she'd be under other circumstances, because she wants to show she's not afraid. *Go ahead, Mom,* she says, *pull the trigger. I dare you.*

Underestimating Anna-Lee all the way. Because Anna-Lee is a Constant Soldier of the Five Principles Movement, and that means *serious.*

The First Principle of the Five Principles Movement states that *Humanity is a pattern of thought, not a side effect of taxonomy,* which means that you're human if you *think* like a human, whether you've got six legs or four arms or two legs like the folks on Earth and Mars.

And then so on to the Fifth Principle, we come to the statement that humanity in all its various forms is intended to occupy every possible ecosystem throughout the entire universe, or at least as much of it as we can reach. Which is why the Five Principles Movement has always been very big on genetic experimentation, and the various expeditions to nearby stars.

I have no problem with the Five Principles Movement, myself. It's rational compared with groups like the Children of Venus or the God's Menu people.

Besides, if there isn't something to the Five Principles, what are we doing out here in the first place?

My problem lies with the sort of people the Movement attracts, which is to say people like Anna-Lee. People who are obsessive, and humorless, and completely unable to see any other point of view. Not only do they dedicate themselves heart and soul to whatever group they join, they insist everyone else has to join as well, and that anyone who isn't a part of it is a Bad Person.

So even though I pretty much agree with the Five Principles, I don't think I'm going to join the Movement. I'm going to keep in mind the wisdom of my good Doctor Sam: *Most schemes of political improvement are very laughable things.*

But to get back to Anna-Lee. Back in the day she married Carlos, who was also in the Movement, and together they worked for years to qualify for the expedition to Barnard's Star on the *True Destiny*. They created Janis together, because having children is all a part of occupying the universe and so on.

But Carlos got the offer to crew the ship, and Anna-Lee didn't. Carlos chose Barnard's Star over Anna-Lee, and now he's a couple light-months away. He and the rest of the settlers are in electronic form—no sense in spending the resources to ship a whole body to another star system when you can just ship the data and build the body once you arrive—and for the most part they're dormant, because there's nothing to do until they near their destination. But every week or so Carlos has himself awakened so that he can send an electronic postcard to his daughter.

The messages are all really boring, as you might expect from someone out in deep space where there's nothing to look at and nothing to do, and everyone's asleep anyway.

Janis sends him longer messages, mostly about her fights with Anna-Lee. Anna-Lee likewise sends Carlos long messages about Janis' transgressions. At two light-months out Carlos declines to mediate between them, which makes them both mad.

So Anna-Lee is mad because her husband left her, and she's mad at Janis for not being a perfect Five Principles Constant Soldier. Janis is mad at Carlos for not figuring out a way to take her along, and she's mad at Anna-Lee for not making the crew on the *True Destiny*, and failing that, not having the savvy to keep her husband in the picture.

And she's also mad at Anna-Lee for getting married again, this time to Rhee, a rich Movement guy who was able to swing the taxes to create *two new daughters,* both of whom are the stars of their particular cadres and are going to grow up to be perfect Five Principles Kids, destined to carry on the work of humanity in new habitats among distant stars.

Or so Anna-Lee claims, anyway.

Which is why I think that Janis underestimates her mother. I think the way Anna-Lee looks at it, she's got two new kids, who are everything she wants. And one older kid who gives her trouble, and who she can give to the Blue Lady without really losing anything, since she's lost Janis anyway. She's already given a husband to the stars, after all.

And all this is another reason why I want to incarnate on Earth, where a lot of people still have children the old-fashioned way. The parents make an embryo in a gene-splicer, and then the embryo is put in a vat, and nine months later you crack the vat open and you've got an actual baby, not a computer program. And even if the procedure is a lot more time-consuming and messy I still think it's superior.

So I was applying for work on Earth, both for jobs that could use computer skills, and also for apprenticeship programs in the fine arts. But there's a waiting list for pretty much any job you want on Earth, and also there's a big entry tax unless they *really* want you, so I wasn't holding my breath; and besides, I hadn't finished my thesis.

I figured on graduating from college along with most of my cadre, at the age of fourteen. I understand that in your day, Doctor Sam, people graduated from college a lot later. I figure there are several important reasons for the change: (1) we virtual kids don't sleep as much as you do, so we have more time for study; (2) there isn't that much else to do here anyway; and (3) we're really, really, *really* smart. Because if you were a parent, and you had a say in the makeup of your kid (along with the doctors and the sociologists and the hoodoo machines), would you say, *No thanks, I want mine stupid?*

No, I don't think so.

And the meat-brains that we incarnate into are pretty smart, too. Just in case you were wondering.

We could grow up faster, if we wanted. The computers we live in are so fast that we could go from inception to maturity in just two or three months. But we wouldn't get to interact with our parents, who being meat would be much slower, or with anyone else. So in order to have any kind of relationship with our elders, or any kind of socialization at all, we have to slow down to our parents' pace. I have to say that I agree with that.

In order to graduate I needed to do a thesis, and unfortunately I couldn't do the one I wanted, which was the way the paintings of Breughel, etc., reflected the theology of the period. All the training with computers and systems, along with art and art history, had given me an idea of how abstract systems such as theology work, and how you can visually represent fairly abstract concepts on a flat canvas.

But I'd have to save that for maybe a graduate degree, because my major was still in the computer sciences, so I wrote a fairly boring thesis on systems interopability—which, if you care, is the art of getting different machines and highly specialized operating systems to talk to each other, a job that is made more difficult if the machines in question happen to be a lot smarter than you are.

Actually it's a fairly interesting subject. It just wasn't interesting in my thesis.

While I was doing that I was also working outside contracts for Dane, who was from a cadre that had incarnated a few years ahead of us, and who I got to know when his group met with ours to help with our lessons and with our socialization skills (because they wanted us to be able to talk to people outside the cadre and our families, something we might not do if we didn't have practice).

Anyway, Dane had got a programming job in Ceres' communications center, and he was willing to pass on the more boring parts of his work to me in exchange for money. So I was getting a head start on paying that big Earth entry tax, or if I could evade the tax, maybe living on Earth a while and learning to paint.

"You're just going to end up being Ceres' first interior decorator," Janis scoffed.

"And that would be a *bad* thing?" I asked. "Just *look* at this place!" Because it's all so functional and boring and you'd think they could find a more interesting color of paint than *grey*, for God's sake.

That was one of the few times I'd got to talk to Janis since our adventure on Titan. We were both working on our theses, and still going to school, and I had my outside contracts, and I think she was trying to avoid me, because she didn't want to tell me what she was doing because she didn't want me to tell her not to do it.

Which hurt, by the way. Since we'd been such loyal friends up to the point where I told her not to get killed, and then because I wanted to save her life she didn't want to talk to me anymore.

The times I mostly got to see Janis were Incarnation Day parties for other members of our cadre. So we got to see Ganymede, and Iapetus, and Titan again, and Rhea, and Pluto, Callisto, and Io, and the antimatter generation ring between Venus and Mercury, and Titan again, and then Titan a fourth time.

Our cadre must have this weird affinity for orange, I don't know.

We went to Pallas, Juno, and Vesta. Though if you ask me, one asteroid settlement is pretty much like the next.

We went to Third Heaven, which is a habitat the God's Menu people built at L2. And they can *keep* a lot of the items on the menu, if you ask me.

We visited Luna (which you would call the Moon, Doctor Sam. As if there was only one). And we got to view *Everlasting Dynasty*, the starship being constructed in lunar orbit for the expedition to Tau Ceti, the settlement that Anna-Lee was trying her best to get Janis aboard.

We also got to visit Mars three times. So among other entertainments I looked down at the planet from the top of Olympus Mons, the largest mountain in the solar system, and I looked down from the edge of the solar system's largest canyon, and then I looked *up* from the bottom of the same canyon.

We all tried to wear blue if we could, in memory of the one of us who couldn't be present.

Aside from the sights, the Incarnation Day parties were great because all our incarnated cadre members turned up, in bodies they'd borrowed for the occasion. We were all still close, of course, and kept continually in touch, but our communication was limited by the speed of light and it wasn't anything like having Fahd and Chandra and Solange there in person, to pummel and to hug.

We didn't go to Earth. I was the only one of our cadre who had applied there, and I hadn't got an answer yet. I couldn't help fantasizing about what my Incarnation Day party would be like if I held it on Earth—where would I go? What would we look at? Rome? Mount Everest? The ocean habitats? The plains of Africa, where the human race began?

It was painful to think that the odds were high that I'd never see any of these places.

Janis never tried to organize any of her little rebellions on these trips. For one thing word had got out, and we were all pretty closely supervised. Her behavior was never less than what Anna-Lee would desire. But under it all I could tell she was planning something drastic.

I tried to talk to her about it. I talked about my thesis, and hoped it would lead to a discussion of *her* thesis. But no luck. She evaded the topic completely.

She was pretty busy with her project, though, whatever it was. Because she was always buzzing around the cadre asking people where to look for odd bits of knowledge.

I couldn't make sense of her questions, though. They seemed to cover too many fields. Sociology, statistics, mineralogy, criminology, economics, astronomy, spaceship design… The project seemed too huge.

The only thing I knew about Janis' thesis was that it was *supposed* to be about resource management. It was the field that Anna-Lee forced her into, because it was full of skills that would be useful on the Tau Ceti expedition. And if that didn't work, Anna-Lee made sure Janis minored in spaceship and shuttle piloting and navigation.

I finally finished my thesis, and then I sat back and waited for the job offers to roll in. The only offer I got came from someone who wanted me to run the garbage cyclers on Iapetus, which the guy should have known I wouldn't accept if he had bothered to read my application.

Maybe he was just neck-deep in garbage and desperate, I don't know.

And then the most astounding thing happened. Instead of a job in the computer field, I got an offer to study at the Pisan Academy.

Which is an art school. Which is in Italy, which is where the paintings come from mostly.

The acceptance committee said that my work showed a "naive but highly original fusion of social criticism with the formalities of the geometric order." I don't even *pretend* to know what they meant by that, but I suspect they just weren't used to the perspective of a student who had spent practically her entire life in a computer on Ceres.

I broadcast my shrieks of joy to everyone in the cadre, even those who had left Ceres and were probably wincing at their work stations when my screams reached them.

I bounced around the common room and everyone came out to congratulate me. Even Janis, who had taken to wearing an avatar that wasn't even remotely human, just a graphic of a big sledgehammer smashing a rock, over and over.

Subtlety had never been her strong point.

"Congratulations," she said. "You got what you wanted."

And then she broadcast something on a private channel. *You're going to be famous*, she said. *But I'm going to be a* legend.

I looked at her. And then I sent back, *Can we talk about this?*

*In a few days. When I deliver my thesis.*

*Don't*, I pleaded.

*Too late.*

The hammer hit its rock, and the shards flew out into the room and vanished.

I spent the next few days planning my Incarnation Day party, but my heart wasn't in it. I kept wondering if Janis was going to be alive to enjoy it.

I finally decided to have my party in Thailand because there were so many interesting environments in one place, as well as the Great Buddha. And I found a caterer that was supposed to be really good.

I decided what sort of body I wanted, and the incarnation specialists on Earth started cooking it up in one of their vats. Not the body of an Earth-born fourteen-year-old, but older, more like eighteen. Brown eyes, brown hair, and those big eyes that had always been so useful.

And two legs, of course. Which is what they all have down there.

I set the date. The cadre were alerted. We all practiced in the simulations and tried to get used to making do with only two arms. Everyone was prepared.

And then Janis finished her thesis. I downloaded a copy the second it was submitted to her committee and read it in one long sitting, and my sense of horror grew with every line.

What Janis had done was publish a comprehensive critique *of our entire society!* It was a piece of brilliance, and at the same time it was utter poison.

Posthuman society wrecks its children, Janis said, and this can be demonstrated by the percentage of neurotic and dysfunctional adults. The problems encountered by the first generation of children who spent their formative years as programs—the autism, the obsessions and compulsions, the addictions to electronic environments—hadn't gone away, they'd just been reduced to the point where they'd become a part of the background clutter, a part of our civilization so everyday that we never quite noticed it.

Janis had the data, too. The number of people who were under treatment for one thing or another. The percentage who had difficulty adjusting to their incarnations, or who didn't want to communicate with anyone outside their cadre, or who couldn't sleep unless they were immersed in a simulation. Or who committed suicide. Or who died in accidents—Janis questioned whether all those accidents were really the results of our harsh environments. Our machines and our settlements were much safer than they had been in the early days, but the rates of accidental death were still high. How many accidents were caused by distracted or unhappy operators, or for that matter were deliberate "suicide by machine"?

Janis went on to describe one of the victims of this ruthless type of upbringing. "Flat of emotional affect, offended by disorder and incapable of coping with obstruction, unable to function without adherence to a belief system as rigid as the artificial and constricted environments in which she was raised."

When I realized Janis was describing Anna-Lee I almost de-rezzed.

Janis offered a scheme to cure the problem, which was to get rid of the virtual environments and start out with real incarnated babies. She pulled out vast numbers of statistics demonstrating that places that did this—chiefly Earth—seemed to raise more successful adults. She also pointed out that the initial shortage of resources that had prompted the creation of virtual children in the first place had long since passed—plenty of water-ice coming in from the Kuiper Belt these days, and we were sitting on all the minerals we could want. The only reason the system continued was for the convenience of the adults. But genuine babies, as opposed to abstract computer programs, would help the adults, too. They would no longer be tempted to become little dictators with absolute power over their offspring. Janis said the chance would turn the grownups into better human beings.

All this was buttressed by colossal numbers of statistics, graphs, and other data. I realized when I'd finished it that the Cadre of Glorious Destiny had produced one true genius, and that this genius was Janis.

*The true genius is a mind of large general powers, accidentally determined to some particular direction.*

Anna-Lee determined her, all right, and the problem was that Janis probably didn't have that long to live. Aside from the fact that Janis had ruthlessly caricatured her, Anna-Lee couldn't help but notice that the whole work went smack up against the Five Principles Movement. According to the Movement people, all available resources had to be devoted to the expansion of the human race out of the solar system and into new environments. It didn't matter how many more resources were available now than in the past, it was clear against their principles to devote a greater share to the raising of children when it could be used to blast off into the universe.

And though the Five Principles people acknowledged our rather high death rate, they put it down to our settlements' hazardous environments. All we had to do was genetically modify people to better suit the environments and the problem would be solved.

I skipped the appendices and zoomed from my room across the common room to Janis' door, and hit the button to alert her to a visitor. The door vanished, and there was Janis—for the first time since her fight with Anna-Lee, she was using her quadbod avatar. She gave me a wicked grin.

"Great, isn't it?"

"It's *brilliant!* But you can't let Anna-Lee see it."

"Don't be silly. I sent Mom the file myself."

I was horrified. She had to have seen the way my Picasso-face gaped, and it made her laugh.

"She'll have you erased!" I said.

"If she does," Janis said. "She'll only prove my point." She put a consoling hand on my shoulder. "Sorry if it means missing your incarnation."

When Anna-Lee came storming in—which wasn't long after—Janis broadcast the whole confrontation on a one-way link to the whole cadre. We got to watch, but not to participate. She didn't want our advice any more than she wanted her mother's.

"You are unnatural!" Anna-Lee stormed. "You spread slanders! You have betrayed the highest truth!"

"I *told* the truth!" Janis said. "And you *know* it's the truth, otherwise you wouldn't be so insane right now."

Anna-Lee stiffened. "I am a Five Principles Constant Soldier. I know the truth, and I know my duty."

"Every time you say that, you prove my point."

"You will retract this thesis, and apologize to your committee for giving them such a vicious document."

Anna-Lee hadn't realized that the document was irretrievable, that Janis had given it to everyone she knew.

Janis laughed. "No way, Mom," she said.

Anna-Lee lost it. She waved her fists and screamed. "I know my duty! I will not allow such a slander to be seen by anyone!" She pointed at Janis. "You have three days to retract!"

Janis gave a snort of contempt.

"Or what?"

"Or I will decide that you're incorrigible and terminate your program."

Janis laughed. "Go right ahead, Mom. Do it *now*. Nothing spreads a new idea better than martyrdom." She spread her four arms. "*Do* it, Mom. I *hate* life in this hell. I'm ready."

*I will be conquered; I will not capitulate.*

Yes, Doctor Sam. That's it exactly.

"You have three days," Anna-Lee said, her voice all flat and menacing, and then her virtual image de-rezzed.

Janis looked at the space where her mom had been, and then a goofy grin spread across her face. She switched to the redheaded, stick-figure avatar, and began to do a little dance as she hovered in the air, moving like a badly animated cartoon.

"Hey!" she sang. "I get to go to Alison's party after all!"

I had been so caught up in the drama that I had forgot my incarnation was going to happen in two days.

But it wasn't going to be a party now. It was going to be a wake.

"Doctor Sam," I said, "I've got to save Janis."

*The triumph of hope over experience.*

"Hope is what I've got," I said, and then I thought about it. "And maybe a little experience, too."

* * *

My Incarnation Day went well. We came down by glider, as we had that first time on Titan, except that this time I told Ground Control to let my friends land wherever the hell they wanted. That gave us time to inspect the Great Buddha, a slim man with a knowing smile sitting cross-legged with knobs on his head. He's two and a half kilometers tall and packed with massively parallel quantum processors, all crunching vast amounts of data, thinking whatever profound thoughts are appropriate to an artificial intelligence built on such a scale, and repeating millions of sutras, which are scriptures for Buddhists, all at the speed of light.

It creeps along at two or three centimeters per day, and will enter the strait at the end of the Kra Peninsula many thousands of years from now.

After viewing the Buddha's serene expression from as many angles as suited us, we soared and swooped over many kilometers of brilliant green jungle and landed on the beach. And we all *did* land on the beach, which sort of surprised me. And then we all did our best to learn how to surf—and let me tell you from the start, the surfing simulators are *totally* inadequate. The longest I managed to stand my board was maybe twenty seconds.

I was amazed at all the sensations that crowded all around me. The breeze on my skin, the scents of the sea and the vegetation and the charcoal on which our banquet was being cooked. The hot sand under my bare feet. The salt taste of the ocean on my lips. The sting of the little jellyfish on my legs and arms, and the iodine smell of the thick strand of seaweed that got wrapped in my hair.

I mean, I had no *idea*. The simulators were totally inadequate to the Earth experience.

And this was just a *part* of the Earth, a small fraction of the environments available. I think I convinced a lot of the cadre that maybe they'd want to move to Earth as soon as they could raise the money and find a job.

After swimming and beach games we had my Incarnation Day dinner. The sensations provided by the food were really too intense—I couldn't eat much of it. If I was going to eat Earth food, I was going to have to start with something a lot more bland.

And there was my brown-eyed body at the head of the table, looking down at the members of the Cadre of Glorious Destiny who were toasting me with tropical drinks, the kind that have parasols in them.

Tears came to my eyes, and they were a lot wetter and hotter than tears in the sims. For some reason that fact made me cry even more.

My parents came to the dinner, because this was the first time they could actually hug me—hug me for real, that is, and not in a sim. They had downloaded into bodies that didn't look much like the four-armed quadbods they used back on Ceres, but that didn't matter. When my arms went around them, I began to cry again.

After the tears were wiped away we put on underwater gear and went for a swim on the reef, which is just amazing. More colors and shapes and textures than I could ever imagine—or imagine putting in a work of art.

*A work of art that embodies all but selects none is not art, but mere cant and recitation.*

Oh, wow. You're right. Thank you, Doctor Sam.

After the reef trip we paid a visit to one of the underwater settlements, one inhabited by people adapted to breathe water. The problems were that we had to keep our underwater gear on, and that none of us were any good at the fluid sign language they all used as their preferred means of communication.

Then we rose from the ocean, dried out, and had a last round of hugs before being uploaded to our normal habitations. I gave Janis a particularly strong hug, and I whispered in her ear.

"Take care of yourself."

"Who?" she grinned. "*Me?*"

And then the little brown-haired body was left behind, looking very lonely, as everyone else put on the electrodes and uploaded back to their normal and very-distant worlds.

As soon as I arrived on Ceres, I zapped an avatar of myself into my parents' quarters. They looked at me as if I were a ghost.

"What are *you* doing here?" my mother managed.

"I hate to tell you this," I said, "but I think you're going to have to hire a lawyer."

\* \* \*

It was surprisingly easy to do, really. Remember that I was assisting Dane, who was a communications tech, and in charge of uploading all of our little artificial brains to Earth. And also remember that I am a specialist in systems interopability, which implies that I am also a specialist in systems *un*operability.

It was very easy to set a couple of artificial intelligences running amok in Dane's system just as he was working on our upload. And that so distracted him that he said *yes* when I said that I'd do the job for him.

And once I had access, it was the work of a moment to swap a couple of serial numbers.

The end result of which was that it was Janis who uploaded into my brown-haired body, and received all the toasts, and who hugged my parents with *my* arms. And who is now on Earth, incarnated, with a full set of human rights and safe from Anna-Lee.

I wish I could say the same for myself.

Anna-Lee couldn't have me killed, of course, since I don't belong to her. But she could sue my parents, who from her point of view permitted a piece of software belonging to *them* to prevent her from wreaking vengeance on some software that belonged to *her*.

And of course Anna-Lee went berserk the second she found out—which was more or less immediately, since Janis sent her a little radio taunt as soon as she downed her fourth or fifth celebratory umbrella drink.

Janis sent me a message, too.

"The least you could have done was make my hair red."

*My* hair. Sometimes I wonder why I bothered.

An unexpected side effect of this was that we all got famous. It turns out that this was an unprecedented legal situation, with lots of human interest and a colorful cast of characters. Janis became a media celebrity, and so did I, and so did Anna-Lee.

Celebrity didn't do Anna-Lee's cause any good. Her whole mental outlook was too rigid to stand the kind of scrutiny and questioning that any public figure has to put up with. As soon as she was challenged she lost control. She called one of the leading media interviewers a name that you, Doctor Sam, would not wish me to repeat.

Whatever the actual merits of her legal case, the sight of Anna-Lee screaming that I had deprived her of the inalienable right to kill her daughter failed to win her a lot of friends. Eventually the Five Principles people realized she wasn't doing their cause any good, and she was replaced by a Movement spokesperson who said as little as possible.

Janis did some talking, too, but not nearly as much as she would have liked, because she was under house arrest for coming to Earth without a visa and without paying the immigration tax. The cops showed up when she was sleeping off her hangover from all the umbrella drinks. It's probably lucky that she wasn't given the opportunity to talk much, because if she started on her rants she would have worn out her celebrity as quickly as Anna-Lee did.

Janis was scheduled to be deported back to Ceres, but shipping an actual incarnated human being is much more difficult than zapping a simulation by laser, and she had to wait for a ship that could carry passengers, and that would be months.

She offered to navigate the ship herself, since she had the training, but the offer was declined.

Lots of people read her thesis who wouldn't otherwise have heard of it. And millions discussed it whether they'd read it or not. There were those who said that Janis was right, and those that said that Janis was mostly right but that she exaggerated. There were those who said that the problem didn't really exist, except in the statistics.

There were those who thought the problem existed entirely in the software, that the system would work if the simulations were only made more like reality. I had to disagree, because I think the simulations *were* like reality, but only for certain people.

The problem is that human beings perceive reality in slightly different ways, even if they happen to be programs. A programmer could do his best to create an artificial reality that exactly mimicked the way he perceived reality, except that it wouldn't be as exact for another person, it would only be an approximation. It would be like fitting everyone's hand into the same-sized glove.

Eventually someone at the University of Adelaide read the thesis and offered Janis a professorship in their sociology department. She accepted and was freed from house arrest.

Poor Australia, I thought.

I was on video quite a lot. I used my little-girl avatar, and I batted my big eyes a lot. I still wore blue, mourning for Fritz.

Why, I was asked, did I act to save Janis?

"Because we're cadre, and we're supposed to look after one another."

What did I think of Anna-Lee?

"I don't see why she's complaining. I've seen to it that Janis *just isn't her problem anymore.*"

Wasn't what I did stealing?

"It's not stealing to free a slave."

And so on. It was the same sort of routine I'd been practicing on my parents all these years, and the practice paid off. Entire cadres—hundreds of them—signed petitions asking that the case be dismissed. Lots of adults did the same.

I hope that it helps, but the judge that hears the case isn't supposed to be swayed by public opinion, but only by the law.

And everyone forgets that it's my parents that will be on trial, not me, accused of letting their software steal Anna-Lee's software. And of course I, and therefore they, am completely guilty, so my parents are almost certainly going to be fined, and lose both money and Citizenship Points.

I'm sorry about that, but my parents seem not to be.

How the judge will put a value on a piece of stolen software that its owner fully intended to destroy is going to make an interesting ruling, however it turns out.

I don't know whether I'll ever set foot on Earth again. I can't take my place in Pisa because I'm not incarnated, and I don't know if they'll offer again.

And however things turn out, Fritz is still zeroed. And I still wear blue.

I don't have my outside job any longer. Dane won't speak to me, because his supervisor reprimanded him, and he's under suspicion for being my accomplice. And even those who are sympathetic to me aren't about to let me loose with their computers.

And even if I get a job somewhere, I can't be incarnated until the court case is over.

It seems to me that the only person who got away scot-free was Janis. Which is normal.

So right now my chief problem is boredom. I spent fourteen years in a rigid program intended to fill my hours with wholesome and intellectually useful activity, and now that's over.

And I can't get properly started on the non-wholesome thing until I get an incarnation somewhere.

*Everyone is, or hopes to be, an idler.*

Thank you, Doctor Sam.

I'm choosing to idle away my time making pictures. Maybe I can sell them and help pay the Earth tax.

I call them my "Doctor Johnson" series. *Sam. Johnson on Mars. Sam. Johnson Visits Neptune. Sam. Johnson Quizzing the Tomasko Glacier. Sam. Johnson Among the Asteroids.*

I have many more ideas along this line.

Doctor Sam, I trust you will approve.


# AFTERWORD: INCARNATION DAY

*"Incarnation Day" was written in response to a solicitation by Jonathan Strahan for his young adult anthology* The Starry Rift. *The finished story was too long for that collection, so "Incarnation Day" went to Gardner Dozois and Jack Dann for their own YA anthology,* Escape from Earth, *and in turn I wrote "Pinocchio" for Jonathan.*

*Every story I write is practice for some other story. Though "Incarnation Day" uses ideas that I have developed elsewhere—the plight of minor children in virtual environments controlled by grownups, and the future in which everything went right (for adults, anyway)—I'd like to think I deployed the ideas here to better advantage. Practice improved things.*

At least one reviewer thought it unlikely that a modern lady like Alison would have an imaginary friend from a century as far removed as Sam Johnson. I disagree. This element of the story is pure realism.

It so happens that when I was younger, Dr. Samuel Johnson was my *imaginary playmate.*

# SEND THEM
# FLOWERS

We skipped through the borderlands of Probability, edging farther and farther away from the safe universes that had become so much less safe for us, and into the fringe areas where stars were cloudy smears of phosphorescent gas and the Periodic Table wasn't a guide, but a series of ever-more-hopeful suggestions.

Our ship was fueled for another seven years, but our flight ended at Socorro for the most prosaic reason possible: we had run out of food. Exchange rates and docking fees ate most of what little money we had, and that left us on Socorro with enough cash for two weeks' food or one good party.

Guess which we chose?

For five months we'd been running from Shawn, or at any rate the cloaked, dagger-bearing assassins we imagined him sending after us. I'd had nothing but Tonio's company and freeze-dried food to eat, and the only wine we'd drunk had been stuff that Tonio brewed in plastic bags out of kitchen waste. We hadn't realized how foul the air on the *Olympe* had grown until we stepped out of the docking tube and smelled the pure recycled air of Socorro Topside, the station floating in geosynchronous orbit at the end of its tether.

The delights of Topside glittered ahead of us, all lights and music, the sizzle of grilled meats and the clink of glasses. How could we resist?

Besides, freaky Probability was fizzing in our veins. Our metabolisms were pumped by a shift in the electromagnetic fine structure constant. Oxygen was captured and transported and burned and united with carbon and exhaled with greater efficiency. We didn't have to breathe as often as in our home Probability, and still our bodies ran a continuous fever from the boost in our metabolic rate.

Another few more steps into Probability and the multiverse would start fucking with the strong and weak nuclear forces, causing our bodies to fly apart or the calcium in our bones to turn radioactive. But here, we remained more or less ourselves even as certain chemical reactions became much easier.

Which was why Socorro and its Topside had been built on this strange outpost of the multiverse, to create alloys that weren't possible in our home probabilities, and to refine pure chemicals in industrial-sized quantities at a fraction of the energy it would have taken elsewhere.

Probability specialists in the employ of the Pryor corporate gene line had labored hard to locate this particular Probability, with its unique physical properties—some theorists would argue, in fact, that they'd *created* it, like magicians bringing an entire universe into being with their spell. Once the Pryors had found the place, they'd explored it for years while putting together the right industrial base to properly exploit it. When they finally came, they came in strength, a whole industrial colony jigsawing itself into the Socorro system practically overnight.

Once they started shipping product out, they had to declare to the authorities where it came from, and this particular Probability was no longer secret. Others could come and exploit it, but the Pryors already had their facilities in place, and the profits pouring out.

Nobody lived in Socorro permanently. There was something about this reality that was conducive to forming tumors. You came in on a three-year contract and then shipped out, with cancer-preventing chemicals saturating your tissues.

"Oh yiss," Tonio said as we walked down Topside's main avenue. "Scrutinize the fine ladies yonder, my compeer. I desire nothing so much as to bond with them chemically, oh yiss."

The local fashion for women was weirdly modest and demure, covering the whole body and with a hood for the head, and the outfit looked *inflated*—as if they were wearing full-body life preservers, designed to keep them floating even if Topside fell out of orbit and dropped into the ocean.

But even these outfits couldn't entirely disguise the female form, or the female walk. My blood seemed to fizz at the sight, and perhaps, in this quirky Probability, it did.

Music floated out of a place called the Flesh Pit, all suggestive dark windows and colorful electric ads for cheap drinks. "Let us sample the pleasures of this charming bistro," Tonio suggested.

"How about some food first?" I said, but Tonio was already halfway through the door.

The Flesh Pit had alcohol and other conventional stimulants, and also others that were designed for our current reality, taking advantage of the local biochemistry to deliver a packaged high aimed at our pumped metabolisms. The charge was delivered from a pressure cylinder into a cheap plastic face mask. The masks weren't hygienic, but after a few huffs we didn't much care.

While getting refills at the bar we met a short, brown-skinned man named Frank. He was drinking alcohol, and joined us at our table. After two drinks he was groping my thigh, but he didn't take it amiss when I moved his hand away.

The Flesh Pit was a disappointment. The music was bottom-grade puti-puti and the women weren't very attractive even after they took off their balloon-suits. After we bought Frank another drink he agreed to be our guide to Topside's delights, such as they were.

He took us up a flight of stairs to a place that didn't seem to actually have a name. The very second I stepped into the front room a woman attached herself to me, spreading herself across my front like a cephalopod embracing its prey. My eyes were still adjusting to the dim light and I hadn't seen her until she'd engulfed me.

My eyes adapted and I looked around. We were in what appeared to be a small dance hall: there was a bar at one end and a live band at the other, and benches along the sides where women smoked and waited for partners. There were a few couples shuffling around on the dance floor, each man in the octopus clutch of his consort.

"Buy me a drink, space man?" my partner said. Her name was Étoile and she wore a gardenia above one ear. I looked longingly at the prettier girls sitting on the benches and then sighed and headed for the bar. On my way I noticed that Tonio had snagged the most beautiful woman in the place, a tall, tawny-haired lioness with a wicked smile.

I bought Étoile an overpriced cocktail and myself a whiff of some exotic gas. We took a turn on the dance floor, then went to the bedroom. Then back to the bar, then to the bedroom. Frank was sent out for food and came back with items on skewers. Then the bar, then the bedroom. I had to pay for clean sheets each time. Étoile was very efficient about collecting. Occasionally I would run into Tonio and his girl in the corridor.

By morning the bar was closed and locked, the dance floor was empty, I was hungry and broke and melancholy, and Tonio's girl had gone insane. She was crying and clutching Tonio's leg and begging him to stay.

"If you leave I'll never see you again!" she said. "If you leave I'll kill my-self!" Then she took a bottle from the bar and smashed it on a table and tried to cut her wrist with a piece of glass.

I grabbed her and knocked the broken glass out of her hand, and then I pinned her against the wall while she screamed and sobbed, with tears running down her beautiful face, and Étoile tried to find the management or the bartender or someone to get Tonio's girl a dose of something to calm her down.

I gave Tonio an annoyed look.

He had driven his woman crazy in only one night.

"That's a new record," I told him.

Étoile returned with an irritated and sleepy-eyed manager, who unlocked the bar and got an inhaler. He plastered the mask over the weeping woman's face and cracked the valve and held the mask over her mouth and nose till she relaxed and drifted off to sleep. Then Tonio and I carried her to her room and laid her on the bed.

"She ever done this before?" I asked the manager.

He slapped at the wisp of hair atop his bald head as if it had bitten him. "No," he said.

"You'll have to watch her," I said.

He shrugged his little mustache. "I'm going back to bed," he said.

I looked at Étoile. "Not me," she said. "Unless you pay."

"It is necessary at this juncture," said Tonio, "for me to confess the infortunate condition of our finances."

*Infortunate.* Tonio was always making up words that he thought were real.

"Then get your asses out of here," said the manager. Étoile glared at me as if it weren't her fault I had no money left.

We dragged ourselves back to the *Olympe*. The ship smelled a lot better with air being cycled in from the station. I wondered if I'd ever be able to pay for the air I was breathing.

"I hope Fanny will recover, yiss," Tonio said as he headed for his rack.

"What did you *do* to her?" I said.

"We did things, yiss. It was Fanny did all the talking."

I looked again at Tonio and tried to figure out yet again why so many women loved him. He wasn't any better-looking than I was, and he was too skinny and he had dirt under his nails. His hands were too big for the rest of him. He had blue eyes, which probably didn't hurt.

Maybe the attraction was the broken nose, the big knot in the center of his face that made it all a little off-center. Maybe that's all it took.

"Listen, Gaucho," he said. He had his sincere face on. "I am aware that this contingency is entirely my fault."

"It's too late to worry about that," I said.

"Yiss, well." He reached down and took the ring off his finger, the one with the big emerald that Adora had given him, and he held it out to me.

"This is the only valuable thing I own," he said. "I desire that you take it."

"I don't want your ring," I said.

He took my hand and pressed the ring into it. "If necessity bides, you can sell it," he said. "I don't cognizate how much it's worth, but it's a lot, yiss. It will pay for docking fees and enough food to peregrinate to some other Probability where you might be able to make a success."

I looked at him. "Are you saying goodbye, Tonio?"

He shrugged. "Compeer, I have no plans. But who knows what the future may necessitate?"

He ambled away to his rack. I looked at the ring on my palm—all the intricate little designs on it, the dolphins of the Feeneys and the storks of the Storch line all woven together in little knots.

I went into my stateroom where I closed the door. I put the ring on my desk and looked at it for a while, and then I went to bed.

When I woke in the morning, the ring was still there, shining like all the unpaid debts in all the multiverse.

I met Tonio when I was working with my wife Karen on a mining concession owned by her family, an asteroid known only by an identification number. We were supervising the robots that did the actual mining, following the vein of gold and sending it streaming out into the void to be caught by the processor that hovered overhead. Gold was a common metal and prices were low. The robots were old and kept breaking down.

Tonio turned up in a draft of new workers, and we became friends. He had his charm, and his strange Andevin accent, and the vocabulary he'd got in prison, where he had nothing to read for months but a dictionary. He said the prison term was the result of a misunderstanding about whether or not he could borrow someone else's blazemobile.

Tonio and I became friends. After Karen and Tonio became friends, I equipped myself with a heavy pry bar and went looking for him. When he opened the door to his little room and saw me standing there, he just looked at me and then shrugged.

"Do whatsoever thou must, compeer," he said, backing away from the door. "For I deserve it in all truth."

I stepped in and hefted the pry bar and realized that I couldn't hit him. I lowered the bar and then Tonio and I talked for about six hours, after which I realized that my marriage hadn't been working in a long time, and that I wanted out and that Tonio could have Karen for all I cared.

After the divorce, when everything had played itself out and there was no point in staying on the claim of a family to which I was no longer tied, I left the scene along with Tonio.

Of the various options, it was the course that promised the most fun.

The *Olympe* isn't a freighter, it's a small private vessel—a yacht in fact, though I'm far from any kind of yachtsman. The boat can carry cargo, but only a modest amount. In practice, if I wanted to carry cargo there were three alternatives. Passengers. Compact but valuable cargo, which often means contraband. And information, despatches so private that the sender doesn't want to broadcast them even in cipher. Usually the despatches are carried by a courier.

Once we docked on Socorro I advertised *Olympe*—I even offered references—but didn't get any takers, not right away. Fortunately docking on Socorro was cheap—this wasn't a tourist spot, but an industrial colony with too much docking capacity—and the air was nearly free. So Tonio got a job Upside, selling roasted chestnuts from a little wheeled grill—and with his blue eyes and broken nose working for him, he soon sold more chestnuts than anyone in the history of the whole pushcart business.

I took my aurora onto the station and went looking for work as a musician. I did some busking till I got a job with a band whose aurorista was on vacation in another Probability, and my little salary and Tonio's got us through the first month even though the puti-puti music bored me stiff. Then I auditioned for a band that had a series of regular gigs in upscale bars, and they took me on. I got a full split and a share of tips instead of a tiny salary, and things eased a bit. Even the music was better. We played popular songs while the tables were full of the dinner crowd, but afterward we played what we liked, and when I got a good grind going, I could make the room sizzle the way my blood sizzled in this little corner of the multiverse.

During our flight I'd had nothing to do but practice, and I'd got pretty good.

A couple of months went by. I didn't see Tonio much—he'd got a girlfriend named Mackey and was spending his free time with her. But he sent a piece of his pay into my account every month, to help pay for *Olympe*.

I didn't have to sell the ring. I put it in the captain's safe and tried not to think about it.

The docking fees got paid, and our air and water bill. I had *Olympe* cleaned and the crudded-up old air filters replaced. I polished the wood and the ornate metalwork in my stateroom till it glistened, and put up some of Aram's old things, in case I wanted to impress a potential passenger with the luxury we could offer. I started stocking the larder against the day it was time to leave.

I began to relax. Perhaps Shawn's vengeance was not quite so hot on our tail. I even spent some dinars on my own pleasures.

Not knowing whether or not it was a good idea, I went back to the place where Frank had taken us that first night. I wanted to find out if Tonio's tawny-haired woman was all right. But I didn't see her, and I had barely started chatting with a couple of the employees when the manager recognized me and threw me out.

Which was an answer, I guess.

There were other places to have fun, though, that didn't come with bad memories. My band played in a lot of them. I met any number of women in them, and we had a good time with the sizzling in the blood and nobody went crazy.

So it went until a friend of Frank's made an offer to hire *Olympe*. Eldridge was a short man with fast, darting hands and genes left over from some long-ago fashion for albinism. His pale hair was shaggy, and his eyes looked at you with irises the color of blood.

Eldridge offered a very generous sum to ship a small cargo out to one of the system's outer moons, a place called Vantage, where a lot of mining and processing habitats were perched on vast seams of ore. The trip would take five days out and five back, and I was free to take any other cargo on the return trip. Half our fee would be paid in advance, half on delivery. The one condition Eldridge made was that the seals on the packages should not be broken.

I'd been scraping a living aboard *Olympe* long enough to know what that stipulation meant, and I knew what I meant to do about it, too.

The band hired a temporary aurora player, and Tonio quit his chestnut-selling job even though his boss offered him a bonus. We had no sooner cleared Upside than the two of us went into the cargo space and broke every seal on every container, digging like maniacs through cushions of spray foam to find exactly what was supposed to be there, bottles of rare brandy or expensive lubricating oil for robots or canister filters for miners' vac suits. We searched until the air was filled with a blizzard of foam and I began to wonder if we'd misjudged Eldridge entirely.

But in what was literally the final container, we found what we were looking for, about forty kilos of blue salt, exactly the stimulant to keep miners working those extra hours to earn that end-of-the-year bonus, to keep them all awake and alert and safe until the salt turned them into sweating, shivering skeletons, every synapse turned to pork cracklings while heavy metals collected in their livers and their zombie bodies ran on chemical fumes.

Well well, I thought. I looked at Tonio. He looked at me.

Vantage would have been a couple months away except that *Olympe* could shift to a Probability where we could make better time, a place where the stars hung in the sky like hard little pearls on a background of green baize. We made a couple course changes outside our regular flight plan, then docked at Vantage and waited for the police to come and tear our ship apart.

Which they did. It was all part of Eldridge's plan. The griffs would find the blue salt in our cargo hold, and we'd be arrested. The salt would find its way from police lockers to Eldridge's dealers on Vantage, who would sell it and give the griffs a piece. In the meantime the griffs would collect our fee from Eldridge in fines, and the money would be returned to Eldridge. I'd be coerced into signing over *Olympe* in exchange for a reduced sentence, and *Olympe* would be sold, with the profits split between Eldridge and the griffs.

It's the sort of trap that tourists in the Probabilities walk into all the time. But Tonio and I aren't tourists.

The griffs came in with chemical sniffers and found nothing, which meant they had to break into the cargo containers, and of course found that they'd been broken into already. "A freelance captain's got to protect himself," I told the griff lieutenant. "If I find contraband, it gets spaced."

I wouldn't admit to actually having found the salt. I didn't know the local laws well enough to know whether that admission would implicate me or not, so I refused to admit anything.

The lieutenant in charge of the search just kept getting more and more angry. I was worried that she or one of her cronies would plant some contraband on the ship, so I made a point of telling her that I'd turned on all the ship's cameras, one in every room and cargo space, and was livecasting the whole search back to a lawyer's office on Upside. If she tried to plant anything, it would be caught on camera.

That sent her in a towering rage, and she tossed all the staterooms for spite, ripping the mattresses and blankets off the beds and emptying the closets onto the deck, before she stomped off.

I planned to unload the cargo and leave the second we could get clearance, but thanks to the griff lieutenant's temper tantrum we had to do some cleanup first. That's why we had time for a passenger to find us. That's how we met Katarina.

Katarina was one of the Pryors, the incorporated gene line that pretty much owned the system, all of Upside and most of Downside as well as every facility on Vantage. She'd been on some kind of inspection tour of the Pryor facilities on the various moons, but she'd been unexpectedly called back to Socorro and needed a ride.

When the message first came that someone wanted passage to Socorro, I'd been worried that Katarina was a plant from the police or from Eldridge, but as soon as I looked at her I knew that she was going to be a lot more trouble than that.

I don't understand the way the gene lines operate internally, with all the cloning and use of cartridge memories and marriages by cousins to keep all the money and power in the same pedigree, but it was clear from the second she came aboard *Olympe* that she ranked high in the structure. She had that eerie perfection that came with her status. Geneticists had sweated over her body years before she'd ever been born. Flawless complexion, perfect black hair, perfect white teeth. Full expressive lips; black eyes that looked at me for a full half-second before they had added up my entire life and riches, found them unworthy of further consideration, and looked away. She wore an outfit that was the opposite of the balloon-suits women wore in Socorro: a dark fabric that outlined perfectly every curve of that genetically ideal body. I got dizzy just looking at her.

She looked at my stateroom—I'd moved my stuff out of it—and spared an extra glance for the painting I'd put over the cabinet door that had been ripped off its hinges by the griffs. The painting was a woman nude on a sofa, with a black ribbon around her neck and a bangle on her wrist. She has a cat and a servant bringing her flowers from the admirer that's obviously just walked into the room. She's looking out of the painting at her visitor with eyes hard and objective and cutting as obsidian.

Aram had that painting in the stateroom when he'd died. I'd kept it for a while but put it away later. It is true that travelers, stuck in their ships for months at a time, like to look at pictures of naked ladies, but not the same lady all the time, and not one who looks back at you the way this one does.

I looked for a startled moment at Katarina and the woman in the painting, and I realized they had the same look in their eyes, that same hard, indifferent calculation. She turned those eyes to me.

"I'll take it," she said. "There's a room for my secretary?"

"Of course." With a torn mattress and a smashed chair, but I didn't mention that.

She left the stateroom to call for her secretary and her baggage. In the corridor she encountered Tonio.

He grinned at her, blue eyes set on either side of that broken nose. Those hard black eyes gazed back, then softened.

"Who is *this?*" she asked.

*Trouble,* I thought.

"I'm the cook," Tonio said.

Of course she was married. They almost always are.


Tonio and I had first come aboard *Olympe* as crew. Aram was the owner and captain—he was a Maheu and had inherited money and power and responsibility, but after eight hundred years he'd given up everything but the money, and traveled aimlessly in *Olympe*, looking for something that he hadn't seen somewhere before.

He also used massive amounts of drugs, which were sent to him by Maheu's special courier service. To show the drugs were legitimate he had doctors' prescriptions for everything—he collected them the way he had once collected art.

Physically he had the perfection of the high-bred gene lines, with broad shoulders, mahogany skin, and an arched nose. It was only if you looked closely that you saw that the eyes were pouchy and vague, that his muscles were wasting away, and that his skin was as slack as his first-rate genetics would permit. He was giving away his body the same way he'd given away his collection.

He was lonely, too, because he would talk to Tonio and me, about history, and art, and poetry. He could recite whole volumes of poetry from memory, and it was beautiful even though most of it was in old languages, like Persian, that I'd never heard before and didn't understand.

I asked him about his gene line, his connections, what he did before he'd started his wandering.

"It was prostitution," he said, with a look at the painting on his stateroom wall. "I don't want to talk about it, now I'm trying to regain my virtue."

These conversations happened in the morning, after breakfast. Then he'd put the first patch of the day on his arm and nod off, his head in Maud's lap.

Maud Rain was his girlfriend. She looked maybe seventeen, and maybe she was. She appeared as if her genetics had been intending to create a lily, or cornflower, or some other fragile blossom, and then been surprised to discover they'd produced a human being. She was blonde and green-eyed and blushed easily, and she loved Aram completely. I was a little in love with her, myself.

Life aboard was *Olympe* was pleasant, if somewhat pointless. We wandered around the multiverse without a schedule. We'd stop for a while, and Aram would leave the ship to visit old friends or see something new that he thought might interest him, and we wouldn't hear from him for anywhere between three days and three months, then abruptly we'd be on our way again. Aram paid us well and gave us a good deal of time off, and once he bailed Tonio out of a scrape involving the wife of a Creel station superintendent.

I don't pretend to understand the chemistry between users and their consorts, and I don't know whether Aram talked Maud into using, or whether it was her own idea. I do know that, like all users, Aram wanted to make everyone around him use, too. He offered the stuff often enough to me and

Tonio, though I never heard him make the same offer to Maud.

Whoever made up Maud's mind for her, she then went on to make a stupid, elementary mistake. She gave herself the same dose that Aram gave himself, without his magic genes and all the immunity he'd built up over the decades, and she screamed and thrashed and went into convulsions. Tonio got his fingers savagely bitten trying to keep the vomit clear of her mouth while I madly shifted the ship through about eight Probabilities to get her to a hospital. By the time we got her there she didn't have much of a brain left. She still blushed easily, and looked at you with dreamy green eyes. She had the sweet-natured smile, but there was nothing behind it but the void.

We left her in a place where they'd look after her, a stately white building on a pleasant green lawn, and *Olympe* resumed its wanderings. Aram deteriorated quickly. He no longer talked in the mornings. We'd find him alone and crying, the tears pouring down his face in silence, and then he'd put a new patch on his arm and drift away. One afternoon we found him dead, with six patches on his arm.

In his will he left all his money to a trust for Maud, and he left *Olympe* and its contents to me. He left Tonio some money. I gave Tonio everything in the pharmacy, and he sold it to someone on Burnes Upside and we gave Aram a long, crazy wake with the profits. The rest of Tonio's money went to lawyers to fix a misunderstanding that occurred during the course of the wake.

When we sobered up, I realized I had a yacht but no money to support it.

Tonio was the only crew I ever had, because he didn't expect to be paid. He did the job of a crew, and when he had money he paid me, as if he were a passenger. When I had money, I shared it with him.

We kept moving, the same kind of random shifts we'd made with Aram.

It was almost enough to keep us out of trouble.

Tonio spent that first night in the stateroom with Katarina Pryor. I tried to console myself with the fact that this was all happening in a whole other Probability from the one Katarina normally lived in. I also tried to concentrate on how I was going to handle Eldridge when I saw him again.

I checked some data sources and inquired about Katarina Pryor. She was about fifty years old, though she looked half that and would for the next millennium, if she so desired. She was one of the Council of Seven that ran Socorro on behalf of the Pryor gene line.

Her husband, Denys, was one of the other Seven.

I let that settle in my brain for a while. Then I sent a message to Eldridge telling him that I wanted to meet him as soon as *Olympe* docked Topside. He replied that it would be his pleasure to do so.

We'd see how much fun he'd have.

I told Tonio of this development as we were walking to the lounge. As he stepped into the room, he gave me the news. "Katarina has invited me to accompany her to Downside on completion of our returnment. I have accepted, yiss, pending of course my captain's sanction."

Katarina's secretary, a young Pryor named Andrew, happened to be sitting in the lounge as we entered, and he looked as if someone had hit him in the head with a brick.

"It's not as if people are going out of their way to hire us," I said, "so the ship can spare you. But..." I hesitated, aware of the presence of Andrew. "Doesn't this *remind* you of anything, Tonio?"

He gave me a look of offended dignity. "The situation of which you speak was on an entirely different plane," he said. "This on the contrary is *real.*"

The conversation was taking place in a Probability where stars looked like spinning billiard balls on a felt-green sky, and he and Katarina were traveling to another place where oxygen burned in their blood like naphtha. Who knew how real *anything* could be under such circumstances?

I asked Tonio if he could delay his departure with Katrina until Eldridge came aboard.

"Oh yiss. Most assuredly."

He seemed perfectly confident.

I wish I could have echoed his assurance.

Eldridge was present when *Olympe* arrived at Upside, and he had brought a couple of thick-necked thugs with him. They were hanging back from the personnel lock because there were plainclothes Pryor security present, waiting to escort Katarina and her new beau on the first stage of their planetary honeymoon.

I called Eldridge from the control room. "Come on in," I said. "Leave your friends behind."

When he came on board he looked as if he was fully capable of dismembering me all by himself, his small size notwithstanding. I escorted him through the lounge, where Katarina and Andrew waited for Tonio to finish his packing job, a job that would not be completed until I gave him the high sign.

His eyes went wide as he saw Katarina. She wore a compromise between the local balloon-suits and the form-fitting outfit she'd worn when she came aboard, which amounted to a slinky suit with a puffy jacket on top. But I don't think it was her looks that riveted his attention.

He recognized her.

"This is Miss Katarina Pryor," I told him, redundantly I hoped, "and Mr. Andrew Pryor."

"Pryor," Eldridge repeated, as if he wanted to confirm this striking fact for himself.

Andrew gave him a barely civil nod. Katarina just gave him her stone-eyed stare, let him know he had been measured and found wanting.

I went to the bar and poured myself a cup of coffee. You had to drink coffee quickly here, because in this Probability it cools very fast.

"Eldridge," I remarked. "I haven't received my on-delivery fee."

He gave me a scarlet stare out of his white face. "The cargo did not arrive intact."

"One crate went missing," I said. "It was probably the fault of the loaders, but since I signed for it, you should feel free to deduct its value from the delivery fee." I made a show of looking at the manifest on my pocket adjutant. "What was in that crate—? Ah, jugs of spray foam mix. Value three hundred—would you say that's a correct value, Miss Pryor?"

Katarina drummed her fingers on the arm of the sofa. "Sounds about right, Captain Crossbie," she said, in a voice that said *Don't bother me with this crap.*

I called up my bank account. "Might as well do the transfer now," I said.

Eldridge's eyes cut to Katarina, then cut back. His lips went even whiter than usual.

If the Pryors decided to step on him, he wouldn't leave so much as a grease spot on their shoes. He knew that, as did I.

He got out his own adjutant and tapped in codes with his one long thumbnail. I saw my bank account jump by the anticipated amount, and I put away my adjutant and sipped my coffee. It was already lukewarm.

"Want some coffee, by the way?" I asked.

Eldridge gazed at me out of those flaming eyes. "No," he said.

"We have some other business, but there's no reason to bother Miss Pryor with it," I said.

He followed me into the control room, where I closed the door and gestured him toward a chair.

"Consider that a penalty," I said, "for thinking I was new to the multiverse."

"The Pryors aren't really protecting you," he said. "They can't be."

"They're old family friends," I said. I sat in the padded captain's chair—genuine Tibetan goat hide, Aram had told me—and swivelled it toward him. He just stared at me, his busy fingers plucking at his knees.

"I'm willing to sell you coordinates," I said.

He licked his lips, pink tongue on paper-white. "Coordinates to what?" he asked.

"What do you think?"

He didn't answer.

We had put the blue salt in orbit around an ice moon, one that circled the same gas giant as Vantage.

"The coordinates go for the same price as the cargo." I smiled. "Plus three hundred."

He just kept staring. Probably that agate gaze had frightened a lot of people, but I wasn't scared at all.

Five days around Katarina Pryor had given me immunity to lesser terrors.

"If you don't want the coordinates," I said, "your competition will."

He sneered. "There *is* no competition."

"There will be if Katarina takes you and your tame police out of the equation," I said.

So in the end he paid. Once the money was in the account, I gave Eldridge the seven orbital elements that described the salt's amble about its moon. Someone from Vantage could easily hop over and pick up the salt for him, and the strung-out miners would go on getting their daily nerve-searing dose of fate.

I showed Eldridge out, and as he bustled away he cast a look over his shoulder that promised payback.

I sent a message to Tonio telling him to solve his packing crisis, and as I returned to the lounge, he came loping out of his quarters, his belongings carried in a rucksack on one shoulder. Andrew raised an eyebrow at the tiny amount of baggage that had taken so long to pack.

Katarina rose to embrace Tonio. I watched as she molded her body to his.

"I am primed, lover mine," Tonio said.

"So am I."

I showed them to the door. "Thank you, Captain," Andrew said, and with an expression like someone passing gas at a funeral, handed me a tip in an envelope.

I looked at the envelope. *This* had never happened before.

"See you later, compeer," Tonio grinned.

"You bet."

I watched them walk toward their waiting transport, arms around each other's waists. People stared. Wary guards circled them. Eldridge and his people were long gone.

I decided it was time to buy and stow a lot of rations. A year's worth at least.

For two fools, running.

But first I wanted to celebrate the fact that I now possessed more money than I'd ever had in my life, even if you didn't count my tip—which was two thousand, by the way, an inept attempt to buy my silence. I couldn't make up my mind whether Eldridge was going to be a problem or not—if I were him, Katarina would have scared the spleen right out of me, but I didn't know Eldridge well enough to know how stubborn or stupid he was.

While I considered this, it occurred to me to wonder how many years it had been since I'd had a planet under my feet.

Too many, I thought.

I opened my safe and put Tonio's emerald ring in my pocket—no sense in leaving it behind for people like Eldridge to find—and then I followed in the footsteps of Tonio and Katrina and took the next ride down the grapevine to Downside. I looked for tourist resorts and exotic sights, and though I discovered there were none of the former, there were plenty of the latter. There were mountains, gorges, and colossal wildlife—the chemical bonding of the local Probability led to plants, even those with Earth genetics, running amok. I saw rose blossoms bigger than my head, and with a smell like vinegar—chemistry not quite right, you see. Little pine trees grew to the size of Douglas firs. Socorro's internal workings had thrust huge reefs of nearly pure minerals right out of the ground, many of which the miners had not yet begun to disassemble and carry away. For a brief time, wearing a protective raincoat, breathing apparatus, and crinkly plastic overshoes, I walked on the Whitewashed Desert that surrounded Mount Cyanide. I bathed in the Red Sea. Then the Green Sea, the Yellow Sea, and the Winedark Sea. The Yellow Sea stained my skin for days. It looked as if I were dying of cirrhosis.

I kept the ring in a special trouser pocket that would open only to a code from my personal adjutant. After a while I got used to the feel of it, and days went by before I remembered it was there.

I'd brought my aurora. Along the way there was music, bars, and happy moments. I met women named Meimei, Sally June, and Soda. We had good times together. None of them died, went crazy, or slit their wrists.

Carried away by the sheer carefree joy of it all, I began to think of going back to the *Olympe* and sailing away on the sea of Probability. Tonio was probably still happy with Katarina, and I could leave with his blessing.

I would be safe. Shawn wasn't after *me*. And Tonio, provided he stayed put, would be as safe as he ever was, probably safer.

I contemplated this possibility for a few too many days, because one morning I woke from a dense, velvety dream to the birdlike tones of my adjutant. I told it to answer.

"Compeer," said Tonio. "Wherewhich art thou?"

"Shadows and fog," I said, because the voice seemed to be coming from my dream.

"There's a party on the morrow. Come and share it with me. Katarina would be delighted to see you."

*I'll bet,* I thought.

The hotel looked like a hovership that had stranded itself on land, a series of swoops and terraces, surrounded by cypress trees the size of skyscrapers, with gardenias as long as my leg tumbling brightly down from the balconies. Katarina had installed Tonio and his rucksack in a five-room suite and given him an expense account that, so far, he'd been unable to dent.

Tonio greeted me as I stepped into the suite. His blue eyes sparkled with joy. He looked well-scrubbed and well-tended, and his hair was sleek.

"Did you bring your aurora, Gaucho?" he said. "Let us repair to a suitable location, with drinks and the like, and partake of heavenly music."

"I thought we were going to a party."

"That is later. Right now we've got to have you measured for clothes."

A tailor with a double chin and a pony tail stepped out of a side room, had me take off my jacket, and got my measurements with a laser scriber. He vanished. Tonio led me out of the apartment and down a confusing series of stairs and lifts to a sub-basement garage. Empty space echoed around us, supported by fluted pillars with lotus-leaf capitals. Tonio whispered a code into his adjutant and turbines began their soft whine somewhere in the darkness. Spotlights flared. A blazemobile came whispering toward us on its cushion of air. I felt its breath on my face and hands. The colors were grey and silver, blending into each other as if they were somehow forged together. The lines were clean and sharp. It looked purposeful as a sword.

"Nice," I said. "Is this Katarina's?" I had a hard time not calling her *Miss Pryor.*

"It's mine," Tonio said. "Katarina purchased it for me after, ah, the incident."

I looked at him.

"There was a misunderstanding about another vehicle," Tonio said. "I thought I had the owner's permission to take it."

Ah, I thought. One of *those* misunderstandings.

"Are you driving?" I asked.

"Why don't you drive? You're better than I am."

I settled into the machine gingerly. It folded around me like a piece of origami. Tonio settled into the passenger seat. I drove the car with care till

I got out of town, then let the turbines off their leash, and we were soon zooming down a highway under the system's fluorescing, shivering smear of a sun, huge jungle growth on either side of the road turning the highway into a tunnel beneath vines and wild, drooping blossoms.

"There's another car behind us," I said, looking at the displays. I was surprised it could keep up.

"That would be Katarina's security," Tonio said. "It is a mark of her love. They follow me everywhere, to render me safe."

And to prevent, I thought, any of those misunderstandings about who owns what.

A blissful smile crossed Tonio's face. "Katharine and I are so in love," he said. "I sing her to sleep every night."

The thought of Tonio crooning made me smile. "That sounds great," I said.

"We wish to have many babies, but there are complicatories."

"Like her husband?"

"He is obstacular, yiss, but the principal problem is legal."

It turned out that Katarina did not legally own her own womb, as well as other parts, which were part of the Pryor family trust. She could not become pregnant without the permission of certain high-ranking members of her line, who alone knew the codes that would unlock her fertility.

"That's... not the usual problem," I said, stunned. I don't know much about how the big corporate gene lines work, but this seemed extreme even for them.

"Can you hire a surrogate?" I asked. "Use an artificial womb?"

"It's not the same." He cast a glance over his shoulder. "Those individuals behind us—mayhap you can outspeed them?"

"I'll try."

I set the jets alight. My vision narrowed with acceleration, but oxygen still blazed in my blood. Alarms began to chirp. The vehicle trailing us fell back, but before long we came to a town and had to slow.

It was a sad little mining town, covered with the dust of the huge magnesite reef that loomed over the town. Vast movers were in the process of disassembling the entire formation, while being careful not to ignite it and incinerate the entire county.

Tonio pointed to a bar called the Reefside. "Pull in here, compeer. Mayhap we may discover refreshment."

The bar sat on its tracks, ready to move to another location when the last chunk of magnesite was finally carried away. I put the blazemobile in a side street so as not to attract attention to ourselves. We climbed up into the bar and blinked in its dark, musty-scented interior. We had arrived during an off-peak period and only a few faces stared back at us.

We huffed some gas and shared a bag of crisps. After ten minutes the security detail barged in, two broad-shouldered, clean-cut, thick-necked young men in city suits. After they saw us, one went back outside, and the other ordered fruit juice.

The regulars stared at him.

I asked the bartender if it was all right to play my aurora.

"You can if you want," he said, "but if the music's shit, I'll tell you to stop."

"That's fair," I said. I opened the case and adjusted the sonics for the room and put the aurora against my shoulder and touched the strings. A chord hung in the air, with just a touch of sourness. The bartender frowned. I tuned and began to play.

The bartender turned away with a grudging smile. I made the aurora sound like chimes, like drums, like brass. Our fellow drinkers began to bob their heads and call for the bartender to refill their glasses. One gent bought us rounds of beer.

The shift changed at the diggings and miners spilled in, their clothes dusty, their respirators hanging loose around their necks. Some were highly specialized gene types, with sleek skin and implants for remote control of heavy equipment. Others were generalized humans, like us. One woman had lost an arm in an accident, and they were growing it back—it was a formless pink bud on the end of her shoulder.

I played my aurora. I played fierce, then slow. The miners nodded and grinned and tapped their boots on the grainy plastic floor. The security man clung unhappily to his glass of fruit juice. I played angry, I played tender, I played the sound of birds in the air and bees in their hive. Tonio borrowed a cap from one of the diggers and passed it around. It came back full of money, which he stuffed in my pockets.

My fingers and mind were numb, and I paused for a moment. There was a round of applause, and the diggers called for more refreshment. A few others asked who we were, and I told them we were off a ship and just traveling around the country.

Tonio had a blazing white grin on his face. "It is *spectacular!*" he said. "This is the true joy!"

"More than with Katarina?"

He shrugged. "With Katarina it is sensational, but she is terribly occupied, and I don't know anyone else in this coincidence of spacetime. People fear to be in my vicinity, and when I corner one they only speak to me because they are afraid of Katarina. I have nothing in my day but to wait for Katarina to come home."

"Can't she give you a job? Make you her secretary, maybe?"

"She has Andrew."

"Her social secretary, then." I couldn't help but laugh at the idea.

He gave a big grin. "*She* knows the social rules, yiss. I am signally lacking in that area of expertise."

"You could be a prospector. Travel around looking for minerals or whatever."

"For this task they have satellites and artificial intelligences." He gazed for a long moment off into nowhere. "I am filled with gladness that you came to see me, Gaucho."

"I'm glad I came." Though I'm not certain I was telling the truth.

Tonio was getting bored with his life with Katarina. A bored Tonio was a dangerous Tonio.

We talked and drank with the miners till Tonio said it was time to leave. Our guard was relieved to follow us out of the bar. His partner had been guarding our blazemobile all this time.

We were both too drunk to drive, so we got in the car and told the autopilot to take us home. Once we arrived, I had a fitting from the tailor, who had run up my suit while we were off enjoying ourselves. I had this deep blue outfit, all spider silk, with lots of gold braid on my cuffs.

"What's this?" I asked Tonio.

"You are my captain," he said, "and now you are dressed like one."

"I feel ridiculous," I said.

"Wait till you see what *I* am compelled to wear."

The tailor adjusted the suit, then gave me the codes so that I could alter the fit of the suit if I wanted to, or add a pocket here or there. In the meantime Tonio changed. His suit was the latest mode, with ruffles and fringes that seemed to triple the volume of his thin body. He looked unusual, but he carried himself with his usual jaunty style, as if he wanted it made clear to everyone that he was only *pretending* to be the person in the suit.

Katarina arrived and wrapped herself around Tonio without caring if I was there or not. I was reminded of my little limpet-girl Étoile.

Katarina began tearing at Tonio's ruffles and fringes. They went off to the bedroom for a lust break. I went out onto the balcony and watched the sun set over the jade forest. The sweet smell of flowers rose on the twilight air.

Tonio and Katarina returned. She wore a dark lacy sheath that was as simple as Tonio's suit was elaborate. Gemstones glittered sunset-red about her neck, and a languid post-coital glow seemed to float around her like a halo. I could feel sweat prickling my forehead at her very presence.

"You're looking very well, Captain Crossbie," she said.

"You're looking well yourself," I said. There was a bit more regard in her glance than I usually got. I wondered if Tonio had been telling her stories that made me seem, well, interesting.

We went to the party, which was in the same building. It celebrated the fact that some production quota or other had been exceeded, and the room was full of Pryors and their minions. Katarina took Tonio's arm and pressed herself to him all night, making it clear they were a couple.

The place was filled with people who were perfectly perfect, perfect everywhere from their dress to their genetics. All the talk I heard was of business, and complex business at that. If I'd been a spy sent by the competition, I would have heard a lot, but it would have been opaque to me.

Don't let anyone tell you that people like the Pryors don't work for their riches and power. They do nothing else.

I was introduced as Captain Crossbie, and people took me for a yachtsman, which technically I suppose I was. People asked me about regattas and famous captains, and I admitted that I only used my yacht for travel. I was then asked where I'd been, and I managed to tell a few stories.

I was talking about yachts to an engineer named Bond—his dream was to buy a ship when he retired, and travel—when a blond man came up to talk to him. I thought the newcomer looked familiar, but didn't place him right away.

He talked to Bond about some kind of bottleneck on the Downside grapevine station that was threatening to interfere with shipments to Upside, and Bond assured him that the problem would be engineered out of existence in a couple weeks. He asked after Bond's family. Bond told him that his son had won some kind of prize from the Pryor School of Economics. It was then that the blond man turned to me.

He had the chiseled perfection that came with his flawless genes, and violet eyes, and around his mouth was a tight-lipped tension that nature—or his designers—had not quite intended for him.

"This is Mister Denys Pryor," Bond said. "Denys, this is Captain Crossbie."

He realized who I was about the same instant that I finally recognized him as Katarina's husband. The violet eyes narrowed.

"Ah," he said. "The accomplice."

"I don't have any response to that," I said, "that I'd expect you to believe."

He gave me a contemptuous look and stalked away. Bond looked after him in surprise, then looked at me. Then the light dawned. Panic flashed across his face.

"If you'll excuse me," he said, and was gone before I could even reply.

That was the last conversation I had at the party. Word about my connection to Tonio flashed through the room faster than lightning, and soon I was alone. I got tired of standing around by myself, so I went out onto the terrace, where a group of women in immaculate white balloon-suits were grilling meats. I was considering chatting up one of them when Tonio came up, carrying a pair of drinks. He handed me one.

"My apologies, compeer," he said. "They are stuck-up here, yiss."

"I've been treated worse."

He looked up at the strangely infirm stars. "I have Katarina by way of compensation," he said. "You have nothing."

"I have *Olympe*," I said. "I've been thinking maybe it's time she and I flew away to the next Probability."

He looked at me somberly. "I will miss your companionhood," he said.

"You'll have Katarina." I looked at the sky, where Upside glittered on its invisible tether. "I hope Eldridge isn't still looking for me," I said.

"You don't have to worry about Eldridge," Tonio said. "I told Katarina all about him."

Hot terror flashed through my nerves.

"What did you tell her?" I asked.

"I told her that Eldridge tried to use us to smuggle his salt, and that we found the stuff and spaced it."

I relaxed a little. The scene that Eldridge and I had played in front of Katarina might not seem that suspicious, if of course she believed her lover.

"You didn't hear the news?" Tonio said. "About that police officer that was found in the vacuum, over on Vantage."

My mouth was dry. "That griff lieutenant?" I asked.

"Her captain. The lieutenant is learning a new job, floating in zero gravity and sucking up industrial wastes with a big vacuum cleaner." He rubbed his chin. "The Pryors don't like people fucking up their workers with drugs."

"They don't seem to mind all those enhanced production quotas, though," I said. "Do you think those come from workers who aren't spiked up?" There was a moment of silence. The scent of sizzling meat gusted past. "What happened to Eldridge?" I asked.

"Don't know. Didn't bother to ask."

If anything was going to harden my determination to leave Socorro as quickly as I could, it was this.

I turned to Tonio. "I'll miss you," I said. I raised a glass. "To happy endings."

Before Tonio could respond there was a sudden brilliant radiance in the sky, and we looked up. An enormous structure had appeared in the sky above Socorro, a vast black octahedron covered with thousands of brilliant lights, windows enabling the 1.4 million people aboard to gaze out at the passing

Probabilities. To gaze down at *us*.

"It's the Chrysalis," I said aloud.

Surrounding the structure were half a dozen birds, each larger than the habitat, long necks outstretched. The storks that were the emblem of the Storch gene line, each with ghostly white wings flapping in utter silence, holograms projected into space by enormous lasers.

Suddenly I remembered Tonio's emerald ring, in its special pocket on the old trousers I'd left back at Tonio's flat.

*Too late*, I thought. Shawn had come for us.

"We can't keep them out," Katarina said. "This Probability isn't a secret any longer, and anyone can exploit it now that it's registered."

I doubted the Pryors could keep the Chrysalis out even if they wanted to. The Pryors maintained a police force here, not an army, and I know the Chrysalis had weapons for self-defense. They had those huge lasers they'd used to project their flying stork blazons, for one thing, and those could be tuned to military use at any time.

We sat on Tonio's terrace the morning following the Storches' arrival, soaking in the scent of blossoms. The Chrysalis was still visible in daylight, its edges rimmed with silver.

Breakfast was curdling on our plates. Nobody was very hungry.

"The Chrysalis is a state-of-the-art industrial colony," I said. "They can park it here and start exporting materials in just weeks."

Katarina gave me a tell-me-something-I-don't-know look.

"They have also made an official request," she said. "They want the two of you arrested on charges of theft and turned over to them."

I felt myself turn pale, a chill touching my lips and cheeks. "What are we supposed to have stolen?" I asked.

Katarina permitted herself a thin smile. "They haven't said. We have requested clarification." She turned her black eyes to me. "They have also asked that your ship be impounded, until it can be determined whether you obtained it by forging Aram Maheu's will."

"That was all settled in the chancery court on Burnes Upside," I said. "Besides, if I was going to forge a will to give myself a yacht, I'd give myself the money to keep it going."

"The request is a delaying tactic," Katarina said. "It's to tie up your vessel for an indeterminate period and prevent you from escaping.,"

"Is it going to work?" I asked. Katarina didn't bother to answer.

The previous night's party had ended with the appearance of the Chrysalis, as the Council of Seven went into executive session and their employees scattered to duty stations to do research on the Chrysalis and the implication of its arrival.

Apparently at some point in the night Tonio had told Katarina about Adora and Shawn, and Katarina must have believed him, because neither of us was being tied to a chair and tortured by Pryor security armed with shock wands.

Katarina rose and gave Tonio a kiss. "I've got a lot of meetings," she said.

"See you tonight, lover mine," Tonio said.

We sat in silence for a while as Socorro's strange sun climbed above the horizon. I turned to Tonio.

"Are you certain," I asked, "that Adora gave you that ring?"

He gave me a wounded look. "Surely I am not hearing what I am hearing, my compeer."

"It wasn't one of those misunderstandings?" I pressed. "Where you're certain she gave it to you, but she doesn't remember doing it?"

"I am certain she told Shawn it was stolen," Tonio said with dignity, "but this is what happened in sooth. He presented her with the ring at their wedding, a sentimental token I imagine. But later she was angry at Shawn for a scene he'd made, where he was complaining about how she had behaved with me at a certain social function, and out of anger she bestowed the ring upon me."

"And when you left and she went back to Shawn," I said, "she couldn't admit it, so she told him it was stolen."

"That is my postulation."

Or that was the postulation that Tonio wanted me to believe.

Tonio had been to prison, and in prison you learn to manipulate people. You learn to tell them what they want to hear. Is it lying if there is no harm intended? If it's just saying the thing that's most convenient for everyone?

*I didn't steal anything.* How often in prison do you hear *that?*

I think Tonio was sincere in everything he said and did. But what he was sincere *about* could change from one minute to the next.

In any case this had to be more than just about the ring. The ring was valuable, but it didn't justify moving over a million Storch employees to this Probability and opening mining operations.

"Why did Shawn and Adora marry in the first place?" I asked.

"Their families told them to. They hadn't met until a few days before the ceremony."

"But *why?* Usually line members marry each other, like Katarina and Denys. It keeps the money in the family. When they merge or take another outfit over, they do it by adoption. But Shawn and Adora were different—each was ordered to marry *out.* The Storches do heavy industry. The Feeneys specialize in biotech and research. What did they have in common?"

Tonio waved a hand in dismissal. "There was a special project. I did not ask for details, no. Why would I? It was connected to Shawn, and when I was with Adora, I had no wish to talk about Shawn. Why spoil a bliss that was so perfect with such a subject?"

"If it was so perfect, why did you leave Adora?" I asked. "When I last saw you together, you seemed so... connected."

"She grew too onerous," Tonio said. "Once we began to live together, she began giving orders. *Go here. Do this. Put on these clothes. What do you want to name the children?* Under the oppression my spirit began to chafe, yiss. She loved me, but only as a pet."

"Still," I said, "you had good times."

"Oh, yiss." There was a soft light in his eyes. "They were magical, so many of our times. When we were sneaking away together, to make love in an isolated corner of the Chrysalis... that was bliss, my compeer."

I looked up at the Chrysalis, hovering over our heads like the Big Heavy Shiny Object of Damocles.

"Do you think she's up there?" I asked. "It was Adora who was the member of the Storch line. Shawn was the Feeney half of the alliance. He could only command the Chrysalis with the permission of his in-laws."

Tonio looked at the sky in wonder. His face screwed up as he tried to think.

I rose and left him to his thoughts. I needed to do a lot of thinking myself.

For the next several days we bounced around the apartment with increasing energy and frustration. The news was grim. Shuttles from the Chrysalis were exploring uninhabited parts of Socorro. There had been one near-miss between a Storch shuttle and a Pryor transport. Fail-safes normally kept ships from getting remotely close to one another, so the miss had been a deliberate provocation

Guards stood on our door and even on the next terrace, sensors deployed looking for any assassins lurking on the horizon. Tonio's blazemobile privileges had been revoked, and he wasn't allowed out of the building.

"I love my little Katarina, yiss," he said one day as he stalked about the main room. "But this is growing onerous."

A bored Tonio was a dangerous Tonio. If he walked out on Katarina, we were both just so much dog food.

"She's just trying to protect you," I said. "It'll only last until the business with the Storches is resolved."

He flung out his arms. "But how long will that be?"

I looked at him. "What if Adora's up there, Tonio?"

He gave me an exasperated look. "What if she is?"

"Do you think you can talk to her? Find out what she wants?"

Tonio stopped his pacing. His startled face began to look thoughtful.

"Do you think I can?" he asked.

"If you try it from here, Katarina will be listening in before you can spit."

"But she won't let me *leave* here!"

"Let me work on that."

His adjutant bleeped, and he answered. His face broke into a look of pure joy as he said, "Hello, lover."

*Go on pleasing them, Tonio,* I thought.

I went to one of the security guards on our door and told him that I needed to speak to Denys Pryor.

"I don't know why I'm even talking to you," said Denys. I had been called into his office, the design of which told me that he liked clean sight lines, no clutter, curved geometries, and a terrace with a water view. He remained at his desk as I entered, and was turned slightly away, so that I saw his perfect chiseled features in three-quarter profile. He wore fewer ruffles in his office than at the party.

There was no chair for me to sit in. Not anywhere in the room. I had a choice of responses—Denys would probably have preferred an awkward shuffle—so instead I leaned on his immaculate white wall.

"I'm here to solve your problems," I said.

He raised an eyebrow.

No wonder Katarina was dissatisfied with him, I thought. She could have conveyed the same suspicion and contempt without twitching a single hair.

"Your Chrysalis problem," I clarified, "and your Tonio problem."

"Tonio Hope," he said, "is welcome to my wife. They deserve each other, and I hope you'll tell them that. But the problem represented by the Chrysalis is rather more urgent." He turned in his chair to face me. "Tell me your scheme, please. Then I can have a good hearty laugh and have you thrown out of here."

Cuckolded husbands, I have observed, are rarely models of courtesy.

"Tell me one thing first," I said. "Is Adora Storch on the Chrysalis?"

"Your friend's former lover? Yes." His tone was bored. "Apparently he stole something from her, but she's too embarrassed to admit what it was."

"Her heart," I said. He looked away suddenly, toward the distant lake.

"What I would like," I said, "is a secure means of communication between Tonio and Adora." And then, at the sudden, sharp violet-eyed look, I added,

"Secure, I mean, from Katarina."

"Start with flowers," I suggested. Tonio contacted a florist on the Chrysalis and sent an extravagant bouquet, with a humble little message. There was no reply. "Just call her," I said finally.

Her secretary kept him waiting for half an hour, while he paced about gripping the adjutant I'd got from Denys. I played quiet, tinkly music on the aurora to keep him calmed down, while I watched the muscles leaping on his face. Finally I heard Adora's voice.

"Tonio! You have the nerve to call me after the way you walked out on me?"

Adora had taken half an hour to work up sufficient anger to decide to confront Tonio instead of just leaving him hanging. Things had worked out more or less as I'd hoped.

Tonio looked at the adjutant's screen. Over his shoulder I saw Adora's brilliant red hair, her flashing green eyes, her pale rose complexion. He didn't reply.

"What's the matter with you?" she demanded. "Have the lies stuck in your throat for the first time in your life?"

"I—I am but stunned, seeing you again," Tonio said. "I know you're angry and suchlike, but—at least the anger shows you still care."

Adora began screaming at that point, and I left the room.

*Just do what you do best,* I told Tonio silently.

I heard Tonio murmur, and more fury from Adora, and then a lot of silence, which meant Adora was doing the talking and Tonio was listening. It went on for nearly two hours.

While it went on I strummed the aurora, volume at a low setting. I really didn't want to know how Tonio did these things: I didn't think I could be trusted with the knowledge.

After the murmuring stopped, I walked back out into the main room. Tonio sat on the sofa, his hands dangling over his knees. He shook his head.

"I'd forgotten what Adora was like," he said. "How beautiful she is. How passionate."

"You've got to tell Katarina," I said. He looked up in shock.

"Tell her that I—"

"Tell her that you're in touch with Adora. Tell her it was my idea, and I made you do it."

"Why?"

"Because if you don't, Denys will. He'll use it to turn Katarina against you."

He rubbed his face with one of his big hands. "This is complicated."

"Tell Katarina the next time you see her," I said.

Which he did, that night. By morning he had Katarina thinking this was a good idea, and the three of us plotted strategy over breakfast.

When, later that day, Denys told her of Tonio's supposed treachery, she laughed in his face.

While Denys was fuming, and Tonio and Adora were cooing at each other with Katarina's approval, I decided it was time to find out as much as I could about the ring. I got free of security by telling them I was going to report to Denys, and took the ring to a jeweler. If I got no answer there, I'd take it to a laboratory.

I could feel my blood sizzle as I walked into the shop. There was a little extra oxygen in the air here, I thought, to make the customers happy and more willing to buy.

The jeweler was a dark-haired woman with a low, scratchy voice and long, elegant hands. She stood amid cases of brilliant splendor, but refused to be distracted by them. Her attention was devoted entirely to the customer.

"Splendid work," she said, gazing at a hologram of the ring as big as her head. "The emerald is a natural emerald, which makes it slightly more valuable than an artificial one."

"How do you know?" I asked. She'd made the judgment a split-second after she'd put the ring into the laser scanner.

"Natural gems have flaws," the jeweler said. "Artificial gems are perfect."

*Imperfection is worth more.* Perhaps that says something about our world. Perhaps that says something about how women relate to Tonio.

"The setting is common gold and platinum," the jeweler continued, "but it's more valuable than the gem, because it's clearly hand-made, and by a master. Let me see if it's signed anywhere."

She called up a program that would scan the ring thoroughly for numbers or letters. "No," she said, and then cocked her head. She rotated the image, then magnified it.

"This is curious. There are letters laser-inscribed in the gem, and that's not unusual—most gems are coded that way. But *this* is a type of code I've never seen." She frowned, and her long fingers reached for her keyboard. "Let me check—"

"No," I said quickly. "That's not necessary."

I only recognized the number sequence because I was a pilot. The numbers had nothing to do with the gem. They weren't a code, they were a set of *coordinates.*

For a Probability. And given how badly Shawn wanted it back, it was almost certainly a *brand-new* Probability.

Feeney researchers must have developed it, very possibly a Probability with one of the Holy Grails of Probability research, like a Probability where electromagnetism never broke into a separate force from gravity, or where atoms heavier than uranium have a greater stability than in the Home Universe, thus allowing atomic power with reduced radioactivity. The Feeneys had discovered this new universe, but they needed an industrial combine with the power of the Storches to exploit it properly. Hence a marriage to seal the bargain. Hence a gem given by one line to the other with the coordinates secretly graven onto it.

I wasn't foolish enough to think the ring held the only copy of the coordinates—the Feeneys wouldn't have been that stupid. But it was the *only copy outside the gene lines' control*. If we gave the coordinates to the Pryors, the Storches would have competition in their new realm before they ever made their investment back.

No wonder something as huge and powerful as the Chrysalis had been sent after us.

I asked the jeweler an estimate of the ring's worth—"so I know how much insurance to buy"—and then I took the ring and walked out of the shop with billions on my finger. The store's oxygenated atmosphere boiled in my blood.

The ring was the best insurance in the world, I thought. Shawn didn't dare kill us until he got his wedding present back.

That night Tonio and Katarina had their first fight. She complained about the time he was spending talking to Adora. He pointed out that he was stuck here in the apartment and had nothing else to do. It degenerated from there.

I went to my room and played the aurora, loudly this time, and tried to decide what needed to happen next. It might be a good idea to get Tonio closer to Adora, just in case he needed a fast transfer from one girlfriend to another.

I went to Denys and suggested that we all go up the grapevine to Upside, in case any face-to-face meetings became necessary. He understood my point at once.

And so we all moved off the planet, spending a day and a half in the first-class compartment of a car roaring up the grapevine. Katarina spent the time adhered to Tonio, who looked uncomfortable. Denys kept to a cubicle where he worked, except for his occasional parades through the lounge, where he was all ostentatious about paying no attention to his wife.

The atmosphere on the car was sullen and ominous and filled with electricity, like the air before a thunderstorm. Even the other passengers felt it.

To dispel the lowering atmosphere I played my aurora, until some pompous rich bastard told me to stop that damned noise or he'd call an attendant. "I'm with Miss Katarina Pryor," I told him. "Take it up with her."

He turned pale. I played on for a while, but the mood, such as it was, had been spoiled. I went to my cabin and lay on my bed and tried to sleep.

I needed to get away from Tonio and Katarina and Denys. I needed to get away from this freakish Probability where my blood sizzled all the time and my skin burned with fever. I needed to get *away*.

"I'd like to move onto *Olympe*," I told Katarina. She was curled around the spot on a lounge sofa where Tonio had just been sitting. He had gone to the bar for a cup of coffee, but you could still see his impression on the cushions.

Her cold eyes drifted over me. "Why?"

"I'll be out of your way. And it's where I *live*." When she didn't answer, I added, "Look, I can't leave the dock without your permission. I'm not *going* anywhere."

She turned away, dismissing me. "I'll tell the guards to let you pass," she said.

"There are *guards?*"

The only answer was an exasperated set to her lips, as if she didn't consider the question worthy of answer.

So it was that I showed the guards my ID and moved back onto *Olympe*. The air was stale, the corridors silent. I stepped into the stateroom and told the lights to go on and the first thing I saw was the painting of the naked woman, staring at me. She reminded me too much of some people I'd grown to know, so I put the painting in storage.

I went to the pilot's station, where I'd talked to Eldridge, and checked the ship's systems, which were normal. I wondered what would happen if I powered up the engines, and decided not to find out.

For a few days I indulged myself in the fantasy that I was going to escape. I filled the larder with food and drink, enough for eight months of flight to whatever Probability struck my fancy. I tuned every system on the ship except the drive. I made plans about where I'd like to travel next.

I thought about putting the ring back in the safe, but I figured the safe was no real obstacle to people like Denys or Shawn, so I kept the ring in the special pocket in my trousers. Maybe Denys or Shawn were less likely to rip off my pants than rip off the door to the safe.

I went to some of the places I'd enjoyed when I was living Topside the first time. All the bars and restaurants that had seemed so bright and inviting when I was just off a five-month voyage now seemed garish and third-rate. Guards followed me and tried to be inconspicuous. Without a friend I didn't seem to be having any fun.

It really was time to leave.

I brought a bottle home to the *Olympe* and drank while I worked out a plan. I'd sell the ring's coordinates to Denys in exchange for our safety and a lot of money. Then I'd sell the ring itself back to Shawn for the same thing. I'd split the money with Tonio, and then I'd run for it while the running was good.

I looked at the plan again the next morning, when I was sober, and it still seemed good. I was trying to work out my best approach to Denys when Tonio came aboard. He was a reminder of everything I was trying to escape and his presence annoyed me, but he was exasperated and didn't notice.

"Katarina is more onerous than ever before," he said. He flapped his big hands. "I am watched every moment, yiss. She says she is protecting me but I know it's all because she doesn't want me to speak to Adora. Yet out of every port I see the Chrysalis floating in the sky, with Adora so near."

"You've got to keep Katarina's trust," I said.

"*Olympe* is the only place where I'm free," Tonio said. "Katarina doesn't mind if I come here. And that's why you've got to help me get Adora on board."

"Adora?" I said. "Here?"

"There's no place else."

"But the ship's being watched. So is the Chrysalis. If Adora comes here they'll see her."

Tonio smiles. "The Pryors and the Storches do not confront each other all the time. Even if they're playing chicken with each other's cargo ships, both the Chrysalis and Socorro possess resources the other finds useful. There are ships coming from the Chrysalis, to purchase certain commodities and sell others and perform transactions of that nature. Adora will come in one of these ships, and when the business is being transacted by her minions she will fly here to me in a vacuum suit, and enter through our very airlock, bypassing those inconvenient guards upon the door."

I was appalled. Tonio smiled. "Adora assures me that it will be perfectly safe."

*For whom?* I wondered.

"I don't want to be on board when this happens," I said.

When Tonio entertained Adora on my ship, I spent the time shopping for stuff I never bought, and when I got bored with that I found a bar and huffed some gas. I didn't return to *Olympe* until Tonio sent me a prearranged little beep on my adjutant.

*Olympe*'s lounge still smelled faintly of Adora's flowery perfume. Tonio splayed on the couch. Energy filled his skinny body. His blue eyes were aglow.

"Such a passion it was!" he said. "Such zealocity! Such a twining of bodies and souls!"

"Glad to know she doesn't want to kill you anymore," I said.

He waved a hand. "All in the past." He heaved a sigh, and looked around the lounge, the old furniture, Aram's brass-and-mahogany trim. "I am glad to bring happiness here," he said, "to counter those memories of sorrow and tragedy."

I looked at him. "What memories are those?"

"The afternoon I spent here with beautiful little Maud. The day before she gave herself that overdose."

I stared at Tonio. Drugs whirled in my head as insects crawled along my nerves.

"You're telling me that—"

He looked away and brushed a cushion with the back of his knuckles. "She was so sweet, yiss. So giving."

I had been off the ship that day, I remembered, making final preparations for departure. Aram was saying goodbye to some of his friends and picking up a new shipment of drugs from the Maheu office. That must have been the time when Maud Rain had finally succumbed to the magic that was Tonio.

And then, in remorse, she'd decided to grow closer to Aram. By becoming a user, like him.

And now she lived in a little white room in the country, her mind as white and blank as the walls that surrounded her.

I stood over Tonio. I felt sick. "Remember you're spending tonight with Katarina," I said.

The glow in his eyes faded. "I know," he said. "It is not that I am not fond of her, but the circumstances—"

"I don't want to hear about the circumstances," I said. "Right now I need to be alone so I can think."

Tonio was on his feet at once. "I know I have made an imposition upon you," he said. "I hope you understand my gratitude."

"I understand," I said. "But I need to be by myself."

"Whatsoever thou desirest, my captain." Tonio rose, and loped away.

I went to the captain's station and sat on the goatskin chair and decided that I had better get my escape plan underway. I called Denys' office and asked for an appointment. His secretary told me to come early the next day.

Tonio had been in prison, I thought. In prison you learn how to handle people. You learn how to tell them what they wanted and how to please them.

I wondered if Tonio had been playing me all along. Telling me what I wanted in exchange for a place to stay and a tour of the multiverse and its attractions.

I had many hours before my appointment, but alcohol helped.

This reality's blazing oxygen had burned the hangover out of my blood by the time I stepped into Denys' office. The geometries of the room were even more curved than his place Downside, and there were even more windows. Outside the office the structures of Upside glittered, and beyond them was the ominous octahedron of the Chrysalis, glowing on the horizon of Socorro.

There were two chairs in the room this time, but neither of them were for me. Both were on the far side of Denys' desk. One held Denys, and the other the black-skinned, broad-shouldered form of Shawn Feeney.

Denys raised his brows. "Surprised, Captain Crossbie? Surely you don't imagine that you and Tonio are the only people who employ backchannel communications?"

He was enjoying himself far too much. Cuckolds, as I've stated elsewhere, are rarely models of deportment.

"I'd asked for a private meeting," I said, without hope.

"Shawn and I have decided," Denys said, "that it's time for you and your friend to leave this reality. We know that your ship is provisioned for a long journey, and we intend that you take it."

"How do I know," I said, "that there isn't a bomb hidden somewhere in my ship's pantry?"

The two looked at each other and smirked. Denys answered.

"Because if you and Tonio disappear, or die mysteriously, that makes *us* the villains," he said. "Whereas if you simply abandon this Probability, leaving the two ladies behind…" He couldn't resist a grin.

"Then *you* are the bad guys," Shawn finished in his deep voice.

I considered this. "I suppose that makes sense," I said.

"And in exchange for the free passage," Denys said, "I'll take the ring."

"*You?*" I said, and then looked at Shawn.

"Oh, I'll get it back eventually," Shawn said. "And I'll get the credit for it, too."

"The Storch line," Denys said, "will have at least a couple years to exploit the new Probability before we Pryors arrive in force. But even so we'll get there years ahead of the rest of the competition… and *I'll* get the credit for that."

Shawn smiled at me. "And *you'll* get the blame for selling our secret to our rivals. But by then I'm sure you'll have lots of practice at running."

"I could tell the truth," I said.

"I'm sure you can," Shawn said. He leaned closer to me. "And the very best of luck with that plan, by the way."

"The ring?" Denys reminded.

I thought about it for a moment, and could see no alternative.

"To get the ring," I said, "I have to take my pants off."

Shawn's smile broadened. "We'll watch," he said, "and enjoy your embarrassment."

Tonio was in *Olympe* by the time I returned. Delight danced in his blue eyes.

"I have received a missive from Adora!" he said. "We are to flee together, she and I—and you, of course, my compeer. She has bribed someone in Socorro Traffic Control, yiss, to let us leave the station without alerting the Pryors. We then fly to the coordinates she has provided, where she will join us. From this point on we exist in our own Probability of bliss and complete happiness!"

I let Tonio dance around the ship while I went to the captain's station and began the start-up sequence. Socorro Traffic Control let us go without a murmur. I maneuvered clear of the station and engaged the drive.

As we raced to the coordinates the message had provided, there was no pursuit. No ships came out of some alternate Probability to collide with us. No lasers lanced out of the Chrysalis to incinerate the ship. No bomb blew us to fragments.

As we neared the rendezvous point Tonio grew anxious. "Where is my darling?" he demanded. "Where is Adora?" His hands turned to fists. "I hope that something has not gone amiss with the plan."

"The plan is working fine," I said, "and Adora isn't coming"

I told him about my meeting with Denys and Shawn, and what I had been ordered to do. Tonio raged and shouted. He demanded I turn *Olympe* around and take him back to his beloved Adora at once.

I refused. I fed coordinates into the Probability drive and an instant later the stars turned to hard little pebbles and we were racing away from Socorro, leaving its quirky electromagnetic structure in our wake.

Tonio and I were on the run. Again. Trapped with one another in Reality, whether we liked it or not.

I had let Tonio play me, just as he had played Adora and Katarina and Maud and the others. Now we were in a place where we had no choice but to play each other.

Tonio was in despair. "Adora and Katarina will think I deserted them!" he said. "Their rage will know no bounds! They may send assassins—fleets—armies! What can I do?"

"Start," I said, "by sending them flowers."

# AFTERWORD: SEND THEM FLOWERS

*"Send Them Flowers" was written in response to a request from Gardner Dozois, for his (and Jonathan Strahan's) anthology* The New Space Opera.

*Space opera is a subgenre that usually involves high adventure in space, featuring highly advanced technology and (very often) interaction with aliens. (In my case, I substituted "really weird humans" for aliens.)*

*I figured the anthology's other contributors would handle the large-scale adventure stories, military epics, and tales of derring-do, which would allow me to do a smaller, more personal story that was nevertheless set against a large-scale space opera background.*

*I realized that I had never written a story of male friendship, so I decided to do that. Because friendship is boring unless it is tested in some way, I created a lot of conflict between the two protagonists. The usual way to put a strain on friendships is to create a romantic triangle, and this I did, but in an unusual way, with the romance lying outside the two principals, not between them. I was also unable to resist complicating the story by creating two triangles.*

*I also decided that, since we don't see very many working-class people in science fiction, that Tonio and Gaucho would hail from the proletariat.*

*The story of a couple pals on the run, with trouble ahead and trouble behind, is not a new one. It is not a coincidence that the main characters are named Hope and Crossbie, and that the story was originally filed under the name "roadpicture." But Hope and Crosby are just milestones on one very long road, and the characters' names might equally as well have been Jack and Neal, or for that matter Bill and Ted.*

*I was sorry, however, that I couldn't make room in the story for Dorothy Lamour in a sarong.*

# PINOCCHIO

Errol has the kind of eagerness that you only see when someone can't wait to tell you the bad news. I can see this even though his hologram, appearing in the corner of my room, is a quarter real size.

"Have you seen Kimmie's flash?" he asks. "It's all about you. And it's, uh—well, you should look at it."

I'm changing clothes and sort of distracted.

"What does she say?" I ask. Because I figure it's going to be, Oh, Sanson didn't pay enough attention to me at the dance, or something.

"She says that you took money for wearing the Silverback body," Errol says. "She says you're a sellout."

Which stops me dead, right in the middle of putting on my new shorts.

"Well," I say as I hop on one foot. "That's interesting."

I can tell that Errol is very eager to know if Kimmie's little factoid is true.

"Should I get the pack together?" he asks.

I stop hopping and put my foot on the floor. My shorts hang abandoned around one ankle.

"Maybe," I said, and then decide against it. "No. We're meeting tomorrow anyway."

"You sure?"

"Yeah." Because right now I want a little time to myself.

I've got to think.

### THINGS TO DO IF YOU'RE A GORILLA
- Make a drum out of a hollow log.
- Look under the log for tasty grubs and eat them.
- Pound the drum while your friends do a joyful thumping dance.

- Play poker.
- Make a hut out of branches and native grasses. Demolish it. Repeat.
- Groom your steady.
- Learn sign language. (It's traditional)
- Do exhibition ballroom dancing.
- Go to the woods with your friends. Lie in a pile in the sun. Repeat.
- Intimidate your friends who are gibbons or chimps.
- Attend a costume party wearing 18th Century French Court dress.
- Race up and down the exteriors of tall buildings. Extra points for carrying an attractive blonde on your shoulder, but in that case beware of biplanes.
- Join a league and play *Gorillaball*. (Rules follow)

I pull on my shorts and knuckle-walk over to my comm corner. My rig is an eight-year-old San Simeon, assembled during the fortnight or so when Peru was the place to go for things electronic—it's old, but it's all I need considering that I hardly ever flashcast from my room anyway. I mostly use it for school, and sometimes for editing flashcast material when I'm tired of wearing my headset.

I squat down on a little stool—being gorilloid, I don't sit like normal people—and then turn on the cameras so I can record myself watching Kimmie's broadcast.

I don't think about the cameras much. I'm used to them. I scratch myself as I tell the San Simeon to find Kimmie's flash and show it to me.

Kimmie looks good. She's traded in the gorilloid form for an appealing human body, all big eyes and freckles and sunbleached hair. She's never been blonde before. The hair is in braids.

She seems completely wholesome, like someone in a milk ad. You'd never know that some time in the last ten days she came out of a vat.

I watch and listen while my former girlfriend tells the world I'm slime. Vacant, useless, greedy slime.

"He's a lot angrier than people think," Kimmie says. "He always hides that."

Unlike someone, I think, who isn't hiding her anger *at all*.

For a while this doesn't much bother me. Kimmie's body is new and it's like being attacked by a clueless stranger. But then I start seeing things I recognize—the expressions on her face, the way she phrases her words, the body language—and the horror begins to sink in.

It's Kimmie. It's the girl I love. And she hates me now, and she'll telling the whole world why.

Kimmie lists several more of my deficiencies, then gets to the issue I've been dreading.

"There was a point where I realized I couldn't trust him anymore. He was taking money for the things he used to do for fun. That's when I stopped being in love."

No, I think, you've got the sequence wrong. Because it was when you started pulling away that I got insecure, and in order to restore the kind of intimacy we'd had, I started telling you the things I should have kept to myself.

### THINGS TO DO WHEN YOU'VE JUST BEEN DUMPED.

- Lie in bed and stare at the ceiling.
- Feel as if your heart has been ripped out of your chest by a giant claw.
- Find the big picture of her you kept by your bed and rip it into bits.
- Wonder why she hates you now.
- Beat your chest.
- Try to put the picture back together with tape. Fail.
- Cry.
- Beat your chest.
- Run up into the hills and demolish a tree with your bare hands.
- Watch her flashcast again and again.

When I watch Kimmie's flashcast for the third or fourth time I notice her braids.

*Braids.* She's never worn braids before. So I watch the image carefully and I see that the braids are woven with some kind of fluorescent thread, that glows very subtly through the cooler colors, violet, blue, and green.

And then I notice that there's something going on with her eyes. I thought they were blue at first, but now I realize that the borders of her irises are shifting, and they're shifting through the same spectrum as the threads in her hair.

I had been paying so much attention to what she was saying that I hadn't been looking at the *image.*

*Image,* I think. Now I understand what she's trying to do.

I was wrong about her all along.

I call my parents. My mom is a hundred and forty years old, and my dad is eighty-seven, so even though they don't look much older than me, they have a hard time remembering what it was like to be young. But they're smart—Mom is a professor of Interdisciplinary Studies at the College of Mystery, and Dad is vice-president of marketing for Hanan—and they're both good at strategy.

My dad advises me not to try responding to Kimmie directly. "You're a lot more famous than she is," he points out. "If you get involved in a he-said-she-said situation, you're both legitimizing her arguments and putting her on an equal plane with yourself. It's what she wants, so don't play her game."

"I never liked Kimmie," my mom begins.

Hearing my mom speak of Kimmie in that tone makes me want to jump to Kimmie's defense. But that would be idiotic so I don't say anything.

Mom thinks for a moment. "What you should do is be nice to her," she said. "Saint Paul said that doing good for your enemy is like pouring hot coals on her head."

"A *saint* said that?"

My mom smiled. "He was a pretty angry saint."

The more I thought about Mom's, the more I liked it.

I decided to order up a bucket of hot coals.

I became famous more or less by accident. Deciding to form a flashpack was one of the things my friends and I decided to do when we were thirteen, for no more reason than we were looking for something to do and the technology was just sitting there waiting for us to use it. And of course everyone and his brother (and his uncles and aunts) were flashcasting, too. Our first flashcasts were about as amateurish and useless as you would expect. But we got better, and after a while the public, which is to say millions of my peers, began to respond.

What the public responded to was me, which I didn't understand and still don't. I would have thought that if people liked anyone, it would have been Ludmila or Tony—Ludmila was much more glamorous, and Tony had led a much more interesting life. But no—I became the star and they didn't.

The others in the pack either accepted the situation or faded away. I think I'm still friends with the ones who left, but I don't see them very often. Being famous has a way of taking you away from one world and putting you in another.

In flashcast after flashcast it turned out that I was good at only one thing, which was explaining to other people what it's like to be me. In our world, where there are very few young people, that turns out to be an important skill.

Kids are pretty thin on the ground. I have a parent who's over a hundred and who looks maybe twenty-five, and who is essentially immortal. If something happens to the body she's in, she'll be reloaded from one of dozens of backups stored on Earth or in space. She won't die as long as our civilization survives.

Neither will anyone else. That doesn't leave a lot of room on Earth for children.

In order to have me, my parents had to pay a hefty tax, in order to pay for the resources I'd be consuming as I grew up, and then demonstrate that they had the financial wherewithal to support me until I could earn my own living. Financial resources like that take decades to build. That's why my parents couldn't have children when they were younger.

So by the time they had me, my parents had pretty well forgotten what it was like to be young. My friends' parents weren't young either. We were a very few kids trapped in a world of the very old. I regularly hear from kids who are the only person in their town under the age of sixty.

Sometimes it's good to know that you aren't the only kid out there. Sometimes we have to have help to remind us who we are. Sometimes it's good to have someone to aid you with all the rituals of growing up, the problems of dealing with friends and rivals, the difficulties of courtship, the decisions of what body to wear and what shoes to wear with it. It's good to have a friend you can count on.

Well, boys and girls, that friend is me.

Q: Do we really have to play gorillaball *naked?*
A: We tried it in darling little blue velvet suits with knickers, but the lacy cuffs got all spoiled.

Next day the pack meets so that we can practice gorillaball. It's a game that we—mostly me—invented, so now we're sort of obliged to play it.

Our team is called the Stars. Because, let's face it, we are.

We practice in the hills up above Oakland, natural gorilla country. The air is heavy with the scents of the genetically modified tropical blossoms that stabilize the hillsides. We crash through bushes, smash into each other with big meaty thuds, rollick up and down trees, and scamper over the occasional building that finds itself in the way. The birds are stunned into a terrified silence. It's a good practice and we end up with our fur covered with dust and debris.

For a while I forget about Kimmie.

We've got grain cameras floating in the air the whole time and everything is uploaded, available for anyone interested in the gorillaball experience. Shawn will edit the thing tomorrow and make a more or less coherent story out of it. We keep uploading as all fifteen of us pile onto the roof of a tram and head back to our clubhouse, waving to people on the street and hanging over the edge of the tram roof to make faces at the passengers.

Our pack headquarters is in the Samaritain, which is a hotel and which gives us the suite free, because the owners of the apartment like the publicity we bring them. We jump off the tram and bound over the pointed iron fence into the pool area, where we splash around until we get the dust out of our fur, and then we lie in the sun and groom each other till we're dry.

You don't want to smell wet gorilla fur if you don't have to. That's one reason for the grooming. The other is social. We're a pack, after all, and packs do things together.

The grain cameras are still floating around us, maybe a hundred of them, each the size of a grain of rice. No single camera delivers an acceptable image, but once the images are enhanced and jigsawed together by a computer you have a comprehensive picture. We're still flashcasting, and for some reason the world is still interested. The splice on my optic nerve tells me that a couple hundred thousand people are watching us as we comb through one another's hair.

Mostly I groom Lisa. I don't know her as well as I know the others, because she's a year younger and new to the pack. She's a member because her older cousin Anatole has been part of the group from the beginning, and he made a special request. He's the brash self-confident one... and Lisa's not. That's about all I know about her, aside from the rumor that she's supposed to be some kind of genius with electronics—even more so than the rest of us, I mean. So I figure it's time I get to know her better.

As I comb through the fur on her shoulders I ask her about what she's studying.

"Lots of things," she says. "But I'm really getting interested in cultural hermeneutics."

Which produced a pause in the conversation, as you might imagine. I imagined tens of thousands of simultaneously calls on online dictionaries demanding a definition of "hermeneutics."

"So what makes that interesting for you?" I say.

"It tells you who created a thing," Lisa says, "and why, and what tools were used, and how it relates to other things that were created. And—" She flapped her hands. "You know, I'm not saying this well."

"Give an example," I urge, because I figured my audience was getting lost.

"Well, look at the headplay *Mooncakes*. It helps to know that it's a rewrite of an earlier work called *The Prodigal*, and that in the original the character of Doctor Yau was a parody of a politician of that period named Coswell.

And that the character of Hollyhock has to do with a fad of that time called mindslipping, where people deliberately inserted a shunt between the right and left sides of their brain, and programmed it to randomly shift dominance from one to the other."

"So," I say, "that's why half the time she's talking like a machine, and the rest of the time her dialogue sounds like some kind of poetry."

"Right," Lisa says. "But people had given up mindslipping by the time *Mooncakes* was released, so much of the audience wouldn't understand the character of Hollyhock at all. So instead of Hollyhock being a comment on a contemporary phenomenon, she was just played for laughs in the remake. And though the Doctor Yau character was more or less the same as the original, the references to Coswell are lost."

"Maybe I'll download it and viddie it again with all that in mind."

"I wouldn't bother." She shrugs. "I didn't think it was that good the first time." She looks up at me. "I'd better fix the hair on your head," she says. "If it dries that way you'll look like Vashti the Dwad for the rest of the day."

She crouches behind me and begins to comb my hair. "So it's flashplays you're interested in?" I asked.

"Not usually. Hermeneutics can analyze any artifact—a book, a video, a building. Any cultural phenomenon. The idea is that you start with the phenomenon and work backwards to try to figure out the people and the culture that produced it."

I looked at her. "You could analyze *me*," I said.

"I could," she said. "But why? You're one of the most analyzed phenomena in the world. Anything I could say has already been said."

"I hope not."

She lowered her eyes. "You know what I mean."

"Yeah. I know. But people say things anyway, even if they're not new."

I shake myself and roll onto my feet and knuckles. I take a breath. What I say now is crucial.

"So has anyone seen Kimmie's flashcast?" I ask.

Just about everyone raises their hands. Lisa didn't, I noticed.

"Let's watch it together," I said. I look at Lisa and wink at her. "See if she has anything new to say."

We roll into the clubhouse. The furniture creaks under our huge gorilla bodies.

People put on headsets or visors or pull their video capes from out of their pockets, and I tell the video walls and the holographic projectors to turn on, and then I look up Kimmie's flashcast and play it. Suddenly Kimmie is everywhere in the room, her image repeated on practically every surface. It's overwhelming.

My breath catches in my throat. I've watched the flash enough times so that I think I've immunized myself, but apparently I'm wrong. A horrible sense of dread seeps into my veins.

So we watch the flash. There's a lot of groaning and laughter as Kimmie offers her revelations. I begin to feel the dread fade. This is a lot better than watching it alone.

By the end people get raucous, and Kimmie's final statements are drowned out by denunciations.

"Hey," I said. "Let's not get angry! This is still someone I have feelings about." I give what I hope is a wise nod. "I know what we should do."

*We should pour a bucket of coals on Kimmie's head.*

"We should all send a message to Kimmie telling her that we love her," I say, "and that we understand her problems." I picture Kimmie's message buffer filling with millions of messages from my audience.

"And while you're at it," I say with a wink, "tell her that you really like that thing she did with her eyes."

*If you're not gorilla, you're just vanilla.*

After we'd sent our messages to Kimmie I ask if anyone has any questions. I'm kind of nervous so I roll to my left, end the roll on my feet, and then roll back to my right.

Simple gymnastics are one of the great things about being a gorilla. I'm going to miss that when I'm back in a standard human body.

Cody raises a hand. "Were you really mad at Albert that time?" she asks.

Everybody sort of laughs.

"No," I said. "I was amused. Kimmie was kind of mad at him, though, so maybe she thought I was mad at him, too."

*Take that.*

I do some somersaults on the Samaritain's deep pile carpets. "Anything else?" I ask.

"Okay," Errol says. "Everyone wants to know if you really took money for wearing the gorilla body."

"I'm not going to answer that right away," I say. I roll to my left, then to my right. It's important that I get this right.

"What I want to do is ask another question," I say. "Now Errol, you've got your visor on, right?"

"Sure."

"And what brand is your visor?"

He blinked. "Esquiline," he said.

"You like it? You think it's a good visor?"

He shrugs his huge ape shoulders. "I guess," he said.

"What if I offered you money for wearing the visor. Would you take it?"

Errol looked at me. "But I'm *already* wearing it," he said.

"So what if I offered to pay you for what you're already wearing? Would you take the money?"

He raised his shaggy eyebrows. "All I have to do is wear it?"

"Right."

"I guess I'd take the money, yeah. If that's all there was to it."

"Okay." I look up into the corner of the room where we've got a camera, and with my visor I tell the camera to zoom in on my face, so that I can look right at my audience of millions.

"What would *you* do?" I ask.


"You've had an eight percent drop in your audience in the last six weeks," my father says.

I put down my forkful of chicken in Hunan sauce.

"It's a blip," I tell him. "It's the part of the Demographic that wasn't interested in being a gorilla."

"The gorilla thing was a mistake," my father says.

Wearily, I agree that the gorilla thing was a misstep.

Wearily, I eat my Hunan chicken.

"The problem is that there aren't any great clothes to wear with a gorilla body," my dad says. "No designer's dressing for the Silverback. Baggy shorts and floppy tees, that's all you had to work with. No wonder you couldn't make it cool."

I wish I could get out of the gorilla body. But I can't, not till after the last gorillaball game.

What happened was that DNAble had sent a vice-president to show me their new body lines. "The Silverback just isn't moving like we thought it would," she said. She looked at me. "It's got a lot of unexplored potential. It just needs somebody like you to show everyone how fun it could be."

I knew right away why the Silverback hadn't become popular, reasons totally separate from the issue of how you fashionably clothe a hairy gorilla. If you want to be an ape, you'd pick a gibbon or a siamang or an orangutan, because those are the ones that can zoom hand-over-hand through the trees. Our pack had already been orangutans, and it was *great*.

By comparison, gorillas just sort of sit there.

But I needed to start something new. My audience was starting to get bored with my current round of parties and clubs and clothes.

"I'll think about it," I said. Already the first thoughts of gorillaball were stirring in my subconscious.

The flattery worked—*Only You can save us, Sanson!*

The VP looked at me again. "I'm authorized to offer you inducements," she said. "If there's a big uptick in gorilla body sales, we can arrange for a bonus."

I didn't answer right away.

But what really happened wasn't quite what I told the pack by the pool. Real life is more complicated than you can express on video.

"Want some more fish?" I ask my dad.

"Thanks."

My dad's body is tall and wiry, and at home he dresses in khakis, very immaculate, as if at any moment he might be called upon to sell something and needs to look his best. He's cooked this whole Chinese meal, with sticky rice in lotus leaves and steamed fish and Hunan chicken and orange peel beef, and since my mom is delivering a lecture series in Milan there's only the two of us to eat it. Huge platters of food cover the antique oak table between us.

Fortunately the gorilla body needs a lot of feeding.

"We've got to figure out a way to grow the Demographic," my dad says.

"The Demographic" is what my dad, the marketing whiz, calls my audience. Every product, according to him, has a "demographic" that forms its natural consumers, and his job is to alert that demographic to the existence and alleged superiority of the product.

By "product," he means me.

My dad's audience has to be alerted by stealth. Nobody has to look at advertisements if they don't want to. In my Media and Society classes I learned that broadcast media used to be full of adverts, but they're not anymore because people can download their entertainment from other sources. You see holograms and posters in stores and public places, but every other form of advertising has to be sneaky. It has to disguise itself as something else.

My dad is a specialist in that kind of advertising.

If you're my age you grow up suspicious. When you see something new you wonder if it's genuine or a camouflaged advertisement for something else.

That's why Kimmie's revelation could be trouble for me. If I turn out to be nothing but an advertisement for DNAble, then the Demographic might never trust me again.

The numbers are important because they can turn into money. Even though my flashcasts are given away free, I get paid for an occasional fashion shoot, or an interview, or for appearing on broadcast video. *Darby's Train* and *Let's Watch Wang* may be silly comedies, but they pay their guest stars very well.

Fortunately I don't have to do any acting on these programs. I appear as myself. I walk on and all this insane comedy happens around me and in the third act I deliver a few pearls of wisdom that solve the star's problem.

Which means I'll be starting my adult life with a nice little nest egg. I won't be rich, but I'll be ahead of the average twenty-year-old.

"So how do we grow the Demographic?" I ask my dad.

"A new love interest always produces a bounce."

"So do babies," I say, "but I'm not going to start one now."

He grins. "Okay. The Demographic is growing older. You need to give them a more mature product. More mature clothing choices, more mature music…"

I want to tell him that my tastes are my tastes, and they've done pretty well for me so far.

Eight percent.

I've got to do *something*, I think.

We all know how lucky we are. There aren't any wars anymore. There's no permanent death. Nobody has to get old if they don't want to. There's no poverty, except for a few people who deliberately go off to live without material possessions and eat weeds, and they don't count. There are diseases, but even if one of them kills you, they'll bring you back.

Our elders have solved all the big problems. The only things left for us to care about are fashion, celebrity, and consumerism.

And the pursuit of knowledge, if that's the sort of thing that appeals to you. The problem being that you'll have to do a few hundred years of catching up before the elders will pay you any attention.

We can change bodies if we like. You lie down in a pool of shallow warm water that's thick with tiny little microscopic nanobots, and the bots swim into your body and swarm right to your brain, where they record everything—every thought, every memory, every reflex, everything that makes up your self and soul. And then all this information is transferred into another body that's been built to your own specifications by *another* few billion nanobots, and once a lot of safety checks are made, you bound out of bed happy in your new body, and your old body is disassembled and the ingredients recycled.

Unless you want something unusual, the basic procedure costs less than a bicycle. Bicycles have moving mechanical parts that have to be assembled by hand or by a machine. The nanobots do everything automatically, and are powered by, basically, sugar.

Our custom brains are smart. We don't have to deal with stupid people or the messes they cause. We *do* have to cope with a bunch of hyper-critical geniuses nitpicking us to death, but at least that's better than having a bunch of morons with guns *shooting* at us, which is what people in history seemed to have to deal with all the time.

Within certain limits our bodies look like whatever we want. Everyone is beautiful, everyone is healthy, everyone is intelligent. That's the *norm*.

But where, you might wonder, does that leave *you*? Who are *you*, exactly?

What I mean is, how do you find out that you're *you* and not one of a bunch of equally talented, equally attractive, equally artificial *thems*?

How do you find out that you're a person, and not some kind of incredibly sophisticated biological robot?

You find out by exploring different options, and by encountering challenges and overcoming them. Or *not* overcoming them, as the case may be.

You learn who you are by making friends, because one way of finding out who you are is by figuring who your friends think you are.

Your friends can be the kind you meet in the flesh. If you live in the Bay Area, like me, there are eight or nine thousand people under the age of twenty, so odds are you'll find some that are compatible.

You can make the kind of friends you only meet electronically, through shared interests or just by hanging around in electronic forums.

Or you can work out who you are by watching someone else grow up and struggle with the same problems.

If you're my age or a little younger, odds are that someone else would be me.

I check out the messages that have been flooding in since the last flashcast. The artificial intelligence in my comm unit has already sorted them into broad categories:

- I'd take the money.
- I wouldn't take the money.
- I wouldn't take the money, and if you did you're evil.
- I hate Kimmie.
- I hate you.
- Gorillas are lame.
- I'm a reporter and I'd like an interview.
- I built the hut, so now what?
- I'd really like a date, and here's my video and contact information.

Some of those last videos are very stimulating.

Stimulating or not, they all get a polite but negative response. Meeting girls is not a problem for me.

And in any case, I can't get Kimmie out of my head.

The messages from reporters I file till later. All they want to talk about is Kimmie anyway.

I pick a representative sample of the rest of the messages and make a flashcast of them. I give some a personal reply. The whole point of flashcasts is that they create a community between the subject and the viewer, and so even the ones who don't like me get their say, and sometimes I'll respond with something like, "Well if *that's* the reason you hate me, you'll probably like Joss Mackenzie, go check out his flashes, I think he's still a snake," or "Sounds like you and the girl in the previous message should be friends."

When they hate me, I don't hate them back. Not publicly anyway. That's not who I am.

(Publicly.)

After the flashcast I take one of my classes. I'm sixteen and should finish college in a year and a half. I don't personally attend class very often, because then the class fills up with people who want to watch me instead of the teacher, so instead I use a headset to project myself into a virtual class.

The class is Media and Society, and the professor is Doctor Granger, who I don't like. He's got a young seamless face and wavy grey hair like sculpted concrete, and he paces up and down and gestures like a ham actor as he orates for his audience.

That's not why I don't like him, though that's probably bad enough. When he found out I was taking his class, he opened up the flashcast to anyone, not just those who had signed up for his class. He knows this is his chance to be famous, and he's not about to miss it. If he realizes how pathetic it is that he, a man in his nineties, is leaching off the fame of his sixteen-year-old student, he has shown no sign of it.

"The chief characteristic of modern media," Granger says, "is the existence of near-instantaneous feedback." He's dressed very stylishly today, with a charcoal-grey turtleneck and a blazer and a white silk scarf that he's somehow forgot to take off when he entered the lecture hall, and that ripples when he walks. Awareness of a worldwide audience has upgraded his wardrobe.

"The reaction of the audience can be viewed by the performers immediately after the performance—sometimes during it. So while performers have always taken their audience into account—always judged their performance and its effects with regard to the public—there is now a special urgency involved. A worldwide consensus on a given performance can be reached before the performance is even over."

I know what the consensus on Doctor Granger's performance is. The Demographic despises him. I wonder if he knows it.

"For those the audience chooses to condemn," he says, "the penalty is oblivion. For those to whom the audience grants its favor, instant fame is possible. But continuing fame depends on continuing positive feedback. Performers have to take their audience into account every minute, and the good ones, like all good performers, anticipate what their audience wants and finds a way to give it to them. But now more than ever a performer has to be careful not to alienate their core demographic."

There's the damn Demographic again, I think.

He turns to me. "Sanson," he says, "do you keep your audience in mind when you're making a flashcast?"

He's always using me in class as an example, another reason I don't like him.

At the moment, however, I purely *hate* him, because he's asked one of those questions for which there's no good answer. If I say I worry about what the audience thinks, then I'm not my own person. But if I say that I don't care what the audience thinks, the Demographic will get mad at me for saying that they don't matter.

"I'm not a performer," I say. "I'm not any kind of actor at all. I just *do* stuff."

"But still you present programs with yourself as the focus," Granger says. "You perform in that sense. So I wonder if you concern yourself with what your audience is going to say after each flashcast."

I feel a little flutter of unease.

"I respect their opinions," I say. "But that still comes afterward. We can all have a big discussion later on, but when something's going on, the only people I'm interacting with is my pack."

Doctor Granger gives me a big smile. "Aren't you worried about losing your audience?"

*Eight percent,* I think.

Let me tell you what it's like. When I was eight my parents took me on a vacation to the Middle East, and we went to the Dead Sea and I took a swim. The water is so dense with salt that it holds you up, and you just lie there with the hot sun shining down on you in the warm water, as if it were the most comfortable mattress in the world, and you know that no matter what happens, you'll never drown.

That what it's like to have the Demographic on your side. There's this outpouring of interest and friendship and love, and they respond to everything you do. There's a whole community there to help you. Anytime you want a friend, a friend is there. If you want information, someone will give it to you. If anyone offers you disrespect, you don't have to respond—the Demographic leads the charge on your behalf, and you can stay above the fight.

You just float there, in that warm saltwater, with the sun shining down, and you'll never drown as long as the Demographic is behind you.

Am I worried about losing that?

I'd be crazy not to.

"It's like any other kind of friendship," I tell Doctor Granger. "There's feedback there, too. But if friends respect each other, they won't tell each other what to do."

Doctor Granger gives a nod.

"You'd better hope they're your friends, then, hadn't you?"

I think of Kimmie and feel a knife of terror slice into me.

She stopped loving me. What happens if everyone else stops loving me, too?


I do some other work and then catch Kimmie's next flash, in which she goes shopping with a couple of her friends. She's wearing big hoop earrings and a wraparound spider-silk skirt, sandals, and a loose-fitting cotton tank with flowery embroidery.

Next, I think, she'll be wearing a headscarf.

She's still wearing the color threads in her hair, the ones that match the color shifts going on in her eyes. It's a subtle style, and not the sort of thing people would notice at once. I'd only spotted it because I viewed her flash twice.

Once I viddied it, though, I recognized it as a statement as clear as a tattoo. Her flashes weren't just a kind of personal electronic diary she was sharing with whoever chose to view them, she had greater ambitions.

Picking such a subtle style meant that she hoped people would notice, only not right away. She was hoping that the whole hair-eyes thing would start small and snowball and become a craze, and that before a few weeks were out, hundreds of thousands and maybe millions of kids would have their hair and eyes in synch.

And after that, after she'd set a major trend, Kimmie was hoping those millions of kids would turn to her for the latest in style, that they would watch her breathlessly for clues as to what to wear, or what music to listen to, or who to be.

That was why I'd suggested that my viewers send Kimmie a note telling her they liked what she'd done with her eyes. It was my way of telling her, *Hey, Kimmie, you're busted.*

It was my way of saying that I know she's trying to be *me.*


I watch as Kimmie walks through shops and looks at clothes and laughs with her friends. She's bouncy and sort of flirting with the cameras.

I feel sick as I remember how she used to flirt with me. *She never loved me*, I think. She just wanted to be around someone who could teach her to be famous.

"Sanson would have liked this," she says, holding up a flirty top. Then she shrugged and put it back on the rack.

Her friends giggle. "That style's so over," she says.

*Given up on subtlety, have you?* I think.

Kimmie nods. "I saw Sanson's mother wearing something like this, once, except it was blue."

"Leave my mother out of it," I tell the video.

She touches her friend's arm. "Sanson and his mother are so cute together," she says. "They're really close. He takes her advice on everything."

I snarl and throw a pillow at the holographic image. Lasers burn Kimmie's image across the crumpled pillowcase.

If there's one thing the Demographic isn't going to want to hear, it's that I depend on the advice of a hundred-forty-year-old parent.

Kimmie has declared war. And I don't know how I'm going to fight back—as my dad said, I can't respond directly without giving her more credence than she deserves.

And besides, what am I going to say? That I hate my mother?

I don't need a bucket of hot coals. I need a cannon.

Next day we have the semifinals in our gorillaball league. We had chosen a field half a kilometer long, with a three-story municipal office building in the middle, plus a row of stores and two groves of pine trees. The six goals were in hard-to-reach places that would involve a lot of climbing.

The Samurai arrive with angry designs shaved into their fur, arrows and snakes and snarling animals—I wish I'd thought of that, actually. Shaved into each of their backs are the words WE LOVE KIMMIE.

They've got a lot of nerve, considering that they're only playing gorillaball in the first place because they're in *my* Demographic.

Before the game starts the Samurai get in a circle and start chanting "*Sanson is a sellout!*"

It goes on for what seems like hours while we stand around and can't think of any way to respond. Eventually Errol starts shouting "*Play or forfeit!*" and the rest of us pick up the chant, but it's far too late. Our fighting spirit has already drained into the dirt, and we look like a gang of lames to our worldwide audience.

The Samurai stomp us. They've practiced a lot, and they have some moves we haven't encountered, and they play rough. The final score is 16-5, a complete rout, and by the end we're dusty and bruised and angry. I'm limping because a couple of the Samurai body-checked me off a building and I didn't catch myself in time. We leave with the *Sanson is a sellout* chant echoing in our ears.

And I'm *still* stuck in the gorilla body till the league finals, which are next week.

I decide it's all Kimmie's fault.

There's a lot of silence in the pool area after the game. I shave an area of my calf and slap on an analgesic patch. Hardly anyone is watching anymore, so I ask everyone to turn off their cameras, and we groom each other listlessly.

When I ask Lisa into my office I run all the detectors that are supposed to make certain that no one is eavesdropping. I don't want anyone to know what I'm planning.

"Kimmie's attacking me in her flashcasts," I say. "And I can't respond to what she's doing, because that would give her more credit than she deserves."

"Okay," Lisa says. "I can see that." She sits on one of the three-legged stools and rubs a bruised shoulder. "All you have to do is wait, though, because sooner or later she's going to make a mistake."

"No," I say. "I want to be able to respond—but I don't want anyone to know it's me."

She looks uneasy. "You want me to make a flashcast attacking her?"

"No," I say. "I don't want anyone in the pack to do it, because then it'll look like I'm just telling them what to say."

Lisa is relieved.

"I want to do it myself," I say.

She stares at me. Though our bodies are hulking gorilloids, our faces are a lot more human, so that there's room for brains behind the forehead and so that people can understand us when we talk, but that also means that we have a nearly full range of human expression. I look at Lisa and I know that she's looking at me with calculation.

"I want to create a false identity," I say. "I want to be somebody else when I start talking about Kimmie."

Lisa considers this. "What exactly do you want to do?"

"I want to create an artificial personality, one who makes flashcasts of his own. Maybe he could be based on Mars or somewhere even farther out." I grin at her. "Anatole says you're good at this kind of thing."

"Maybe I am," Lisa says, "but nothing I do is going to be foolproof."

"Lots of people make anonymous flashcasts."

Lisa looks dubious. "I don't think very many of them are as famous as you are."

"I won't do it for very long."

"All right," she says. She still seems doubtful. "If anyone really *wants* to find out, they will."

"Let's do it," I say.

"Let me look into a few things first," she says. "Before I start, I want to make sure I'm not going to make a mistake and wreck things."

I agree. I like the fact that she's being careful.

I start making plans for what I want to say.

"You've lost another fifteen percent of your audience," my dad says.

Tonight's meal is Italian. There's stuffed tomatoes, herring artichokes, squid salad, ravioli stuffed with pheasant, braised beef in the Genoese style, and a ricotta pie. And again it's all for the two of us, because my mom's giving a talk in Peru.

"I know," I say.

"You're a trend-spotter," he tells me. "What trends look good?"

"I've been looking around. But with everything else I'm doing—"

"How about the whole neo-barbarian thing?"

"No legs," I say, my mouth full of squid. I swallow. "Besides, after being a gorilla I don't ever want to have to deal with fur coats ever again."

"You need to find some coincidence of fashion and culture—video or music." He waved a ravioli on his fork as he repeated his mantra. "No modern cultural phenomenon ever lasted unless there were great clothes that went with it."

"I know," I say.

"And a new dance style always helps."

"I know."

I know. I know more than he does. I'm the one who's a slave to the Demographic, not him.

So I start casting about for trends. I stay up nights listening to music from all points of the solar system, and looking at the flashcasts of obscure designers. For a while I think about getting a second pair of arms, like some of the asteroid miners, but then I realize how much I'm longing to inhabit a basic human body again.

I keep looking. Put *this* style with *this* music with *this* dance. I've done it before. How hard can it be?

It's hard. Especially because I hear in my head what the Demographic is going to say about it. *You want me to wear* those *heels?* Or, *These people are singing in* Albanian! Or, *Hell, I'd rather be a gorilla.*

But in the meantime we have to deal with the last gorillaball event, the Samurai versus the Night People, the other Bay Area team that survived the semifinals. I've viddied their games and I don't think they stand a chance.

I appear in person to award the league trophy, which is a huge, fierce gorilla head chomping with its fangs on a ball. Since I don't want to go alone I bring the whole pack.

"Hey, a question," I say to the Samurai captain at the coin toss. "If you like Kimmie so much, how come you haven't gone blond?"

He doesn't have an answer for that, but wins the toss anyway.

I watch with the pack as the Samurai begin one of their patented jackhammer attacks and commence their long afternoon's humiliation of the Night People. The score is 4-1 when I look at Deva and give her the nod.

She quietly leaves, and takes the league trophy with her, out of range of anyone's cameras.

After the Samurai finish, they find that the trophy has been replaced by a piece of paper pinned down by a large pinecone. The rest of us are in our vehicles. (I have new but deliberately downmarket Scion. I'm not legally allowed to drive it, but I can always program it for a destination and let the onboard navigator take over)

"Hey!" the captain says. "Where's the trophy?"

"It's gone for a walk," I say, "but it left behind a clue as to its current location."

What I'd written on the paper was this:

> *There once were gorillas of note*
> *But overly tempted to gloat.*
> *They played ball without peer*
> *Till a brave Mutineer*
> *Carried them off on his boat.*

### HOW TO FIND THE LEAGUE TROPHY

- Scratch your heads in puzzlement until someone watching the flashcast sends you a message informing them that Errol's mother owns a boat called *Mutineer.*
- Troop down to the marina in Alameda, and then stand around like a bunch of apes until you finally notice that the boat is flying flag signals.
- Decode the flags and follow directions across the Bay to Sausalito.
- Spend the next several hours tramping back and forth across the Bay, knowing all the while that millions of people are watching

your purgatory in realtime, and that Sanson and his pack are in their clubhouse rolling on the floor with laughter.

- Finally find the trophy in a pine tree on the field where the Samurai had beaten the Stars, and realize that the pine cone was a clue that you were too dense to get.
- Limp off into darkness and obscurity, knowing that millions of people are laughing at you, and will laugh for years to come.

After we stopped flashcasting, Lisa came over to me and said in a low voice. "You know that thing you asked me to do?"

"Yeah?"

"I've done it."

I take her into my office and she gives me the codes. "All you need to do is decide what your avatar is going to look like," she says.

"Magnetic," I answer.

That's how the Duck Monkey begins. A Martian, the Duck Monkey gazes down from the sky and examines the cultural scene on Earth with mixed amusement and scorn.

The Duck Monkey examines all of Kimmie's flashcasts. He mocks her fashions, and shows ridiculous people in history who had worn similar clothing. He points out similarities between her flashes and mine, and suggests that she's nothing but an imitator. He closely examines her ideas and expressions and provides links to the originators of those ideas and expressions. He makes fun of her friends. He points out that it's tacky to use information I gave her in private.

No one could survive such scrutiny with her dignity intact. Not Kimmie, not me, not anyone.

Nor does the Duck Monkey stop with Kimmie. I don't want him to be a one-note critic, or the electronic equivalent of an obsessed stalker. The Duck Monkey also hates the singer Alma Chen and the actor Ahmose. He likes the band Peninsular & Orient, and because I want him to be different from me I have him like al-Amin even though I personally think he's pompous. The Duck Monkey likes classical music, to which I'm mostly indifferent, and praises a number of virtuosi. (I look up their reviews to make sure that what I was saying was plausible to someone who actually knows that scene.)

Other than Kimmie, I never attack anyone who isn't big enough to take the hit. Ahmose has millions of fans—why should he care what the Duck Monkey thinks?

He does, though. He makes a few vicious remarks about the Duck

Monkey in an interview and gives my Martian avatar instant credibility. The Monkey's numbers jump.

A pro like Ahmose, you'd think he'd know better.

I really love being the Duck Monkey. I can say anything I want and not have to worry about the Demographic. I can be as sarcastic as I like, and if I love something, I can say so without having to worry about whether my opinion is sufficiently fashionable.

But in the meantime, I also have to be me. And that isn't nearly as much fun.

My new human body isn't beautiful. Beauty isn't interesting when anyone can be beautiful. People my age have grown up around physical beauty and we instinctively distrust it. Besides, I've been beautiful in the past, and I don't like the way it makes people look at me.

What I want instead of beauty is *sincerity*. I want to blink my dewy eyes at the camera and have the Demographic believe everything that comes out of my mouth.

At first I plan on straw hair and blue eyes and then I realize everyone's going to think I'm imitating Kimmie. So my next has olive skin and a sensitive mouth and soulful brown eyes, and that's the face I see in the mirror as soon as I climb out of the vat.

I look at myself carefully. Hey, *I'd* believe me.

I give the rest of the pack a few days to choose and settle into their new bodies, and then we have a Style Day. I'm always getting sent stuff—clothes, shoes, hats, accessories—by designers who hope I'll popularize it for them. There's quite a backlog after our two months as gorillas, so we unpack it all by the pool, and model it for each other. We flashcast it all live, and the Demographic send in their comments and instantly rate each item.

There's nothing very exciting. The designers seem to be going through a dull patch.

Wakaba makes a nice cream-colored shirt that fits me, with a standing collar that brushes my ears. It's got French cuffs so I can use a pair of chunky lapis cufflinks that I've had around for months. I find a thin black tie with a gold stripe, by Madagascar, and tie it around the standing collar with a simple four-in-hand knot. Then I find a navy blue silk jacket designed by Desi, with braided lapels and a single vent.

No need to bother with a mirror. I just check out the feed from the others' headsets.

I mostly like what I see. The style is kind of severe, but its very plainness invites the use of jewelry. And the look is mature. I remember that Dad wants me to find an older look.

"You look like a schoolboy from Bombay," Anatole says, which deflates me a little.

"Wait a minute," said Lisa. "I know what he needs."

Lisa has acquired the body of a Taiwanese basketball player, tall and rangy, with almond eyes and long black hair. She walks to one of the white metal poolside tables, rummages around the packages for a moment, then returns with a pair of sunglasses. I can feel the warmth of her breath on my cheek as she perches the shades on my nose.

"Ooh, nice," says Deva. I check her video feed. The shades are gold-rimmed wraparounds with deep jade-green lenses, and they've got camera pickups for flashcasting. Wearing them I viddie like a cross between the Bombay schoolboy and a dapper young gangster.

"Now you look like a vicious lawyer," Lisa says. I sneak a look at the online poll and seventy percent of the Demographic approve the look, with a furious twenty-five percent hating it. And even the twenty-five percent *care*.

"I like this look," I say. "We should become the Pack of Vicious Lawyers."

I sense a certain resistance in a few of the pack members, but after all I'm the star—so we all adopt the style, or something similar, and for the next several days the Pack of Vicious Lawyers crosses the Bay Bridge to a series of clubs in San Francisco. (As a loyal citizen of the East Bay, I refuse to call it "the City" like the natives do.) We invade clubs en masse, listen to bands like Sylvan Slide and The Birth of China, and are invited into the V.I.P. rooms by management eager for the free publicity. I meet and chat with famous people like the artist Saionji—who invites us all to his opening—and the producer Jane Chapman, who asks the name of my agent.

Considering that none of us can even drink legally, this isn't bad at all.

I regain a third of the audience I lost during the gorilla fiasco, but then the numbers begin to slide again. People have seen me go to clubs before.

I know the Pack of Vicious Lawyers is only a transitional phase. It's too mature a style for all the Demographic—a fourteen-year-old couldn't pull off the Vicious Lawyer look. And there's nothing in the package but clothing and style—the Vicious Lawyers don't *do* anything, they just stand around in groups and look intimidating. I hope it will last till I can find the new style that will bring the Demographic screaming back into my camp.

I start to sweat. I want all the love back. I'm knocking myself out looking for the next trend—and of course I'm going to college and being the Duck Monkey as well. Time is running out, and so for that matter is my audience.

And then I think I find it. The music is from Turkmenistan, coincidentally where my mother gave a lecture series a few years ago, and is called Mukam. It's descended from a traditional form that goes back for centuries, but everyone in Southwest Asia has been trading licks and musical styles for ages now, so in addition to using the flute and the two-string lute native to the area, the Turkmen imported the double-ended *dhol* drum from the Punjab along with modern electric instruments and insanely rigorous vocal styles from places like Tuva and Mongolia. The musical forms are incredibly complex, but the *dhol* drives the music forward and makes it compulsively danceable, at least if you can dance to 5/4 time or 6/8 or the even more complex polyrhythms native to the area.

And the clothing from the region is terrific. Baggy tops and drawers, and riding boots of leather or felt, and long fur-trimmed lambskin coats. Some of the coats have lace and trim and frogging that would do credit to a nineteenth-century drum major, and others are ornamented with wild, colorful felt appliqué.

The only element I don't care for are the huge fur hats the size of beach-balls, which make people look like giant dandelions. I reckon we can do without the headwear.

The Turkmen style had everything. Music, movement, fashion. It had all that was needed for it to become a major trend, everything except exposure.

Exposure I could provide.

I call a meeting of the pack and specify that no cameras are to be worn. I draw the blinds on the clubhouse and play the music and show videos of the clothing.

"That's great," Anatole says. "But how are we supposed to dance to any of this?"

"People have been dancing to this music for hundreds of years," I point out.

Errol just gives me a blank stare. "*How?*"

I don't have an answer for that one. "Let's look at the videos again," I suggest.

The videos don't help—they're all of professional dancers who are infinitely more skilled than we are. They even look good in those huge fur hats.

Lisa approaches me later, after we broke up in confusion. She is still very shy and doesn't like talking in front of the whole pack, but I guess she's comfortable with just me.

It's those trustworthy brown eyes, I decide.

"We could do research on the dancing," she says.

"Yes," I say. "But we don't want to do old stuff."

"It doesn't have to be new," she says. "It just has to be *new to your audience*."

I look at her for a moment. "You're right."

Lisa goes into the computer archives and digs up information about the sort of dances they were doing in Central Asian clubs about forty years ago. I find old instructional videos. Most of us aren't very good at it, but Lisa turned out to be a natural.

I'm the star and I get to pick my partners, so I dance with Lisa for most of the afternoon, and get her to tutor me. I ask her why she's so good at it.

"It's just a matter of counting. For most dances, all you have to do is count to four. For the waltz, you count to three. And for this... well, the left side of your brain counts to eight while the right side counts to five."

"Right."

But everybody's smart these days, and after a few more afternoons of practice, I get so I'm good at counting exactly that way.

Autumn comes on, wet and chill. My mother leaves for Mars, where she'll teach for a semester, and leaves me with Dad and tons of fresh-cooked gourmet food, which no longer being a gorilla I could not eat nearly fast enough.

We all get good at dancing like Turkmen. Clothing appears at the clubhouse. We listen to hours of music and pick our favorites for our debut, which we decide is going to be at the Cryptic Club down in the Castro—the management is happy to comp us for a night and play our music in exchange for all the free publicity.

I don't let anyone take video of any of our practice sessions. Not only because we don't all look particularly expert, but because I don't want any pictures getting out into the world. Nobody's going to know about the Turkmen style till I sprang it on the world Saturday night.

We make appointments to get hair extensions. I've decided that long, wild hair is going to be part of the look.

I'm on top of the world. I'm having enormous fun being the Duck Monkey. Kimmie's audience has stabilized at about a quarter the size of mine, and isn't getting any larger. I know that I'm about to popularize a style that will sweep the world and bring the Demographic back.

And I'm seeing a lot of Lisa. She isn't part of the pack because she wants to be around me, or to be famous, but because her cousin Anatole had talked her into it. That makes her different from the others. Lisa has friends outside the pack that she spends time with. She has a mind that analyzes and categorizes everything that goes on around her, including me. Sometimes I think she looks on me as just another artifact to be studied.

But sometimes when she looks at me it isn't analytical. I'm not analyzing her, either. I like the way she dances, the way she feels in my arms, her scent. Sometimes I want to lean over and kiss her, just to see what might happen.

I begin to think about that. I don't hurt so much anymore when I think about Kimmie. I think maybe Lisa's a part of that.

But Lisa and I are doomed. The Demographic would hate her—she isn't their style at all. They want me to go with strong, outgoing personalities who also happen to be really beautiful. If I start seeing Lisa, my numbers would start to slide.

And she'd get a ton of hate mail. I don't know whether she could cope with that. So for all sorts of reasons I don't kiss her.

But still I enjoy thinking about it.

The catastrophe happens on a Friday evening, the night before we're due to premiere our new style at the Cryptic. Tonight the pack is at Errol's place up in Berkeley looking at music videos the Demographic sent us. We listen and watch and give our verdicts, and the Demographic watches us and responds to what we're saying.

We're watching Fidel Nuñez lament the state of his *corazon* when I get a message on my headset from Deva. *Check Kimmie's new flash. Don't say anything.*

I look at Kimmie's flash through the splice on my optic nerve, and I feel like someone's just slammed me in the head with a crowbar.

Kimmie and her pack—there are only seven of them—are flashing live from a club I recognize, Toad Hall on Treasure Island, and they're wearing long fur-trimmed Turkmen coats and baggy pants and tall riding boots. They carry horse whips, and they're dancing to Mukam using the same steps that we planned to use. They have a different playlist than the one we built, but it has a lot of the same songs.

I sit in Errol's media room and watch my whole next phase crumble into dust. If I show up tomorrow night at the Cryptic, everyone will think I'm imitating Kimmie. I can't even prove the idea originated with me because I'd been so strict about not recording anything.

My head swims and I feel as if I'm going to faint. Then I realize that for some time I'd completely forgot to breathe. I take in some air, but it doesn't make me feel any better.

Fidel Nuñez finishes his song. There's a silence and I realize that the rest of the pack have been watching Kimmie's flash too.

"What do we think?" Errol asks. His tone is anxious.

There's more silence.

"I think it's *boring*," I say. I stand up and I reel because I'm still light-headed. "I think we need to get *moving*."

There is a certain amount of half-hearted approval, but mostly I think most of the pack are as stunned as I am.

I look at the pack and wonder which one of them told Kimmie about the Turkmen style.

One of my friends has betrayed me.

"Spending a Friday night looking at videos?" I ask. "How pathetic is *that?*"

"Yeah!" Anatole says. "Let's get out of here!"

We go outside and the cool night air sings through my veins. There's a heavy dew on the grass and mist drifting amid the trees. I turn back and see Errol's house, with its red tile roof curving up at the corners like a Chinese temple, and the trellises carrying twining roses and ivy up the sides of the house, and the tall elm trees in the front and back.

"You know," I say, "this place would be great for gorillaball."

Errol looks at the house. "I'm glad you didn't say that back when—"

"Let's play now!"

Errol turns to me. "But we're not—we're—"

"I *know* we're not gorillas," I say. "But that's no reason we can't play gorillaball. Let's have the first gorillaball game without gorillas!"

Errol's horrified, but I insist. Errol's parents, who actually own the house, aren't home tonight, so they can't say no. I captain one team, and Errol captains the other. We choose up sides, all except for Amy and Lisa.

"I'm not playing," Lisa says. "This is just crazy."

Amy agrees.

"You can referee, then," I say.

We set up one ladder in the front and another out back. We put one goal in a tree in the front, another in a tree in the back. I win the toss and elect to receive.

The ball comes soaring over the house and Sanjay catches it. He goes for the ladder and I lunge for a trellis. Errol and his team are scrambling up the other side.

Sanjay reaches the roof but already two of Errol's teammates are on him. He passes the ball to me and I charge. I knock Michiko sprawling onto the roof tiles and then I hit Shawn hard under the breastbone, and he grabs me to keep from falling. So now we both fall, sliding down the tiles that are slippery with dew. As Shawn goes off the roof he makes a grab at the gutter, something he could have done easily as an ape, but he misses. I get the gutter myself and swing into a rosebush just as I hear Shawn's femur snap.

Thorns tear at my skin and my clothes. I drag myself free and run for the elm tree that overhangs the street. I grab the goalkeeper's foot and yank him out of the tree, then climb up myself and slam the ball into the bucket we've put in a crotch of the tree.

"*Goal!*" I yell.

The others are clustered around Shawn. I'm limping slightly as I join them. Blood thunders in my veins. *Which one of you ratted us out to Kimmie?* I think.

Errol turns to me.

"Shawn's smashed his leg up bad. Game's over."

"No," I say. "You're down one player, so we'll give up one to keep it fair." I turn to Sanjay. "You can take Shawn to the hospital. The rest of us can keep playing."

Lisa looks at me. "I'm going, too. This is insane."

I look at her in surprise. It's practically the first thing she's said in public.

"Go if you want," I said. "The rest of us are playing gorillaball."

And that's what the rest of us do. No more bones are broken, but that's only because we're lucky. By the end of the night I'm bruised and cut and bleeding, with sprained fingers and a swollen knee. The others look equally bad. I've scored seven points.

The trick, I decide, is not to care. If you don't care who you hit and who you walk over you can score a lot of points in this world. You could be like Kimmie.

We should have fought the Samurai *tonight*, I think. We'd have crushed them.

The ratings are great. Many more people watch us live than watch Kimmie. And when I edit the raw flash into a coherent, ninety-minute experience the next day, the number of downloads are as good as anything I've done.

Gorillaball leagues start forming again, only without the gorillas. People are inspired by the madness of it.

I'm back on top.

But only for a short ride. I have to cancel the Cryptic appearance, and after the gorillaball blip, my numbers resume their slide. And word gets out about Kimmie's new style, so her numbers start to soar.

She's riding the trend that should have been mine.

We trade in the Vicious Lawyer look for Byronic. It's one of the styles I'd considered, then rejected in favor of the Turkmen look. Byronic is all velvet suits and lace and hose with clocks and beads and braid and rickrack. It's the sort of thing that the part of the Demographic who enjoyed being gorillas would hate.

The true weakness, though, is that Byronic music is boring. They're supposed to be sensitive poets, but all they really do is whine. *I'm young in an old world.*

Yeah, tell us something new.

My numbers continue to sicken. I try not to think about the fact that I'm losing thousands of friends every day. I try not to want their love but I do.

The crowning insult comes when Dr. Granger gives me a B in my Media and Society class. He decided that my understanding of the media scene was "insufficiently informed."

I complain and flash the complaint. It gets me a lot of sympathetic messages, and a notice from Dr. Granger that he's decided, after all, to fail me.

The swine. It's a piece of petty malice beyond anything even the Duck Monkey has ever done.

He must have read what the Demographic was saying about him.

I have nothing to lose. I make another flashcast, this time telling the world what a pathetic old geezer Granger is, sucking up to me as long as he thought he could vamp a piece of my fame. For a moment, my downloads blip upward again, then start to slide.

It's then that the management of the Samaritain decides to repossess our clubhouse. I'm passé, and they don't want anyone connecting their expensive hotel with passé.

I'm told that they've decided to repaint and redecorate the suite, and that we should get our stuff out.

"So you're getting rid of the furniture and the carpet and everything?" I ask.

They assure me that this is the case.

I call a pack meeting—the pack is down to eleven now—and we rendezvous at the Samaritain for one last live flashparty. The hypocrisy and opportunism of the Samaritain's management has got me in a rage. I show up with buckets of paint and brushes and knives and crowbars.

"Since the Samaritain's going to redecorate," I announce, "I think we should help them. They don't want any of this stuff anymore."

Most of the paint ends up on the walls, though a lot gets ground into the plush carpet. We smash the furniture and cut up the pillows. Foam padding falls like snow. We rip out paneling with crowbars. We tip the couch in the pool, and then skim the paintings onto the water. We're in our Byronic finery as we do this, and all our clothes are ruined.

We leave the Samaritain singing, and head to my place.

After the cameras are turned off we groom each other as if we were still gorillas. I sit at the foot of my bed as Lisa sits behind me and tries to comb the paint out of my hair.

I check the ratings and announce that they're stellar. Anatole gives a little cheer.

"They're only watching to see you fall apart," Lisa says.

I give her an annoyed look over my shoulder. *What's wrong with that?* I want to say.

If the audience wants me to fall apart, I'll fall apart. If they want me to cut off my hand, I'll cut it off and flashcast the bleeding stump.

Anything to get the love back.

"Maybe you should decompress," she says. "Just be a regular boy for a while."

"Don't know how," I say. Which happens to be true.

"You could learn."

"Who wants to be normal anyway?" Anatole asks. I agree, and that torpedoes the subject.

We talk about other things for a while, and then Lisa bends over me and murmurs in my ear. "You know that project we're working on? Some people are getting very interested in it. I've been able to hold them off by routing everything through the moons of Saturn but it's not going to last."

"Okay," I say.

"You've got to stop it," she says.

Errol is looking at us strangely. Maybe Lisa whispering in my ear made him think we might be an item.

"Soon," I promise.

But I'm lying. The Duck Monkey is my only consolation. By now he's become the whole dark Mr. Hyde of me. The Duck Monkey doesn't have to worry about the Demographic or my pack or anyone. He can just be himself. He eviscerates everything he looks at, Kimmie in particular. There's a whole subculture now who view Kimmie's flashcasts, then check the Duck Monkey to see what he says about her.

The pack descends on the opening of Saionji, the artist who'd foolishly invited us to his opening. We're in our wrecked Byronic outfits, shabby and torn and splattered with paint, a complete contrast to Saionji's art, which is delicate and fluttery and imbued with chiming musical tones. Saionji is polite but a little distant, knowing he's being upstaged. But I have some intelligent things to say about his pieces—I've done research—and he warms up.

Over the buffet I meet Dolores Swan. She's petite and coffee-skinned and wears a short skirt and a metallic halter. She's got deep shadows in the hollows of her collarbones, which oddly enough I find the most attractive thing about her. I'm vaguely aware of her as a model/actress/flashcaster/ whatever, and even more vaguely know that she was last employed as the host of a chat show that lasted maybe five weeks. We make polite sounds at each other, and then I'm off with the pack to ruin the tone of a long series of clubs.

It's a week later that Jill Lee dies playing gorillaball in a human body. Even though they return her to life from a backup, there's a big media flap about whether I'm a good example for youth. I point out in interviews that I never told Jill Lee or anybody else to play gorillaball without a gorilla body. I point out that she was dead for what, sixteen hours? Not a tragedy on the order of the *Titanic*.

The consensus of the media chatheads is that I'm not repentant enough.

That wrangle hasn't even died away when the Duck Monkey is unmasked—by that cheeseball Ahmose, of all people, who paid a group of electronic detectives to dig out my identity. Ahmose is *shocked* that a celebrity with such a wholesome image would say such bad things about him. Kimmie tells the world she's so terribly, terribly hurt, and she cries in front of her worldwide audience and scores about a million sympathy points. I'm besieged by more interviewers. I answer through the Duck Monkey.

*While I am flattered that some people claim that I am Sanson, I am in fact a completely separate person, one that just happens to live in Sanson's head.*

The chatheads agree that I'm insufficiently apologetic. My ratings jump for the sky, however, when the Duck Monkey takes a scalpel to Kimmie's interview with the Mad Jumpers, the number one band from Turkmenistan. I mean, when you're doing an interview, you're supposed to talk about something other than *yourself*.

The Duck Monkey thing is at its height when Dolores Swan drives up in her vintage red Hunhao convertible, the one with the license plate that reads TRY ME, and invites me to elbow my way through the mass of flashcasters and personality journalists camped out in front of my house and drive away to her bungalow in Marin.

Next morning, I've got a new girlfriend who's forty years older than me.

### THINGS TO DO WHEN YOU'RE CRACKING UP
• Fly to Palau for a romantic honeymoon with your girl-friend.
• Have a drunken fight the first night so she runs off to Manila with a sports fisherman named Sandy.
• Throw up in the lobby fountain.
• Console yourself with a French tourist called Françoise, who looks fifteen but who turns out to be older than your mother.
• Have Dolores catch you and Françoise in the bed that she

(Dolores) is paying for, so there's a huge scene.
- Make up with Dolores and announce to the world you're inseparable.
- Throw up in the swimming pool.
- Record everything and broadcast live to your worldwide audience of millions.
- Repeat, with variations.
- Repeat.
- Repeat.
- Repeat.
- Repeat.

The ratings are *great*.

By the time I make it back to the East Bay, there is no longer any debate about whether I'm a bad influence on youth.

A consensus on that issue has pretty much been reached.

The thing with Dolores is over. She's got enough of a bounce off our relationship to get a new job with the Fame Network as an interviewer and fashion reporter. When I last saw her she was on her way to Mali.

After the suborbital lands in the Bay and taxies to shore, I walk to the terminal through a corridor lined with posters for KimmieWear. Her clothing line, now available worldwide. Even *I* never managed that.

I wonder if Kimmie has ripped out all the parts of me that had talent and taken it all for herself.

My dad takes me in, and makes three pizzas. He doesn't reproach me for running off because, face it, my ratings are as good as they ever were. He talks about his new viral marketing campaign, which sounds just like the last forty years of his viral marketing campaigns.

I've got a whole new Demographic now. Hardly any of my old audience watches me anymore.

The new viewers are older. My dad wanted me to find a more mature audience, but I'm not sure he had in mind my present assembly of celebrity junkies, scandal watchers, sadists, and comedians. The latter, by the way, have been mining my life for their routines.

*Q: What's the good news about Dolores breaking up with Sanson?*
*A: She'll never accuse him of stealing the best years of her life.*
*Q: What's another good thing?*
*A: She'll never complain he was using her. She was using* him.

Oh yeah, that's funny all right.

Dad offers ideas for growing my Demographic, like I need another legion of perverts in my life.

I get a good night's sleep. My current wardrobe of tropical wear is un-suitable for a Bay Area spring, and I can't stand the sight of any of my old clothes, so I go shopping for replacements. I buy the most anonymous-looking stuff available. Everywhere I go, there are holograms of Kimmie laughing and pirouetting in her Turkmen coats.

I remember that laugh, that pirouette, from the Fashion Days our pack used to have.

The day wears on. I'm bored. I call the members of the pack. It's been three months since I flew off with Dolores and they've all drifted away. They're all in school, for one thing, the spring semester that I blew off.

I wondered whether, if I called a meeting, anyone would show up.

I leave messages with people who would once have taken my call no matter what they were doing. I talk briefly to Errol and Jeet, who promise to get together later. I call Lisa and am surprised when she answers.

"What are you doing?" I ask. "Want to come over?"

She hesitates. "I'm doing a project." I'm about to apologize for bothering her when she says, "Can you come here?"

I program my Scion for Lisa's address. As I drive over I think about how Lisa's the only person I knew who didn't want something from me—at-tention, a piece of my fame, an audience, a boost in their ratings. Even my dad seems to only want me around to test his marketing theories.

I think about how she had danced so expertly in my arms. I think about how I hadn't kissed her because I'd thought the Demographic wouldn't approve.

I don't care what the current Demographic thinks at all. They're all creeps.

Lisa's sharing an apartment in Berkeley with a girl friend, and when I come in she's sitting cross-legged in the front room, with different video capes around her, all showing different flow charts and graphs and strange, intricate foreign script.

"What's up?" I ask.

"Fifteenth-century Persian manuscripts. I'm trying to work back from illumination styles to a vision of manuscript workshops."

"Ah."

I find a part of the floor that isn't being used yet, and sit.

"So," I say, "you were right."

"About what?" Lisa's frowning at one of her flow charts.

"About my audience watching only to see me fall apart."

She looks up. "I probably should have phrased that more tactfully."

I shrug. "I think you voiced the essence of the situation. You should see the kind of messages I get now."

Once I felt this whole swell of love from my audience. Now it's sarcasm and brutality. Invitations to drunken parties, offers of sex or drugs, suggestions for ways I could injure myself.

"The thing is," she said, "it's a feedback loop you've got going with your audience. They reinforce everything you do."

Positive feedback loops, I remember from my classes, are how addictive drugs work.

"You think I'll succeed in kicking the habit?" I ask.

Lisa's expression is serious. "Do you really want to become a real boy?"

I think about it.

"No," I say. "I don't. But I can't think of anything else to do. Where can I go in flashcasting once I've mastered the art of being a laughing stock?"

She doesn't have an answer for that, and goes back to her work. There is a long silence.

"Can I kiss you?" I ask.

"No," she says, without looking up.

"Does that mean *No,* or does that mean *Not Yet?*"

She looks up and frowns. "I'm not sure."

"Tell me about your work," I say.

So I learn all about the hermeneutics of Persian manuscripts. It's interesting, and I love the intricate, complex Arabic calligraphy, whole words and phrases worked into a single labyrinthine design. There are charming little illustrations, too, of people hunting or fighting or being in love with each other.

Lisa offers me a glass of tea. We talk about other subjects till it's time for me to go.

I think about those Persian designs all the way home. I think about how you could base a whole style on it. I can see the clothes in my head. I wonder what kind of music would go with it.

When I get home I hear my dad in his office talking to some of his colleagues. I go into my room and watch other people's flashcasts. They're all inane.

The Duck Monkey could rip them to shreds, but they don't seem worth the bother.

It's a strange thing, but the Duck Monkey's ratings have held steady, fed by a stream of celebrity gossip from Dolores and her friends. The Duck Monkey has a completely different demographic from my own audience. They're smarter and funnier, and they're not trying to get me to kill myself in some horribly public way.

It's like the Duck Monkey is some kind of viral marketing campaign for something else. A new Sanson, perhaps, one who comes swinging back into the world with a style based on Persian manuscripts.

Or maybe the Sanson who's a real boy.

I lie on my bed and think about Lisa and the Duck Monkey and Arab calligraphy. I wonder if I can live without the love of all those people who made up my Demographic for all those years.

I decide I'll try to get the love of just one person, and if necessary go on from there.

I send a message to Lisa to tell her I'd like to see her again.

# AFTERWORD: PINOCCHIO

*This story was written for Jonathan Strahan, as a substitute for "Incarnation Day," which proved too long for his* Starry Rift *anthology.*

*"Pinocchio" was inspired by a television documentary about former child stars. I was depressed by the desperate need of mature forty-year-olds to recapture their glory days, when they werse ten or eleven, and I began a meditation on the nature of celebrity. I combined these ideas with reflections on the instantaneous feedback that is such a prominent characteristic of twenty-first-century media, and gradually developed the story of Sanson, the media puppet who was trying desperately not to become a real boy.*